THE PLEIADIAN EXPERIMENT

THE PLEIADIAN EXPERIMENT

PART 2 OF PORTAL 106

GEORGINA FATSEAS

CITIOFBOOKS, INC.
3736 Eubank NE Suite A1
Albuquerque, NM 87111-3579
www.citiofbooks.com
Hotline: 1 (877) 389-2759
Fax: 1 (505) 930-7244

Ordering Information:
Quantity sales. Special discounts are available on quantity purchases by corporations, associations, and others. For details, contact the publisher at the address above.

Printed in the United States of America.

ISBN-13:   Softcover   979-8-89391-532-7
           eBook   979-8-89391-533-4

Library of Congress Control Number: 2024904480

Table of Contents

The Editor's Notes

There are some references to towns and cities in Australia and Finland. There are some Australian expression used in this book. British spelling is used.

The Author's Notes

The author has taken creative licence to use real constellation, galaxies, and star names to be names of the planets in this book. All galaxy names in this book are fictitious.

The author has used a small part of the ancient Sumerian mythology as inspiration for the story. Ancient written records in the Sumerian language are incomplete. Time has eroded or destroyed parts of the myth. What has survived and is readable needs to be supplemented with imagination even by historians. Other scientists have looked at the mythology to investigate the information provided is true or not. As time passes and more information is translated from the clay tablets, there is indication that some events may have taken place.

Prologue

At the start of the invasion, the Planets of Sirius B, Andromeda and Pleiades searched through ancient records for techniques on warfare, a skill lost to them through a thousand years of peace. Knowing their warfare skills were limited, the governments of these planets sent their people to other uninhabited planets in other galaxies.

In their searches of old records, the Pleiadeans discover corrupted and incomplete records of a once thought mythical planet called Tiamat far away in The White Galaxy. Before the information could be used in a meaningful way in war, the three planets were destroyed. However, the Pleiadeans took the information they discovered to their new planet, Beta Cancari.

For twenty-five years the different refugee colonies would send teams of people to assist the human underground surviving on the undestroyed planets to fight the Lacertians and their overlords, the Draconians. No progress was being made. The Draconians had developed technology to track communication that made direct interaction between the colonies and the resistance fighters almost impossible. The conditions for humans on the planets in Oberon were becoming worse.

On Beta Cancari morale was dropping, and resources were becoming low. President Findlee ordered an exploration ship to be built in a bid to boost morale and to locate planets with resources. Included in the first explorative mission to go to the White galaxy to see if it was possible to locate the planet of once thought mythical planet of Tiamat by using the corrupted ancient maps.

CHAPTER ONE
The Explorer

President Findlee watched with pride at the very first long-distance spaceship was loaded for its maiden flight. This massive ship before him was supposed to be a joint venture between the survivors of Pleiadean, Siriusian and Andromedan nations which in the past were close friends. But now, it was time to bite the bullet and go it alone on this venture. To find a resource rich planets or find evidence of a once fabled planet, Tiamat, or the location of refugees from Amada Galaxay theorised to be in the same galaxy, the White Galaxy. Any find would be deemed as a successful mission.

Findlee watched his adopted son, Ashton, walk up to him. "Hi Dad!" said Ashton with a broad grin. President Findlee smiled as tears threatened to escape his eyes. "Hello. Just watching this." He waved his hand towards the ship. "I wish I could go with you on this adventure. It is so exciting to see this happen. It was a long battle to get this off the ground." He turned to Ashton. "What time do you officially leave?"

"Tomorrow morning. Everyone has to report to the check point at some ungodly hour," Ashton replied.

Findlee nodded. "I will be here to see you off. Now, go and say good-bye to your friends staying behind. Don't get so drunk that you miss your flight."

Ashton patted his father on the back. "There are only a handful of people I want to see. How about dinner tonight at home? The last home meal for the next year and a half.

Findlee smiled. "I would appreciate that."

The next morning President Findlee and Ashton walked to the visitor's deck near the check point. As groups of people were marked off, Findlee allowed a tear to roll down his face. He sniffed. "Your group is coming up soon. You better join it." He gave Ashton a hug, "Goodbye, son. I will miss you. The hardest part is the zero contact."

Ashton nodded as he gave his father hug. "Yeah. The Lacertians have made long distance communications be impossible without us revealing where we are." Father and son released themselves from the hug, shook hands before separating permanently.

Findlee waited until Ashton walked up the ramp to the door. He saw Ashton stop and wave back. He reciprocated. He remained on the visitor's deck until the spaceship rose slowly into the sky, and then suddenly sped away in a blink of an eye. Findlee whispered his anxiety as he walked away, "Just come back safe and sound. One lonely year and half for me. The trip will change him forever." A tear rolled down his face as the loneliness instantly became a reality. "Pull yourself together," he mumbled to himself.

Seven Months Later.

Commander Jalon of the Pleiadean ship, The Explorer, had called a meeting for the head of staff from every division in the crew. "As you know we have come across this inhabited planet bustling with life and technology. This is the first planet which we have come across showing any form of advancement." The crew nodded their agreement. "I propose we stay and investigate this planet." A few eye-brows raised, and people sat up straighter showing their renewed attention. "With your agreement we stay to observe this planet and learn its ways. We can hide behind this planet's moon by linking to its rhythm and movement patterns around the planet. I hand you over to the Captain Keka."

"We can stay in the moon's orbit and in its shadows as we explore the planet. We can do this for three months and after that we must return to Beta Cancari."

Neo, the head of security, voiced his concern, "Only three months? That will not be enough time. We won't have time to sort the place out. May I suggest we stay for five months. We have mapped the route for our return. We won't be spending precious time plotting pathways and facing the unknown. To get a better idea how this planet functions, we can send one of my team down."

"Just what are you proposing?" Keka asked with a horrified look on his face.

"An experiment. What we can see, the people on this planet are varied in colour and body shape. One person can go and live amongst them. In this way we will be able to assess this planet much better than sitting in this place. True it will be an experiment and maybe fraught with danger. Safeguards will be taken to ensure the person is safely returned."

Commander Jalon shook his head. "No. Too risky. There is at least a language to be learned. I don't think you have thought this through properly. No. I won't allow it."

Dr. Haiten drummed his fingers on the desk. "The gravity is stronger than what we are all used to. That will take a toll the person's body. The air quality is another consideration. I know water will not be a problem as we have all seen it is abundant but is it drinkable? Not to mention issues with the food. It could kill a person."

Neo smiled. "My team can overcome all of that. True the language is a stumbling block. But these kids are the fastest language learners you could ever come across. Let them have a go. What an experience it would be for anyone who goes down." Seeing Commander Jalon and the others were not convinced. "Okay a compromise," said Neo.

"We stay for four months observing from afar. But if my team cracks a language code in one month or less, we stay for the rest of the three-month time slot and observe how our person copes. If there is the slightest hint of trouble, we extract the person immediately. We monitor and record every movement and every word the person says." The group sat in silence contemplating Neo's suggestion.

"Okay, it's a compromise," said Jalon. "Give me the files on all your team members. Get them started immediately while I go through their background. Meeting adjourned."

Jalon looked at the files on his private computer. Eight young adults trained at the academy for espionage and covert work against the Lacertian ruled planets in Oberon and Amada which were once their home galaxies.

- Ichiro. Twenty-one. Two missions to drop supplies to three groups of rebels in Carnel, the former capital of Daraxon. Both missions succeeded.
  One mission to Octophoria to help structure the rebel groups to be more effective in their attacks. Fluent in Daraxon and to a lesser extent in Octophoria.

- Frode. Twenty-one. One mission to Lacerta. Planted bombs in Hydra, the capital city of Lacerta. Two bombs exploded in the main city square. The bombs were positioned in a way that would make Lacertians run in a predetermined direction. In reality, the lacertians ran towards two more bombs which exploded minutes later. The four bombs killed three hundred and fifty-two Lacertians and injured many more.
  Two smaller missions delivering supplies to Genobolan rebels. Fluent in Lacertian.

- Garyth. Twenty-three. Two missions to Nubia to deliver supplies. Participated in combat against Lacertians. Both times freed Nubian slaves in the food farms destined for the Lacertian Draconian tables. Over two hundred slaves freed. One mission to Beta Genobola. Bombed one small Lacertian food factory making canned and preserved human for their population. Fluent in Nubian and Genobolian.

- Kora. Twenty-one. The only female to qualify. Computer genius. Two missions to Nubia. One mission to assist the underground rebels to release water through the city to all suburbs except the areas with high concentration of Lacertians, namely the city centre and the immediate surrounds. She altered the automated water distribution codes to ensure the water would flow continuously. She also inserted a virus which would always revert to her original codes after ten hours should the Lacertian succeed in diverting the water to their quarters.
  The second mission to Nubia was on the other side of the planet where she assisted rebels to break into the main medical

production plant. She altered the computerised manufacturing program to include toxins in the formulas. Unknown number killed. Fluent in Nubian.

- Nodin. Twenty-two. Two missions to Centaria to deliver supplies and assorted medical equipment, to a known group of underground fighters. That mission included bombing the brand-new Lacertian library as a diversion to free sixty Centarians destined for the Lacertian and Draconian dinner tables.
The second mission was to assist in blowing up a Lacertian high school where human children were used for dissection in biology lessons before being consumed. Fluent in Lacertian. Still learning the Centarian language.

- Eraton. Twenty-one. Two missions to Genobola to assist the rebels in bombing the mines bearing rich minerals. The minerals were used by the Lacertians and Draconians to build their crafts. The second mission resulted in two truckloads of weapons and ammunition being stolen and contents distributed to the rebels. Assisted rebels in attacking an overnight holding bay for slaves. Over one hundred Geobolan slaves were freed. Fluent in Genobolan and Lacertian.

- Ashton. Twenty-two. One mission to Turbia, the very first legitimate colony of the Lacerta. In Turbora, the capital city, bombs were scattered around the city heart and surrounding suburbs. The first explosions killed sixty percent of the politicians while the Lacertian parliament was in progress. In less than thirty minutes, the bombs planted in the suburbs at major municipal buildings exploded. This included an arena where people were being auctioned for Lacertian dinner tables or for slavery. The arena collapsed causing a forty percent instant death rate. Unknown numbers died later from flying debris and panic to leave the venue. Suspected of having mind control abilities but refuses to be tested. Not fluent in any of the Oberon and Amada languages but manages extremely well.

- Eldon. Twenty-one. One mission to Isobola, a former incarceration planet. With the planetary shift caused by the destruction of Pleiades, Sirius B and Andromeda, the planet's angle changed. It is now a holiday resort. Eldon with the assistance of some Genobolans blew up the major space port killing over six hundred Lacertians and Draconians. Tourist travel was suspended for six months.

One mission to Daraxon. He altered the chemical formula for the balls of 'sniff' to make them toxic for the Lacertians. This costed the vegetarian faction of the Lacertian government millions in compensation. The number of Lacertian deaths was estimated to be over two thousand before all the paint balls were recalled. Fluent in Lacertian and Daraxon

Jalon drummed his fingers on the desk and pondered just who in the group would best be suited for the task. He re-read the files looking for more details and became frustrated at the lack of access to Beta Cancari's community and academy records. He leaned back on his armchair staring at the ceiling as if some answer was up there. He smiled as an idea came to his mind. He called Neo and Keka into his office.

A few hours later, the youthful group had assembled in the gym. Neo, Keka, and Jalon watched as Dr. Haiten established the biological base lines before attaching weights around their bodies to simulate the extra force the gravity will be exerting on their bodies. Dr. Haiten explained, "Every morning you people will be put through different exercises with the weights. In the afternoon you're free to go to the communications room and work out a language from that planet we are all studying."

On their third afternoon in the communications room, Eraton made a breakthrough. He pushed on the communications button which went directly to the flight deck. "Sir, I've managed to intercept clear pictures and speech coming from two satellites. Please come to the communications rooms and see what I have discovered." Both Keka and Jalon went to the room to see half of the screens lit up with a myriad of foreign faces speaking strange languages. "Sir, we have tapped into television programs but what is puzzling us is the language. Ashton believes there are a variety of languages rather than just one. We are trying to sort out which is the most dominant one for us to focus on."

Ashton looked up from the three screens in front of him. "This place is amazing. I don't know how these people can communicate; look at the sounds and the scripts. I have worked out there are over fifty scripts. I am trying to isolate one."

Kora called out, "Look over here. I have what I believe to be a children's program matching sounds or words with individual letters or scripts." The room focused on the screens Kora was watching. Ashton smiled and planted a kiss on Kora's forehead. "That's the one we will focus on. What frequency are you on?"

"Frequency delta two nine four coming from the satellite situated at three degrees seven four six." Jalon and Keka nodded at the progress and left the group to their language lessons.

Everyone in the room fine-tuned their equipment to pick up the same information. Like children in a classroom from centuries past, they began imitating, chanting and writing. When the program ended some replayed it while others searched for other children's programs. From that day on, the team located thirty programs, but it puzzled them as accents were different and at times the scripts and words were also different. Kora, then realised they were confusing themselves as they now found different languages used the same script in different ways. She pointed the problem out and re-directed everyone to one find one language which could be dominate. Two more days went by before they settled on one. The group was now focused on English. Between themselves they practised speaking but were never sure if they had the language right in all aspects.

Within two weeks of listening, imitating and writing, the group developed a clique. They started to watch assorted shows but decided they loved action movies best of all. Rapidly the language unlocked, and they paid more attention to the script. Within days they mastered that as well. They knew the spelling was frequently incorrect, but it didn't bother them.

Keka walked into the communications room and saw group speaking and correcting each other in the new language. He smiled at their progress and thought, *Neo was right. They are good. Very Good.* He watched them looking at the screens watching some sort of electronically transmitted entertainment and wished he could join in their delight. He flicked the light switched off and on to gain their attention. "Screens off and everyone to the gym," he ordered. He heard a few groans and strange words what he surmised cussing in the new language.

This time in the gym the group was surprised not to be face with strenuous work outs. Smiles lit their faces as they were handed bits of equipment. "Put the earpieces on and turn on the microphones," ordered Dr. Haiten. Each placed a clear plastic blob into an ear. Out of the translucent ear blob came a near invisible cord which was then hooked over the back of the ear. The cord came to an end about halfway down the jaw line. It had a small clear ball which they twisted until a voice could be heard. Instructions came via the earpiece. "Please speak your name and give your room number." Each gave their details. Each engaged in minor conversation with an unknown voice. Each was then instructed to turn off the equipment and place it in a personalised location for collection later.

Next, they were instructed to remove their shirts and put on a plain white T-shirt. Kora moved herself to a semi-partitioned area for the change of clothes. Next, they were given tan coloured trousers. Dr. Haiten explained the shirts and the trousers. "These look like common clothes as seen on the screens you have been watching. It will look normal to the people on the planet but to us it is high tech. While you have been learning that language, the bioengineers have been busy developing these clothes. The fibres are hundreds of bio-physical readers. They read every body output; sweat, muscles exertions, dryness, heartbeat, and so on. Each of you will be monitored two at a time so we have some comparative vitals. Whoever goes down will be biologically always be monitored for their health at all times." Haiten read out the first pair and the set task all will be doing. After forty minutes the base lines were established.

"Next test. Take off your shoes and put these shoes which look like the shoes worn on this planet." Dr. Haiten waited until everyone put the shoes on. "Pair up. One walk around the gym in pairs. When you get back here then jog one lap and then run as fast as you can for one lap." When everyone had completed their laps, Dr. Haiten picked up a pair of unworn shoes sitting to one side. "Did any of you not find the shoes comfortable? Don't be shy pointing that out." He looked around the group. They seemed satisfied.

Haiten held up the spare shoes. "Now the surprise bit. Maybe it is the fun bit for some of you." He smirked. "Stand in a line shoulder to shoulder then spread out to be two shoulder widths apart." He pointed to the structural beams above. "See that beam. Tap the tip of each shoe once on the floor. That will activate a vertical jump from a standing position. If you are running, you have to stop just for a second before tapping the tip of the shoes. Both shoes must be tapped but not necessarily at the same time or in a certain order. Let's see if you can jump up and hang onto the beam."

Garyth looked puzzled. "Just how are we to get back down without injuring ourselves?"

"That, my son, is a good question. Hang under, let go and drop down for the others to catch you or find another way down. It's called problem solving." "You're kidding!" said Garyth.

"I am not. Just let go," confirmed Dr. Haiten as he surveyed the room. "One at a time."

Eraton went first but fell short of the beam by a metre. Next Nodin tried and came close. Kora tried but failed miserably. Garyth tried and cursed as he lost composure and landed on the floor in a heap. Eldon succeeded to grip the beam and hung before allowing his body to drop. He smiled as he landed. Frode missed the beam to sail beyond its height and came crashing down landing on top of Eraton and Nodin. Ashton found himself just going beyond the beam's height to land on the beam itself. He slipped but managed to grab the beam and curl his body around it.

Looking like a snake curled around a tree branch, he stayed there wondering what to do. Dr. Haiten yelled, "Don't waste time. Get down!" Ashton pulled himself to a sitting position on the beam and looked around. Slowly he stood up on the beam, walked across it towards a vertical round post and slid down. Dr. Haiten clapped. "Well done. That was problem solving."

Ashton wiped away beads of sweat from his face. "Thank you, Sir."

Ichiro tapped his shoes. He flew up in a beautiful acrobatic style and landed gracefully on the beam. He climbed down to hang by his arms under the beam and then dropped as gracefully as he had landed on the beam. Dr. Haiten smiled at his style. *An acrobat,* he thought. Haiten ordered all of them to find a location in the gym and keep practicing and landing for the next twenty minutes. As he watched the group, those monitoring their body vitals, kept recording.

"After lunch we come back here. Keep those clothes on. We are still collecting data. Be back here in one hour. As the group left the room and headed down the hall to the mess room, people they passed turned their heads at the group wearing strange attire. No one asked a question, and the group felt relieved not having to answer.

When they returned to the gym, they were told to continue their jumps for the next ten minutes. Neo joined Dr. Haiten and addressed the group. "Those shoes have another built-in feature. See the design on the side? With a hand on each shoe press the button in the centre and run. I want you all to run through the ship going down this path." He held up a map. "Here to the engine room going down these corridors, one lap in the engine room and back going down these other corridors before coming back here. We are going to time you and cameras along the route will be watching. Do not run into anyone or equipment. You will leave in pairs. Find yourself a partner and leave on my signal. First pair. Ready? Go!"

Kora and Nodin bent over and pressed the button in the motives on the shoes. They could feel some power wanting to propel them out of the room and down the prescribed path. They bolted out of the room, down the first corridor, down a set of steps, down another corridor and nearly collided with people coming out of a room. They ignored the startled people who were shaking their heads. They reached the engine room circled it once before returning on the almost identical path. On the way back, they nearly collided with Eraton and Ichiro. Later they came across Forde and Garyth before their route ended and meeting Eldon and Ashton who were just leaving the gym.

Neo looked at the timer. "Impressive. Very Impressive. Just three minutes to cover that distance. Take a break." A minute later Eraton and Ichiro came in only puffing slightly. Frode and Garyth bolted through the door laughing and puffing occasionally. Neo signalled them to rest. "Three minutes. Was it that entertaining?"

Garyth looked up to Neo and nodded. "Fantastic to go like the wind." A minute later Eldon and Ashton came through the door also slightly puffing.

"Wow," said Frode punching the air with delight while looking at the others. "The best run ever." Neo looked at the time as Eldon and Ashton came through the door. "You two were the slowest at three minutes fifteen seconds."

"Look at the recording and see our obstacles," Ashton retorted.

Neo asked for a play back on the gym screen. The first three groups had a perfect run, almost no one was about. Then he watched the recording of Ashton and Eldon. People were in the corridors and the two of them weaved their way around. Then both stopped and hit the tip of the shoes. They flew over the oncoming crowd which scattered and screamed their way to alcoves or the walls of the passageways. Neo looked at the flying action. "The jump is supposed to be vertical. How did you make it go horizontal?" He paused the play-back.

Eldon smiled. "Lean forward not up. It was an experiment we did together. It worked."

Ashton laughed. "It was fun scaring the others. Can you please re-run those jumps? I love seeing the faces on the crowd."

Neo debated in his mind before giving into the indulgence. He played the clip back in slow motion. Surprised looks and scattering people brought a smile to his face. But he was focusing on the body angle before lift-off and the angle of landing. *I will have to show the tech people this,* he thought. Eldon said at Neo, "Re-play the rest."

Neo continued the play back. Ashton and Eldon were about to go down the stairs to the engine room but found their path blocked by people struggling with equipment on the stairs. Ashton and Eldon vaulted over the rail. They completed the circuit only to find the struggling people had barely moved two steps. They went to the side of the stairs, tapped their shoes to fly up. They vaulted over the rails again before disappearing. Their actions distracted the people with the equipment to a point they nearly lost control. Neo smiled. "Very creative. Well done. Tomorrow, we meet here again at eight. New equipment to test. Change your clothes. Dismissed." The group left the gym. In the corridors, they paused like one mind. They ran through the corridors scattering all coming towards them.

At eight in the morning, Neo and Dr. Haiten had already laid out wrap-around sunglasses. Haiten stood back allowing Neo to take control as he observed the group's actions. Neo ordered, "Put your glasses on and wait for a few seconds. Keep still while your DNA is matching the glasses to you." Neo received word from somewhere else in the ship.

"That process is complete." "To test them, make a swap." The group made several swaps. "You will notice that only you can now use your own sunglasses. If anyone else tries them on, it will be like a blindfold. Swap back. Take them off again and look at the design at the front."

He waited until all the glasses were returned to their owners. He directed the group to look at the circular designs on the glasses. "They have important functions. On the top just were the arms meet the frames you can see a circle on either side. These are cameras; what you see is what we see. On the arms, just beside the cameras is a small indentation. These are the voice activation controls. The centre circle is fun and games part which will require you to practise. At the back of the room there are some metal boxes where you will find items for practising on. Follow me."

Neo slipped on his glasses and stared at the target. "This is harder than it looks. The maximum distance between you and your target is three metres. That is the best we could do in such a small apparatus. The glasses are your main tool kit. Line up. Face your target. Look at the target and say 'Red'. A beam of light will shoot out from the middle circle. It will be hard to predict how and what will happen to any object you point to. Some objects will catch fire instantly. Some objects will melt, others will misshapen and be rendered useless. Some components of an object will melt inside to cause a malfunction. The person holding any weapon pointed at you is most likely to drop it before they develop a severe burn. If they are stupid enough not to let go, the object will leave a permanent brand on their hands. There is a time variable as it depends on the object being fired upon. Aim for the centre. Go." Neo and Haiten allowed them practise. Each person adjusted the beam until they hit the target consistently. At the end of the session, they inspected the misshapen objects.

"Now we go to orange. Orange will cause a mechanical object to mal-function or just stop working no matter what the object does. Like before, speak the word. Neo demonstrated. "Orange. A narrow beam will shoot out to break the object." He aimed at a perfectly good light tube. "You have a pile of objects in front of you. Let's see you wreck them before they are recycled into something else on this ship." The team continued practising until lunch time. Neo nodded. "I think we can have a break while the room is refitted with equipment. See you all back in two hours for a long session. I need to keep these glasses with me." He pointed to a pile of boxes each having a person's name.

"Find your sunglasses," ordered Neo. The next colour we are going to do is yellow. You're going to like this one. Instead of using a stationery target you're going to play a kid's game of tag. One blast of yellow stuns a person or animal for thirty seconds. Two blasts for up to a minute and so on but don't go beyond four blasts in one succession as it may permanently injure a person. Two blasts and a break of ten minutes then two more will be safer for the victim."

Kora asked, "Just how does it stun a person?"

Dr. Haiten answered, "Each of the beams shoots ionising and non-ionising rays. The red beam are the two rays combined with microwave rays. The orange is combined with ultrasound pulses. The yellow is just pure ionising and non-ionising rays. We do not want to injure the person or animal which receives the blast. We only want to stop them from injuring you. Nothing more. I will tell you how the other beams work when we introduce them to you."

Dr. Haiten cast his eyes around the room. "Garyth you're going to be the first victim. You have to dodge the shots. If you get hit, you can't move no matter how much you try. When Garyth is caught then it will be Eraton's turn to be the victim. I want each of you to feel the stun effect, and to realise how annoying and frustrating it is. For some, it can be scary. Garyth, when you come out of the stunned state, you can immediately join in to try to shoot Eraton. Remember we are monitoring all body responses. Garyth are you ready?" asked Haiten.

"Not really."

"Give Garyth five seconds to move away and then on my command," Neo said.

Garyth jumped over equipment noticing flashes of light just missing him. He ran close to a mirror then dived. The beam reflected back to the shooter. The shooter, Ichiro, was stunned but Garyth continued bobbing around the gym equipment. Kora took aim trying to anticipate Garyth's movements. She hit him on the hand. Garyth was stunned. Neo called out, "Stop!" Just as he did so Ichiro started to move, stiffly at first and then with more ease. Neo walked over to him. "Can you explain to the others how it felt?"

"You can hear and see everything around. It was downright annoying being trapped in your own body. You could have warned us the mirror would reflect the beam," he said angrily.

"Sorry. We didn't know for sure," replied Neo.

Garyth gave a groan as he slowly recovered. "That was horrible." He took a few wobbly steps before he was able to walk normally. "I saw you all run around. I could hear you speaking to Ichiro, but I couldn't do a thing but move my eyes. Scary."

"Shall we continue?" Dr. Haiten asked. "We still have to establish base lines. "Eraton, you're next."

Eraton just looked at the group. "Ashton just shoot me so I am over and done with."

Dr. Haiten shook his head. "Movement. No short cuts." He leaned forward and yelled, "Run!"

Eraton touched the motives on his shoes and ran around the gym at the same time ducking and swerving. Frode took aim as he neared the weights. The beam bounced off the weights and hit Eraton in the back. Arched in a very uncomfortable stance, Eraton stood helpless. Nodin walked up to Eraton and lifted Eraton to another position of the room. Nodin could see Eraton's eyes staring back, helpless. Nodin then tried to move parts of Eraton's body then he realised exerting force would break a bone. He stopped and waited for the affect to wear off. Seconds later, Nodin was able to move one of Eraton's arms with ease but still Eraton was unable to resist. Neo and Dr. Haiten raised an eyebrow. "When he recovers which will be soon, you're next."

Nodin prepared himself for some revenge from Eraton. He tapped the tip of his shoes for a vertical jump onto the beam above then ran across the beam doing a couple of summersaults before jumping onto another beam. Nodin just managed to grab the beam when Eraton hit him. There he stayed until the effect wore off. Dr. Haiten walked over ready to catch him just in case he lost balance. Nodin recovered and fell landing on top of Kora and Dr. Haiten. Nodin pulled himself up from the human pile. "Thanks for the catch." Dr. Haiden and Kora slowly picked themselves up from the floor. Kora whispered as she rubbed one of her legs, "Any time."

Neo called out from the other side of the room, "Kora your turn." Kora waved back to Neo and ran behind some equipment, jumped over other bits when Garyth fired hitting her mid-air. Ashton, who was just behind her, ran to catch her before she landed hitting the hard equipment. He safely positioned her between two pieces of protruding bars and whispered with a broad grin and a wink, "Now I know how to stop you from yapping." Kora eyes faced him with frustration. She just wanted to kick him for the comment but couldn't. As she recovered, she yelled, "Ashton, you're in for it!" Ashton grinned knowing well what she meant. "I hope so. My room or yours?"

Before he could move or say anything more, Kora shot him at close range much to the amusement of the others. She whispered in a smug manner, "Sucker."

Neo and Haiten chuckled to themselves. "This is what I like about this group. One can expect the unexpected," said Neo to Haiten before he slowly approached the group. They waited for Ashton to recover before moving on. Neo looked at the group. "I see you all have now mastered the aim. This time we are going to move out of the gym and cause havoc. The next colour is green. Green is again the ionising and non-ionising beams with electro-magnetic pulses. We are going to walk around in one group and use the green beam to open locked doors or start things up. He demonstrated by shooting a beam at the locked gym door. The locking mechanism clicked and broke. He pointed to the broken lock. "Maintenance is going to be busy. Shall we proceed?"

Neo and Dr. Haiten led the group down the corridor and stopped near a vending machine. "Ashton, this machine doesn't always work." He pushed a few buttons. Nothing happened. "Make it work." Ashton stood in front of the machine. "Green." The lock on the door clicked. Ashton opened the door and helped himself to a few snack bars which he passed around.

Eraton smiled. "Now that is more like it."

"Shall we move on?" suggested Dr. Haiten as he peeled the wrapper off the bar he was holding.

As they passed doors to various rooms, each took a turn to unlock the door. The doors with the electronic swipe pads which normally shone red to indicate it was locked now shone green. The doors just with knobs fell apart. The group walked away pretending to be innocent of any wrong doing.

They entered the laundry room. "Line up in front of a machine and fire at will." Ten large machines which had completed their cycles restarted. A lady came rushing in scolding them, "Those clothes were just completed. Why did you start the cycle up again?" Looking around to see all but two wearing the wrap-around glasses, she summoned up courage. "Get out! Get out you creeps. Get out before I call security!" Neo smiled but didn't say a word knowing he and the small group were the security. He ushered the smiling group out. "Just one more practise shot. Up to the games room," said Neo.

When they entered the games room only two people were there operating the only two workable machines. "Maintenance hadn't come to this section for days as it is low on the list." Neo ordered, "Find yourself a machine and make it work. The two people in the room spun around with relief thinking at last the other machines with different games were going to repaired at long last.

Green beams shot out. The consoles started up but died almost instantly. Neo repeated, "Fire up and keep the beam running so you can play for a bit. The longer the beam stays on, the longer you can play. If the beam shuts down, so does the machine." After an hour, Neo ordered the team to leave the room.

The original two people walked over to the now silent machines and saw they were just as dead as they were before. Disappointed, one whispered, "Who were they? And how did they do it?"

The other person shrugged. "Don't know. Maybe they are a privileged group. Neo said keep the beams going. What beams was he talking about? I didn't see any beams, did you?" The other person shook his head.

Dr. Haiten and Neo led them back to the gym. They noticed the door of the vending machine was wide open and the contents gone. When they entered the gym, Dr. Haiten noticed the door was repaired, *that was quick* he thought.

Neo ordered them to their target areas as before. "The pieces of junk you created before, I see has been left here. Not a problem. The next colour is blue. Blue has the ionising and no-ionising pulses mixed with gamma rays. Blue will slice through metals of any description. It is most effective on pieces no thicker than two centimetres. Do not use this beam on any life form as it will kill the animal or person. Go ahead. Practice slicing the scrap metal and see if you can create a shape or sculpture." Dr. Haiten and Neo watched the group and noted the concentration levels on their faces.

As the group practised trays of food and drink were brought in.

Neo set the next training session up.

After thirty minutes he called their attention for the next task. "This will be a bit easier and slightly more enjoyable. Take three different glasses of liquid each and set them in the target area. You should have one water, one juice, and one of cooking oil. The idea is to freeze the liquids. Different liquids will take different times to freeze. The same principle applies like the green beam making a broken piece of equipment activate. The colour is purple. Purple shoots out the ionising and non-ionising pulses with an atomic imitation of a coolant measured at minus forty degrees. You can start."

Dr. Haiten examined the liquids, as he did so Kora asked, "Would the purple beam freeze a person or animal?" Haiten contemplated the question. "Small creatures for sure but I wouldn't know what effect it would have on larger animals or people."

With a wink. "Do you want to volunteer to be a victim?"

"Err. No Sir. Just curious," Kora replied.

"As a guess, the larger the life form, the greater the amount of beam time would be required. It may drain the energy source or make the glasses redundant. It would freeze metal and as you know a person touching frozen metal can be stuck there until it thaws, or they risk pulling their skin off and that would be painful. Some types of thin frozen metal can be smashed with a hammer."

Neo called out to the group, "The next task is freezing these bits of food. Make your own ice blocks and you can eat them if you wish. Neo saw a few smiles as each took a tray of food to the target area. Again, they aimed their beams to the bite sized morsels. Most found the size challenging their focus abilities. When all pieces were frozen, Neo examined each tray. "Are you going to eat that or will you have a go heating them up with the red beam?" Eldon selected two items to suck then switched to red to practise thawing. He groaned at his attempt which burnt the food.

Ichiro decided to eat one of the items of food. He tried hard to focus on the small area but found he incinerated the most. Kora looked at the results of Eldon and Ichiro. *One short blast should do it,* she thought. She concentrated on a short blast from a further distance. It worked. One item was perfectly cooked, and a tiny bit of aroma turned Ashton's head. "Can you do that again to make sure it wasn't a fluke?"

"Watch and learn from the chef," she teased. Another perfectly cooked morsel was on the plate. As she was bringing it up to her mouth, Ashton's swooped his mouth over the food and ate it off her fingers. She laughed at the prank pulled on her. "I suppose we're even now?" With a stuffed mouth he nodded his head and sucked in air to cool his mouth. "Ho-ot." He swallowed as Kora burst out laughing and planted a kiss on a reddened cheek. "Now we're even?" Ashton nodded.

The next day Dr. Haiten and Neo spoke to the group regarding their biological results. "You don't make it easy for us. The results are almost identical. We've never had such a homogeneous group before any mission. Today, we are going to try harder to sort you out. All of you are worthy to go to the planet but we realise if a group went, it would draw attention or suspicion. Today we are testing you out in a different way. You have fresh shirts and trousers to put on. It's black this time. It does the same task as the ones you have been wearing for the last few days. The one's you are taking off now are going to the laundry." Neo waited for the change of clothes to take place. "Put your communication systems on."

He handed over the sunglasses. "This time you will not be using the ray beams. You will only be using the standard glasses with your earpieces. This is to give the person supervising your actions, practice in recording and communicating with you." The object of this task is to find on this ship two cubes." He held up a cube for all to see. "There are only two on the ship. The cube is this size, white with a green dot on two sides. There are ten other cubes hidden on the ship. They are decoys. You won't get any prizes for finding and bringing in the decoys. You can leave the decoys where you find them or bring them in to the gym. That decision is yours. The decoys are similar in size and colour but have green dots on all sides. Take a very good look at this cube for it will be this cube which will advance you to the next level. You will need a partner for the task because you will need a second pair of eyes to help with the search. Partner up now." Neo waited until the group had formed four pairs.

He handed each person a card. "The card I gave you has all the parts of the ship where you can enter to search for the cubes. As you can see, you are permitted to search each other's rooms, our rooms and the personal rooms of those who gave permission for this test. They are mostly people who have been recording your statistics. Take a minute to read through the list. Feel free to ask questions."

Frode was the first to speak, "This is half the ship! One day to find two small cubes? That's a big ask." Haiten sighed. "If you are not up to it, you can sit this out."

"No. No. I am up for it. It's just the expanse."

"That is why you are in pairs. Two eyes can be better than one," said Neo. "Take a torch from the bench. Remember, your supervisor may speak to you and give instructions. It is also a team effort with your supervisor, your partner and their supervisor. Two cubes to be found, two teams will miss out and will be barred from advancing to the next level. Your time starts now," said Neo.

The teams quickly grabbed a torch and tuned into their supervisor. The supervisor paired themselves to match pairings. The teams quickly planned their routes and rooms to search and raced to their starting point. Room by room they searched. Icherio found a fake cube under Commander Jalon's bed. He cursed as he moved on to Haiten's room. Ichiro and Frode searched the rooms of the other team members. When they left the officer's quarters, they left the rooms tidy but when they searched their colleague's rooms, they left the mess of upturned personal effects. They reasoned if the room was a mess, the following teams would either not bother or re-search the room but would be slowed down with the disorder. Like vultures moving from one room to the next, the teams searched the permitted areas.

Kora and Eldon who had teamed up, were first to search the mess hall and the kitchen. Much to the annoyance of the kitchen staff they entered freezers and fridges, pulled out cutlery and cooking utensils, searched the storerooms, benches and everything that could be big enough to hide a cube. While they were searching, the staff yelled at them to get out and threatened to complain to higher up when Kora and Eldon ignored them.

Just as they were leaving, Garyth and Nodin burst in to repeat the search. Then the kitchen staff picked up large knives and chased Nodin and Garyth out, "The place was searched seconds ago. This is not the place for your childish games. Get out! Get out!" Garyth and Nodin pressed their shoe logos and bolted out of the kitchen before any of the staff there decided to swing the knives around. As they fled, the kitchen staff who all stopped working shook their heads at the intruders and their super-fast exit.

As Nodin and Garyth departed in haste, they saw Kora and Eldon had already moved into the mess hall and had begun to examine every chair and table to the annoyance of everyone trying to eat a meal. The other crew questioned them what was going on but received no answer. Then Kora and Eldon climbed up the cross beams above examining every nook and cranny. The people below gasped and started to become anxious. When Garyth and Nodin joined them on the beams at the opposite end, the growing crowd became more concerned and wondered if there was a threat. The two teams left the mess hall to enter another room before each going in different directions.

Garyth and Nodin entered the refuse section and searched the walls and looked at each other, "Toss you. The loser goes swimming in that smelly rubbish," said Nodin as he pulled out a disk.

"Don't bother," said Garyth as he reached into a corner and pulled out a cube. He smiled, "It's the right one. White and two green dots. Let's get out of here and back to the gym." They reported their find and held up the cube for the supervisors. All the other teams were notified of the find. The pressure was turned up a notch.

Ichiro, Frode, Kora and Eldon kept becoming frustrated. They found several fake cubes and were beginning to wonder if a second even existed. Ashton and Eraton started at the flight control deck where the staff had been pre-warned of the test. They left the room and ran to the living quarters to see their rooms as well as everyone else's room in a total mess. They ran to the food propagation area and searched. As they entered the kitchen the angry head chef yelled, "You people were here earlier today. The others did a search for whatever you are looking for and found nothing. Get out!" Again, a knife was held up to make sure the intruders were not welcomed.

Ashton found himself a bench in an alcove. "Let's think about this." He crossed off the rooms that were obviously inspected and showed no results. "What did Haiten say? There are two identical cubes. The way he said it sounded like three: the one he was holding as an example and two more making a total of three. But if we twist the words; two cubes, one out there that looks like this. And he said,' this is the one which will advance you.'"

"What do you mean?" Eraton asked as he ran his fingers through his sweaty hair.

"It means, only one is out there and that was found. Haiten has the other. He had it all the time."

"So we've been running around all this time and for nothing? He must be laughing his head off," said Eraton.

Ashton nodded his agreement as he smiled. "The old guy is throwing us off the scent. The two cubes are identical, so he displayed one under our noses and we all ran off half-cocked looking for two when we were already looking at one. Back to the gym."

They ran back to the gym. Neither Neo nor Haiten was there. They asked their supervisor where the men went. An unknown voice said, "Neo has gone to his quarters. Haiten has returned to his surgery." Eraton looked at the list. His surgery was out of bounds. Ashton said, "Search the gym. It's here. I'll take the beams." Eraton and Ashton searched the room pushing aside and lifting the equipment. When Ashton finished the search on the structural beams, he gave Eraton a hand moving the heavier equipment. Ashton called a stop. "Where was Haiten standing?"

"About here," Eraton replied as he moved over to that part of the room.

"What did he do after that?"

"He watched us all bolt out like idiots while he was tossing the cube up in the air like a toy," said Eraton. Ashton imitated Haiten action and tried to think what Haiten would do. "He either put the cube back in his pocket or planted it somewhere between here and his surgery. We need to check the two possible routes he would have taken. If we don't find it, then we visit him in his surgery."

Ashton and Eraton searched the passageways. There was no result. They knew the others were searching except for Garyth and Nodin who would be tidying up their rooms or having a drink at the ships' only bar. Ashton looked at the list of rooms they had crossed out. The surgery was off limits and Haiten was inside. Eraton said, "We have to lure him out. I'll fake an injury, a possible broken arm when I fell off the above beams at the gym. Give me a minute to get there." Ashton waited for five minutes before knocking on Haiten's door.

"Sorry to disturb you. Eraton has injured himself in the gym. He was searching the beams when he slipped. I think he broke an arm." Haiten quickly grabbed some equipment and walked quickly with Ashton towards the gym. When they reached the door, Eraton was sitting on a bench nursing an arm. When Haiten reached Eraton, Ashton and Eraton grabbed him. "The cube please," said Ashton. There were only two cubes not three." They let go of Haiten. "Neo was right. You kids are clever." He pulled the cube out of his pocket and smiled with delight as he handed over the cube. "Good to see we have thinkers. I'm impressed with the scheme to get me out of restricted area." Haiten reported in that the second cube had been found.

"Ashton and Eraton, you make a good team. Tomorrow will be the final test for the four cube finders."

In the afternoon Eraton, Ashton, Nodin, and Garyth were called to Commander Jalon's office. The small office looked crowded as Captain Keka, Dr. Haiten and Neo were already inside. No sooner after Eraton, Ashton, Nodin and Garyth were inside, Jalon said, "Follow us to the lab where you will face the final test." The men walked out of the office to the research laboratory two floors below. Ten pairs of eyes looked up from their work benches as the groups were introduced to each other. The technicians inside had been briefed earlier in the day as to what was going to happen. They had three hours of preparation time; important projects were locked away while the minor projects remained on the work benches to be repaired. The team of four was taken outside for their briefing as the doors locked behind them.

Jalon addressed the group. "Put your glasses on as you will be monitored by your supervisor. Also, we will be watching through the above observation deck. There are twelve cameras in the room observing every move and every angle. Your task will be timed for three minutes and then it is all over. The people inside have been prepped for your invasion so they will be on guard. Your task is to steal at least one item from the room. If you are caught by a technician or by us, you are out of the running." The doors to the laboratory reopened. Neo, Jalon, Haiten and Keka entered the room Eraton, Garyth, Nodin and Ashton followed behind. As Neo, Jalon, Haiten and Keka disappeared up the stairs to the observation deck, the group of four dispersed themselves through the laboratory.

As individuals, each spoke to the technicians working on some object that was previously put on the back burner. Ashton and Eraton flirted with some of the most junior females as Garyth and Nodin took interest in some equipment two senior men were repairing. The group moved around the room and passed each other on occasions. The three-minute buzzer sounded. Everyone looked up at the observation deck. Jalon spoke into the speaker. "Time up. Please come up to the observation deck and wait until you are called into the temporary interview room."

The group of four each took a seat lined up in the observation deck just outside the make-shift room. Nodin was called in first. He looked at the panel sitting behind a long narrow white plastic table which looked like it was from the mess hall. Each officer sat behind with a notepad showing details of their past and the results of the last week. Nodin stood silently and waited for one of them to ask a question. Jalon looked at Nodin. "Did you manage to steal anything?"

Nodin put his hand in his pocket and pulled out three screws and a copper coil. "That is all, Sir."

"From whom did you take that equipment?" asked Keka a bit disappointed at the result.

"From one of the senior men working on what looked like the mechanism of the vending machine we vandalised a few days ago."

"Leave the parts here in this small bowl. Send in Eraton. Dismissed." Nodin placed the parts in the bowl and walked out.

Eraton walked in and looked at the panel. "What did you steal?" asked Jalon.

Eraton put his hands in his pocket and pulled out a microchip. In another pocket he pulled out a screwdriver. "From whom did you steal these items from?"

"The microchip from one of the young ladies and the screwdriver was between two people on one work bench. Neither was using it at the time," said Eraton.

"Exactly what does the microchip do?" asked Jalon.

"Something to do with a laser gun. I'm not sure which of the two microchips it is. Both look exactly the same except for the coding on the back. I would need a manual to know which microchip goes where," replied Eraton.

"Put the pieces in the bowl. Call in Garyth. Dismissed," said Jalon.

Garyth walked in the room not feeling confident. "What did you steal?" asked Neo noticing the nervousness.

"The only thing I took is now missing. I stole a small tube containing specks of mixed iron and copper shaving. It is no longer on my person. I also have memorised information. The code to the storeroom is two, two, five, eight, eight, zero, D."

Neo was impressed. "Exactly how did you come across that information?"

One of the workers entered the storeroom. Each digit and letter has a unique sound. It is just knowing what sound goes with what number and letter."

"So you would know all door codes on this ship?"

"Most, Sir."

"Just to test you out, tell me a room and what is the code."

"Commander Jalon's room is D,E, three, six, two, Captain Keka's room is four, two, five, E, A.

The flight deck is E,D,C, four, six, five. The…"

"That's enough," said Jalon as he held up his hand to stop him.

"How long does it take for you to learn the room codes?"

"As soon as I hear the sounds."

"If the sounds were altered, how long then?

"Not long. Maybe a couple of minutes."

"If they were altered to glow, how long would it take then?"

"About a minute."

"If you saw a sequence of events, would you be able to accurately recall them?"

"I would say near perfect."

"That is all. Send in Ashton," ordered Jalon as he raised an eyebrow.

Ashton walked in and looked at the panel before him. Dr. Haiten asked, "What did you steal from the room."

Ashton looked squarely without blinking. "Nothing directly from the workers." He put his hand in his pocket and pulled out an assorted array of objects. "The tube is from Garyth. The switch from Eraton. The light bulb from Nodin."

"Only Garyth mentioned the missing tube. The others didn't say a word about other missing objects," said Jalon.

"They didn't have to as they qualified with the other objects stolen."

"Exactly what did you steal for yourself?" asked Jalon trying to hide a smirk.

Ashton reached into his trouser pocket and pulled out a handful of objects. "Commander, I believe this security card is yours." Ashton returned the card to the Commander. "Neo, this mini photo of your wife belongs to you." Neo looked stunned as the plastic encased photo was returned.

"Dr. Haiten, this stylus is yours. It is really a bad habit to wear styluses on your ears." Haiten blushed after he touched both ears before accepting his stylus. "Captain Keka. This is yours - your credit card." Keka's mouth dropped. "How did you get these?"

"The rules said anything in the room from anyone. All of you were in the room for close to ten seconds. The people inside were expecting theft. All of you were not and that included the other three outside. It is easier to go for the unsuspecting."

The men were still looking stunned as they stared at their returned items. Neo managed to say, "Dismissed."

Ashton started to walk out of the room then stopped halfway and returned. Trying to look exasperated he turned to Haiten. "Sir, what is it with you that you can't keep your styluses?" Ashton held up the stylus for Haiten to take for the second time. Ashton turned again to walk to the door. Neo called out, "Okay light fingers hand over my watch."

"Sir, are you accusing me of stealing your watch? You should be asking Captain Keka that question after all he is the one wearing it." Ashton gave a cheeky salute and walked out of the room.

Keka pulled up his shirt sleeve and looked stunned. "How did he do that?"

"We better make checks to see what we own just didn't walk out of the door. Findlee said he was cheeky and full of mischief. Where's my notebook?" asked Jalon.

"Ashton!" they chorused loudly.

Jalon walked quickly to the waiting group and held his hand out for the notebook. Ashton pulled it out of his clothing much to the surprise of the other three. "Are you trying to get yourself into some kind of detention?" asked Eraton.

"No. Just had enough of these tests. I'm going back to the communications room to practise that foreign language. Anyone coming?"

Jalon was soon joined by Keka, Neo and Haiten. As they walked back to Jalon's office to discuss the results, Haiten looked to Neo. "I didn't know the academy was teaching young adults to be criminals."

Neo considered the comment before replying, "It depends on your perspective. To many, these young people are heroes; certainly, to the various resistance groups in Oberon and Amada. They remain invisible to the general population in those galaxies and even on Beta Centari. The Lacertians will regard them as the worst kind of criminals and if they were caught, they would face a dreadful death. Yes, we do teach some criminal activities, but it is for their survival. Past students were killed because they were not clued up enough. Stealing is one survival skill which helps them and the resistance groups to cause disruption, frees slaves and frees prisoners. Stealing a key or a gun saves lives."

Jalon added in jest, "What Ashton did was actually entertaining. I am going to re-play the events in the laboratory and see how they each stole items and the interview at the end. Ashton is on a different level when it comes to thieving. Entertaining. Garyth is on a different level when it comes to break in and entry." He smiled as he recalled the brief information he read in each of their files. *What a dangerous team. Thank God, they are on our side.*

CHAPTER TWO
Earth
Daraxon Technologies Inc.
Headquarters
Same Time Period

In the small observatory, the modified mini telescope which contained extra sensitive auditory equipment slowly spun on its base to trace an unusual sound. The person on duty was Lenax, one of the first settler-refugees to Earth. He called out to his younger brother, Egan, "Hey! We have something unusual here. The scope is tracking it now." Egan looked up from his computer and switched on the record button.

"Do we get dad up here?" asked Egan recalling what his father had always pressed into their minds, anything unusual, call him no matter what or when.

"Just give it a minute before we pull him out of bed. I want to make sure it's not a false alarm," replied Lenax as he focused on the strange signal with the moving telescope. He frowned at the noise, *mechanical*, a sound he hadn't heard for over twenty years. "Okay! Wake the old man up. We have something worthwhile."

Minutes later and still dressed in his pyjamas and gown, retired General Tayee jogged up the steps to the telescope. "What have you found?" Lenax and Egan smiled. "Something none of us have heard since the ship from Genesis arrived about twenty years ago. The scope is pointed towards the moon. Whatever or whoever was tracked to the dark side of the moon. It has anchored behind it. Egan played back the visual and auditory recordings."

The room was silent except for the mechanical noise. Tayee's face was a mix of concern and delight.

"I have heard that sound before. It's not Daraxon or Centarian. With luck it maybe a ship from one of the other planets in Oberon or Amada. Monitor it carefully. I will have to call in other guardians to see if they know the signature. I pray it is not the Lacertians. We can't have the Lacertians coming here."

Tayee left the room and drove as quickly to the main office and started phoning all the guardians of Earth and then phone Jed and his family. Jed raced to the office and smiled when he saw Tayee in his pyjamas, "That important?" he gestured to Tayee's clothes. Tayee smirked back, "Yes." I am getting the others online now. We need a major meeting as soon as possible." When the fifteen links were set up, Tayee now joined by Hammond and Jed to listen to the mechanical noise coming directly from the observatory.

Patron, the only member to represent the Pleiadean nation, smiled on the video link as tears escaped his eyes and trailed down his face and then his face sprung back with confusion and concern. "Some parts of the signature sounds like Pleiadean and then it changes. It is not a true Pleiadean signal. Remember how Alcyn tricked the Lacertians by changing the ships signal to by-pass them so he could attack the Lacertians on the planets which they occupied. We must exercise caution."

"I agree," echoed half the people on the video link.

Hammond suggested, "We will have a major and compulsory group meeting. It is too risky to do this by links. We will recall everyone from around the world. Would four days be enough time for everyone to come back here?" Hammond saw a mixture of nods and shakes.

Dalmon, the only survivor from Sirius B offered, "Make it five days to allow a few of us to catch flights from the more distant locations."

Jed nodded. "I will arrange for the mess hall to be reconfigured for the meeting. We will have to hire some chairs. How many should we expect?"

Without hesitation Patron answered, "Five hundred."

Tayee looked concerned. "The room is designed for three hundred. Some people just might have to sit on the window ledges. We will work something out. Make sure to emphasize that this is a compulsory important meeting." Not long after, the meeting was terminated. Tayee sighed, "We have our work cut out. I will slip back home and change and tell the misses what is happening. I'll be back within two hours to help monitor that possible ship."

Five Days Later.

As people entered the converted mess hall jammed with closely placed chairs and very narrow passageways, and the main table for the Daraxon Technologies Board and Refugees Council heads looked dwarfed and sandwiched. A video link with a large screen housed the overflow housed in a marquee. At seven p.m. sharp the meeting began. Jed gave a formal welcome and apologised for the suddenness. He introduced the council mostly for the benefit of the younger generation. He was followed by Lenax and Egan who explained the findings in the early morning five days ago and their constant monitoring since then. They replayed the sound and the accompanying visual recording from the telescope. Lenax finished, "The sound is continuing. Every so often we hear a different sound like a signal emanating from 'it', for want of a better term. I will now play those back and if anyone can identify that, please say what it is. I'll put the visuals on the screen so you can see the variations of intensity and frequency." Leanax played the filtered sound.

Titus, one of the original child refugees, now an adult, stood up. "I know that sound very well. NASA has them all the time. It is someone tapping into satellite. The small click is a connection. Most connections are legal as various nations and media outlets have paid for them. The preceding noise, I am not sure about. And you say it is coming from the position behind the moon?"

Egan nodded and said loudly for the benefit of those who couldn't see from their seats, "Yes."

"Do you want me to get satellites focused towards the moon? NASA or the European Space Agency wouldn't mind if they knew something was up," said Titus.

Patron stood up. "Help would be nice but not until we are sure what ship - I call it a ship for want of a better word - is hiding behind the moon. If we can't sort this out by ourselves in three days, then we ask for help. There is a chance the Russians have picked up the sound as well. I will do some sniffing to see which countries have also located the signal. Are you returning to NASA after this meeting?"

"No. I am taking official holiday leave plus more. That's eight weeks. I am considering returning here and helping out." From the rear, Mark stood up and clapped. "Good we can catch up. If this is a friendly spaceship, I want to see it and be on one. If it is an enemy ship, then, I'm ready to shoot it down."

Sue, his mother stood up. "Since the time you and Jenny smuggled yourselves on Alcyn's ship and Hammond had to return you, you have been obsessed with returning to the stars. The space station trips are nerve wrecking enough. To another galaxy? Over my dead body young man." The minor domestic scuffle caused laughter around the room. Mark blew his mother a kiss. "I love you mum."

That made people in the room laugh louder.

The meeting went on for two more hours. Within that time, plans were drawn up for two possible scenarios. Plan A was if the craft was friendly. Plan B was if it was an enemy. Then the people broke up into teams listing their names for a welcoming committee or for a war committee.

When it was time to go, Hammond approached Mark. "How is the space station going?"

"Much better with Daraxon know-how. Alcyn was right. It would never have finished without Daraxon help. How is the reconstruction of the portal system going?"

Hammond groaned before answering, "Zantha, in her haste, left behind the microchip designs. Everything else is built but we are stumbling with the chips. The chips are made, tested and stored for reference. Then we have to make sure each chip is in the right location and that is endless testing. The wrong chip in the wrong place just breaks that part of the portal system. Then we have to rebuild the broken parts. Slow, expensive, exhausting and frustrating. Mind you, Alcyn and his family took two generations to master it. Having all the other plans have accelerated the process by one generation. I just wish the portal transporter didn't blow up when Alcyn arrived. I still remember that day."

Mark recalled. "Yeah. I remember the sound of the blast. I was in the make-shift correspondence school when we were all quarantined. I still recall the crater it made, the ground shaking and the trees shredded to match sticks. We were all shocked."

Hammond placed an arm around Mark's shoulder as he said, "That was a day we all remember well. Alcyn was taken to hospital with leg injuries. Did you know the doctors pulled out over thirty bits of tree and metal from his legs?"

"No way. Are the bits still around?" asked Mark.

"In the boardroom's office in a drawer just below a picture of Alcyn. Why?"

"Just wondered," asked Mark. "Are all the pieces of the transporter still stored in the shed?"

"What was left and recognisable. They are in the old horse shed with other bits of junk."

"Tomorrow I want to take a look at the original transporter pieces and the junk. I want Titus to take a look too. Fresh eyes may see something," said Mark.

Hammond released his fatherly grip from Mark's shoulders. "You and Titus are like a puff of fresh air. Have you considered staying here and giving up the work on the space station? I have a surprise for the both of you which may sway you. We are at a point where we may need your skills. See me in my office about eleven tomorrow and I will show you both at the same time. I will organise I.D. badges and clearance status for you both." The men shook hands before parting.

Mark walked up to Titus, "Your father wants us in his office at eleven. He's got something important to show us."

Titus smiled back. "I know he was working on something besides the reconstruction of the portal system and transporter. Maybe he's ready to show us something that actually works. Are you heading home now?"

"Not immediately. How's Astra?" asked Mark.

"Ah, you still like my little sister," said Titus.

"She's still the prettiest around and the bulk of the others are related, too young or too old".

"I am sure there are a lot of pretty women in your work," Titus said.

"Some are married and are off limits. The ones still on the shelf are high maintenance or catty. Not my type," replied Mark.

"Well, she's somewhere over there." Titus pointed to a large group of young adults. "Since you have been away, you have a bit of competition these days."

Mark raised an eyebrow at the information as he walked over to the group.

Astra smiled at Mark as she grabbed his hand to pull him closer to the group and introduced him. Mark couldn't help but notice an arm belonging to a younger cousin of his, Andrew, slipped around Astra's waist. Mark deliberately placed his arm around her shoulders as if reclaiming her. To his surprise Andrew's arm remained firmed and gently pulled Astra closer to him. Astra felt squeezed and stepped away from both. She held up her mobile to take photos of those around her and then shoved the immediate cousins together to form a family portrait. In Daraxon she said, "Smile for the camera."

At eleven the next morning Titus and Mark met at Hammond's office. Both were wondering what was so important. Hammond ushered them into his office and gestured for them to sit. Hammond handed them their I.D. badge clearly stating clearance level four. Titus and Mark clipped the badges on. Both said softly, "Thanks."

"Titus you know I was working on another project. It was needed to keep my sanity from the regular failures of the portal system. Therapy so to speak. That project is all but completed. Just a few more days and a few more tests. Follow me to the new shed beside the old horse shed. It is stored there. Besides high-tech security, we have guards are on duty twenty-four seven."

Hammond stood in front of the medium sized hangar and pushed a button for the doors to open. The doors slid in the tracks barely making a noise. Titus's and Mark's mouths dropped open as they stood still. The two men working inside turned to see who was entering.

Before Mark and Titus was a mini jet. Black wings spread out with subtle curves similar to a bird. Its triangular over all shape looked ominous in the shed. Hammond ushered them in towards the set of steps which led to the cockpit. "Have a look inside. Take your time." Titus and Mark inspected the craft from all angles and climbed over every aspect like children in a playground inspecting a new addition.

Titus was first to speak, "It's beautiful. How far does it go?"

"To space in less than five minutes. Almost uses no fuel. No toxic emissions. This is the future of Earth's space flights to and from the space station. This is the prototype. The next one will be larger and will be able to go much further," said Hammond feeling proud of the creation.

Mark jumped in the cockpit. "Does it go to the moon?"

"This particular model, no. But the next one should be able to do a round trip to the moon. As you have already seen, this one has a carrying capacity for cargo and room for one passenger," Hammond said stating the obvious. "You both have pilot experience. We need pilots to test run the vehicle. Both of you can go together for the first spin as Earth kids say." Hammond spent the next twenty minutes going through the specifications and other details. "We can give it its first test run now if you like."

Mark looked around the shed. "Where are the space suits?"

"Not needed. If you crash in space, you will not survive very long. Are you both ready?"

Mark jumped in the pilot's seat. Titus was more than happy to be a passenger knowing Mark had far more experience than he had. Hammond said, "Test one is just going vertical, hover for five minutes and back down again. I better let Lenax and Egan know so the telescope can be locked in on the moon."

Minutes later Hammond gave a signal all was clear. Mark taxied the craft out of the hangar about two hundred metres away. He gave Hammond a wave before pushing the button with the up arrow. The craft gave a soft hissing sound as it lifted slowly at first to two hundred metres and then disappeared from view. Mark hit the button with the horizontal line for hover. The craft made a soft *shhh* noise as the engine function changed. The craft floated as the timer built into the hover button glowed and digital clock face replaced the straight line on the button. When it reached five minutes he hit the down for button. There was a soft change in the engine before the craft slowly lowered itself back to Earth with a whisper and kissed the ground gently.

Titus and Mark changed places. The process was repeated. Hammond waited for the engine to switch off before approaching. Titus lifted the cockpit cover, with a broad smile, "Beautiful. Just beautiful. Smooth, purrs and comfortable."

Mark echoed his agreement. "We went as far as the start of space. Do you want us to try again going further out?"

Hammond shook his head. "That is enough for the day. Taxi it back to the shed. Mark, you mentioned you wanted you and Titus to rummage around the transporter remains. Do you still want to poke around?" Mark and Titus nodded.

When the craft was locked away in the hangar, Hammond led Mark and Titus to the old horse shed. "This is all what we could salvage." He pointed to one alcove. "The big pieces which are mainly the outer shell are here." He pointed to a row of shelves containing boxes of charred matter. Around a table were four chairs. The tables and chairs were placed in front of the shelves. "The tip bits as much as we could find at the time," said Hammond as he pointed to the boxes. "Most of the transporter disintegrated from the intense heat. You're welcome to go through the remains."

After examining the large and identifiable pieces which were significantly buckled and now covered in dust, Mark and Titus turned their attention to rows of shelves housing boxes of miscellaneous fragments. Systematically going through every box only two pieces were removed and placed on one table. Before leaving the shed, they carefully placed the two pieces into a dusty jar for further examination.

Titus and Mark were at Hammond's office door holding the jar containing two bits of semi-charred items. Titus and mark were signalled to come in Titus said, "We found something which may help with the transporter. I won't be sure until I see it under a powerful microscope. Is there one around?" asked Titus. Hammond stood up from his desk. "Follow me to a lab down the corridor."

When Mark and Titus were ushered into the foyer of the laboratory, they were each handed robes, disposable gloves and disposable caps. After putting on the garments and entering the laboratory for the first time in years, Titus commented, "It's cold in here."

"We have to keep it cool and sterile. We can use the microscope near the back wall," said Hammond. He pointed to one of two microscopes not being used. Hammond focused the microscope over one of the chips and studied it for a couple of minutes. He looked up disappointed.

"Take a look. Nothing." Mark gestured for Titus to go first. Titus looked for a few minutes while manoeuvring the chips around. He looked up. "Dad, do you have a register of the chips you have already designed and failed?"

"Sure. I'll get a copy. Why?" asked Hammond.

"I think I may have spotted something." Hammond went to a set of shelves to the front of the room and pulled out four binders. Titus looked surprised at the number of chips that had been designed and ruled out as failures. Each design had a chip enclosed in a pouch. He opened one book and marvelled at the work and attention to detail. Titus looked through the binders until he found something that resembled the partial chip under the microscope. He pointed to it as his eyes darted back and forth, double checking all visible aspects. He placed the binder aside with the page opened. The damaged chip was placed next to it. He moved the folder with the damaged chip to a cleared bench beside them.

Titus put the second chip under the microscope and like before moved it around to examine all aspects. He carefully flipped through the folders looking at each and making comparisons, as much as the undamaged parts would allow.

"Dad you did re-create two chips. The one over there is on the bench is a match. The one still on the scope is almost a perfect match. The charred rim on the left is a bit of a question mark. Under other types of equipment, you may identify the rest." He tapped the page. "You did that last year going by the date written on the page."

"They still didn't work. The components didn't fire up," said Hammond somewhat frustrated. Titus stood aside. "Dad, take look. You did create one chip, but you left something out." Hammond's interest piqued. "What did I miss?"

"Look carefully at the edges and tell me what you see," stated Titus with a grin and hoping his father would see it too. Hammond frowned and then admitted defeat. "I don't see it. What do you see that I can't?"

Titus said three words, "High grade crystals."

"Where?" asked Hammond.

"The chip is encased in high grade crystals which act as a power source for the chip. I think all the chips were coated with crystals. The evidence is at the sides on both chips. The rough edging is crystals and over the other side is a partial coating of the remains of a crystal layer," said Titus. Hammond took a second look and gave a broad smile. "How did I miss such a basic thing? Daraxon had mountains of high-grade crystals. I feel so stupid." Titus placed his hand on his father's shoulder.

"No dad. You had nothing to go by. You're never stupid. Tell me how many people have done what you have done?" Hammond didn't answer but the words felt comforting.

Mark looked at the microchip under the microscope. He saw the uneven glittering edges. He asked, "Which part of the portal or the transporter does it belong to?"

Hammond looked puzzled. "All the hardware is constructed. That has been done for some time. Now it is a matter of finding which chip goes where. Now we know they have to be coated with crystal, the task maybe easier. We will remake and test every chip with a coating and insert it with every part requiring a chip. Not as easy as it sounds. We just may have the chip which was programmed from here to Daraxon. Alcyn said he blew up the palace before coming here. We simply don't know if the palace was rebuilt or something else is in its place. Knowing Alcyn and his dislike for the Lacertians, he would have made sure the palace would have vaporised. The explosion of the transporter was a fine example of his thoroughness. He was adamant that the portal system should never be in the hands of the Lacertians. Do you two want to join me in the next few days to test out the microchips?"

"Sorry dad. I think we both prefer the space craft. Can we do more testing with that?" asked Titus.

"Not for a few days. Still some glitches. Going up and down was all we were one hundred per cent confident on," said Hammond sensing their excitement to fly. "What will help is you two going through that rubbish again and finding more chips. I vaguely recall there were over 100 chips in the control system alone for the transporter. Less parts were for the viewer section. The viewer, like the transporter is replicated. The viewer's deflector works but that is about all. One thing that was never done was a scan over the area for buried pieces." Hammond sighed. "We were all so busy adjusting to the new life and later we just forgot about the search. Mark can you contact Jenny and see if she can borrow some ground penetrating radar equipment from the university. That place owes her a few favours." Mark nodded.

Jenny gave Mark a quick lesson in using the equipment over the area where the transporter stood many years ago. They initially avoided the crater now filled with dirty water. A pump was installed and was pumping for nearly four hours draining the pond as Jenny and Mark preferred to call it. In this time, Jenny made a grid with cords and stakes on three sides while the pump spat the water out on the unmarked side. Mark and Jenny took turns pulling the radar over marked squares. Mark was becoming bored with the process and wondered how Jenny could do such painfully slow work.

On the second day, in the early afternoon they started on the edge of the now empty crater. Mark noticed the audible difference, and the screen attached to the radar started to flicker with zigzags. He called out to Jenny, "I think I have something." Jenny got off her chair, grabbed a red pennant before running over to Mark. She looked at the screen. "That is something alright. Well done." She stabbed the pennant into the ground where the machine showed the most activity. "Take a break. I am going to be here for an hour. A cold drink would help when you return." Mark didn't argue as he looked at their old home now a rest area for workers in this area of the property.

Jenny put her archaeology skills to work. She dug, shifted, and carefully disposed of tailing and brushed away dirt. An hour later, Mark returned with a cold bottle of water and handed it to Jenny. He brought the chair Jenney was sitting on earlier closer to where Jenny was digging. He sat on the chair and engaged in idle chatter as Jenny became dirtier and dirtier. "You always did like playing in the mud," he commented. She looked up allowing the comment to wash over but still she retorted, "You were always the one scared of a bit of dirt." She tossed a hand full of tailings in his direction. Mark dodged the flying dirt which still managed to land on his shoes. "See," said Jenny.

She continued digging. Now she was close to forty centimetres down. She scrapped the hard-reddish dirt when she spotted something to the side of the hole. "I think I have found something." Mark moved off the seat and peered down the hole. He couldn't see anything, but Jenny's trained eye detected a sharp edge. She reached for the trowel and brush, and slowly removed the baked soil where a protruding edge became more defined. After thirty minutes, she pulled out a cube which looked fully intact. She smiled and then jumped up and down like a child holding a well-earned trophy. She handed the cube to Mark. "I'm going to clean up and pack this stuff up. Help me with the packing. Then we'll both take it to Hammond. He might know what it is."

Hammond was in the office with Titus when Jenny and Mark walked in carrying the now cleaned up cube no bigger than ten centimetres. Jenny handed the cube to Hammond. Hammond's eyes lit up. "That is a tremendous find. It's like, how should I put it, the core energy source of the transporter part of the portal system. We have been trying to get the one we made to work but have failed…chip issues." He carefully placed the cube on his desk. The exterior had a few minor dints, but he instantly knew it would work. "Come with me to the lab."

Titus, Jenny, Mark followed Hammond who had a very distinct spring to his step, to the main laboratory. He ran a few preliminary tests, but the cube failed to fire up. He drummed his fingers on the workbench pondering what he had done wrong or overlooked. He snapped his fingers when he recalled from those long-lost days, "Leave it in the sun for the next the next twenty-four hours. Let the sun do its work. Then we run the tests again."

The next day Jenny, Mark and Titus watched patiently as Hammond gave the cube a test. The cube gave a soft glow at the start, then it became brighter and brighter. When the light became intense all in the room began to shield their eyes. Hammond stopped the test. "It works. Now we have something to reproduce." Mark asked about the progress of the other chips. "They are all now remade and are currently being coated with crystal. It will take a couple of days." To Jenny, "Do you think you could recover any more buried parts?" "I'll try. It always takes time. The depth factor is always unknown. Forty centimetres is as starting point, but things could be either shallower or deeper. It's always random," explained Jenny.

Jenny took Titus to the site and taught Titus how to use the radar. Like the day before with Mark, they alternated. Titus pulled the ground penetrating radar going closer and closer to the centre of the drained crater. Jenny heard a beep from her chair and yelled out, "Stop!" As she stood up, she grabbed a few pennants before running towards Titus. "Wave it again. There." She put a maker on the spot shown by indicators on the machine. The beeps on the machine and the zig zag confirmed something else was below them. Titus continued dragging the radar for another two minutes. She yelled again, "Stop." She placed another marker. She turned off the machine and told Titus to take a break. Titus left her and walked over the hangar where the spacecraft was stored.

Jenny dug the first hole but this time only going down thirty centimetres before she spotted something. Something had a cord which had withstood the red dirt encasing it. Carefully, she scraped and brushed away until there was enough dirt moved for her to ease the item out. It was a tote bag. She frowned. Before opening it up she washed her hands using the water in the water bottle beside the chair. She gently opened the bag, gave a peep inside before slowly pulling out its contents. She burst out laughing, "It was a picture of Alcyn as a child with his parents. Inside were other family photos. She looked carefully at the well-preserved images before reinserting them in the grubby bag. "Nice find. Not what we are looking for."

She dug around the same area slowly inching her way to the second flag in close proximity. She found some fragments which she catalogued and bagged. As she came closer to the second flag she saw an object. With more excitement she dug the soil away. She looked around for Titus. She saw him coming out of the shed. She yelled as loud as she could. "Titus! Titus! I need help with this." Titus barely heard he calls but saw her waving her arms. He immediately ran over to her. "Got something big here. I need some help. Get me the other shovel." Titus brought the shovel over and slammed it in the ground. "What now?"

"Dig of course!" Jenny said in broken Octophorian.

One hour later, they stopped digging and scraping as the formation of a chair emerged. Titus burst out laughing. "I remember sitting in one of these chairs. Dad is going to love this especially if the insides are intact." He pulled out his mobile and called. Hammond couldn't get there fast enough. His car nearly ran into the crater before coming to a stop. He jumped down the hole and punched the air and tears started to well up. "The chair is important. It holds the body together in neutrino travel. A precious find. He grabbed both Jenny and Titus in a bear hug. Let's get it back to the lab for analysis." Hammond lowered the back seat of his car to make more room for the chair. Jenny smiled as Hammond drove back to the laboratory. To Jenny it was like watching a child receiving his most wished for Christmas present from Santa.

A few days later Hammond told Titus and Mark the space craft was ready for another test run. "We have notified air traffic control all the way around this country, NASA, the space station and the ESA are also monitoring the test. One lap around Australia. Satellites will be focused on you, data from all monitoring groups will be collected and correlated. Flight time is at noon. Are you ready for the maiden flight?" Hammond then thought to himself, *that was a stupid question. They have been itching for days.*

At twelve, Mark and Titus climbed in the cockpit. The craft taxied out. Mark pushed the up button. Like before the initial climb was slow and then it sped up in a blink of an eye. Mark looked at the pre-programmed flight plan. "It's south to Sydney, to Melbourne. Oops! They missed out Tassie. Do you want a quick fly over to Tassie?" asked Mark thinking of ways to prolong the test flight.

"So tempting. Better stick to the flight plan or we could get grounded," said Titus.

"Spoil sport," ribbed Mark.

In one hour the pre-programmed at medium speed, the trip 22,000-kilometer trip around Australia was completed.

When they landed, they were not met with just Hammond but a small crowd: Jed and Sue who were Mark's parents and Jenny his sister, Hammond and Stella, Titus' parents and sister, Astra, Tayee, and all his family. "It went like a dream," said Mark as he and Titus were climbing out of the craft.

"The next flight," Titus said, "Me at the controls." Stella, his mother raised her voice, "You don't have the same flight experience as Mark. I don't want you crashing that thing."

Titus frowned. "That thing can be driven by a two-year-old. It is far simpler than the standard air force jets or navy jets. And I dare say easier than driving a car." Astra tugged on her brother's arm, "Shhh. She's been on tender hooks since the announcement of the possible ship hiding behind the moon. She is so jumpy at the moment."

Titus took in the information and diverted everyone's attention. He suddenly grabbed Astra and tossed her in the air. She squealed her delight but as she came down her weight was too much. Both went down in a heap. Mark saw the opportunity to pull her up. She took Mark's held out hand saying in a posh manner, "Thank you kind Sir."

"Any time, m'lady," said Mark putting on a bad British accent.

*

Jed, Tayee, Lenax and Egan had virtually locked themselves in the observatory while the four senior guardians of Earth phoned every three hours for updates. NASA and the European Space Agency were also monitoring the strange sound as it was no longer possible to conceal the information. Titus frequently spoke to his bosses at NASA asking them to check the clicks of someone tapping into the satellites circling the Earth. They and the ESA by now had heard the sounds and ran various system checks and cross referenced all the paying companies using the satellites systems. Everything came back as normal. Only one colleague in NASA suggested someone could be piggy backing on someone else's account. They ran checks for extra data usage. Nothing.

"Strange," said Tayee. "What I recall all those years ago, the Lacertians didn't hide or monitor planets. They just plundered it and thought afterwards. Maybe they learnt from that tactic to watch, wait and see."

Patron and Dalmon, two of the senior Earth Guardians, disagreed. "Do you recall those Expansion Day Suits? They planned that well in advance," said Dalmon recalling the conference where they were informed how product inspectors were planting bombs in the products before being boxed for sale.

"Point taken," said Tayee. "Still, we will keep monitoring the moon's general area. "Were the military of the other countries informed of the situation?" Patron shuffled his notes before replying. "The U.S.A., Canada, New Zealand, the European Economic Community, Russia, China, Japan and Indonesia are on guard. Alerts are going out to the South American, African countries and all of the smaller nations."

Tayee nodded. "Thanks. How are the preparations going?"

"For the possibility of it being a Pleiadean ship, we can't do much until we know for sure. We have sourced out venues, entertainment, and all the party bits in four possible countries," said Dalmon.

"If it is Lacertian," said Patron, "and we hope it is not, the military of all nations will be prepared. Until then our hands are tied. We are keeping in daily contact. When any communications are broken or satellites are taken out, then we will know for sure it is Lacertian. All that can be done in preparation is in place now. What each government is planning equipment-wise is up to them, but we need to be coordinated. We are still working on that aspect. All we can do is keep watch on the moon."

Lenax said in an excited voice to his father, "Dad, come and look at this. Hurry! I am picking up movement from the moon. It looks like a small ship!"

"What? Whoever is up there is sending a reconnaissance craft!" said Tayee as he peered at the screen. Tayee alerted Dalmon, Patron, Hammond and Jed. Jed and Hammond volunteered to contact everyone else, and both stayed on standby for updates. Patron and Dalmon referred to their plans made days before moving towards the observatory.

Tayee and Lenax had all the tracking devices showing movement coming from the direction of the moon. Egan began to prepare the communication links with various space agencies around the world which he knew were focusing the assorted equipment towards the moving object. It was now a cooperative effort between the agencies and Daraxon Technologies in tracking the fast-moving object coming to Earth.

Tayee stood by the phone ready to report anything as he watched as Egan and Lenax going about their tasks. One hour later Egan spoke, "It's halfway here already. That thing is really moving."

Mark and Jenny came into the observatory to watch firsthand the drama unfold. Tayee looked tense as his started to call the main office where Jed and Hammond were stationed. "The thing is halfway," he said in almost a whisper and not taking his eyes of the main screen.

One hour later, the tracked reconnaissance craft circled the Earth and with each revolution it came closer and closer. NASA and the ESA picked up the trail and started calculating the estimated entry point.

The two other agencies contacted Tayee directly to confirm the object will be landing south-east from Daraxon Technologies. Tayee relayed the message to the main office.

Mark bolted out of the room taking a pair of high-powered binoculars with him. He looked up at the blue sky above. Then he ran to the tallest building in the complex, took the lift to the top floor and ran up the stairs to the flat roof which doubled up as the helipad. He stayed there searching the sky with the binoculars glued to his face and not even wanting to blink in case he missed the object. A flash went passed as it descended to the south-east. It didn't go pass the horizon. *It landed somewhere close by,* thought Mark. He did some rough trajectory calculations in his head before returning as fast as he could to the observatory. "Get me a local map on the screen now. I have a hunch as to where it landed."

Egan switched a laptop to Google Earth before handing it over to Mark who was now shaking with excitement. "If I am right, it has landed in the Lamington National Park or close by."

"How did you come to that conclusion?" asked Jenny.

"Pilot's calculations, trajectories etcetera. Maths stuff you were not too good at," he teased.

Jenny ignored the ribbing as she knew he was right. Mark was always good at advanced maths while she levelled out in twelfth grade.

Then she said with dismay, "The Lamington Park area and all the other nearby parks cover over five hundred square kilometres: dense forest, steep hillsides and the rest. A needle in a haystack." The others spun around and looked at her contemplating the size of the area. "We need to send a craft over the area looking for damaged forest as the first step. Then we need to send out search patrols keeping to all types of roads and bush tracks as much as we can before going into virgin dense bush. Then there are no guarantees of anything. "

Egan spoke slowly not sure if anyone would like to hear what he was going to suggest. "Jenny, you have the bush skills. You have been in jungles before chasing and sometimes finding needles in a haystack. I suggest you lead the recovery team."

Jenny looked shocked. "I have only done small area searches after data from satellites virtually pinpointing where to go. Nothing this big or elusive. I will need lots of help, satellite information and lots of teams. One won't be enough!"

Mark said, "We have a big advantage to speed things up; permanent helicopter in the sky directing a team to the landing site."

Tayee picked up the phone as it rang. Hammond was on the line. "Tayee here. The craft has landed in the in the Lamington National Park or one of the other parks surrounding it. We are discussing a recovery team with Jenny leading the search."

Hammond switched the phone to speaker to allow Jed and Sue could hear. Sue replied, "I want Cassie and Jamie involved. Jamie as the coordinating helicopter pilot and Cassie on standby to hoist anybody out for extraction for any reason. They have been doing this type of rescue work for years."

"Agreed," said Jenny finding more confidence knowing her aunt and uncle would be helping out.

CHAPTER THREE
The same time period
Beta Cancari

The alert signal sounded over the city. The Pleiadean people living on Beta Cancari, stopped what they were doing. Turned off the lights and proceeded in an orderly manner to the basement of the building in which they were in. In the past, this was well rehearsed drill and there was always notice it was a drill. This time, there was no notice. Anxiously, the people looked at each other in questioning silence.

When they reached the basement of each building, they walked to what appeared to be a blank wall. The internal computer scanned their faces and electronically marked each person. Then each person walked to another wall which by now opened to reveal a secret passage. The passage was wide enough for people to walk four abreast but through practice drills, it was found faster and more efficient to walk in pairs.

The tunnel pathway was flat for the first three hundred meters and then it slowly sloped upwards. This signalled to the population they were now entering the numerous caves discovered in the days of early settlement. The cave walls were now lined with reinforced concrete and painted white to help reflect the soft lighting. Every so often the walls would have a number - a countdown to the main chamber.

The main chamber was like a small theatre; seats neatly arrange where the people would sit and face the narrow stage. This time there was no one on the stage. A large screen appeared, and an image of President Findlee formed. From his room in the administration building, he directed people to settle quickly. He patiently waited for all the seats to fill. There were multiple chambers in the cave system and he waited until all but the skeleton crew above ground had confirmed all the citizens were accounted for. Silence filled each chamber.

"The observatory has tracked a ship of unknown origin. Until we are sure with what we are dealing with, all citizens are to wait inside the chambers." Then he gave directions for the certain staff to turn on the extra power sources for people to access food and drinks from the pre-installed machines. Other doors which were always shut were opened. A small passageway led to three more chambers which were bigger than the one which they were all in. Here bunker beds four levels high were separated by narrow walkways. Each room held over two hundred bunks. Signs around the edges indicated where other facilities were located: bathrooms, hydroponic gardens, entertainment and education facilities. It was almost a duplicate set up of the world outside.

President Findlee and the remaining crew monitored the sky above. The incoming data slowly began to form a picture. The signature was confusing. One part matched the old signals from Sirius B and other parts matched Andromeda then there was another aspect which didn't match anything.

Findlee and the skeleton crew braced themselves for the worst. More data came in and then there was static appearing on the communication screen. A picture formed of an Andromedan person and a Siriusian person. Findlee and his staff gasped in horror. Beside the two recognisable people was a small built female Lacertian. The images were soon accompanied by voice.

"Greetings people of Beta Cancari I am Commander Abyr from the planet of Segmar. To my right is Captain Zan from the planet of Xion. To my left is Kyrina from the planet of Lacerta.

Segmar is the colony populated by the refugees from Andromeda and a sprinkle from Nubia and Genobolia A and B. Xion is populated by refugees from the Sirius colonies and a few Nubians and from Genobola A. Kyrina and her small group of Lacertians are trusted rebels against the occupation and slaughter of humans in Oberon and Amada. We come in peace. We have been searching for you for nearly ten years."

Findlee and the staff looked in shocked silence, not quite believing what they were seeing or hearing. Findlee cleared his throat and stuttered at first, "Greeting Commander Abyr, Captain Zan and Kyrina. Please can we establish identification codes as set up by our deceased leaders of Andromeda, Sirius B and Pleiades?"

Abyr agreed to the complex identification procedure. Findlee felt better but was still being cautious, He asked. "Kyrina please give me your background."

Kyrina gave a toothy grin and her voice was sincere, "I am the granddaughter of the deposed President Kyros. When my grandfather and his family and all the politicians and their families were disposed and dumped somewhere in our galaxy, I was saved by a neighbour. I was being childminded at her house when Supreme Commander Aramadus, General Yin and friends raided our home. They took everything that wasn't nailed to the floor. Our neighbour at the time declared I was one of her children and she raised me as one of her own. She and her other children never divulged I was a family member of Kyros. The small group of renegades who are with me now have fought against the current regime. We were a small group of five which has slowly expanded to one hundred. Yes, President Findlee, there are Lacertian who are disgusted about what has happened to the people of Oberon and Amada. Our small skirmishes have been blamed on renegade Pleiadeans, Siriusian and Andromedans. It has been my small group who have been slowly feeding accurate information to Pleiadeans, Andromedans, Siriusians and when we can, to Genobolans. When we meet in person, I will explain how my small group has assisted the information being fed to your people."

Findlee was mute for a few seconds trying to process the information. He looked across the room to gauge how the others were responding. "This is all a bit of a shock. I do not want to be rude, but we need a few minutes to discuss this matter in private." He switched of the communication system and to be sure of privacy, he ordered a person to disconnect the system from the power source.

After debating and discussing the situation and possible scenarios which could play out, President Findlee reconnected the communication system. "Thank you for your patience. Commander Abyr, Captain Zan and Kyrina, I seek permission for myself and a small delegation to board your ship." "Permission granted. Please land your craft on dock two. That is the VIP dock and is located just under the flight deck. We will open the doors when you signal to us of your near approach," confirmed Abyr.

"Thank you. We will advise you when we are near," replied Findlee.

He switched off the communication system. To the small group who were going to accompany him, "Be prepared for anything. Pack and conceal well one miniaturised weapon. The rest of you, you know the drill: turn on the shield over the city, warn the people in the caves of the events. If we don't come back, prepare for attack."

President Findlee and his five diplomatic assistances docked on the ship now hovering a quarter of a lightyear away from Beta Cancari. They were met by Zan and Kyrina who ushered the small delegation to a conference room. Findlee looked around the room and noted the plaques accompanied by pictures decorating the walls – fallen Andromedan and Siriusian people. To one side were three others, Lacertians who had suffered a similar fate. He swallowed hard when he saw four plaques with names, no picture, no date of birth and deaths. Ashton's name appeared with Eraton, Kora and Garyth.

Kyrina picked up on the distraction. "We know of them. Only heroes go on this wall. We pray they are never found. These Lacertians died a few years ago. That was a bad year, three down in one go. They were close friends who assisted the resistance in Genobola. They gave the Genobolans information where to find a factory making fighter jets. The information led to the factory jets being fitted with delayed time explosives. When the fighters were in space, they blew up one at a time; different distances and different times."

Kyrina noticed Findlee's eyes go back to the four Pleiadeans. She smiled and said with sincerity, "Good men. Cleaver tactics. If my rebel group ever meet them, they will be treated like royalty; and respected equally as Alcyn. It was a pity he died in his palace. As a child, I was told he blew up his palace when a ship landed on its roof. There was nothing left of the place; just a crater and still today the area is radioactive. I would like to have met him. I was told by my adopted mother; my grandfather had a deep respect of Alcyn. My grandfather's dealing with Alcyn were constantly blocked by the military and other powerful business people."

Abyr walked into the conference centre. "Welcome aboard. You people were hard to find. Ten years it took to find you."

Findlee looked firmly into Abyr's eyes. "We did send out search parties in between raiding planets in Oberon and Amada. Beta Cancari is not resource rich. Building crafts is a problem. Anyway, we were all supposed to be difficult to find."

Zan, Kyrina and Abyr chuckled. "We had difficulty finding each other. Xion is mineral rich but is low on suitable agricultural land. It is hydroponics for us. Segmar is bountiful with water and plants, but we are constantly fighting the native creatures. They occupy the water supply and jungles. We compete with them for edible plants. Nothing is perfect." There was a knock on the door. A junior officer walked in carrying a tray of drinks. He was shortly followed by two others each carrying a tray of food. "Try our other new food," Abyr gestured to the trays now sitting on the conference table.

When Findlee and crew returned to Beta Cancari, they went directly to the underground caves. To make the planet appear more populated than the skeleton crew, about five hundred men and two hundred women went back to the surface and resume their routines. A handful of teenagers of different ages returned to resume classes and to give a small appearance of normality. The cover for such a small population of children was the people had difficulty conceiving since coming to the planet. The cribs still holding unborn children were permanently stored deep in the cave system. Very few knew the actual location, but all knew when children were born via the regular communal announcements. To Findlee, the unborn were precious.

The next day, Abyr, Zan and Kyrina landed on Beta Cancari. They noted the small delegation and small population moving about the planet. The numerous buildings didn't match. Abyr didn't comment about the buildings and observed population ratios. Findlee did pick up on the expression and the unsaid words. "We built these building in hope of filling them up with people. Then we discovered our fertility rate dropped. So now we have an over-supply of accommodation and other buildings. We have halted any more construction. No expansion to other parts of the planet either. There is no point for more settlements."

Abyr nodded but felt he was slightly misled. True, this was the only settlement he could see as he and his delegation approached the planet. He didn't question further. On Segmar and Xion, there were now five cities and all well populated. Beta Cancari by comparison, was like Segmar or Xion some fifteen years ago.

When Abyr, Kyrina and Zan returned to their ship, they flew towards the galaxy boundary. They crossed into the void and set their course towards Xion, the closet plant in the galaxy of Normaria, their new galaxy home. Segmar was in the same system but was much further away, almost to the centre.

The alarm system sounded. Abyr placed the ship into battle mode. A Lacertian mothership came at them. Abyr and crew fought and lost. Many of the fighters were lost either exploded or disabled in space to drift forever into oblivion. Those still on board the ship, were either dead or near death. Kyrina could see Abyr and Zan slumped over the controls. She struggled towards them; both her legs were injured – one was profusely bleeding. She pushed Abyr aside and flopped into the commander's chair. She released a probe no bigger than a shoe box. The probe would fly towards a void and hover for a year before self-destructing. This probe was pre-program to go towards Beta Cancari, but not close enough to expose the planet. Before she could utilise any of the other controls, she passed out leaving the ship to wobble through space.

The commander of the Lacertian ship ordered reconnaissance jets to circle the lame ship enemy ship. As the jets circled, they gave observational reports. Commander Loric ordered the pilots back and then turned on the magnetic field. The damaged ship before them stabilised. Minutes later Commander Loric with a small contingent of soldiers boarded the ship. As they moved towards the flight deck, the soldiers shot every person. To them it didn't matter if the person was already dead. The laser blasts from the guns were insurance.

When commander Loric opened the door to the flight deck, his men fired on the remaining crew. His jaw dropped in shock when he saw a female Lacertian at the controls. He slapped Kyrina's face. She didn't stir. His attention was pulled away when a sergeant said, "Sir, you better come and look at this. There is something very interesting in the conference room." Loric looked at another soldier, "Watch her. Makes sure she stays there until I come back." The soldier nodded and raised his gun. The commander pulled himself away from the unconscious female Lacertian and puzzled as to why she was here.

The sergeant guided the Loric to the conference room. His jaw dropped when he was directed to look at the plaques on the wall. He stared at the array – Andromedan and Siriusian which he recalled from the news flashes. Then he felt ill when he saw Lacertians were alongside. "What? We have traitors assisting our enemy?" He stared in silence trying to comprehend the discovery. He then saw four plaques with names and no pictures. He took the three Lacertian plaques down as he ordered the sergeant, "Pack all these pictures up and put them in my office." Loric strode back to the flight deck.

He heard Kyrina groan. He leaned towards her face and slapped her again. "Wake up." He shook her vigorously and yelled, "Wake up." Kyrina groaned more as her eyes struggled to focus on the face just centimetres from hers. She felt another slap and a man's voice yelling, "Wake up, bitch!"

Kyrina slowly rubbed her aching jaw. She stared in horror when her now focused eyes saw a Lacertian commander staring aggressively at her. He slapped her again. She tried to rub her jaw again but felt two strong hands grab each of her arms to restrain her. Terrified, she sat staring at the commander. Loric pulled out the three pictures of the deceased Lacertians. "Who are these dead Lacertians?" Kyrina said their names as each picture flashed in front of her. "Why are you and these dead Lacertians keepsakes on this ship?"

Kyrina lied, "Commander Abyr has a warped hobby. He collects pictures of the dead Lacertian he personally killed."

She earned another slap across her face. "Don't give me that. It was in that makeshift hall of fame. I shall remind you, lying to any officer is very punishable under our laws." Kyrina stared back definitely as she felt a trickle of blood slip down her throat. "Yes, Sir. I know the law."

Loric snarled, "Good. What are you doing here?"

"I was captured and made prisoner."

"Ha! Do you really expect me to believe that?" He slapped her again. She struggled against the two men restraining her. They held her firm.

He questioned her more. He slapped her more. Her face was very swollen. Karina struggled to speak.

Loric turned to his attention to the picture-less plaques he had seen on the wall. "Who are these people? These obviously not dead people."

"Abyr called them the undead heroes walking," spat Kyrina.

"You mean spies?"

Kyrina nodded and then shrugged. "Spies likely. No one knows what they look like. That's why there are no pictures."

Loric looked at the plaque and then back at Kyrina. "I think that were the most truthful words you have uttered in the last ten minutes. What are you doing on the flight deck?"

"You attacked the ship. I escaped from my room and headed here trying to steal the ship."

Loric was calmer when he asked, "Just how did they capture you?"

"I was lured. Stupid trick. I had heard this Kora person was hiding in a known rebel camp. I went to investigate. Stupid me fell for the trap." Loric grunted. "Take her back to our ship. Lock her up."

One of the soldiers who was going through the fight deck records drew Loric's attention. "Sir, come and look at this recording. This ship has been in contact with another planet. Guess who was a willing assistant?"

Loric watched the recording. He was fuming and shocked. It never occurred to him; any Lacertian would side with humans. He, like the rest of the group in on the flight deck, were again shocked to discover a person directly related to Kyros was still alive. He issued new orders, "Put the bitch in maximum security. Get me the location of this planet. Get our navigator here like yesterday. There has to be more humans." Loric looked around the flight deck filling his time as the others worked out how the controls work.

A navigator from the Lacertian ship boarded the captured ship. He went through the navigation system. "Sir, the system has been tampered with. The information box is missing. Someone has removed the navigation memory box and all its information. We have nothing but an empty compartment."

Loric fumed, "I know who removed the information." He stormed out of the room and boarded his waiting jet.

When he arrived back to his own ship, he went directly to the cell where Kyrina was held. She was cuffed to a bench. She sat up when Loric walked in. He began his interview by punching Kyrina's injured legs. As much a she could, she held back the screams of agony. She wasn't going to give Loric any satisfaction. He stopped assaulting her, quietly admiring her resistance. "More of that will come if you don't start being honest." Kyrina nodded.

Loric began, "How many Lacertians are assisting the resistance?"

Kyrina shrugged and lied convincingly, "Ten thousand, maybe more. I don't have exact numbers. Some are killed, some are replaced with new recruits. Ten thousand sounds about right, give or take a hundred."

Loric grunted, "That is maybe plausible but exact numbers will be beneficial to your health. How many?

Kyrina answered with a question, "How many soldiers and pilots do you have on each planet?" Loric immediately saw her point. He didn't know the exact figures himself except they were over the million mark per planet. He changed tact.

"On which planets are your traitor friends on?"

Again Kyrina lied, "On all of them; all main planets, all former and new colonies, all fully occupied planets. They are everywhere."

"Which planets have the most traitors?" Loric leaned close to her face in a threatening manner.

"Hard to tell. They move around a lot. Most work alone."

"Where are the highest numbers?"

Kyrina remained silent. Loric slapped one of her injured legs three times. "Just reminding you of your obligations."

Kyrina remained silent trying to think of answers to more questions. Loric slapped a leg again.

"Okay, on Turbia and the colonies, on Isobola and on Centari."

Loric thought about the answers for a few seconds, "What ranks do they hold?"

Kyrina whispered as she saw Loric hold a hand up ready to slap her legs again.

"All ranks of government, all political sides, all main manufacturing, all main food supplies, and all main water supplies. They are everywhere." Loric stormed out of the room.

"Sir, do we execute this traitor now?"

Without looking back, he called out, "No. The bitch has more to give us. Keep her alive and attend to those injuries but make sure she is always restrained.

Kyrina rolled onto her side and faked crying. She was taunted from one of the outside guards, "What do you expect?" he spat out, "Traitor!" Kyrina didn't respond. She laid back down on the bench and turned her back to the guard and grinned through her pain. *The witch hunt will start, and disruption will occur through mistrust. They will only find corruption not resistance* she thought. She dropped off into an uneasy sleep knowing the chaos she had caused.

The small box released to Beta Cancari was detected by the observatory on the planet. The signal activated when it was less than a thousand lightyears away from the planet. The alarm across the settlement sounded again. Again, people filed their way to the tunnels. Findlee's and his skeleton crew listened to the message beaming towards them. Findlee cursed. "Send someone up to retrieve that box before it is found by anyone else, namely Lacertians." He waited until the reconnaissance craft left the planet. Then he ordered, "Don't give orders for the people to come out until we know what is happening. They will stay there until further word is given."

The reconnaissance craft returned. The box was rushed to the control tower where President Findlee and the others were stationed. The box was opened by using a laser beam. Inside were three items.

The first contained navigational maps, Segmar, Xion, the new positioning of some planets in Oberon and Amada, Lacerta and its four original colonies – Turbia, Sefus, Marnef and Indulos. The second contained information regarding previous attacks by rebels and those currently being planned. This also contained valuable information regarding Lacertians, their buildings, their time schedules. Many were politicians or scientists. Findlee and the select group counted twenty planned attacks would occur in the next few days. Over one hundred would occur in the next few months. Some may never occur as information was incomplete.

The third and smaller file was a list of military personal in all areas of the armed forces. Ranks above sergeant, the location of bases on the planets. There was a sub file buried in this file. It contained pictures of companies with their directors. It was obvious to all; the military and corporate files were incomplete – information was added as it was discovered. It was clear the research on what company did what was comprehensive and complete. "Make two copies. Hide one in the caves, inside the gestation cribs. One copy remains in my office but in twenty different segments spread out through the room. This original," Findlee thought for a while, "Give it to me. I alone will hide the file. If Ashton and Commander Jalon return, they will know where to look. The less people who know where it is hidden, the better." He saw the others exit the room.

He stared outside the window which overlooked the city. He thought of Ashton and the conversations he frequently had with him. He made sure Ashton and Jalon were the only people aware if anything had gone wrong, any original information would be buried in a secrete chamber under the library. The chamber was directly under the copy of the Orris's instructions to form a new independent colony. To Findlee, the declaration of a new colony was most important display in the library.

Ashton and Jalon knew the one-way access was via a panel in the basement below this building. A panel different to the existing escape routes which everyone knew. But only Ashton knew of a second exit from the chamber. It was one way and that led towards the basement of the control tower. From there, was a set of steps which led the way to the caves. He taught Ashton how to navigate the cave system. He prayed, Ashton and the crew on the Explorer would never arrive home to a destroyed city. He went back inside to plan strategies. He found it hard to concentrate as his mind flipped back and forth from the task in hand to Ashton and the Explorer crew.

CHAPTER FOUR
Earth

Ashton slowed the craft down to a near crawl as he searched for a place to hide the one-man craft. From the pod he could see the extreme denseness of the forest below; trees, bushes and vines fighting each other for sunlight and space. He understood immediately the area was uninhabited and that suited his purpose. After not being able to find a suitable landing space in the immediate area below, he turned the pod around and headed towards a chasm he passed by earlier. From above, he turned the sonar on to scan for a cave or indentation which would offer a hiding place for the craft.

He followed the chasm until it gave way to a valley where a spring slowly trickled water out of the ground to form an ever-widening creek. Ashton noted the further he went along the valley, the creek widened before levelling out in width. He flew above the creek, until he noticed a path running parallel two metres above the creek. After following the path for a few minutes, he noticed the path widening and eventually giving way to an isolated, run-downed building sitting on a small rise. He turned the pod around and went back to the depths of the chasm which offered greater seclusion. Now, travelling at a lower height and halfway along the chasm, the sonar beeped indicating an indentation or possible cave.

He directed the pod to a small outcrop of rocks giving a very crude and dangerous landing area. He lowered the craft to be just thirty centimetres off the outcrop, stabilised it in hover mode before opening the door. As the door opened, he felt the rush of warm air and the unfamiliar bush odours assaulting his nose. He coughed before carefully lowering himself to the rocks below. He stood still feeling the extra gravity tugging at his feet and wondered if he could possibly walk. He took one step on the uneven surface and felt as if he was carrying extra heavy gym weights on his legs. Step by step he moved towards the spot where the sonar indicated an opening but not visible to his eyes. He pushed his way through the bushes which were growing out of the cracks in the rocks. He smiled. The sonar was right, there was a cave.

He walked in the cave examining it for height and depth. The pod would protrude by less than ten centimetres. He looked at the front bushes concealing the entrance. He considered what to do. *Go over the trees where the canopy from the tree below covered the front. Chop down the two front bushes and trim back the two bushes at the sides.* He used his glasses. "Blue." The laser shot out as he controlled the cutting of the bushes. When it was done, he pushed the bushes over the edge only to land on the upper parts of the canopy of the tree below. He went back to the pod and to manoeuvre it to the cave entrance, rotated the pod so it would face outwards, and slowly reversed into the cave. Should he had to exit the planet quickly, the pod was ready.

He spoke to the flight deck on the spaceship, "I've landed. The pod is secure."

"Haiten here. Get some rest. Your body is indicating high levels of stress. Rest in the pod overnight before you do anything else. We will monitor your vitals as you sleep. "

Ashton looked around the pod before reclining his seat to its maximum position. "Will do. This gravity is exhausting." He sat in the craft watching the sky slowly change from blue to indigo and then to black. He noticed the temperature dropped by four degrees offering him a more comfortable sleeping temperature. He chewed on a bar of food, drank half of his water while he studied the very different night sky. He felt disorientated as it didn't resemble anything he known before. When the moon started to show itself an hour later, it offered some comfort and allowed him to settle down for a sleep. He removed his glasses and spoke, "Goodnight up there. Going to get some sleep now." He switched off all communications before there was a reply.

The early morning sun streaming through the pod window woke him up. He looked around as he rubbed his eyes. For a second he forgot he was in the pod and where he was. He was about to curse the joker shining a bright light into his room. He righted his seat and stretched. He picked up his duffle bag and rummaged through it looking for some morsel he would like to eat. He selected one with a pale green wrapper, a protein and vegetable bar. As he slowly ate the food, he looked out of the window as he shaded his eyes from the invading sun. He switched on his communication system and put his glasses on.

Haiten spoke again, "Good morning Ashton."

Ashton mumbled with half a mouthful of food, "Morning."

"As you were sleeping your body has made some adjustments to the gravity. But don't try to exert yourself just yet."

"Okay. But I have to relieve myself. I am not using the inbuilt facility and leave it here for months unattended," said Ashton as he put away the wrapper into to waste receptacle.

"Get yourself out of the pod and take everything with you. Relieve yourself outside." Ashton gathered his equipment.

Ashton sipped on his water bottle before placing it in the duffle bag with his food supply. He mentally went through the back pack: two other changes of clothes, one jacket which looked like leather but was in fact a bullet proof vest with disguised bits of armoury for emergency, spare sun glasses, spare headset, one distress signal pack with a homing signal to the pod, one levitator, one miniaturised carry bag which would open fivefold when the side button was activated and toiletries. He placed the two bags outside the pod before locking the pod. He walked outside to the small ledge he stood on the afternoon before, looked down and the then up and thought, *I am not going anywhere.* He pulled out the levitator and strapped it to his waist. He picked up his two bags before he flicked the switch only to find the gravity was much heavier than he thought. He turned the dial to three quarters. He felt himself rise into the air. He smiled before directing the levitator away from the ledge before lowering himself to the ground some fifteen metres below.

When he landed, he looked up to where the pod was concealed. The metallic grey machine blended in with the brown and dominating grey rocks around. The surrounding bushes and the canopy from the tree below gave more coverage. It was almost impossible to see from ground level. He gave the homing beam a test. He aimed the gadget towards the sky. The gadget gave a series of beeps indicating the pod was close by. The small screen then gave a picture of its location. He switched off the hand-held set comfortable in knowing it worked. He turned to retrace the pathway which he travelled the day before. From ground level it looked so different. He spoke to Haiten watching him from the spaceship, "Would you mind giving me a bit of privacy so I can relieve myself?" He heard a click confirming the viewing and communication was shut down for a couple of minutes. He took off his sunglasses just to be sure.

He waited until Haiten completed some testing his biological data and much to Ashton's relief, testing only took a few minutes. He walked slowly heading towards the source of the creek he saw the day before. It was only three kilometres away but to Ashton it started to feel it was much further. The sun was beating down and the tug of the gravity on the uneven surface made progress slow. He stopped frequently to wipe away sweat streaming down his face and sipped on his almost depleted water rations.

When he came upon the source of water, he laid on the ground and scooped up handfuls washing his sweaty face which was now showing early signs of sunburn. He rested at the spring while Haiten ran more tests. "Haiten here. Most readings are fine. Take out a shirt in your bag and drape it over your head. The back of your neck and your head in general are showing signs of burning." Ashton did as advised and instantly noticed the difference. He removed the shirt he was wearing and doused it in water before putting it back on. He scooped up more water, but this time drank it. He sighed at the refreshing feeling. He scooped up more and refilled his bottle, and said into his microphone, "The best water I have tasted for months."

Haiten's voice came over the system, "You should have tested the water before drinking it." Ashton nodded and retorted, "It's clearer than anything on the ship, and come to think of that better than the water on Beta Cancari." He scooped up more water into the bottle and splashed his face again. He stood up again and took slow steps to allow his legs to re-adjust to the gravity.

He noticed six crude steps made from rough rocks and dirt lead up to the path. He knew instantly people did come this way to the source of the creek. *Civilisation wouldn't be that far away* he thought. He went up the steps and followed the narrow path which slowly fanned to a metre in width. The path took him very close to a run-down timber building. He diverted to the shack.

He knocked on the door and called out in his accented English, "Hello! Hello! Anyone home?" There was no answer. Cautiously, he turned the knob and opened the door. The building was small and only had the one room. It was a shell with only one table with two rickety chairs one on either side. There was wooden slat bed with a few missing slats and devoid of mattress and any other bedding. As he walked into the room, the floorboards squeaked with every step. He felt something scurry across one of his shoes. He jumped back and felt his heart race.

Ashton looked up and saw more creatures looking down at him from the exposed rafters. His first instinct was to burn the place down but that would draw attention. He called out, "Purple!" As he did so, the beam shot out to freeze one animal. Ashton moved his head keeping the purple ray going under his control. The assorted animals froze. He decided to exit building but a voice on the other end stopped him. "Haiten here. I'm extending my watch."

"Yes, Sir," said Ashton somewhat surprised.

"Ashton, I want you to jump up and bring down one of those creatures you froze." Ashton hesitated, "This building stinks of those creatures. You want me to pick up one of those things so you can have a better look? Normally, I wouldn't disobey an order but this time I am. If you want a creature, come and get it yourself. I'm leaving the building before I get some disease." Ashton hurried out of the building allowing the door to slam behind him. He took a few steps away from the door before vomiting to the side of the entrance. "You should have picked up those signs of me becoming ill. Who is reading the data?"

Haiten's voice sounded apologetic. "Sorry, I got carried away with what I was observing and forgot to check the stats."

Ashton slowly followed the path for another two kilometres. At this point, the path gave way to a wider path bordered with rocks. He followed that for another five minutes when he heard a strange mechanical noise approaching. He took cover under a tree shading a large boulder as it offered the only protection. He frowned at the low flying machine. The helicopter swooped and circled near where he was hiding before leaving to follow the path and back to the isolated building.

Ashton remained hidden not wanting to move away just in case the machine returned. His hunch was right. Some five minutes later, the helicopter returned and this time, it circled much lower than before. He could see people inside; a pilot and two others looking at the ground both using binoculars and a fourth person further inside sitting at a screen. He gasped when he saw the imperial logo for Daraxon - possible co-incidence. He recalled the history lessons of Prince Alcyn and his neutrino-based transport system he and his family had invented. He recalled refugee ships in Amada escaping to colonise another planet. To Ashton, it didn't make sense. Colonies were always on unoccupied planets. This planet was very occupied. Just maybe Alcyn was able to convince these people they could share the planet. His mind raced with other assorted possibilities and wanted to investigate further. As the helicopter left, he asked the people in the spaceship, "Did you see that? I mean the logo - the imperial logo of Daraxon."

Haiten's voice came through, "Yes. We are replaying the footage, and we will be definitely examining it carefully. It's most likely to be a co-incidence."

Ashton left the safety of the hiding place to continue walking along the path which now gave way to a two-way bitumen road. He walked for another ten minutes before coming across a small convoy of cars. From the passenger side of the first car a middle-aged lady called out, "Hey You!" Ashton looked around thinking the lady was addressing another person. "Hey you! The one looking around. The one with the two bags." Asthon then realised he was being addressed and pointed to himself for confirmation. "Yeah you. The early bird." She continued speaking, "Were you camping in the valley over night?"

Ashton looked puzzled. She repeated the question before Ashton answered in accented English, "No. I was up at dawn to do this walk." Ashton could see she wasn't convinced.

"Did you see anything in the sky late yesterday afternoon or last night?"

"Birds only. Every night I see stars, planets and the moon, some clouds. You see more stars from the southern hemisphere than in the north. Days ago, I was camping in another section of this ...jungle but

I was put off by waking up to see creatures sharing my sleeping bag." replied Ashton. "Did you see the helicopter this morning?" asked the lady lifting a bottle of water to her lips.

"Yes. That thing is gone now," replied Ashton he pointed to the general direction, "That way. Why?"

"Didn't you hear on the radio or TV that a spaceship landed?" Ashton gulped, "When I go travelling, I don't carry such things. I switch off and try to reconnect with nature."

"Thanks." She and the driver drove off shaking their heads. The convoy behind her continued their journey to the end of the road.

It was early afternoon when Ashton reached the first building which showed signs of life. He read the sign outside, "O'Reilly's Chalet" Opening hours 10 a.m. to 8pm. Ashton looked around and noted the chalet was a part of a much larger complex which was bustling with activity.

He walked up the small flight of six steps before reaching the wide timber veranda. Groups of people occupied most of the tables now being exposed to the afternoon sun. He saw a teenage boy slipping coins into the vending machine and pushing a few buttons. The machine went into operation and the boy placed his hand in a compartment to retrieve the request. Ashton wished he had coins to try the machine out for himself. Using the green beam was out of the question with so many people around.

Ashton watched the people on the veranda: coming, socializing, eating and drinking light refreshments, relaxing before moving on either back to their cars or inside the chalet before finally departing in their assorted vehicles. He couldn't help but notice when he purposefully eavesdropped or couldn't help overhearing rowdier conversations - the main topic was a possible spaceship had landed. Theories, beliefs and denials were abundant as he listened from a table where he was the sole occupant.

He looked up when a young lady carrying a tray, cleared the tables and wiped them clean. She had been out numerous times before but now as there was a drop in the crowds she approached him for the first time. Ashton knew she had noticed him sitting quietly on his own, drinking from his own water container, and ate his own supply of bars. She smiled at him. Ashton nodded back. "Sir, do you want a drink?" she asked.

Ashton reached for his now near empty drink bottle, "Can I have this refilled?"

"Sure." The young lady took the bottle and returned a minute later with cold water. Ashton thanked her and sipped the water thinking how fortunate he was drinking such pure water.

It was close to five-thirty when the bulk of the afternoon crowd had died down. The young lady returned to Ashton's table curious that he was there all afternoon, sitting and watching and hardly saying a word. "Are you waiting for someone to pick you up?" she enquired to begin the conversation.

"No. Just relaxing. I will be moving on, later. How far is it to the nearest town?"

"I hope you have no intentions of walking. You will be walking for a good part of the night. Beaudesert will be a good two hours of walking. From Beaudesert you can catch a bus or train to Brisbane. If you catch a bus and if the traffic is heavy, it could take up to an hour and a half. By train, maybe an hour give or take a few minutes."

Ashton nodded his appreciation. "Where are you staying?" asked the young lady seeking some courage to be forward.

"Nowhere yet. Nothing permanent. Just passing through. What is going on out here? Helicopters have been flying around all day?"

The lady said, "Apparently a space craft was detected and everyone is out searching. It was supposed to have landed in this area or a part of the national parks system; three huge parks. They have a very large area to search if there are no big areas of flattened trees to guide them. If anyone finds them, I hope it is Daraxon Technologies. The military from anywhere or paranoid locals would be disastrous for the creature that landed."

Ashton smiled for the first time since arriving at the chalet. "My name is Carrie." She held out her hand. Ashton partially stood up from his chair and shook it, "Ashton."

"Where are you from?"

Ashton didn't want to answer the question and hoped his vague reply would suffice, "From far, far away." *Much further than you could ever imagine,* he thought.

Carrie looked at Ashton thoughtfully, "I am actually quite good at pinpointing where people come from just by their accents and a few other give-a-ways such as colouring etcetera. I would say you're from one of the Scandinavian countries. Which one Sweden, Norway or Finland?"

Ashton nodded and gestured at her attempt and flashed a smile all the time thinking, *where on this planet are they? Look it up.* "Finland," replied Ashton.

Carrie grinned, "See. I told you I was good at guessing."

Ashton burst out laughing, "Okay. You're good."

Carrie was beginning to feel bolder and gave a slight flirtatious smile. "You should smile and laugh more often; it becomes you." Ashton didn't know what to say but was sure Kora was puffing with jealousy as he heard a gasp through his headset.

"You mentioned Daraxon Technologies would be better for the creature from space. Why?" enquired Ashton.

Carrie commented, "Because they are the only people with experience with intergalactic stuff."

"How come you know that?" asked Ashton as he leaned towards her.

"Mum and dad sometimes do some work with them. Today they were in the Daraxon helicopter with my two cousins, Mark and Jenny. In my uni breaks I go over and do some work as well."

"Like what?" asked Ashton with growing interest.

"Mundane stuff like cleaning, cooking for staff or anything else they need another set of hands or when other staff are away. I was there last month when they had a big meeting. Everyone was there and the party that followed was great."

"Do you know what the meeting was about?" pushed Ashton.

"Buying out my parent's land to expand the place," she lied. Ashton detected the lie but played along.

Carrie excused herself as she spied more tables being vacated and items left on them. Ashton watched her continue her cleaning duties. He spoke to the spaceship. "Did you people get any of that conversation?"

Kora who was translating for Commander Jalon stood back, "Interesting. See if you can find your way to Daraxon Technologies and have a good look around. Find out what you can and move from this place you've occupied. You've been there for hours."

"Will do," replied Ashton as he saw a large super shiny black four-wheel drive pull up.

Carrie returned to the table holding a full tray of rubbish and plates. She put the tray down for a brief moment, took out her order book and wrote her phone number on it. She handed it to Ashton. "This is my phone number give me a call when you find a place. I will be happy to show you around."

Ashton looked surprised and accepted the note. "Sorry, I don't have a number to give you. But I would be interested in having a tour through Daraxon Technologies if they have tours."

Carrie said, "No tourist stuff there that I know of. I doubt if I could get you a private tour. Only big corporations, government ministers and the military seem to get the tours and then that is by invitation and limited to twice a year. The last showing was four months ago but recently the place is buzzing with activity with a possible sighting of a spacecraft." Carrie picked up the tray before disappearing inside the chalet leaving Ashton to his solitude.

Ashton watched as the tall middle-aged man climbed out of the car. Carefully, he closed the door and placed the keys in the back pocket of his trousers of the expensive navy-blue suit. The man removed his sunglasses as he went up the stairs and went directly inside the chalet.

After admiring the car for a few minutes, Ashton left his table and walked over to the vehicle to check it out. Minutes later, the man came out of the chalet holding a rum and coke in one hand while the other was pushing the door open. He called out to Ashton, "Look, but don't touch!" Ashton spun around. "Forgive me. I was admiring your car. Beautiful."

By this time the man was almost standing at the top of the steps. "The best and the most expensive of this type on the market," he boasted.

"It looks new," commented Ashton.

"It sure is. Just four days old," replied the man with a grin.

Ashton nodded. "Very nice indeed. Just curious how long did it take for you to save up for one of these?"

"With a good paying job, not long. Then of course it depends on the job," said the man looking intently at Ashton. With hesitation Ashton asked, "I'm heading to Brisbane. Can I be so forward and ask for a ride?"

The man was taken aback by the forward request but quickly composed himself. "Tell you what. I will be leaving here in twenty minutes, but the ride is going to cost you."

"How much?" asked Ashton now feeling uncomfortable.

"You can work off the ride by doing a job for me when we get to Brisbane," replied the man.

"What do I need to do?" asked Ashton sensing something was amiss but couldn't put his finger on the problem.

"I want you to deliver two parcels for me. One parcel as soon as we get back, and the next the following morning. Then we call it even," replied the man. "Since we are going to be temporary travelling companions, my name is Martin. What's yours?"

"Asthon."

Ashton agreed and watched Martin go into the chalet. When Martin returned, he was carrying a parcel and a briefcase. He tossed them on to the back seat of the car and directed Ashton to place his tote and backpack on the floor of the back. "Jump in the front," said Martin.

CHAPTER FIVE
The Motel

The black four-wheel drive turned into the underground car park of the William Street Metro Brisbane Motel. Martin pulled out a card from his wallet and inserted it into the box at the side. The long wooden arm at the entrance lifted. Martin drove through towards another gate where he repeated the process. The second gate carried a sign: management staff. "We are here at my main place of work. Come inside and look around. Have you anywhere to stay?"

Ashton picked up his bags as he looked around the dark surroundings. "Not yet. I haven't booked in to anything yet."

"Don't worry, I can get you a discounted room. Follow me," said Martin.

Ashton didn't move. "Sorry, Martin, I don't have enough money for such a place. I am backpacker level for accommodation. Thank you for the lift. I did appreciate it. And that first job?"

Martin nodded. "Well at least come inside and I will give you details. And then you can go slumming it at the backpacker's. Have a drink on me or even a meal." Ashton thought about the idea, and it did appeal. "A light snack. Thanks."

When Martin entered the foyer carrying his briefcase and parcel, the staff jumped to attention. Ashton's eyes scanned the place absorbing the mix of opulence and history which collided into unimpressive décor.

Martin called Ashton's attention before they started moving into the dining area. One of the male staff members approached. "Sir, sorry to disrupt you and your guest, we have a small problem. Can I please have your attention for a couple of minutes?"

Martin quickly instructed Ashton, "Wait here. I'll be back." He signalled to a female behind the desk and read her name tag, Dayna. "Please look after Mr. Ashton. Take him to the gaming room while I attend to this matter."

Dayna smiled at Ashton. "This way, sir." Ashton followed Dayna to the large gaming room. Ashton stood looking blankly at all the machinery and the unfamiliar noises they were making. Dayna saw his expression and quickly explained the three payment systems, coin, token or card. "Mr. Ashton, would you like to try a poker machine?"

Ashton snapped out of his trance. "Sorry. I have no coins, and I do not understand the rules." Dayna reached for a token in her uniform pocket. She walked up to a vacant machine and explained the rules of the game. Ashton watched. Dayna fished out another token and handed it to Ashton. "Your go."

Ashton did as instructed as guided by Dayna. This time ten tokens rolled out. Dayne grabbed the small winnings and reimbursed herself and handed the rest to Ashton. "All yours."

Ashton took the tokens and one by one fed the machine to lose all but one. *This is a mug's game*, he thought, *feeding a machine and going broke. I wonder.* As he put the last coin in the machine, he said in Pleiadean, "Green." The machine dials spun around until the jackpot sounded around the room.

Ashton grinned. "I believe beginners luck." Dayna stood shocked as the amount read twenty thousand dollars. "Mr. Ashton, I believe you have just won a mini fortune. Congratulations. It is rare for such an amount to come up. Follow me to the desk and I will pay your winnings into your bank account or credit card."

Knowing he didn't have either facility, Ashton replied, "I will just have it in cash."

Just as the last dollars were being counted out, Martin appeared at the counter. He had heard of the jackpot and was surprised to see the winner was Ashton. "Congratulations Mr. Ashton. Now you don't have to slum it in the back-packer's accommodation. You have enough for two weeks stay here and in one of our more luxurious rooms."

Ashton replied, "I don't need expensive accommodation; one standard room with just the basics." Martin leaned over the desk. "Give him what he wants."

Dayna checked the system. "Room 412 is available. Sir, I can arrange for your luggage to be sent up."

"No. I will keep it with me." replied Ashton unfamiliar with the service.

"As you wish, sir. Enjoy your stay," said Dayna as she handed over the pass card in a white cardboard sleeve.

Ashton pulled out his extra carry bag still in the backpack. He opened it manually so not to draw attention and stuffed the money inside. He placed that bag onside one of the bigger bags.

Ashton said, "Now that meal, Mr. Shields. I'm famished."

On their second attempt to the restaurant, Martin's phone rang. "Excuse me," he said to Ashton as he moved away and turned his back. A minute passed when Martin returned and this time managing to get into the restaurant. Martin automatically guided Ashton to a rear table which was reserved for staff. He gave Ashton a menu while he ordered drinks. Over the meal Martin and Ashton engaged in conversation mostly about the motel and the first delivery job. "Take your belongings upstairs to your room and meet me down here at the main street entrance." Martin nodded the general direction. "I will then give you this parcel for delivery." He nodded towards the parcel now placed on a chair still under the table.

Ashton entered his room and looked around and smiled and thought, *if this is basic, then I would like to see what luxury is.* He unpacked his tote bag containing food and placed all his clothes in the provided cupboards. He looked at the bag of cash, now containing a little less because four days accommodation was paid in advance. He removed close to five hundred dollars in cash and placed it in his zip up pocket in his jacket. In the privacy of the room, he pushed the bag with the cash to deflate. Looking a bit thicker around the centre, he stuffed it into a compartment in his tote bag. His voice activated the inner seal. The money dematerialised. Then he replaced some of his food items back in the bag. The bag was in the cupboard near his handful of clothes.

He went down to the foyer to see Martin holding the parcel. He gave Ashton directions on a note paper and the address. Martin gave a few verbal directions, smiled and shook Ashton's hand before walking away. Ashton read the note and the directions. The place wasn't far, just on the other side of the bridge and to a side door of another motel bearing a similar name. There he would knock on the door and ask for a man called Baker. Baker would then give him another parcel which will be given to Martin who would be working in his office. *Job one down,* thought Ashton. *Job two tomorrow and then free of the debt.*

The following morning Ashton entered the small guest computer room. There were three computers connected to one printer. All three were in use by elderly people. He observed as he waited his turn.

He punched in Finland. Still not sure where in the world it was, he brought up a map of the world. "Ugh. That's on the other side of the planet," he whispered. He brought up Finland again and checked out the tourist sites to gain information about his supposed home land. He found the capital city to the south and the large lake to the north. He noticed, the further north one went, the towns were more isolated. All were connected by roads and small airports, but not all were connected by train.

Then he typed in Daraxon Technologies. Very little information came up:

Founded twenty-five years ago by Jed Lawson and his family. They make revolutionary domestic products employing some of the best scientists and engineers of the world. They have their own observatory and space research centre which they share information with E.S.A. and N.A.S.A. Inventions by Daraxon Technologies: All in one laundry unit: washes, dries and irons clothes. Available in two sizes: individual and family sizes. Solar power units for most watercrafts: ferries, hovercrafts, boats of all sizes including ocean liners and naval ships. Improved systems for water extraction from air and irrigation technology. Specialises in advanced space technology research and communication systems.

That was it. Very hush hush. He stared at the logo. It was the same as the old imperial logo he had learned about in school on Beta Cancari. It was the same logo that was eradicated from the two galaxies of Oberon and Amada. Now, it was the symbol of the resistance movement. And here it was on the screen associated with a company developing space technology. He recalled what Carrie said, tight security and limited access. *A co-incidence,* he thought. *Maybe, not.* Now Ashton was more determined than ever before to visit Daraxon Technologies.

Ashton enquired at the desk if Martin Shields was available. The young lady looked at her computer.

"No Sir. Are you Mr. Ashton?"

Ashton replied, "Yes."

"Mr. Shields has left this briefcase for you. Here is a written message. Mr. Shields won't be in for another hour and a half." The lady handed over the brief case and the letter. Ashton took the case and the letter, walked a few paces away before opening the letter. The instructions included a mud-map of the next delivery.

Ashton delivered the briefcase to a shop in the city. The man accepting the briefcase made Ashton wait while he checked the contents in a back room. The man made an electronic payment using his computer. The man returned. "All is fine." The man placed the briefcase on the counter and slipped a copy of the electronic transaction inside. Ashton took the briefcase. The man said, "Give both items to the receptionist at the motel if Mr. Shields is not there." Ashton nodded. He walked back to the motel and enquired again about Martin Shields. The same lady served him. "He's not back. Just leave the briefcase here. I will give it to him." Ashton nodded. "Thanks." and walked away.

Ashton decided to leave the motel for the unfamiliar street outside. As he neared the door, Martin who had just arrived, called out to him. "Good morning Mr. Ashton." He walked closer to Ashton before speaking much softer, "I believe you made a delivery today."

Ashton nodded. "The envelope and the briefcase are at the desk. I believe my transport debt is paid in full." Ashton made a few steps towards the door.

Martin walked closer to Ashton. In a much softer voice, Martin asked, "Mr. Ashton, I was wondering if you could do two more delivery jobs later today. This time it is payment in cash." Ashton felt he was being reeled into something unsavoury.

"No. I am more into security work than delivery work."

"Security, Eh? This place always has openings for security work. The turn-over is quite high. Shift work is the problem. See me tomorrow morning at my office about nine. A job interview. Deal?" Ashton smiled and felt better with the idea of security work. "I'll see you at nine." Ashton left the building quickly trying to avoid any more interruptions.

At nine a.m. Ashton waited outside Martin's office door. He was ushered in after ten minutes of delay. Martin stood up and shook Ashton's hand, then motioned for Ashton to sit down. "Tell me about your work experience," asked Martin.

Ashton invented a story of his work in Finland, ex-army moved into security work. Martin swallowed every word and nodded his approval. "Now for the paperwork formality." He handed Ashton a form. Ashton eyes scanned the form, and he filled out what he could. The form was partially filled out when he handed it back to Martin. Martin noticed the numerous blanks. "Some of these can remain blank but a couple cannot. I need your passport details. That is the most crucial one. Can I see your passport, please?"

Ashton became uncomfortable then lied. "I can't supply that yet. I was mugged in Sydney before moving up this way. I am waiting for a replacement which will take a few more days." Martin could see Ashton was lying and, on the surface, dismissed it. Inwardly was delighted. "When you get the new passport, we can add the details." He pushed the intercom system and said, "Ms. Newton, please bring in Mr. Wesley."

Mr. Wesley was ushered in and introduced to Ashton. Mr. Wesley was in his mid-sixties, medium height and a little tubby around the middle. "Mr. Rod Wesley, this is Mr. Ashton, another new recruit."

Mr. Wesley gave a warm fatherly smile which Ashton appreciated and Ashton returned a warm smile and gave a small nod. The warmth reminded him of his father back on Beta Cancari. "Nice to meet you," said Ashton as he extended his hand. Martin looked at the two men. "Mr. Wesley will show you the ropes and where everything is. Rod will show you around today and get you fitted for a uniform. There is lot to learn. Today and tomorrow and for the next week, shadow Mr. Wesley." Martin dismissed the two men.

When the men walked out of the administration area, Martin immediately used his private mobile and texted a message:

Found male, illegal entry to the country. He's done two deliveries. Needs convincing to do more.

He switched off his phone to focus on his legitimate work.

As Rod Wesley escorted Ashton to the locker room, they passed a staff service desk. A much older man looked up from the newspaper he was reading and smiled at Rod. "Good morning, Rod. And who may this recruit be?" Rod introduced Bill Bickford the man in charge of uniforms for the men who worked at the motel. "A measure up for security uniform, thanks," said Rod. Bill looked Ashton up and down. He found his tape measure and measured Ashton. He pondered for a while. "Not sure if we have one to fit. What will fit in width will be too short in length." He rubbed his chin in thought then rummaged around for a few shirts as a trial size. Ashton put them on over his Pleiadean T-shirt.

"Just as I thought," said Bill. "Too short. Just a minute. He returned to his desk and asked, "Who was the person who gave you this job?"

"Martin Shields," replied Ashton.

Bill phoned Mr. Shields. "Sorry to disturb you, Mr. Shields. This young lad you sent down with Rod for a security uniform has a problem."

Irritated at the intrusion, Martin snapped, "What's the problem?"

"Sir, the uniforms don't fit. We will have to get them specially made."

"Okay. Get two only. How long would it take for them to be made?"

"About a week," Bill hesitated.

"Get him the uniforms. In the meantime, he wears his clothes with an I.D. badge. No other uniform issues until the proper uniform arrives." Bill proceeded to make an identification card for Ashton. Bill said, "Wear that at all times. When you get the proper uniform, you will get the rest of the stuff like Rod is wearing." Ashton looked at Rod's clothing and the paraphernalia surrounding his waist. Ashton nodded.

"Follow me. We're going to the surveillance room. I'll introduce you to the crew in there. You will be supplied with a communication system for two-way conversations. You will have to remove all the head gear you are wearing. No music earphones or any other gadgets while on duty."

Ashton retorted, "It's a hearing aid. Ear damage from being a bit too close to a bomb while serving in the army."

Rod looked at Ashton and shook his head in sympathy. "I want you to watch what goes on in this room," Rod said as he led the way.

Rod introduced Ashton to a large group of men monitoring four screens each. Each flashed their eyes back and forth between screens. Ashton watched one of the monitors assigned to Paul. Shyly Ashton spoke, "Wind back this screen. I am sure that well-dressed man with the blue shirt and yellow tie just pick pocketed the lady's handbag." Paul looked surprised at the request, shrugged before speaking, "Are you sure you saw him take something?"

Ashton looked firmly at the screen and watched the man move to the next victim, "Never been so sure. He's a pick pocket." Paul wound back the footage and played it back in slow motion. Ashton was right. In slow motion two fingers slipped into the lady's bag, quickly rummaged around, sorted out the cash from the cards and withdrew cash before walking away." Rod and Paul gasped and looked at Ashton. Paul gave Ashton a broad smile and without taking his eyes off the four screens, "Welcome to the team." He shot his eyes to Rod as he reached for the communication button, "Is Ashton assigned to this room?"

Rod looked around. "Shields has assigned him to the floor in plain clothes until he gets a uniform." "Good idea and with those sharp eyes, we need some help on the floor," Paul replied before giving instructions to four men on the floor in the same section to move on the spotted pick pocket.

From the security room all could see the pick pocket beginning to walk quickly away from the area. When he saw the two security men directly in front of him, he turned around and saw two more directly behind him. Knowing his time was up, man struggled and waved his arms changing the intended discrete removal to a noisy scene.

Ashton looked intensely at the screen and pointed. "The man has just planted the evidence on the rear guard with the dark brown hair." As the man was dragged away, Paul spoke to the security guards on the floor, "Graham, check your pockets. In the scuffle, the man slipped something into your rear pocket." Graham checked all his pockets and drew out a fist full of notes, waved and mouthed thank you before joining the others giving the criminal a firm push towards an interview room. Paul and the other men in the team clapped Ashton. "That was very impressive. Welcome to the team," said a voice from the far end of the room. Rod gave Ashton a friendly slap on the back. "Maybe having a plain clothes person on the floor is a good move." He placed his arm across Ashton's shoulders and led him out of the room to show him other parts of the motel; parts which were generally out of bounds to the public.

After three hours of touring and introductions, Rod Wesley directed Ashton to the last port of call. "This is the most important part of the job; report writing for the shift. I will show you the process. Because you spotted the pick pocket, there will be extra things to write up and Paul will have a copy of the video clips on a flash drive. Also, a copy of the interview with the thief will be added to make a complete dossier for the police and then to court later on." Ashton gave an inward groan. He hated formalised paperwork. Rod patiently assisted him with all the procedures and double checked his work. Rod noticed Ashton's spelling was a bit wanting. "Not that great with the spelling bit for the reports, are you," commented Rod.

"Not everyone can spell perfectly in a second language," replied Ashton hoping it would suffice.

"Maybe if I did an audio report instead. Would that be acceptable?"

"Not sure," replied Rod sympathetically.

The next day Rod and Ashton met at ten, the start of the Ashton's first shift. Rod tested Ashton's memory as to which staff only door went where and how to link the back areas. Then they went to their assigned area to supervise the patrons. Rod spoke to him on and off pointing out the regulars and past trouble makers who were permitted to return under strict rules.

Bob and Ashton walked around the motel. Bob introduced Ashton to other floor walkers who were not there yesterday. When no one was about, Rod spoke casually of other social matters and revealed he was close to retirement age. He wanted a quiet time without much drama for the next two months. Then he asked, "What's with your very dark sunglasses?"

Being caught off guard, Ashton fumbled around for a response before saying, "A light sensitivity problem since that bomb blast with night vision glasses. Can't handle light anymore. It was the same bomb blast that wrecked my hearing. The bomb was too close, but I count myself lucky not to have lost more. That bomb killed one of my friends in the same unit."

Rod shook his head. "Well, it obviously doesn't stop you from any other visual activity. What you did in the surveillance room yesterday was brilliant. Who trained you?" Rod asked with genuine interest.

"Military training," Ashton recalled the lie he told earlier. He was thrown off guard again.

"What division?" asked Bob.

"I am not sure how you say it in English, undercover work but I spent most of the time just watching through binoculars in ISIS territory. It got boring being on high alert and just watching," Ashton replied hoping the line of conversation would stop at this point. Rod chuckled. "That's what I want over the next two months, boring. That will suit me fine."

It was close to one in the afternoon when all security staff received an alert. There was a disturbance in the underground car park. Four men were engaged in a fight. The security staffs were already advised while the ambulance and the police were on their way. All car entries and exits in the car park were in the process of being locked down. Then the staff received an alarmed call through their earpieces, "The men have drawn guns and are shooting at each other. Do not approach. Take cover watch and observe." Rod spoke into his microphone, "Just got to the car park door two. Ashton is with me."

"Stay. Do not approach." Ashton waved Rod down to the ground as he opened the door no more than ten centimetres hoping to get a view of the unfolding drama. Ashton could see one injured man on the ground holding his arm and defiantly shooting at one of the attackers. He closed the door and reported to Rod. "Stay here. I can round these men up before the police get here." Rod looked horrified and pulled Ashton back. "Are you bloody crazy?"

"I've seen worse than this. Don't follow me. You'll distract me. Stay put," Ashton said as he noted Rod's concern and anger for the disregard for the instructions.

Ashton went on all fours crawling between cars. At times he paused summing up the exchange of shots. He sneaked up to the injured man holding a gun and aiming it at the opposition. In Pleiadean he said, "Orange" The gun mal-functioned. While the confused man looked at the broken gun, Ashton came closer. Ashton took off his glasses and said firmly, "Look at me. Look at me. When you see me with or without my glasses, you won't see a face but that of in crazed grizzly bear. To escape me, you have to pay dead." Ashton put his glasses on and in Pleiadean said, "Yellow." The man felt a strange sensation creeping over his body. Unable to move, he felt helpless as he felt his body being dragged between cars and going towards the stairwell. He tried to scream but his vocal cords were equally stiffened. The man was just starting to regain his movement when Ashton repeated, "Yellow." The man was paralysed again. Ashton crawled back to the stairwell door pulling the man behind him. He opened the door. "Have you got something to tie one up. He's waiting outside." Rod opened the door as he pulled out the cuffs from one of the pouches on his belt. Rod looked at the man and then at Ashton. "What did you do? He's stiff like a board."

"A little hypnosis which is going to wear off in fifteen seconds. Cuff him." Ashton crawled away again but returned. He glared at the cuffed man before opening the door where Rod was hiding.

"You win. It is a war out there made worse by both sides not being able to aim straight. Bullets are burying themselves into the cars or ricocheting off pillars."

"Tell me about this hypnosis thing," asked Rod as he opened the door to see if the injured man needed further help. "Dad was an amateur magician who did hypnosis tricks as a part of his act. It took him years to master. He taught me. Just watch. I'm going to open the door and look at the man. Just watch how he reacts to seeing me." Ashton opened the door just ten centimetres. He popped his head through the opening. Rod placed his head through the door to watch. Ashton muttered softly, "Yellow." A beam zapped the man again. The man stiffened again. Ashton and Rod pulled back and closed the door. "When he sees me, he sees a grizzly bear. That was plant number one. To survive a grizzly, you have to play dead. I planted that in his head as well. He's playing dead for thirty seconds."

"But you said something to him. What did you say?" asked Rod who was not entirely convinced.

"I gave him a warning which he responded to," lied Ashton.

Rod and Ashton received a message from the control centre. "The police and an ambulance are here." There was pause. Seconds later the sound of the car park doors rolling up were heard. The police were yelling out to the three men. There were more verbal exchanges and then silence. Through their earpieces, Ashton and Rod heard, "The police are rounding up the three men. Rod, Ashton, just wait a bit," said Paul from the control room. They waited another minute. "Okay heroes. You can approach the police and tell them to collect the man having a love affair with the rail."

Rod opened the door and stepped out. He looked at the cuffed man hanging on to the rail for dear life. He was crying and babbling incoherently. Rod turned to Ashton as he stepped out of the stairwell. The man looked at Ashton and cried out, "No. No. Keep away from me. Keep away from me." Sweat and froth formed at the man's mouth. Ashton knelt down to look at the wound. "It's only a graze. A bit of a wash and a few stiches and you'll be a new man." The man shook with fear at the sight of Ashton. Ashton's touch was now like a bear rubbing against him. The voice was a contorted growl; a bear trying to speak. It was too much; the man wet his trousers from fear.

When a policeman approached the cuffed man, the man looked up, "Get me out of here." He looked to Ashton. "Keep that animal away from me. Don't let him come near me." The policeman uncuffed him from the rail, returned Rod's cuffs and placed his own cuffs on the man who gratefully said "Thank you for saving me from that mad grizzly bear." The man gave a sigh of relief. The policeman looked back at Rod and Ashton who both shrugged.

The policeman didn't have to nudge him forward. "So, you had a bad day at the office?" The man nodded. "Keep that animal away from me. You should be taking that thing to the zoo." Again, he began to babble incoherently. The policeman led him to the ambulance where a paramedic was waiting. "Take him to get this grazed arm fixed and then get a psych test. He wasn't as strong as he thought he was. He's unhinged." The paramedic nodded. The arresting police man climbed into the back of the ambulance to accompany the man at every step of medical assistance. He would remain on duty until relief came.

Rod and Ashton walked back inside of the motel. Rod eventually asked, "That hypnosis thing worked well. But geez, it has some side effects. Never seen a man so scared at the sight of another. Are you as good as your father with this hypnosis thing?"

"No. I only manage to get the person to act for thirty seconds. Dad gets them for two minutes," said Ashton.

"To be a good as your father with this instant hypnosis thing, how much more practice do you need?"

Ashton shrugged. "Maybe a wealth of people who are willing to be practice subjects. Do you want to volunteer?"

Rod grinned. "I'll pass. Does it work on cats and dogs? There's a real vicious over indulged mongrel living down the road from me. He would be a perfect practice subject. I would like the wind knocked out him."

Trying to end the conversation, Ashton directed Rod to the report writing room. "Let's get our reports done first."

Paul entered the report room with copies of the CCT of the events in the car park. "We need triplicates this time; one for our permanent storage, one for the management and one for the cops. Make sure each has a CCT copy. Nice work boys."

*

Back at the station, Detective Kirkwood completed the interrogation of the three men now occupying a holding cell at the police station. "I'm going over to the P.A. The injured man is finished with his medical attention to his arm. Symms says the man is off his rocker. They want to do a psych test tomorrow. I want to see how bad this man is," he said to a sergeant who was given directions earlier to keep an eye on the trio.

Detective Kirkwood was ushered towards the hospital room door by Sergeant Symms. "You won't have much time with him. The doctors are going to give him a sedative. He's been alternating between crying and yelling out some incoherent garbage." Kirkwood nodded at the information and peered through the window before entering the room.

As soon as the man saw Kirkwood enter the room, he whimpered, "Are the zoo people going to capture and kill that creature running around out there?"

Kirkwood raised an eyebrow. "Can you tell me about the animal?"

"Big. Hairy. Scary. Ugly. Bear."

"I am sure the zookeepers will be able to track it down. What is your name?"

"Len, Len Pierce," replied Len.

"Date of birth and age?" asked Kirkwood.

"Nineteenth of July, 1987. Twenty-nine," replied Len giving a grimace.

"How is the arm going?"

"Painful."

"Tell me in your own words why you went to the motel and how did the fight start."

Kirkwood listened and interrupted where he needed more details. There was a knock on the door. A nurse came in holding a small tray with a needle on it. Before the nurse could speak, Kirkwood moved back from Len's bed. "Okay Len. I think that will do for now."

"Don't forget about catching the bear," whimpered Len as he felt a needle being injected into his arm.

Kirkwood nodded. "I will see what I can do."

When Kirkwood was outside the room two more police officers came by. "Symms, we're your relief."

"How is he?" asked one of the relief officers.

"The nurse is giving him a sedative. He's really in Wonderland. Not violent. Scared of his own shadow." replied Symms.

"I was just in there with him," said Kirkwood. "Some things were very coherent, but the man is convinced he was attacked by a grizzly bear. Scared out of his wits. Don't say boo or growl. It might trigger him off again."

Ashton went to his room, undressed before allowing the shower run for a long time over his body. He washed his Pleiadean work clothes in the hand basin rung the as tight as he could. He then hung them up to dry in the shower recess. He dropped off to sleep but woke up two hours later. He spoke into the Pleiadean microphone, "Hello up there. Who am I talking to?"

"Neo," came the reply. "How are you feeling?"

"Better after a sleep. I need a bit of help. Tonight, I'm going down to the computer room and research how to get a passport. I need to get to the other side of the planet to create some papers to make sure the passport is legitimate and to legitimise myself here at work and in this country. I don't think I will have time to go to my pod, do all the stuff I need to do, hide the pod again and be back in time to do everything else. I will get back to you while you organise a four-man pod to come."

"Do you want anyone in particular to help?"

"Any two from the team. We are all about the same. I'm going to the computer room now."

Martin Shields was in his four- wheel drive watching the video feed from Ashton's room to his mobile phone. He cursed in a soft voice, "He's a cop. Undercover. He's speaking in some code to his superiors. Or he could be from a rival gang doing undercover for them." He drove out of the car park and went directly to his home. He thought about the events, where and when they met. Always pleasant. Always obliging. Not a hair out of place. He thought, *those sunglasses and the headset he always wears are obviously not what he said to me in the drive back from the chalet. Sensitive eyes to light? Specialised hearing aid? What a load of crap.*

At home Martin took out his copy of the reports Ashton and Rod lodged regarding the pick pocket. He crosschecked it with Paul's report. He placed the flash drive in his laptop to see the pick pocket in action at normal speed. He replayed it at increasingly slower speeds until it reached the maximum: sixty-four times slower than normal speed. "Christ," he whispered to himself. "The man has eyes sharper than a cat or some other wild animal of prey."

Then he reviewed the scene in the car park. There were bits of Ashton crawling unarmed around cars. He played the whole scene and repeated the parts where Ashton appeared crawling on the ground. He enhanced and slowed down the screen. Ashton said something to the man and then the man stiffened like a piece of timber. Martin replayed the scene in a bid to lip-read the words. He was clear in 'look at me' but the rest was impossible. The slight tilting of the head was enough to have the camera at the wrong angle. He saw the door open, and Rod's and Ashton's heads appeared. He made a note to get the footage in the stairwell. Martin drummed his fingers on the dining room table and thought, *He has to be a cop.* Martin looked at the reports by Ashton and Rod. He scoffed, "Hypnosis. What is this world coming to? It wasn't even a decent lie."

He picked up his mobile phone. "Baker, are you free tonight?"

A gruff voice replied, "Yeah. After eight."

"I got a job. It will take all night. Two hundred now and another two when finished. I want you to tail and get photos. Nothing more. Keep your distance as the person is really mean and has no qualms about killing," said Martin.

"Distance, photos and nothing else. Gotcha." repeated Baker.

"I'm sending you details now. He is at the motel. Tail him when he leaves." Martin hung up before another word was spoken.

CHAPTER SIX
Finland

Greg Baker was more than keen to follow Martin Shields's orders. Earlier Shields had filled him in as to what had happened in the car park to his younger half-brother and was now resting in hospital under guard. Knowing Len was getting shrink attention rubbed against him; *he isn't nuts, just a criminal like me.*

Greg Baker and Kerry Smith followed the cab Ashton was in going up to the Mt. Gravatt Lookout. They pulled over to the side of the narrow two-way road when the empty cab passed them coming down the mountain. They were less than twenty metres from the car park entrance when Greg Baker pulled over to the side of the road. "We walk from here."

"What?" questioned Kerry.

"Shields said this guy is a killer. Distance and photos only. This is distance now and photos soon." Kerry nodded disliking the entire task at hand and mumbled, "Who the hell comes here this late at night besides teen-age lovebirds screwing each other?"

As they neared the top, Greg pulled Kerry aside and directed him into the nearby bushes. While they crouched behind the bushes, Ashton walked towards a parked car and peered inside. They could see Ashton go to each window checking for occupants. Ashton turned and walked around the area and slowly broadened his search for the missing people. Kerry and Greg ducked when Ashton came towards them. Looking satisfied there was no one about, Ashton went to the centre of the car park.

Greg and Kerry continued to watch Ashton going to and from the centre and return to the parked car. Most of the time they observed Ashton looking into the sky, slowly rotating as he did so. They imitated Ashton's actions of watching the sky but not knowing what to look for. Eventually, they saw Ashton focus to one point in the sky. Greg took photos of Ashton looking up at the sky but still couldn't see what Ashton was looking at. Kerry tugged at Greg's shirt. "Get photo of that car just in case the owner causes trouble. We have a reference." Greg agreed and using the telescopic lens focused the camera briefly on the number plate and took a photo of the car.

Through the lens Greg Baker saw Ashton smile towards the west. Greg switched to video mode on the camera in time to see Ashton raise an arm while holding something in his hand. Ashton shot a pink beam into the sky and kept the beam going for ten seconds before he switched it off. A pink beam shone down towards the Earth. Ashton pushed a button on his belt and floated up and into the pink light. As soon as the light covered his entire body, he disappeared. Greg and Kerry gasped not quite believing what they saw. They played the recording back before running towards their car to drive down the mountain as fast as the narrow twisting road would permit. Kerry Smith spoke to Martin on the mobile, "You better see what we have on this guy. Can you meet us in twenty minutes at the coffee shop on Park Rd.?"

Martin sleepily replied, "I'll see you in thirty."

"Make sure you do. There was one other car which looked empty but that doesn't mean the people or person was absent. If someone else saw what we saw, it is going to be on the net. That is, if it is not already on the net," said Kerry.

"I guess it will be incriminating, is it?" Martin said with piqued interest as the tiredness floated out of his body.

*

Ichiro opened the door of the four-man pod. Ashton couldn't get in fast enough as his lips were blue, "Thanks," he shivered. Ichiro threw a thermal rug over him as the pod rose higher into the sky. Ashton produced a map of the world and pointed to an isolated Finnish town at the southern end of Lake Inari. "There. That's where we start. Got some warm clothes because we are going to need them?" Ashton asked as he felt his body warming up. Eraton who was at the controls asked, "Why so far away?"

Ashton calmly said, "This world has so many different mixes of people, black, brown, white and lots of variation within those. Apparently, we look like people who come from a group of countries called Scandinavia and our English accents are similar. Passports are a legal document required for working in foreign lands. A bit like the old interplanetary identifications which use to exist and were heavily used before the war with Lacerta. I need to be legitimised here, or the experiment will be over. As we don't know anyone who could forge one of these passport books, we have to get legitimate ones. Finland, here we come."

"You could have picked a place not so isolated. How cold is it there?" Ichiro asked not sure what he was expecting to see.

"Deep freezer cold," said Ashton.

"The more isolated the better. It's the only isolated town in the area which can supply the documents. The place virtually shuts down over the winter months so there won't be many people around apart from caretakers, and a handful of others. And be careful the gravity takes a bit of getting used to. Baby steps and the levitator at three quarter strength," said Ashton forewarning them.

The pod landed in a car park half a block away from their intended targeted building. The pod immediately sank into the snow. "Well done," Eraton cursed to himself as he saw the wall of snow rob him of fifty per cent of his vision.

"Just a minute. I have to put it into hover if we are going to get out."

Ashton and Ichiro donned on their thermals. Eraton rotated the pod looking for anyone who could be approaching. No one could be seen - no street lighting either. "As much as I want to join you two, I will stay with the pod just in case we get a visitor." Ichiro and Ashton nodded.

"See you in ten minutes," Ashton said as he put his hand on Eraton's shoulder. The door of the pod opened to allow a freezing gush of cold air inside. Eraton shivered, "Shut that door! Hurry up!"

Ashton led the way to a small council building. It was two stories high. At the ground level an awning overhung the entrance. A small motion camera clicked on as Ashton said, "Blue" to cut the hinges off the door on one side and the latch on the other." They carefully moved the door aside triggering the silent alarm. Ashton directed Ichiro upstairs to where birth, marriage and death certificates were supposed to be stored. Ashton rummaged through the cabinets to locate blank birth certificates. He took a bundle but only intended to fill in one. He saw a folder on the counter and opened it up. He saw it was another birth certificate, and it was stamped and initialled. "Damn. We need to find a stamp," he said to Ichiro who was distracted by the array of family photos on two desks.

"Now I see. We do look like these people. It makes sense to come here," he replied slowly dragging his eyes off the photos. Impatiently, Ashton hissed, "We need to find a stamp like this. Help would be nice."

On one desk Ichiro saw a holder with assorted stamps dangling in a rough circle around a middle handle. "Would any of these help?" he asked.

Ashton looked at collection and hoped one was right. He drew out a piece of paper and stamped each one until he found what he wanted and double checked it against the one on the on the prepared birth certificate. "Make yourself useful, stamp the bundle of birth certificates in the corner and make sure the stamps are the right way around," ordered Ashton as he busied himself by copying the filled in form but inserting his name and estimated date of birth.

He nudged Ichiro, "Time to go. Six minutes is up." Ichiro put the stamp down and scooped up the now stamped birth certificates and stuffed them down his shirt front. They went outside and this time they heard the whirring noise of the camera, both looked up, "Shit, we're on camera. Let's move it before the police come. Red" The camera melted. Ashton looked down the street to see two men on skies and each holding a rifle coming in their direction. "Company is coming," Ashton said as he tapped Ichiro's shoulder to gain his attention. Quickly Ashton and Ichiro turned on their levitators. They flew up three metres off the ground, down one side street before levitating to a higher level before zooming back to the pod.

"That was close," said Ichiro relaxing more as he felt the pod take off.

The pod lifted vertical before heading south to Helsinki. Ashton saw the police on the ground had stopped skiing while watching them escape.

"Did you see what I just saw?" asked the police man who was in his early thirties.

"Good, you saw it to. I thought I had one too many beers. What did they want in the council building?" asked the older policeman.

"Let's find out," replied the younger policeman.

They looked at the opened door, their mouths dropped with shock. The door was intact and the two side hinges and the bolt were history. "Never seen a break-in like that before," said the younger man. From the doorway both looked around the room and noticed the lower section was in order. The younger police man looked at the camera and pointed to the molten mess. "That's a new way to wreck a camera. I hope there is some footage before that happened." The men patiently waited outside until Maria arrived.

Maria Birger was the town's mayor. She was in her forties and was a person who didn't tolerate any nonsense from anyone. She wasn't very happy about being dragged out in the middle of the night, a cold night at that. She greeted the two policemen. She was shown the unique way the door was opened and the melted camera. She looked at the perfectly intact downstairs room. "Let's go upstairs," she said.

When they entered, they could see open cabinets and assorted papers missing, and the set of stamps had been moved from one desk to the front counter. The folder which was ready for a family to pick up was now confiscated as evidence and would be brushed for prints. Maria walked to the safe and saw it was still locked. The older police man cursed, "They were making identities using genuine blank documents. It would be simpler if they stole cash from the safe. No, they had to make our life complicated. Bastards."

"Maria, we need to get all the footage from the cameras and see what these two men look like. They got away," said the younger man.

"Just how?" asked Maria fuming at the administrative inconvenience the event had caused.

"Err, um. They had a thing which flew. They flew away," the older policeman said with hesitation.

"Jet packs?" she asked becoming impatient.

"No. Something far more sophisticated and so much quieter. Actually, it didn't make a damn sound. With luck it may be on the CCT. Let's play it back and get hard copies."

Within minutes of starting the playback, they cursed the recording of the front door camera. Ichiro's and Ashton's action of slowly moving their heads along the two lengths of the door, and then moving the door to one side were captured. There was no clear evidence of a cutting tool. "They are using head mounted laser beams," said the younger policeman guessing at the technique the burglars used. "I didn't know laser equipment came in miniaturised formats." The first internal camera saw them go directly upstairs and back down again. The upstairs camera saw them rummaging through the cabinets and bring out a bundle of blank forms. The stamp was used on some but not on all. At the front door was a clear picture of their faces; both turned towards the camera. There was a reddish glow spreading across the two captured faces before the camera went dead. The break-in took exactly six minutes.

Maria and the police officers went outside to examine the broken camera. "That will be evidence as well," said the younger policeman. The older policeman searched his bag for a camera and went over the scene taking photos. He then pulled out tape to cordon off the area. "Call a carpenter to fix the door. That has to be done now. We'll come back in the morning and process the site. The forensic team won't be able to come for a few days as the roads and rail tracks are blocked and the snow on the runway will take time to shift. We have to do it ourselves, well at least collect evidence under their guidance."

At the police station, hard copies of Ashton's and Ichiro's faces were made and sent to the main headquarters in Helsinki with a report. They had debated whether the escape vehicle they witnessed should also be included. With no recording of the escape, they doubted their last statements would be taken seriously. They wrote on a separate page what they had witnessed when the two men escaped but didn't include it in the main report. It worried them that the new break and enter technology was now available on the market, somewhere on the net. For the next two hours, they were on the net trying to locate the source of the technology. They did find laser cutters, but these were large bulky machines. The men noted the manufacturers and would contact them later.

*

In Helsinki, Ashton pointed to the building a kilometre below. "That's the place. The stuff we need is at the ground floor. Ready to jump?" asked Ashton who was now going through an adrenaline rush. Ichiro shook his head, "Nope. But here it goes." As they neared the ground, they switched on their levitators which placed them gently in an alley way next to the targeted building.

Ichiro and Ashton spun around at the sound of voice going. "Arh". Ichiro grinne., "Boo!" With that, the homeless man who witnessed their landing in front of him ran down the alley towards the main street. The man tossed his bottle of alcohol over his shoulder while yelling out in Finnish, "Bad batch of booze." The bottle cashed at Ichiro's feet. The smell of the alcohol filled the air. Ichiro grinned.

"I have no idea what the man is yelling but he obviously thinks his drink was bad." "I have tried some of the alcoholic drinks here. Some of it is disgusting. Others are brilliant and would make a fortune on Beta Cancari," grinned Ashton as he recalled two very different experiences.

Ashton led the way, up a few steps before stopping at the door. Both looked at the double doors and simultaneously said, "Blue." They cut the toughened glass doors and gently pushed the glass. The glass exploded on the floor inside. They stepped through; the silent alarm was triggered and the motion cameras activated. The counter was sealed off with security screens much too thick for their beams to cut through. They ran the length of the long counter and noticed the entrance was blocked off by a locked door. They hastily cut the bolts as they did in Inari, pushed the door to the side. Ichiro opened as many draws and cupboards as he could while Ashton rummaged around trying to find what he wanted. Nothing was forth coming. Ichiro nudged Ashton and pointed to another door, a much thicker door.

The door was locked but that didn't hold them back as the hinges and bolts were sliced. Ashton looked around and spotted a safe and swore, "Which do we use?"

"Try green," suggested Ichiro.

"Green," said Ashton. The beam shot out, but nothing appeared to be happening. Another silent alarm was triggered. Ashton tried again and this time the door to the safe gave a series of clicks. Ashton pulled the door open and reached in. He found what he wanted. He and Ichiro grabbed a handful of passport books each. Ashton took one to the front counter where he earlier saw a few books in a stand ready to be collected by their owners. He used one as a reference before making his own book.

Ashton and Ichiro stopped in their tracks when they heard police sirens screaming towards them. "We go upstairs to the roof," said Ashton as both pressed the logos on their shoes. They were just at the top of the stairs when the police burst in with guns aimed. One policeman called out when he heard footsteps above. "This way." Half the men followed while the rest remained guarding at the crime scene.

Ichiro was still feeling the effects of the gravity. It slowed him down. He turned to face the oncoming police, "Yellow! Yellow! Yellow!" The police in the lead were stunned into statues temporarily blocking the any progress of those following behind. Ashton smashed a window opened. "We won't have time to get to the roof. Ready to jump?" Ichiro nodded as he puffed. Both jumped out of the window but instead of doing down, they flew upwards. Ashton looked down to see three policemen with mouths agape looking up at them. Ashton gave them a wave as another shocked policeman leaned out of the broken at the window. All the police saw the two criminals disappear into a pink beam of light. They all recorded the disappearance on their personal cameras.

Seconds later, Ichiro and Ashton broke into the Australian Consulate office which was halfway across town. Ichiro broke open the doors by shooting blue rays. As they entered, the silent alarm sounded in the office of the company monitoring the alarm system. Ashton broken open locks of cabinets by shooting green rays and flicked through the papers searching for the items he wanted - visas. He pulled out several application papers and stamps but cursed at the array. He gambled on a student application visa. "Got it!" He stamped his book. They ran out of the front door and stopped dead in their tracks. A convoy of police cars had arrived without the sirens announcing their arrival. Ichiro pushed the distress button. A pink beam shot up. Another pink beam of pink light came down. They disappeared in front of the stunned police.

*

At the Helsinki police headquarters, the police chief was called to the station. The events of the night warranted senior police to be involved from the start. The chief heard the verbal reports before ordering formalised written reports. Upon hearing and reading the almost identical methods of entry and escaping he sat at his desk drumming his fingers as he thought; *coordinated raids by two sets of twins...or brilliantly crafted masks...what are the chances of that? High tech equipment, gadgets to make them fly and disappear, police frozen on the steps and now reduced to a babbling mess, targeted items were passports, visas and...*" he was interrupted, "Sir, just received from Inari a similar break in. This time it was birth certificates. We have some photos of two criminals. You're not going to believe this; they look exactly the same people who broke into the Immigration Office and the Australian Consulate."

"What? Not possible," The chief took the report from the detective's hand and made a quick comparison to the footage from the three locations. He frowned and muttered, "Six men wearing masks. It is not possible to be Inari and then here in a space of two minutes. The roads and trains are shut, and all flights are cancelled. These guys are very well organised, very coordinated and we can't determine yet if they were filling orders or doing this to sell on the black market. Geez." He looked up at the detective. "Organise a full station meeting immediately. Include the patrols that attended both sites and arrange a video link with the Inari station."

The meeting at the station was into the first five minutes when a sergeant knocked on the door. "Sir, we have a homeless man who claims to have seen the two criminals just before they entered the Immigration office."

"I'll take that. I'll borrow these for a few minutes," said the detective as he removed the two photos received from Inari, the clearest pictures of the duo.

Minutes later the detective returned and pinned the pictures on the board. The chief and the others looked at him. "It was a positive I.D. by a homeless man. The same two men were Inari two minutes before doing over these two places. I already contacted flight control at the airport. They reported one craft going to Inari and coming back this way to Helsinki. The craft was doing at an extraordinary speed and failed to respond to requests of identification." He looked at largish group before him. "As this is going to shape up as forged identities going by the items which were stolen, contact Interpol and give them everything we have to date. Put their faces only on social media but that's all. Maybe someone can identify these people. The big question is, when they disappeared where did," the chief searched for a word, "this gang of six magicians go to hide? Who was piloting the aircraft? What type of craft flew through or over a storm?" A murmur spread across the room.

A voice from the back called out, "Sir, we should contact our counterparts in Australia about visas. They went to the consulate office so that could mean Australia is high on the list." People around looked at the voice as the chief craned his neck to see a very young officer who had not long graduated from the academy. The voice continued, "It is not possible to go from Inari to Helsinki in minutes unless it is in some air force jet and that would be very noisy; everyone would hear it. The craft was silent and obviously high up. It is not possible to go to Australia from here in less than thirty hours unless you are in the space shuttle. The space shuttle can do it in an hour. I very much doubt the NASA would hire out the shuttle." There was a chuckle around the room.

"Point taken. All international airports need to be notified at once," said the detective. "We can notify the Australian counterparts immediately. No doubt their consulate office is already on to their immigration office and that will filter down to their federal police and their spy force. I think the latter is called ASIO. But it wouldn't hurt for us to make contact."

CHAPTER SEVEN
Brisbane

Ashton directed Eraton and Ichiro to the Brisbane International Airport. He jumped from the pod and using the levitator slowly edged his way to a side door at the international terminal. When on the ground he tried opening the door but couldn't. "Green." The door unlocked. The mechanism broke beyond repair. Ashton pushed it open and wiped his prints off the handle. After a few false turns he found his way to where passengers were lining up to have their passports stamped. He noticed all were holding a green form and the flight ticket. He purposefully bumped an elderly Asian lady and lifted her boarding pass. He went to a counter lining one side of the passageway where he found the green declaration form, filled it in and joined the line of passengers at the numerous gates. As he was waiting, he then realised his ticket didn't have his name on it. His heart jumped as he thought about what he was going to do. As he approached the desk he just handed in his passport and the green form. The officer looked at the passport and then back and then made a quick search on the passenger lists. His name didn't show. "Sir, your name is not on any of the flights."

Ashton removed his glasses and stared intently at her. "It is there. Have another look." The lady complied and smiled. "Sorry Sir. Ah! Yes. There it is. I missed it." She stamped the passport and ushered him through. "Have a nice stay."

Ashton smiled back. "Thank you." Ashton moved as quickly as he could through the terminal and caught a cab back to the motel.

He walked to the desk and asked to see Mr. Shields. Dayna said, "Mr. Shields should be in shortly. He's due to start at six-thirty. You look very tired. A big night out? Eh?" Ashton nodded.

Dayna asked, "Working today?"

"Not until ten," replied Ashton. I'm off at six," she looked at her watch. "That is in a few minutes. Would you like to join the staff here for breakfast?" She indicated three of the four reception staff.

"That would be nice. I'll just freshen up first. See you soon."

Just then Martin Shields walked in. He was early. He gave a greeting wave to the staff. He waved to Ashton and indicated for him to come with him. When they were in the privacy of the office, Ashton waited a few minutes for Martin to unpack and set himself up for the day. "I have my passport. I went to Sydney late yesterday and collected it," said Ashton. Martin pulled out the unfinished paperwork from three days ago as Ashton handed over the passport. Martin filled in the details but noticed it was a student visa and that was limited to twenty hours of week of work. "I didn't know you were going to study here. What course are you enrolled in?"

Ashton said the first word that came into his head, "Engineering."

"Where?"

"At a university. Where else?"

"Which university?" questioned Martin.

Ashton searched the room for clue and noticed a business degree hanging on the wall behind Martin's desk. "University of Queensland."

Martin nodded not believing it. He handed back the passport. Ashton left the room with a feeling there was something dark behind Martin Shields.

Martin sat at his desk as he muttered, "That passport was the best fake one I have ever seen. He must have good contacts." He leaned back in his chair and switched the television for the early morning news. He gasped at first and watched in shocked silence.

Breaking News from Finland.

A well-coordinated gang wearing masks broke in and robbed three Finnish Locations. The first was in the snow bound town of Inari on the southern end of Lake Inari and two minutes later the gang broke into Finnish Immigration Office and seconds later they broke into the Australian Consulate Office. Genuine documents from all offices were stolen; no doubt destined for the black market. Here is the only clear photo of the masks they were wearing.

There was Ashton and a friend staring back at him. Martin sat stunned at the events in Finland. He compared Ashton's face on his phone with the faces of the two men on the TV. He laughed and shook his head. *Well the passport is real. Ashton is definitely one of the gang. A rival gang ever so tech smart. Leaps and bounds ahead of anything I could do.* Then he thought, *not possible to be in Finland and back in eight hours.* He pressed the intercom to the reception. "Could someone find Mr. Ashton and send him back to my office please."

The male voice on the other end replied, "I believe he is in the restaurant having breakfast with other staff. Shall I get him now?"

"Yes. Thanks."

Minutes later Ashton stood in front of Martin's desk. Martin showed Ashton a picture of himself now on a news app. "Is that you? It looks like you. The photos in the news clip are definitely you and I see you have a friend."

Ashton looked at the news clip and at the photo before replying,, "No. Not possible. Can't be there and in Sydney at the same time."

Martin looked firmly. "Are you sure? One of the masks is remarkable like your face. Look again." Ashton looked and said nothing. He didn't even make a twitch. "Is this what you wanted me for to verify I was in Finland? Finland is on the opposite side of the world, and it is not possible, except by space shuttle to go that distance and be back in time to start work. I don't own a space shuttle. How many people do you know who does? It is just a coincidence that the mask and my face are the same."

Martin grunted, "Your passport stamp says different."

"What do you mean?" asked Ashton hiding his concern.

"You said you were robbed in Sydney a few days back but the stamp shows today's date. Now confess. That was you and a few of your gang or friends, whatever you want to call them, on the news now circulating the world."

Ashton looked disgusted. "Sir, I would never jeopardise my life or career in such a stupid stunt even if I could carry them out. The embassy issued me a new passport with new dates. I am not in control of that. May I go now?"

Martin looked firmly at Ashton. "No. I know it was you. You are a born liar. And now I see you are a criminal on top of that. But I want your services not just here but for other duties. That courier job I mentioned, you are going to do three deliveries for me. Important deliveries. Do your normal roster in this place and call me at this number." Martin wrote down his private mobile number.

Ashton walked to the door and stopped. "I don't have a phone, and I can't drive."

"Then you buy a phone and you better learn to drive." hissed Martin.

Ashton heard a voice on his Pleiadean headset, "Keep cool. Don't let this man wind you up. Don't go against him. Pretend to go with him. Going against him, could make him injure or kill you."

"I am not going to be your message boy in delivering what I suspect is drugs."

"Who said anything about drugs? I have a recording of you disappearing into a pink light. It is not on the net yet, but I can put it there. Others have it as well. I can go to the police with all the information," smirked Martin.

Ashton looked firmly. "You wouldn't risk blowing your drug distribution ring apart."

Martin hissed, "You make the deliveries, or I will implicate you as a major player in that gang forging identities."

Ashton walked back to Martin's desk and leaned over it. He took off his glasses and stared intently at Martin. "Look at me. Look at me. Do you think you can make me deliver more of your rubbish?" Martin sat in his chair staring back. Ashton continued, "Take out a note paper and a pen. Write down all the people you regularly use to make deliveries. I want their names, addresses and numbers." Unable to resist the instructions, Martin complied. He handed over a list of ten people. Ashton put the list in his pocket. He continued staring at Martin. "Now I want you to delete the picture of me disappearing into a pink light. And tell me who else has the video." Martin said one word, "Baker." Ashton waited until the task was done. "Now you are going to forget I was in here now and you are going to go home with a major headache which will make you stagger when you reach the front door of your home. The headache is going to be so big; you will drink several bottles non-stop of your favourite alcoholic drink or other drinks in one sitting. Then you will go to bed and remember nothing."

Ashton left the room but waited outside not far from the reception desk. Martin packed up his bag and walked out of the motel oblivious to all around him.

*

In New York, Patron was watching the news. He gasped as he watched the footage. When it finished, he immediately picked up the phone and dialled Daraxon Technologies. "Patron here. I need to speak to any of these people urgently. Hammond, Dalmon if he is still there, Jed or Tayee."

"Patron," said Sue sensing the urgency in his voice. "Hammond is here." She switched him through.

"Hammond speaking."

Patron spoke quickly and with concern. "Did you see hear the news about the raid in Finland?"

"Yes," replied Hammond but found himself being cut off with Patron's urgency.

"The people are Pleiadean. We have to find them quickly before they get themselves into more trouble with the law. I didn't think the war with Lacerta would change Pleiadeans or even Siriusians into criminals. Maybe they had to do drastic things in order to survive. I hope they were not followed to this planet."

"We started looking locally but it has drawn a blank. Where do we start looking?" asked Hammond. "They could be anywhere in this world. Well, one thing is for sure, it's a Pleiadean ship hiding behind the moon."

"I'm coming over. I have an idea. But search the south-east corner more before going too far afield. The craft is supposed to be close to your part of the world. It can't be far. No, not a craft but a small pod or a one or a four-person pod. They won't risk being too far away from that. See you in a couple of days."

Hammond spoke to Tayee who now seemed to be living in the observatory.

Tayee was flustered. "Hammond, we have been tracking quite a bit of movement. The two objects which were about halfway here went back to whatever is hiding behind the moon. Then last night a slightly larger craft came to the Brisbane area. It hovered for about three minutes before heading north by northwest. NASA and ESA tracked it over Finland. It made one stop in the far north near Lake Inari and a slightly longer stop with a tiny bit of movement over Helsinki and then back to Brisbane about five a.m. this morning. Then the craft was traced back to space to go behind the moon. Then two small craft came back and are hovering in their original positions. The interesting thing is the stops over Finland match the same three stops that are in the news for the robberies. Are the robberies and the space craft we're tracking linked?"

"Most likely. Patron said the people doing the wrong thing are Pleiadeans and was worried that the war has converted these people into criminals. He wants them found immediately and brought here," said Hammond.

Tayee considered the idea. "We'll keep trying to find the person or people here before they get into more trouble. That craft you built, can it go the moon and back?" asked Tayee.

Hammond sensed Tayee's urgency. "It may need some further adjusting but doable. I will get a team on the extra adjustments now. As for the people looking for the Pleiadean person or the two of them, I will call a meeting to re-structure the group. We need to inform the governments the craft behind the moon has been identified as Pleiadean but caution is still required."

CHAPTER EIGHT
Cleaning Up Brisbane

Ashton purchased a phone then spent the next twenty minutes playing around with it to learn what it could do and its limitations. He entered all the numbers and addresses Martin's supplied. Then he entered Carrie's number. He thought he would give it a test and dialled Carrie's number. Carrie picked up the phone with an unknown number. "Hello, Carrie speaking."

Ashton spoke slowly not being used to the Earth device. "Hello, Carrie. This is Ashton. We met just over a week ago at the chalet where you work."

Carrie was surprised as she recalled meeting the tall loner with a sunburned face on the veranda. "I wasn't really expecting you to phone since you didn't have a phone. How is the holiday going?"

" Good. I have accommodation and even found a job," Ashton said hoping he would not need to say more on that. "Would it be possible for us to meet up again? I am still trying to sort out transport so it may be a bit easier if you came into the city and we could do some sight-seeing here with you being my guide."

Carrie was surprised by the straight forwardness of the request. "Can I phone you back? I need to check out my work and uni schedules."

"I'll be waiting by the phone for your call," Ashton ended.

He walked back to his room. While he was charging up his new phone, he pulled out a bottle of cold water from the bar fridge. As he sat sipping, he heard a voice come through on his Pleiadean head set.

"Ashton. It's me Nodin. How are things going?"

"Nodin. What are you doing talking to me?"

"Keka, Neo, Jalon and Haiten are not happy with the way things are going," Nodin informed him.

"Add me to that list. Things here are just so much more complex than what we saw on the television programs we tapped into. No doubt you heard that I am trying to meet this young lady I met at the chalet. I am hoping meeting someone away from this environment would give me a fresh view of things," Ashton said in between sips of water. "I must say the water here is terrific. That is one compensating factor. Excuse me. The lady is returning the call."

"Ashton, speaking."

"Carrie, here. I can meet you in two days - in the afternoon about five. We can catch up for a couple of hours before I am picked up by a relative who is going to pick up a good family friend from the international airport."

"That sounds fine. Can you meet me at the mall at Hungry Jacks? I would like a mini-tour and for you to show me a nice place where we can get a meal."

"Okay. I will think of a place. See you at five, on Thursday."

Ashton looked at the first contact supplied by Martin. He dialled it.

"Baker here. Who's this?" asked Greg Baker frowning at the unknown number and frowned deepened at the voice coming through.

"The delivery boy you met a few days ago. Meet me in Queens Park near the statue of Queen Victoria. Meet me tonight at seven. Another delivery and payment. Bring one thousand."

At seven Baker was leaning against the statue waiting for a delivery. The cash was neatly enclosed in an envelope tucked into his tattered casual jacket. Ashton was carrying a box with fresh grass clipping from the rear of the motel and weeds he had picked from an unkempt garden not far from the park. He gave the box to Baker and held his hand out for the cash. Baker recalled this was the man who flies and disappears into pink light. He was instantly alert and frowned at the box and tried to open it. Ashton put his hand on the box and shook his head. "Are you crazy?"

"Where's Shields. He normally does the organising. This box is very different from his style." Ashton looked at Baker and said, "Shields is sick. I'm filling in until he recovers."

"What's wrong with him?" asked Baker.

"Took too much of his own stuff," lied Ashton.

"I didn't know he was a user. Live and learn," said Baker feeling both suspicious and surprised at the revelation. Baker gingerly handed over the cash and took the box from Ashton.

"Come with me to the river's edge of this park," said Ashton. "I want to show you something." Greg Baker followed keeping a slight distance from Ashton. When Ashton stopped walking, he pointed to a group of men. "See that group?"

Baker nodded. "They come here every week. Poofter's pick-up place. Keep away from that mob." "Follow me to the bench and sit down." When they were seated, Ashton took off his glasses and said in a soft but commanding voice, "Look at me. Look at me in the eyes." Greg Baker felt the compulsion and looked at Ashton in the eyes.

"Give me your phone." Ashton held out his hand. "Your phone, please."

Baker handed over his phone. Ashton found the video of himself on Mt. Gravatt where he stepped into the pink beam of light. He deleted the video. "Is there another copy of this event on Mt. Gravatt?"

Baker nodded. "The main camera has the original copy."

"When you leave this park tonight, you will delete the original film." Baker nodded.

Ashton repeated the instruction. "When you go home delete the original film of what happened at Mt. Gravatt."

"Yes Sir. I will do as you command."

"Now one last thing. You are to sit here and be counselled by a group of friendly men. You can leave them or join their group if you so desire. That decision will be up to you." Baker nodded. Ashton zapped him with yellow and returned his mobile.

While Baker was still immobilised Ashton walked to the group of gay men.

Ashton introduced himself with a false name and nodded towards Baker. The group turned to where Baker was sitting. "See that guy over there on the bench. He's shy about coming out. Have a chat to him, but only a chat. I will raise my hand for you to come over." Ashton walked towards Baker. He gave Baker another zap of yellow and waited a few seconds before raising his hand. Ashton walked away. When he neared the statue, he looked back to see Baker crying like a baby and the now sympathetic men trying to assist. The more they tried to counsel him, the more Baker cried. Ashton thought as he grinned, *one down nine to go.*

Ashton phoned the next number. Kerry Smith looked at the unknown number and answered the phone. "Kerry here. Who is this?"

"You met me a few days ago. I made a delivery," replied Ashton.

Ashton could hear Kerry catch his breath. "I do some work for Martin. Martin is sick so I'm filling in."

"You mean Martin is dead and you are taking over," retorted Kerry Smith.

"Those two thoughts hadn't crossed my mind. Thanks for the ideas. Remind me to promote you when I take over. I have a delivery for you. Meet me in King George Square Park in an hour. I will be at the Adelaide Street underground car park entrance. Bring one thousand dollars."

An hour later, Kerry Smith slowly approached Ashton and recognised him as the man who disappeared into a pink beam of light. Kerry nervously introduced himself to Ashton while keeping a distance. Recalling what Martin had said about the man before him and knowing the man could disappear, nervously he handed over the cash without a word. Ashton placed the money in his jacket pocket. "Where's the stuff?" Smith demanded.

"Follow me. This place is too exposed," said Ashton as he sipped on a bottle of beer. Kerry followed Ashton into the car park and headed towards the electric car refuelling bays which were now empty. Ashton placed the beer bottle near the rear wall where he had earlier placed a brown paper bag containing Asprin Clear tablets and a needle in a sealed packet.

He handed the bag over the Kerry who frowned at the different method of drug delivery. He was about to say something when Ashton zapped Kerry with a yellow beam. While Kerry was paralysed, Ashton stripped Kerry down to his underwear, removed Kerry's wallet with all his identification papers and placed them in a separate pile well away from the clothes. Kerry was coming out of his paralysed state when he was zapped again with yellow. Kerry was staring at Ashton with fear. Ashton waved him a piece of paper with four names, phone numbers and addresses on them. He commanded, "When the police and the fire brigade come, you will insist they check out these men. They are medium ranked drug dealers who also sell guns on the side. Do you understand? I am putting this paper into your wallet." When Ashton completed the task, he broke up two Asprin Clear tablets and shoved them into the beer. The beer frothed to overflowing. Ashton held the mini-beer-based volcano over Kerry's head to allow the displaced beer flow over his body. He smelled drunk. Ashton handed Kerry the bottle. "Hold this for a minute will you." Then he called from his early lessons that manipulating limbs could result in broken arm. Instead, he shoved the near empty but still cool bottle down the front of Kerry's underpants with the top half poking out. Unable to move a muscle on his own accord, Kerry felt helpless as he watched Ashton place the remaining tablets back into the brown paper bag. The paper bag was left at Kerry's feet.

Ashton glared at Kerry. "Don't move a muscle or I will vaporise you. Do you know what you have to do?"

Kerry blinked his eyes. Ashton took off his glasses and demanded in a soft voice. "Look at my eyes. When you see my face with or without glasses, you will always see an alien with red eyes. The red eyes shoot fire. Now, you will cooperate with the police and give the names of these dangerous men. You're going to be an informer; a good reliable informer." Ashton repeated everything to be sure Kerry understood the instructions. Ashton slipped his glasses on. He made his hands into the shape of a gun and pretended to shoot Kerry. To make his point clear about aliens shooting fire, Ashton set Kerry's clothes on fire with the red beam. Instantly, the smoke alarm sounded. Ashton walked casually to the stairwell exit just metres away from Kerry.

Kerry didn't move or say a word until he saw the two policemen arrive. Without moving Kerry called out a warning, "Keep away from me. There is a creature from out of space who is going to vaporise me if I move. He burned my clothes." Kerry pointed with his fingers and eyes to the wallet. "In my wallet is a paper with address where the other spaces creatures selling drugs are hiding." The officers glanced at each other giving a look which said, high and off the planet. One officer went to the wallet and sorted through the identification and assorted cards. "Kerry Smith?"

Kerry nodded but still remained frozen to the ground. Tears began to pour down his face. The other officer approached and quietly said, "Come with us. The creatures are no longer here. You're safe with us." The officer slowly picked up the bag at Kerry's feet without taking his eyes off Kerry. The unmistakeable smell of beer assaulted his nose. Trying to keep in a quiet and friendly manner, the officer removed the near empty bottle of beer from Kerry's underpants. "It's okay. Shhh. It's gone." Kerry whimpered, "If I move, I will vaporise."

The officer who had picked up the wallet said in a reassuring voice, "He wouldn't dare touch you anymore. We can shoot him if he comes near." He gave the other officer a wink. "We shot one of these creatures before. They are scared of us. We can get you out of here and to safety of the station. The creatures are terrified of the station." Kerry gave a sigh of relief. He pointed to the burnt clothes. "The creature burned my clothes as a warning. Are you sure it has gone?"

The officer holding the wallet looked around. "I don't see it. The fire brigade is here. The noise of the siren scared the creature away." A couple of firemen entered the car park with a hose extended. "See!" said the policeman as he signalled the firemen back and said in a loud enough voice for the firemen to hear. "The firies are here too. They will squirt the creature away with their hose on full blast. The alien creatures don't like water."

Kerry relented and with the assistance of the two police officers slowly walked past the firemen.

Kerry called out to the firemen. "Be careful. The creature starts fires by shooting red beams from his eyes."

"Thanks for the warning. We will keep watch," said one fireman who didn't look back at Kerry but was suppressing a laugh. He whispered, "High on something. Burned his own clothes."

From across the street and hiding in the growing crowd, Ashton stood watching the drama. He saw Kerry yelling out, "There are alien creatures in the city. They set fire with red beams coming from their eyes. I thank the police who saved me from the creature and are taking me to safety in the station." The crowd laughed and shook their heads. When the two firemen holding a hose appeared from the car park the crowd clapped. Kerry saw them, "Thank the firies. They can kill the creature with their water hoses!" The surprised firemen looked at the crowd. One of them cottoned on as to what was happening and gave a quick bow. The arresting policeman spoke softly to Kerry, "Come on Kerry. The faster you can get in the car, the safer you will be." Kerry couldn't get into the car fast enough.

Martin was standing on the balcony of his apartment which overlooked the dark snaking river dividing the city. He had been drinking most of the day. The alcohol was now oozing through the pores of his skin. He had depleted his small supply of rum and was now swaying as he raised a new and fourth bottle of scotch to his lips. He swayed as he fumbled to reach the phone nestling in his shirt pocket. "Ashton here," announced Ashton in a cheerful voice. How are things going?" "Fuck off. You're," Martin slurred and burped loudly down the phone. "Yah fired from being a delivery boy." Burp. He swayed more and sipped from the bottle.

"Good. I didn't like that work. I'm taking over with my team of people," Ashton replied with determination in his voice. Upon hearing those words, Martin almost sobered up instantly and slurred as he yelled drawing attention from people two balconies away. "Like fucking hell, you are," Through blurry eyes he saw the lady go inside while her husband observed Martin. He swayed more as he leaned dangerously over the glass balustrade. He looked across at the man staring and growled, "What are you fucking staring at?" The man watching him yelled out, "The door is the other way! Behind you!" Martin swayed as he turned around. "I know where my bloody door is!" He raised his glass to salute the man before stumbling inside. He fell over knocking his head on the coffee table. The world went blank.

It was close to eleven at night when Ashton looked at the last four names on the list. All lived at the same address. Ten minutes later he arrived at the address and ordered the taxi that he was in, to pick him up in thirty minutes but at the street corner.

He looked at the old house before him running a plan through his head. As he opened the squeaky rusted iron-gate, an Alsatian came running and barking to warn the occupants of the intruder. "Purple," said Ashton. The dog froze in mid-leap and fell to the ground. "Good dog," whispered Ashton and dragged the frozen animal to the side and place it under an unkempt bush. Ashton hid under the veranda as two lights turned on. A voice from inside called out, "Thor! Thor! Who's there? Thor!"

Another voice inside, "It must have been a cat or possum." The lights went out.

Ashton crept around the house surveying the surrounds. Four motor bikes all in pristine condition were at the rear of the house. He aimed the red beam at the ignition until each melted or misshapen ensuring no key could start the bikes.

He walked back to the front of the house. Starting one third of the way down the steps, he sliced every second step almost through the thickness of the tread and approximately in the centre with the blue beam. Rather than walk up the non-sliced rickety steps, he levitated up and placed himself two steps down from the top, just a metre away from the small landing. He used his green beam to unlock the door. The external knob fell from its position, made a loud a clucking noise before rolling and bouncing down a few steps to disappear into the long grass underneath. The noise disturbed an occupant who had not yet fallen asleep after Thor had woken two of them. Ashton levitated back to three metres as soon as he saw the glow of a light shining through the window near the door.

The man who had first turned on the lights, grabbed a baseball bat. He preceded to knock on each occupant's door as he walked down the hallway. More lights turned on. When the first man saw his friends were behind him, he pushed the front door open. Their eyes were directed straight ahead; a tall blond man floating in front of him. The group rubbed their eyes to ensure they were not dreaming.

"Hi," said Ashton. "Sorry, about the door. Thor is sleeping like a baby. I didn't want to disturb him. Nice dog." The men's eyes glanced around looking for Thor.

The first man called out, "Thor! Thor!" Silence. "What did you do to the dog?"

"Nothing. He's just sleeping," replied Ashton.

"Sleeping like dead?" quizzed the man who eyed Ashton with suspicion and growing hatred.

Ashton shrugged. "Don't know."

The first man now moved to the centre of the door to allow the other three men squeeze their heads around him. Four angry faces stared back and summing up the situation. Ashton bobbed his head around and gave them a friendly wave. "Hi guys." No one answered. The first man growled, "Who the fuck are you and what the fuck do you want?"

"I'll introduce myself. I'm Kaiser. I'm replacing Martin Shields."

A man from the rear replied, "How come we heard nothin' about this?"

"You're not high enough up the chain," replied Ashton.

One of the men reached into his pocket and pulled out a mobile. Ashton shot the phone with an orange beam. Some parts of the broken phone fell to the floor. The four men's mouths were agape. "Which of you is Garry Baker?" There was no response. "I thought I would let you know, Greg has joined the gay community and is loving every minute. Kerry Smith has been certified crazy and is sitting in the police station babbling on about creatures from out of space. Martin Shields took too much bad stuffed mixed with alcohol. He became unreliable. So, management sent me to take over. If you have objections, this is the time to sort it out now."

"Kaiser is it?" growled Garry. "You come from nowhere and get the job when we have been working our way up for years? What makes you so fucking good? You look like a puppy."

"This," said Ashton. He bowed before shooting a red beam to set the bat on fire. The flaming bat was dropped on the steps and rolled down a few before disappearing into the grass below. A small flame threatened to spread. Ashton doused it with a purple beam. The men ran towards Ashton. When their feet hit the pre-cut steps, they fell to the ground beneath. When the men disentangled themselves, they automatically lined up cursing the man who called himself Kaiser. Slowly they inched their way towards Ashton. Ashton seared the ground around him with a red beam. Fire rose up temporarily keeping the men at bay. When out of danger, Ashton doused the fire with a purple beam. The men looked around. Ashton was now at the top of the stairs. "That is why I have been selected. Stay where you are," he commanded. "No one needs to get hurt." Ashton could feel their anger radiating. "Calm down now. I want you to walk up the remaining steps. They are safe. I want you to collect every bag of drugs and place them on the landing." Ashton levitated up and away from the house to let the men inside. One didn't move. Ashton levitated closer and hissed, "Move or I will make sure you end up in the funny farm like Kerry."

Three, two-kilo bags of drugs were placed on the landing. Ashton looked at the haul. "And the rest." One of the men drew a gun on Ashton. He pointed it with the trigger cocked. "This is a scam. I've had enough of this two-bit magician trying to steal our stuff."

Ashton frowned and then broke into a smile. "Excellent. Just excellent. You've passed the test! Congratulations to you all. Welcome to the inner ring." Now, completely baffled and the man with the gun lowered it a fraction. Ashton glided around the confused group. "Garry, you have your own territory. It is the entire Sunshine Coast area. Tony Spinner." Ashton looked around. "You have the entire Gold Coast area. Jack Wilson. You have the entire west and north Brisbane. Shane Wilson. You have the entire south and east of Brisbane." Ashton saw the smiles on their faces. "One more surprise to help you out. Each of you will be given crook cops which will turn a blind eye or rig any found evidence that can put you away. If they can't keep you out, they will do their best to have everything minimised. Also, you have access to a free lawyer when the time is needed, if ever needed." Ashton lowered himself to the ground. "Put all the drugs, any incriminating evidence and guns in the ceiling. The contacts who will be coming tomorrow will do a search and will ignore that location. They have to do a search to make it look legitimate." Ashton floated over the fence before lowering himself to the ground. As Ashton walked away, he heard the men run upstairs.

He went down the street to catch the waiting taxi. "Take me to the cab rank in William Street, just near the motel." Ashton walked towards Victoria Park. In contrast to earlier in the evening, there were only a handful of people in the area. Ashton walked towards the bench where he had left Greg earlier. He sat down and dialled the police. He gave them details of the four men and their haul of drugs and guns stowed in the ceiling. He walked close to the water's edge with the intention to toss away the SIM card he had bought earlier in the day but was distracted by a groan coming from the bushes to his right. He went to towards the bushes to see Greg naked with his ripped clothes dumped at his side. Greg had been badly assaulted. Greg feebly groaned, "I can't handle any more." He cried out and curled himself into a foetal position. Greg cringed as Ashton bent down.

"Who did this to you?" enquired Ashton.

Realising the voice was different, Greg cried, "Some big arse bald poofter sadist bastard. He wasn't part of the group. When the others saw him, they fled. This mongrel bashed me up before raping me twice and calling me a whore because I didn't agree to be his woman. I can still smell his bad breath and feel his dirty skin touching mine."

"Got a phone," asked Ashton.

"Yeah." Greg rummaged around and cursed. "I can't find it. My eyes are too puffed up to see anything clearly." Ashton looked around and found Greg's phone.

"It's broken," said Ashton as he handed the phone back to Greg. Greg sobbed as he took the broken phone. "I'll help you get dressed and call the cops," said Ashton as he reached over for the Greg's clothes. While Ashton called the police and the ambulance, he looked at Greg and thought, *this was not supposed to happen. No one deserves that. Just as bad as the Lacertians.* He removed the cheap SIM card and tossed it into the river. He stayed with Greg just long enough to see an ambulance arrive at the roadside of the park. He told Greg, "The ambulance has arrived first. The cops can't be far behind. You'll be okay now." Ashton disappeared into the night.

***

At the police station Detective Kirkwood looked at the night's events. He knew he had his work cut out for the next few days. Kerry Smith was brought in earlier screaming about aliens shooting red beams. The man insisting, he take the list of names in his wallet for they were the names and addresses of drug and gun selling aliens hiding in Brisbane. And now a report had come in. Greg Baker, the older half-brother of Len Pierce, who was hospitalised just days ago after a shooting incident in the motel underground car park, had been raped and savagely beaten in Victoria Park. Len showed signs of mental disturbance. Greg was significantly worse than the other he considered loopy, after the attack. Greg had supplied the attending police with a detailed description of an oversized bald man with tattoos. The man was linked to other attacks – women and men alike. The monster had struck again with the same amount for ferocity. Kirkwood pulled out a composite picture of the possible attacker and sent the picture electronically to police now guarding Greg's hospital door. When shown a composite picture of the attacker, Greg squinted through puffed up eyes before nodding vigorously. He cried uncontrollably. When the confirmation came back, *"The man needs to be off the streets fast,"* thought Kirkwood.

As for Kerry Smith, Kirkwood placed him in the same basket as Len Pierce; raving terrified lunatics. Both men refused to leave the safety of their temporary accommodation and making excuses as to why they should remain. Len wanted the hospital. Kerry refused to leave the watch house cell.

Kerry had given him four names of aliens who were supposed to be drug dealers. Kirkwood considered the drug factor seriously but dismissed the alien bit as delusions of a man who had taken a possible new designer drug. He wondered if Len had taken the same drug, a new dangerous illegal street drug.

Detective Kirkwood checked the four given names. Nothing but minor offences. They appeared to be clean and well off the radar. *The worst type,* he thought. Now, coupled with a well-known address coming via crime stoppers which gave details as to where the drugs were stashed, he wondered if there was vigilante in the city or it was a cover for a new gang moving in. Getting rid of the opposition by gifting them to the police was a unique way to gain territory. Alternatively, it was a start of a turf war. It was too early to tell. He felt there was a link to all the men involved but he just didn't know how. He would find out.

He leaned back on his office chair and placed his feet on the desk and his hands behind his head. He closed his eyes. There was a pattern, and he wasn't seeing it. After ten minutes it dawned on him. He sat up again and started a name search in the data base before contacting his counterparts in the drug squad.

The next afternoon the station was buzzing with activity. Two simultaneous raids brought all eight men in with very incriminating evidence: a tidy drug haul yet to have the street value applied, an assortment of guns, some lab equipment and a heap of assorted phones and computer equipment.

Kirkwood read the reports and replayed the questioning to date. He tossed the information over in his mind. A new name came up by the four men at the Milton raid. Kaiser who was high up in the ring or was branching out on his own. He took a second look at the reports by the four Milton men. He considered the facts and tried to piece a picture. *Tall and very thin, blond and wore wrap around glasses which shot beams of light via voice activation. He had a gadget which allowed him to fly or levitate. He thought about Kerry who had made himself very comfortable in the watch house cell. Kerry said the man shot a beam of light from his eyes. The same signature. Not an alien but a vigilante or a new drug lord moving in.* Kirkwood considered, *the unknown man as fearless liar who faced danger head on and to walk away leaving his victims in the police hands. He somehow killed a dog, instantaneously. Forensic said, snap frozen while the animal was in full attack mode. How?*

He tossed the information over in his mind as he went to the coffee machine to make himself a latte. A sergeant was using the machine when Kirkwood was taking his cup from the cup holder. "Sir, have your seen and heard the news from Finland? A gang stole genuine identification papers." The officer placed his drink down and pulled out his mobile phone to show the new wanted men. Kirkwood gasped. Instantly, forgetting about making his coffee, he grabbed the officer's phone and rushed off calling over his shoulder, "I'll bring it back soon."

The officer called out as Kirkwood waited at the lift door, "Apparently there are six guys wearing two styles of masks. The gang is supposed to heading our way."

Kirkwood called out, "Thanks for the information." Kirkwood stepped into the lift. He muttered, "As if we need more crap filling the detention centres or cells. Have a holiday in Australia! Free accommodation, free English lessons, air-conditioned rooms, free gym membership, meals to suit any diet or religious requirements - only catch – no smokes and drugs, no grog, no birds and do as you are told until you holiday is over. Geez. "

Kirkwood walked to the cells in the station. Kerry was awake and looking at the ceiling. He gave a gentle coughed before opening the unlocked door. Kerry immediately sat up. Kirkwood introduced himself. "Can you tell me everything you know about last night?"

Kerry grumbled, "I said it all earlier to the other cops. I am going to sit here until that thing is caught or dead."

"It's not a creature but a man wearing some glasses which shoots laser beams," said Kirkwood in an assuring voice. Kerry gave a sceptical look. "It was a creature. I can still see it in my mind." Kirkwood stood up. "You're free to go. It was a man wearing some high-tech glasses. Others have seen him" Kirkwood showed him a picture of a man wearing wrap around glasses.

Kerry froze, "That is not the exactly the same alien creature, but he looked a lot like him." Kirkwood swiped to show another picture. "Kerry yelled in fear and tears welled in his eyes at the same time. "That's the monster that shoots out beams of fire."

"Calm down," ordered Kirkwood as he put the picture away. "It's of a criminal wanted overseas." Kerry was unconvinced, "That's the alien monster. Believe me, he ain't human. It's wearing a disguise."

Kirkwood stood up. "Thanks. You can leave any time you want. The door is unlocked."

Kerry shook his head. "I'm staying right here where it is safe. That's the alien creature I saw in the car park. I told you there were more of them."

Kirkwood said softly trying to calm a clearly distressed Kerry, "We have a group downstairs. These guys have seen a man with wrap around specks shooting a red beam from his high-tech glasses. Before I go down there, I will run their names by you. Maybe you know them."

Kerry listened to the names.

"Garry Baker. Do you know him?"

Kerry nodded. "Greg Baker's brother."

Kirkwood looked up. "Greg is in hospital. He was attacked by a jumbo bald man with lots of tattoos."

"You mean Mad Dog," said Kerry showing concern as he wiped away a tear.

"You know him?" enquired Kirkwood.

"Just by reputation. Nasty arsehole. Needs a bullet, not a cell. A real psycho. What did he do to Greg?"

Kirkwood coughed and delayed responding, "Bashed him up and raped him. Greg's a mess and is in hospital." Kirkwood saw Kerry's face showing a mix of horror, anger and shock. Kirkwood was silent for a while allowing time for Kerry to recover.

Gently Kirkwood asked, "Do you know Len Pierce?"

Kerry nodded. He tried to hold back forming tears, "He's Greg's and Garry's half-brother. Haven't spoken to 'im for a few months. He joined some bikie gang. None of us liked the idea. Has something happened to 'im too?"

Kirkwood brushed his hair back with a hand and drew a breath. "He's in the psych ward at the P.A. getting assessed. He's claiming there is a grizzly bear around town. He was also treated for a gun wound. Just a graze. That was the easy part for the doctors. Does mental illness run in the Baker family?"

Kerry drew back in anger and disgust, "Na."

"Your family?"

"Nup," said Kerry.

"Is there someone selling a new drug out there?"

"Not that I know of," said Kerry feeling a bit agitated.

"Sorry. I had to ask," said Kirkwood. "Do you know any of these men?"

Kirkwood pulled out a list of names from his pocket.

Tony Spinner?" asked Kirkwood.

"Know the name. Never met 'im. Rumoured he makes stuff in a lab."

"Jack Wilson?" asked Kirkwood.

Kerry shook his head.

"Shane Wilson?"

Kerry shook his head again. "Sounds like them are brothers."

"They are," confirmed Kirkwood.

"Garry, Tony, Jack and Shane are all downstairs having a rest in the cells. There was a raid, and we found lots of drugs and a few guns and knives." Kirkwood saw Kerry's face drop.

"Just what is your role with these men?" asked Kirkwood knowing from past ranting Kerry had made and seemed somehow compelled to tell the truth.

"Me? Small fish. Do the small stuff. I know me place. Do as you are told and no trouble. That's me. Small stuff."

Kirkwood looked down the list further. The men on your list, do you know them?" Kirkwood showed him the remaining four names.

Kerry glanced at the list and said quite openly, "Read them names out. Me reading ain't that good without specks."

"John Towers? Bobby Singh?"

Kerry nodded. "Know Singh. Scrawny Indian. Thinks he's Elton John. Tries to sing the songs but sounds like fingernails down a blackboard. Elton John would piss in his pommy dacks if he knew his songs were being murdered. I guess half of 'em singers would chunder in their brekky if they heard fans like 'im singing. Put them fakers together and you have a sound like bullfrogs in matin' season. On second thought, that would insult the bullfrogs. As for what Mr. Elton John-Singh does, not sure. Could be a hit guy. Likes to show off his guns and other weapon shit. You don't piss 'im off. Short tempered bastard, he is."

"The next name on the list. Your list. Larry Holmes?"

"Never met him. Chinese whispers say he has connections everywhere."

"The last name. Simon Ballaton?"

"Yep. Met the arsehole. Big prick with lots of balls. Treats women like dirt. Ya' don't treat women that way. Loves himself and thinks he can do no wrong. Never pull him up for anything. You get a bullet sooner or later. Carries grudges like telephone posts and when yah hear he is going to dump one, yah run. Being in another country ain't going to save yah. Chinese whispers again, drugs and horses. Loves them horse races and is not shy to rig a race or two. Is that 'em all?" Kirkwood nodded. "Just who gave you this list?"

"I told yah. The alien did. The one you showed me on the phone."

Kirkwood sighed. "All these people are downstairs as well. Are you sure you don't want to go home now?"

Kerry looked around the room. "If they are down there, I'm going home. I'll take my chances with the aliens. At least the aliens let me live in spite of a warning he would kill me. If I keep my gob shut, then I will be okay. The mob downstairs don't care if the gob is open or shut. They do you in either way." With that, he stood up and followed Kirkwood out of the cell and to the front door.

Kirkwood just sat down on his office chair and read a memo. He became suddenly alert at the contents: joint investigation with the feds concerning a criminal wanted in Finland and had been confirmed to be in the Brisbane area. Kirkwood rubbed his hands and immediately compiled a report on all the collected information. A positive identification of one man. The other seemed to have vanished. He joked to himself, "Yeah, gone back to his planet or spaceship."

CHAPTER NINE
In Brisbane with Carrie

Ashton completed his shift, freshened up before meeting Carrie at Hungry Jacks. Carrie was punctual and arrived at Hungry Jacks merely seconds after Ashton had arrived.

"Nice to see you again," he smiled. "Here, let me carry that backpack for you." Carrie gladly handed over the bag at the same time smiling back. "Good to see you."

"It's a bit early to go to a place I selected for a meal. Come with me to The Botanical Gardens. These are not just any Gardens, they are haunted."

Ashton burst out laughing. "Since when do ghosts haunt gardens?"

"It's a part of Brisbane's history. Lots of angry souls playing out their roles in life but don't know how to stop. The restaurant is around that part of town, so it is a short walk from the Gardens to the restaurant."

When they passed through the Botanical Garden gates, Carrie directed Ashton to the side path which would circle the outskirts and down to the river. Carrie stopped about ten metres from the river bank. "Here's the creepy history of this place. When the first people arrived, this area was swamp or marsh land. The prisoners from England were treated like slaves by their violent jailers. Food was scarce so the jailers made the prisoners drain all this land we have been walking on because they considered it to be the most fertile to grow crops. They had to grow their own food as they were over eight hundred kilometres away from all civilization. No transport of any kind except ships. The job was made tougher because the prisoners and the jailers wore inappropriate clothing made from a thick warm fabric called flannel. It was a bad choice of colour and fabric. The pristine white flannel quickly turned yellow from body sweat and brown at the legs from mud stains. Many prisoners died from the heat, starvation, infections and disease caused by being in the muddy waters for extended period of time and from insect's bites which became infected or carried some dreadful disease. Hygiene wasn't great either. Lots of illness such as diphtheria and cholera were common. Come this way." Carrie pointed to a cluster of exotic native trees.

"Here is the most active ghost spot. The ghosts come at any time of day or night wearing their yellow and mud-stained prison uniforms. This place was active because these trees were used to hang some prisoners who were continually perceived to be trouble makers." Ashton looked at the trees and at the surrounds.

"Exactly what do the ghosts do to people?" asked Ashton not quite sure if he was being led on and literally up the garden path. "They sometimes interact with people but in a very creepy way. People who have seen them say the eyes are all white, no pupils. Some ghosts try to talk to people. Others actually chase them with knives or gardening tools and try to try to kill people."

"Oh, come on. You expect me to believe that?" laughed Ashton.

"Cross my heart. It's the honest truth. The police have records going back to the 1920's.

The ghosts show up at random times and dates. There hasn't been a reported sighting for nearly ten years. If people have seen them, they are not reporting them because of the fear of ridicule."

"You mean like the small group of men using gardening tools near the garden bed just over there?" Ashton pointed to the bed he was referring to. Carrie went a shade of white then laughed almost immediately when she realised, she was sucked in by the prank.

She looked at her watch. "We better go. The restaurant will be opening soon. It is about five minutes away from the gates," Carrie said still laughing at herself being caught out.

It was close to nine. Carrie was waiting with Ashton outside the restaurant. She noticed Ashton hadn't removed his sunglasses. It kind of bothered her. "What's with the sunglasses?"

Ashton repeated the lie he told others before, "Got to close to a bomb blast when wearing night vision glasses in the Middle East. The eyes are very sensitive to light. The ears are also messed up. Bit deaf."

"How sensitive to light are you?" asked Carrie.

"Very," confirmed Ashton. Before he could say anything more, Ashton felt the glasses disappear off his face and saw Carrie was wearing them. "Christ Almighty! They are like blind folds!"

Ashton took them back. "They're made especially for me."

Jokingly, she said, "Now you are going to say they are D.N.A. activated?"

Ashton was surprised by the astute guess. "Not exactly."

Carrie took the glasses back. "Humour me. Stick your tongue out. Come on play along with me. Stick that tongue out." Ashton gave in and stuck his tongue out.

Carrie quickly swiped the glasses across Ashton's tongue and placed them on her face. For a fleeting few seconds she saw through the glasses.

"Wow. Boy, do you look surprised. The clarity is brilliant...for a fleeting few seconds. So, they are D.N.A. controlled. Clever."

Ashton took them back and placed them on his face. "So much for technology," he muttered in Pleiadean.

Carrie gave a wave as a white four-wheel drive pulled up. "My ride home," she said to Ashton. Ashton bent over and gave a wave to the three occupants inside. He opened the door for Carrie and quickly greeted the people inside. "Carrie, please introduce us?" asked Patron.

Carrie looked in the car as the two in the front turned their heads. "This is my father Jamie and one of his close friends, Tayee. Here in the back seat and just fresh from New York is Patron, who I consider a surrogate grandfather."

Ashton extended his hand to each. "Nice to meet you all." To Carrie, "I won't hold you up as I know you all have a long way to go, maybe we shall meet again in the near future." Patron smiled and nodded. "I hope so and maybe sooner than you may think." In Pleiadean he said, "Good night, Ashton."

Ashton was thrown off balance but in English he said, "Good evening to you all."

Ashton watched the car pull away and gave a short wave. He saw Carrie turn around and wave back.

*

Before they even reached the freeway entrance, Carrie's father, Jamie, asked, "What is he like?" "They're always polite as much as possible one the first date. He has a sense of humour which I like. For some strange reason, I don't understand why, he's so much like a younger version of Patron." She turned her gaze to the old man and held his hand. Patron took the cue to quiz her more in a very gentle manner. He contemplated her answers and tossed them around in his head. "I don't think he was from Finland. I think he's the Pleiadean Hammond, Tayee and the rest of us are looking for."

"What makes you say that?" asked Carrie.

"Just something about him. As you Earth people put it, a vibe, an air, a gut feeling; that something that's undefined. When I said good evening in Pleiadean, he was thrown off balance for a few seconds. But he responded in English. Just before the war with Lacerta, spies were well trained and knew never to speak their own language. I bet he's a Pleiadean spy. And above all, his face has been on the news."

"Oh! Patron. Pull my other leg," laughed Carrie. Patron pulled out this mobile and flipped to the two stored pictures from the news clips. Tayee turned his head to the back seat.

"Carrie, if Patron is right and he's Pleiadean, it will be a great opportunity to find out what has been happening over the last twenty-five years. Also, we need to save him from more trouble than what he is in. The only way to find out is to invite him over for an informal dinner. If he is not Pleiadean, then still be wary".

Jamie kept his eyes on the road as he suggested, "How about we arrange a meeting on Sunday night. He can stay over. The guest room rarely gets used."

"I thought Patron is staying with us," said Carrie.

"This time I am staying with Tayee," replied Patron.

Tayee said, "I have been pushing for a couple of years that the complex builds a ten-bedroom guest overnight facility. With all the recent activity, people just might listen now. The local motels are not the best options since they are frequently full and are inconvenient for most of our people."

"I'll call Ashton tomorrow. What time? Give me a few time options just in case he is working, and we need to shuffle around that."

Jamie quickly added, "Lunch about twelve thirty, afternoon about three or in the evening about seven. If he comes in the evening, he brings an overnight bag. Public transport stops about ten."

*

When Ashton arrived at the motel, the man on late night shift at reception called him over. "Ashton. This envelope has arrived for you." Ashton accepted the large envelope but was very puzzled as to who could have sent it.

When he locked the door to his room, he opened up the envelope. Four photos of himself with Carrie were spread out across the only, but small table in the room. Two photos were in the park, one going into the restaurant and another inside. He thought for a while, who *around him had taken out a camera or even used a phone. One group to the right consisted of six people celebrating a birthday. They took photos all night. The angle was wrong.* He ruled them out. *There were two men further away. They were discussing some business - some papers were spread across the table. May be that was a cover. One used a phone to make calls and could have taken a photo when I wasn't looking. They left much earlier than Carrie and I did. A possibility.* Ashton placed the photos back in the envelope. He looked around his room and wondered.

He spent well over an hour searching for any devices. He was just about to give up when he decided to check the glass door to the balcony. The curtain wasn't drawn over the handles of the glass doors. On one of the handles was a small round disc. The disc had been facing him all the time since he was back from the restaurant, or it was planted much earlier. He searched further. On the television set and disguised as one of the coloured circles forming a logo, was a listening device. Ashton smiled at the two pieces of equipment, *interesting* he thought. *I wonder what the range is.* He picked the two items up and tossed them out onto the street below.

Ashton spoke to the person on duty at the spaceship. "Hello up there. Who am I speaking two?" "Kora. Translating for Jalon." " You heard the conversation and saw the pictures?" "Yes. Not a good situation. Check your personal stuff just in case something was added to that," said Kora as concern entered her voice. Jalon spoke in Pleiadean, "Patron who you briefly met in the car, spoke Pleiadean. Find out more about him. If my history is right, he was on one of the diplomatic teams just before the war. He was assigned to Genobola or Beta Genobola. How he got here is a mystery. History isn't always accurate when there is such an upheaval in society. Information is second or third hand, or it can get twisted to suit the ruling government. That Tayee man, if he is who I think who he is, then he was Prince Alcyn's top advisor in the military. That would make sense that they would use the Daraxon logo for their organisation. There could be more people from Oberon and Amada. Maybe we accidentally found the refugee colony which somehow convinced these people to share their planet. It was a rule and a good rule, never to occupy a planet already inhabited. It saves tension and conflicts. Now, this is something to report back to Beta Cancari." Ashton soaked up the information. "You know I am being watched, not just by you but by people down here." "Yes. Lose them. If need be, quit that security job." "Okay. I can give notice. Normally it is two weeks' notice but a week should be okay. I will need to top up on cash before I go. This place is a bit expensive. I think it is the boss, Martin Shields who is watching me with spy equipment. I have given him enough cause. Since the photos received tonight, I am concerned with Carrie's safety. Shields may perceive her as a softer target than me. She could be used as bait. Just to make sure she is safe I'm going to meet her in the mornings at the station and walk her to the bus stop and wait with her until the uni bus comes. She goes to uni three days a week. She crams all her lessons and tutorials into those three days. Then she is free for the rest of the week. Tomorrow is the last day of lessons for the week."

*

Martin was now sporting a stitch over his left forehead. His monumental hangover had cleared but he was still feeling some after effects. He had called several of his delivery men. The most used people were not answering. Those he used less frequently were leaving town or wanted extra pay. Martin sat back in his lounge chair and turned the television on. Instantly, he knew why there was no response. Two raids in Brisbane done at the same time. He recognised eight men rounded up. Another news article mentioned Greg Baker's savage attack and was now in hospital. Martin left the apartment to go to the nearest vending machine containing an array of SIM cards, headphones and other assorted equipment.

Back at the apartment, he was about to replace his old SIM with a new phone number when the phone rang. He saw the name Ashton on the screen. He hit the reject. The phone rang again. Three more rejects. On the fourth he answered in a grumpy voice, "What!"

"Ashton here. Thanks for the photos. Very nice souvenirs of a great evening. Very thoughtful of you. You can tell your photographer-cum-spy, he can pick up his equipment off the footpath anytime he or she chooses."

"Do you know what you have done to my business?" sneered Martin.

"Yes. I have a deal. We go fifty-fifty and I won't hand you over to the cops."

"Over my dead body," Martin said with more venom.

"That can be arranged," teased Ashton. "

I've lost most of my staff. My name is poison with everyone. No one wants to make deliveries because of you. Ten people gone in one night! Why?" hissed Martin.

"No one wants to work for a person who takes his own medicine. It makes a few screws go lose."

"I don't take the stuff, and you know it," snarled Martin.

"They don't know that. Bad news always travels faster than good news. All they know is you're washed up as a boss for this area," teased Ashton.

Martin turned off the phone and inserted the new SIM. He wondered if Ashton would show his face at work. He will roast him there and make sure rest of the staff would hear.

CHAPTER TEN
Police Headquarters
Friday Morning

Superintendent John Gilbert, had called an early morning meeting. At seven a group of twenty people sat before him. To his left were a group of ten federal police. He quickly introduced the federal police to his own team then he let his counterpart in the federal police, Superintendent Michael Chisholm begin. "Many of you may recall the news item about the gang of six who broke into the Finnish immigration department and our consulate in Finland." He looked around the room and saw all had heard about the event. "I will begin showing you all the clippings of CCTV received from the Finnish police. None of this has ever released to the public in case copy cats decided to do the same series of stunts. I say series and you will see why."

Chisholm played all the footage of all three locations in Finland in their chronological order. Then he directed the group to the two clear photos of two men captured on the Inari CCT footage before the camera melted. Chisholm replayed each film clip and stopped each to point out the unique anomalies. "The men look at the camera in Inari. A red beam of light is seen coming from the centre of the sunglasses." He stopped the clip and highlighted the feint beam. "The beam melted the camera but not before the Finnish police got two clear pictures of these two high tech thieves."

Then he replayed the first clip from Helsinki. "One of the external cameras faces the door to the building. Look carefully at the technique of opening the doors. Clean precise and very little damage. They use this time the same glasses but a blue beam to slice through metal." Again, he stopped the clip and pointed to the near invisible beam. "When they broke into the safe, a green light shines out and breaks the locking mechanism in a very unique way." He again stopped the film clip and pointed to the faint beam captured by an internal camera. "The safe lock had to be replaced." Then, he held up the busted door lock from the international airport. "Same beam and a sample of the results."

"Now look at the police giving chase up the stairs. The ones in front freeze like statues. When interviewed, all the men had side effects which are slowly wearing off. All the police officers affected said they were shot by a yellow beam coming from their glasses. The police offices coming from behind were all slowed down by the immobilised police on the steps.

"If that wasn't enough, also caught on police body cameras were the two men smashing through the glass windows to escape. Instead of going down they floated up. There were no ropes or grappling hooks or even mark created by grappling hooks. They floated. A pink light shone down, and the two men disappeared." Chisholm replayed the events at the consulate. They break into the Australian Consulate using the same technique - we see the pale blue light coming from the same wrap around glasses. And when caught on the front of the consulate's steps, the same pink light shines down. Then they are gone again.

"Now keep this in mind, the town of Inari was snow bound – no trains, nor roads and no flights in or out. There was a major snowstorm which isolated the town. By air on a normal passenger flight, Inari to Helsinki is about one hour, give or take fifteen minutes. It depends on the weather. The Finnish traffic controllers plotted one craft flying at an incredible speed coming from the south-west going over Helsinki to Inari. It was at supersonic speed but gave no sound. It disappeared for a period of time, exactly six minutes, and the same time which is a coincidence of the Inari town hall raid. Then it was tracked again going over Helsinki where it hovered for a few minutes in one location and adjusted itself for a few more minutes. Then it disappeared at incredible speed. The air traffic controllers tried to communicate with the craft, but there was no response."

John Gilbert held up his hands for quiet. He added. "We know for sure one of the gang members is here in Brisbane. I have read a very interesting report compiled by Detective Kirkwood. The face of one of these criminal magicians has been identified by a group of local criminals." He pointed to the picture of Ashton. "Open your folders and you will see a summarised version of Detective Kirkwood's report. There are quite a few things which are in perfect alignment with the information sent to us by the Finnish police. We have sent a copy of our findings to them. The other five criminals have not been found here or anywhere else.

A few days before these Finnish events, there was a shoot-out in the car park at the William Street Metro Motel. One man who suffered a bullet graze, Len Pierce, was zapped with the yellow beam a few times. He is in the psych ward. Doctors say he is physically well enough to leave but keeps ranting on about a grizzly bear wandering the streets of Brisbane. He refuses to leave the hospital. Apart from that claim, the doctors say he is perfectly sound in mind. Then after the Finnish incidents, a minor drug pusher, Kerry Smith was found traumatised and babbling on about aliens shooting red beams out of their eyes.

"For some reason, Kerry Smith, a minor player in a small drug ring, has now turned the tables and has become an informer; a quite good informer who gave us four names of people who were well off the police radar. If that wasn't enough, another four dealers are now in custody. They claimed a man by the name of Kaiser, made a visit to their home. He conned them into displaying their drugs and guns and told them to hide the stuff in the manhole. We believe it was Kaiser who contacted Crime Stoppers with detailed information. All four men said, Kaiser floated or levitated, chopped up their steps but they didn't know how as there was no noise, and set the baseball bat on fire by shooting a red beam from the glasses, broke a mobile by shooting an orange beam and made a protective ring of fire with red and doused with purple. All done by shooting beams of light from some wrap-around sunglasses. Their Alsatian dog was found dead, frozen. Forensics don't know how it was done but all concede the animal was snap frozen. We need to find Kaiser and all his buddies and their equipment. From our investigations, we know this Kaiser guy, a fake name for sure, frequents is the William Street Metro Motel. That's where we will start. Surveillance to find where his buddies are. Let's round up Kaiser's gang."

John Gillard continued, "This Kaiser character with his high-tech gear, is acting like a vigilante. Cleaning up the streets or is planning a takeover. We don't know which. Because the equipment is high tech, we are going to approach Daraxon Technologies. It may be one of their pieces of equipment that grew a set of legs, and they haven't reported the theft. It won't be the first company not to report stolen plans or equipment - too embarrassing for them. They prefer to hire their own private investigators. We have searched the net for the equipment. No one sells the multifunctional glasses, that is why it could be a Daraxon Technology project gone missing.

The head of ASIO, Peter Dewy, will be accompanied by Blake Granger who is assisting Dewy with the changeover. It was Granger who suggested we contact Daraxon Technologies for assistance. I do believe Daraxon Technologies has always been on the watch list for Blake Granger."

Chisholm added, "Read the information provided in the folders: the Finnish police report and our discoveries to date. We have sent our information via Interpol to the Finnish police. I bet they are happy we have the problem in our back yard. Or we have a vigilante cleaning up a drug ring or a new group muscling in and will be causing a gang war. But we all have the problem for genuine documents going to identity thieves. I think the drug problem is easier between the two." As Chisholm walked out of the room. There was a flap of papers and murmurs.

Kirkwood looked at his file and cursed softly to another detective sitting beside him. "Working with the feds is hard enough. But with ASIO is a pain in the butt: the word cooperation doesn't exist. I have heard about the Granger guy, a bastard who carries a twenty-five-year grudge against Daraxon and still calls himself normal!"

CHAPTER ELEVEN
Daraxon Technologies Inc.

Martin sat on his outdoor lounge chair on his penthouse balcony. He looked at the night sky, the city lights, and down towards the black mass of the river which meandered through the city reflecting the lights from the skyscrapers. At the start of the fresh bottle of his favourite expensive scotch, he gulped it down by mouthfuls drinking directly from the bottle in a bid to calm his nerves. But now he was mindlessly sipping as he reflected over the last conversation with Ashton, a conversation which had looped in his mind since it occurred. There was some agreement, not a good one but a crude truce.

Martin scrolled down his second list of contacts. This group was his back up for when the other ten couldn't do the work he wanted. They were rougher and demanded higher fees and they got their request. Martin dialled each person and became frustrated by their replies; busy, too dangerous, leaving town, already out of town and so on. He was three quarters down the list when he struck a yes.

Tony Smith, also known as Smithy, was eager to go. He had heard what has happened to his much younger cousin, Kerry, and was itching to have a go at Ashton. Smithy contacted his friend Hugh Mc Intyre. Martin met the two men at a bar in Auchenflower. He gave them photos of Ashton and of the unknown young lady. "We go after him first. Leave the lady out for now. If he is too difficult, we go after her."

*

Ashton met Carrie at the station. She was surprised to see him. "I hope you don't mind. I thought I would walk with you to the bus stop where you catch the bus to uni," said Ashton.

"Delighted by the company. I have a request to make. Patron, in particular, and my parents want to meet with you. They are a bit old fashioned. They want to meet the people who I associate with, they want to know if you can come out to our place on Sunday for either lunch or dinner." Ashton pulled out his phone to check the calendar. "I finish my shift at two. How about dinner? Tell me how to get out there."

"Catch the Beenleigh train from this station. Go to Beenleigh, that's the last stop. The journey takes about thirty minutes. Bring a change of clothes as you will be staying over. Public transport thins out after eight and none after ten. Give me a call when you get on the train. I will meet you at the Beenleigh station."

As they waited at the bus stop, Ashton pulled out a small parcel. Shyly he said, "I got you something. It is a bit of an impulse buy. I hope you don't mind." As he handed the small box to her, he said, "Open it. Something of a thank you for the other night."

Carrie took the box as she said, "This is not necessary. It was a pleasure." Ashton shrugged and waited until she opened the box. She eyed the butterfly pendant. Ashton offered, "Here, I will help you put it on." Carrie allowed him to clip it on. She quickly played with the butterfly pendant with her fingers and gave Ashton a quick peck on the cheek. "Thank you. It is lovely but really unnecessary."

Ashton just grinned. "It is necessary. A nice lady needs to wear something nice." Ashton saw Carrie leave on the bus and he walked quickly to the motel.

He looked at his watch. Fifteen minutes late. He signed in. Rod looked at his watch as Ashton walked quickly over to him. Rod wasn't happy. "Hello," he said rather gruffly. "I think you owe me an explanation."

"About what?" asked Ashton.

"Cops are all over the place asking lots of questions and showing your picture. They said the man is wanted in Finland. You're from Finland. What have you done and running from?"

"You heard about the Finnish incident?" Rod nodded.

"Well, I was in Sydney collecting my replacement passport. I was mugged a few days before coming here. How can I be in Sydney and in Finland at the same time? The mugging was recorded at the Sydney police station. The cops here obviously didn't contact the Sydney police. They didn't even bother to contact the Finnish consulate in Sydney to verify the incident. Now, they just assumed I did the heist. I prefer to be straight. Life's simpler. Besides I don't fancy time behind bars. What is it you say? Don't do the crime if you can't do the time. Best advice ever." Rod nodded and began to relax.

"Cops are everywhere in plain clothes," said Rod as he nodded towards two men at the bar and another two in the lounge area sipping of coffee. Ashton made a mental note.

"Excuse me," said Rod as he walked over to a lady who was having trouble picking up her walking stick.

For the very few moments Rod was away, Ashton was approached by two men who were sitting in the lounge. They flashed their badges. "We would like to have a talk with you," said one in a soft voice.

"Sure," replied Ashton as he led them back to their lounge chairs and waiting half consumed coffees. He sat down with them. Ashton coughed loudly and turned his back. In that short time, he swapped his glasses for another pair bought locally which were nearly identical. He had bought the glasses just in case someone else wanted the check out his real wrap around pair. The incident of Carrie conning him by sticking out his tongue to collect his DNA was not going to happen again. "Sorry about the bout of coughing." He sniffed loudly. "What can I help you with?" One of the men pulled out a photo. "This is you, isn't it?"

Ashton didn't say a word but pulled out his passport. "This is me." He flashed the passport and told of the attack in Sydney. He mentioned the date of the attack and the trip to Sydney to claim his new passport. They frowned with suspicion. They would check later. "We would like to look at your glasses," requested the other man. Ashton took off the glasses and handed them over. They examined them and compared them to the information they had received. They were close but not a match. They handed the glasses back. One noticed Ashton holding his hands over his eyes.

"Just what are you doing?" asked one police man.

"Protecting my eyes. I was in the Middle East when a bomb exploded while I was wearing night vision goggles. Since then, my eyes and have become super light sensitive. My ears are also damaged. That's why I wear an earpiece which is not security. Need to hear things. The police officer handed them back.

"Ex-army?" asked one policeman.

"I didn't think the Finnish people were over there," said the other.

"A small contingent attached to the Danish forces. Surveillance only work."

"You look so much like the man in the photo. Sorry to have bothered you." With that the men stood up and walked away. Ashton watched them leave the room.

He walked over to the bar where the other two policemen were watching the whole scene. "Cops," he muttered just loud enough to be overheard by a man who was obviously drowning sorrows by the glassful. He asked the bar tender, "Water please." Ashton felt the police policemen's eyes burn into him as he started to move away. He looked into the mirror above his head and noted they were following him. He led them to a corner out of the line of cameras. When he had them where he wanted them, he turned and gave an intense stare after removing his fake glasses he was still wearing. "Look at me carefully. I am not the person you are looking for. Now leave the Motel. Repeat that." Ashton waited.

When his shift was completed, Ashton changed out of his uniform before leaving. As he walked away from the motel, he looked into shop windows and noticed in the reflection he was being followed. When he stopped, they stopped and turned around. He thought, *"Amateurs. Let's see how good you really are."* He led them down a dirty side lane - a dead end. He turned and beckoned them forward. He saw them glance at each other as if they were conferring and then nodded. They were close to arm's reach when Ashton tapped the tip on his shoes to jump over their heads and on the way down, he purposefully hit the back their heads. The two men went flying face first onto the grimy alley way. When Ashton landed, he tapped the logo on his shoes. He ran away leaving the men slowly pulling themselves up from the ground. Ashton didn't look back and headed towards the mall.

Ashton saw them again some ten minutes later. They were weaving their way towards him. Ashton spotted a policeman patrolling the mall and walked towards the officer. He pretended to be a tourist asking for directions. He watched the men circling as they edged slightly closer and stopped when they saw Ashton beside the policeman. Ashton deliberately engaged in conversation with the police man and walked beside him for a short distance. When he left the policeman, he weaved his way through the crowd before coming up behind one of the men and followed him. He lifted the man's wallet before moving away to enter a store. He rummaged through the wallet. Hugh Mc Intyre on the driver's licence. Two debit credit cards and a small amount of cash. He used one card once and the other two times both times using the tap to pay and keeping well below the one-hundred-dollar amount. He bought himself a cap, and a shirt which he threw over his current clothes. From another shop, he bought a bottle of wine intended for Kora and himself to share when he returned to the spaceship and another bottle to take to Carrie's home. He gulped when he saw Hugh walk pass him only a metre away. Hugh was distracted by searching his pockets looking for his missing wallet. Keeping his head down, Ashton walked beside Hugh and returned his wallet minus the cash.

Ashton was heading towards the motel with the intention of placing his growing number of gifts in his room, when he spotted the same two men again guarding the front entrance. Ashton diverted to the car park entrance, entered the motel, and then to his room via every back entrance he knew. He placed the wine in the small fridge and checked his room again for bugs. He found new bugs and placed them in his pocket. He went to the foyer to see if the men were still waiting outside. Hugh Mc Intyre was still there and now drinking a bottle of water. He looked for the other man through other glass panelling but couldn't see Hugh's partner. Ashton walked outside.

"Hi." The man spun around and looked at Ashton with a surprised look. Ashton pointed down the street. "You'll have a better chance of getting a cab by going down there. Most cabs pull up down there."

Hugh nodded. "Not waiting for a cab. My ride will be here soon," said Hugh trying to remain calm and distant from Ashton knowing the man could jump better than most Olympians. He rubbed the back of his head at the recall of the slamming he had earlier received. He nodded towards an old blue Ford. "It's here," said Hugh as he moved towards the slow-moving car. Ashton slipped the devises he found earlier in his room into the man's trouser pocket. Ashton bobbed down and saw it was the other man who was also in the alley. Ashton gave a wave, "Hi, there." Ashton could see the man's face go white and he beckoned Hugh in. Before Hugh could shut the door, the car started to accelerate but not before Ashton shot the car with a red beam. The car came to a sudden stop and smoke began to pour out from the engine. The traffic piled up behind as the two men jumped out of the car and lifted the bonnet. Ashton disappeared into the growing crowd and traffic jam.

From a coffee shop, Ashton tried to text Martin, but the text failed. Ashton decided to go to Martin's apartment. He knocked on the door and waited. He knocked again and this time he heard Martin's voice call out, "Coming. Give me a minute!"

Martin opened the door as far as the security chain allowed him. He shut the door in Ashton's face. Ashton knocked again and said in a slightly loud voice. "Hi partner. Let me in or I'll let myself in." Martin yelled, "I would like to see you try. The door has a few security features."

Ashton took a few steps back. "As you wish." With the blue beam he cut the bolts and the hinges and pushed the door open. The door slammed down in the apartment. Martin stood there stunned into silence. Ashton moved towards Martin. "Listen here business partner, it is very rude to ignore the other half. I came to tell you; it stinks with distrust when you send people to follow me." Martin still remained silent as the bottle slipped from his hands and broke on the floor spilling its contents.

Martin slowly pointed to the door and stuttered, "How, how did you do that?"

Ashton shrugged. "Doors don't stop me." He sneered, "Partner!" Martin took a few steps back. "Now, are we going to be honest with each other? Or do you want to join the rest of your gang at the cop shop?"

Martin gulped as he slowly recovered, then gave a small smile as a myriad of thoughts raced through his mind. "Can you get into any building? And break any lock?" Ashton looked at Martin suspiciously before answering. "I prefer to be straight but if I get, as you people express, pissed off, I can get a bit angry and be destructive. Don't piss me off again or this room goes up in smoke."

Martin's growing smirk disappeared instantly. "I'll certainly remember that. I was wondering if you could use that bad temper and get into posh houses with some very nice items and information off computers. We could make a fortune."

Ashton looked firmly at Martin. "In your baby dreams. Why go after small stuff when the big stuff is waiting for the taking?"

Martin gulped agai., "What big stuff are you talking about?"

"Big businesses like the big motels with their casino areas and the expensive items in the shops inside. Not to mention very posh rooms with women wearing expensive everything."

"Have you been planning an inside job?" asked Martin.

"Retirement funds," said Ashton bluffing his way through the situation. "No more amateurs following me. No one else but you and me. These things take planning. You can start by stopping the attempt of drowning yourself in alcohol and get into shape. I will see you in the motel gym tonight at six. One hour of workout. You need to get rid of the growing spare tire around the middle. Being fit, just may save your life." Ashton walked out of the room by deliberately walking over the downed door. "You might want to get the door repaired."

Ashton signed off on his Sunday shift. He packed his backpack and the bottle of wine and headed for the station. As he walked to the station, Ashton looked over his shoulder a few times to make sure he wasn't followed. He sent Carrie a text message he was on the way.

When he was about halfway to Beenleigh, he had a feeling of being watched again. He looked at each person in the carriage before looking towards the next train carriage behind his. Soon he identified who was following. It wasn't either of the men who followed him before. He didn't return to his seat but sat beside the man.

"Nice day," said Ashton. Silence. The man moved uncomfortably. "I saw you looking at me." He held out his hand for a handshake. "I'm Shane." The man wasn't sure what to do and remained quiet and didn't take Ashton's hand. "I thought at the next stop we could head into the men's room and have a bit of fun." Ashton slipped his arm around the man's shoulder and gently pulled the man close while his other arm lifted the man's wallet, and another item form the man's jacket. Ashton could see the man going pale. The man pushed Ashton's arm away before standing up to move away. "Don't ever touch me again," sneered the man. Ashton whispered, "Sorry, I didn't realise you were taken. Being very faithful is highly commendable. Lucky person."

At the next stop the ash-faced man disembarked. Ashton saw him use his phone and look back at the train. Ashton peaked inside the wallet and lifted half the cash and looked inside the other item. He groaned. It was an undercover federal police officer. Ashton drew the officer's attention by giving a loud whistle and threw back his wallet and I.D. through the now opened window of the train going back to Brisbane. Ashton saw the man go whiter as he ran to pick up his items while still talking to someone on the phone. "You dropped them on the floor!" yelled Ashton and waved as the train pulled out of the station.

Ashton gave Carrie another text:

At Eden's Landing. Two stops from Beenleigh.

Carrie text back:

Just parked the car. Going to the station now. See you soon.

When Carrie met Ashton at the station she directed him to her car. Carrie explained, "Tayee and Patron insisted one of Daraxon security people follow us home." She pointed to a small green Mazda car. The man behind the wheel gave him a wave. Ashton gave a wave back. "Daraxon sending their people to look after you?" asked Ashton.

"Yep. Close family ties."

The car turned down a very narrow two-way road which was not well maintained - patches were covering patches. "We're just over halfway," said Carrie. The car bounced and Carrie reduced her speed. Ashton saw another old deep green Holden following and was directly behind them. The security car was now two cars back. The old green Holden burning oil from its tail pipe had been following them for about ten minutes. Ashton looked in the passenger's side rear-view mirror as he spoke, "We have a new person tailing us." Carrie glanced into the mirror and dismissed the car, "It's a narrow road with not much opportunity to pass."

"Let's test this person out. Just follow my instructions," said Ashton.

Carrie frowned. "Relax will you. You are being a bit paranoid."

"I'm not paranoid. Your family are. They were the ones who sent security to follow."

"Um, ah. It is easy to break down and become isolated. Being isolated here at night can be a bit creepy," said Carrie.

Ashton gave a grin. "Nice try. Get ready to follow my instructions. When we get around the bend, speed up a little."

Carrie sped up. The Holden behind sped up. "Slow down now," instructed Ashton. Carrie slowed down and the car behind slow down. "Is there a safe place on this narrow road to pull up? If the person is not following, they will drive pass. They will drive pass if they have brains." A minute later Carrie found a wider shoulder and pulled over. The car slowed down to a crawl and then stopped in the middle of the road to nearly cause the security car to crash behind. "Stay in the car and get down. Start making phone calls. I will handle this," said Ashton as he climbed out of the car. Carrie bent down and started to phone home. She peaked over the car seat to see Ashton walking towards the Holden. The security man following had also stopped and was reaching for his gun as he slowly moved out of his car.

Ashton acknowledged the security man's action while he walked to the man in the car stopped on the road. "Hello. We saw that you are having car trouble. Did the engine finally stop?" The short semi-bald man with a Polynesian like tattoo on his face looked surprised.

"Been having trouble for a long time. Can't find the problem. Goes good for a day or two and then plays up," lied the bald man.

"Can I take a look at the engine?" asked Ashton knowing all too well he didn't know a thing about cars. The man lifted the car's bonnet and grinned smugly. Ashton took one peak and moved his hands over the engine without touching anything. He quickly pulled a button grenade off his jacket and slipped it into the engine where it wouldn't fall when the car moved. He put the bonnet down. "The motor's very dirty. That can make an engine run hot. You better get it to a service station quickly. I don't like the look of the engine. Very dodgy." The man grunted.

Ashton saw the guard standing outside his car and watching every move while his gun was in his hand but pointing down to the ground. Ashton called out, "It's okay. Get back in your car. The car's engine is so bad it could blow any minute. Keep your distance." He turned to the man, "The engine is so bad, and it could blow. Drive slowly. The car following could assist you if you break down altogether. We would stay but we have a tight schedule." Ashton walked quickly to Carrie's car and ordered Carrie, "Drive as fast as you can. Just go!"

Carrie didn't argue. The man with the run-down Holden started the engine. There was a loud bang followed by a cloud of smoke which drove the occupant out of the car. From the mirrors in the car, both Ashton and Carrie saw the guard assist the man and speak on the phone. "Just keep driving," ordered Ashton.

"What the fuck did you do to that car?" asked Carrie who was both shaken and frightened.

"Nothing. The heap was burning oil, and the engine was running far too hot. It would have eventually blown or break down completely. I didn't expect so soon." Ashton said in a calm matter-of-fact manner.

"We should go back and assist," demanded Carrie.

"No. Your security person is capable of handling the situation. Besides, the man is dangerous. There was a small packet of bullets on the passenger's seat and a rifle on the back seat," lied Ashton. "Just keep driving," Ashton ordered. "Something tells me, he wasn't out here to shoot roos."

Carrie's car pulled into the driveway at her home. She directed Ashton, "Follow me. We are going around to the back of the house to the barbeque and entertainment area."

Ashton's eyes popped. It wasn't a small crowd of about six people he was expecting, but a tribe close to twenty people.

He pulled Carrie back. "I thought this was going to be just a few family members plus Tayee and Patron."

Carrie didn't respond immediately; she introduced her mother, Cassie and re-introduced her father, Jamie and then her twin brothers Andrew and Reuben. Then she directed him to Tayee's family, Jed and his family, Hammond and his family and then to Dalmon and finally to Patron. Ashton was still holding the now warm bottle of wine when Carrie decided to take it and place it in the refrigerator. He moved around the group awkwardly at first, but he noticed Patron and Dalmon were watching him all the time.

About halfway through the evening, Patron and Dalmon approached Ashton. "Come with us to the pergola. We want to have a private chat without all the noise." Ashton followed the old men to the dimly lit pergola; all sat down on the padded bench. Patron was direct and spoke in Pleiadean. "Tell me young man, the ship hiding behind the moon, is that Pleiadean?" Ashton frowned and pretended not to understand. The old man grinned. "My, oh my. You are well trained. Relax. This is the safest place you could ever be on this planet. Home among Oberon and Amada refugees." Ashton didn't know what to say. Commander Jalon spoke to Ashton, "My God. Ashton don't blow this. Get more information. We finally found some of our people. Speak in Pleiadean. I am putting this through the ship."

Ashton gave a sigh. Then he spoke in Pleiadean answering all of Patron's and Dalmon's questions. Tears had formed in their eyes. Carrie noticed and grabbed four serviettes before she approached the trio. "What's wrong," she asked Dalmon and Patron as she slipped an arm over Dalmon's shoulder and handing them serviettes. The old men wiped their faces. Patron sniffed, "We've been found. We are no longer isolated. The ship is friendly. Tell Tayee and Hammond. We even spoke to the commander of the ship. We have been found." He forced a smile through the tears. Patron wiped away tears with the back of his hand. "We never dreamed we would be found. We gave up hoping years ago." Patron tapped Ashton's leg and pulled Ashton towards him for a hug.

Carrie looked up to see Hammond and Tayee talking to each other. She called out to come over. When they were close, she gave them the news. "Please keep this quiet for a couple of days," said Hammond. "There is a lot of work to do before we make any announcements. If this gets out too early, the press will be here. Then they will be followed by the well-intentioned but annoying people and the crazies - not to mention every government and every agency. We can delay the circus and plan our strategy."

Tayee said softly to Ashton, "You better stay a few days, not just overnight." With that he walked directly to Cassie.

Ashton filled in the present group of refugees as to what he and his people had been doing over the last twenty-five years. They gasped and cried at the continued horror all Amada and Oberon people were continuing to experience. Both elderly men cried knowing their planets no longer existed and the whereabouts of the Siriusian and Andromedan refugees was still unknown.

Tayee and Hammond escorted Ashton around some parts of the Daraxon Technologies complex. They avoided the research and development area except for the jet sitting in the large hangar. Ashton picked up on the other omission. He didn't ask why, nor did it matter that much. They had their reasons, and it was their business. He was a guest, and he was going to behave that way. The last thing he needed was to draw suspicion and more attention for all the wrong reasons. While they were walking around the complex, Patron quizzed him about the people now long gone. He hoped he would come across someone mutual. Patron gave his story of escape.

"President Orris, the now last president of Pleiades, gave orders to me. I was to be the new diplomat on Beta Genobola. My wife, Loana and my two daughters, Lonon and Palo accompanied me to the planet. We flew by private charter. The pilot was the most brilliant pilot I had ever the pleasure to fly with. His name was Captain Pallaton."

Ashton interrupted, "You mean Captain Pallaton? The man who shot down over sixty Lacertian fighters?"

Patron asked, "Did he shoot down over sixty Lacertian fighters? My, My. The best pilot I have ever known. When we were over halfway to Beta Genobola we came across ten Lacertan fighters in formation heading directly for Isobola. He detoured and hid the craft we were flying in behind large piece of space debris. We stayed there for several hours before we continued to Beta Genobola. Do you know of him?"

Ashton went a bit bashful. "He was my father. Commander Findlee, now President Findlee is my guardian-cum-father."

Patron's face lit up like a Christmas tree. "Pallaton was one of the best young men I had ever met."

Patron leaned back on his chair and began assessing Ashton in a different way. "You say Findlee is your guardian?"

"Yes. Well technically not anymore since last year. He is the only father I knew. He is still dad to me although I have long known about my own biological father and mother." said Ashton.

Ashton gave a cough. "My mother also died in the war. I was told she was a geneticist nurse who flew two missions from Beta Cancari, our new colony, back to Pleiades to load up on gestation cribs and more refugees. She died landing a battle beaten craft. She had suffered injuries.

Findlee tells me he was amazed how she got the ship back and everyone else arrived safely, but she and the other pilot died."

"Her name?" asked Patron double checking to make sure he was thinking correctly.

"Ashira," replied Ashton.

Patron eyes popped. "Are you sure it was Ashira?" Ashton nodded.

"Come here young man. Lean closer." Patron gave Ashton a tight hug and tears rolled down his face.

"Your mother's father and I were brothers. I can't believe it. A relative. No wonder Carrie said you were like a younger version of me. Family traits can show up in different ways. And she was smart enough to see it first."

Ashton was lost for words. He let Patron hug him a touch longer before pulling away.

It was the early hours of Tuesday when Carrie knocked on Ashton's door. "Time to get up. You have to catch the train back to the city."

Ashton groaned. "Too early. I am not in a hurry to go back." Carrie opened the door just wide enough to pop her head through. "Sorry, but we have to get going. What time do you start work?"

"That's a horrible thought. Nine."

"Then you better move it," said Carrie. Ashton put the pillow over his head. His voice was muffled and like a child protesting about going back to school, "I don't like the place. I don't want to go."

"Then leave. No one is holding you there, are they?" asked Carrie.

Ashton pulled the pillow off his head. "You're right. I can quit any time."

Jamie came to the door. "Ashton, get up now. What's the hold up?"

Ashton was now half up and leaning on his elbows, "Nothing. Just procrastinating."

CHAPTER TWELVE
The Motel

Ashton signed in for his shift at the motel. "There's a message for you," said one of the reception staff. Mr. Donaldson wants you in his office as soon as you come in." Mr. Donaldson was one of two other managers of the motel. Unlike Shields, it appeared to Ashton the man was more at peace with himself. The man was much shorter than Shields and walked with a sense of authority.

Mr. Donaldson ushered him in. "Please take a seat." Ashton sat in the unfamiliar office. His file was already on the desk and showed signs of it being read. Mr. Donaldson asked various questions and listened carefully and watched Ashton's gestures to make sure words and gestures matched. "Today you will be working in the surveillance room. We are down three staff in that area and that is unusual. There seems to be a spat of illness and family emergencies of late. Paul will give you a quick briefing but going from your records, you won't need much coaching." Ashton left the room and went to the surveillance room.

Paul greeted Ashton and placed him in one of the three vacant chairs. He gave Ashton a few quick instructions before leaving Ashton to work. Ashton's eyes flicked from one screen to another. He remained silent as the other men occasionally engaged in conversation. Still focused on the screens Ashton heard the gossip about Martin Shields and the conjecture of his now frequent absenteeism. Ashton smiled and thought, *I wish that was so true.*

Paul noticed Ashton smiling. "What's got you grinning?"

"Nothing," replied Ashton.

"A grin like that comes from a good week-end with a bird," said Paul giving a wink across to the other staff member, Gordon.

"In your dreams," said Ashton. "Met the family and went through the third degree."

"How long have you known her?" enquired Gordon from the far side of the room.

"Just a few days after I got here," replied Ashton.

Gordon whistle., "Gee, you know how to move fast. That's hardly time to be in the sack and you're at the folk's place."

"They're just old fashioned," sighed Ashton.

"Watch out for those types. They are like Rottweilers. They sink their teeth and claws into you and don't let go. Or spit you out like toxic matter."

"Relax. That is not going to happen," said Ashton as his eyes flicked to another screen.

"What makes you so bloody sure?" asked Gordon.

"Through the interrogation we discovered we are distantly related," lied Ashton. "That is a major damper in itself. So, it is strictly friendship."

"That's a real bummer. Got a picture of her or the family? Generally, when that happens, the cameras go wild," said Paul.

Ashton pulled out a group photo.

"See the old man in the corner? That is where the link is. My grandfather's long-lost brother," said Ashton. "He's been here for twenty-five years, give or take a few and started his own clan."

Paul looked at the photo a bit longer. He frowned. "I have seen two of these people in the media a couple of times. He clicked his fingers hoping the memory would crystallise. He pointed to Jed and Hammond. "These two, I'm sure are bosses of Daraxon Technologies. If your girlfriend is connected to these people, no wonder you got an early third degree. Did you get a tour of the place?"

"Only parts. Spent a long time with the old uncle, Patron."

"You mean the Patron, the ambassador?" asked Gordon. Ashton nodded as he continually watched the screens. Ashton heard a series of whistles and loud breaths.

"I didn't know he was an ambassador," said Ashton who had an inkling the old man's role on Earth was somewhat important but didn't know in what capacity.

Paul looked at Ashton. "If he is related to you, then what the fuck are you doing here? You should be in Daraxon. You got upper-end skills to be there. They only take the best. The staff are so well looked after, that no one ever wants to leave. One hundred per cent loyalty." Just then the door to the room opened. Martin Shields walked in. Everyone stared.

Martin looked ill and swayed. "Ashton, in my office in five." He slammed the door behind him. Everyone stared at Ashton. Ashton just shrugged and gave a blank look to the others. Before Ashton left the room, Paul offered, "Do you want me to come as a witness? He looks like trouble on a mega scale."

"Thanks. I think I can handle this. Just be aware, Shields is not all what he seems to be. If I need help or look as if the conversation is going downhill, I will definitely call. We better do a number swap so I can call you immediately." They made a swap. Ashton assured him, "If I start dialling, just come." Paul nodded. He waited until Ashton left the room before he contacted Mr. Donaldson.

A few minutes later both Paul and Gordon saw through the screens, Martin and Ashton leave the motel. Gordon said in a soft voice, "Something is not right between those two men." He replayed the screen with Paul watching. Ashton looked at every camera and mouthed, "Help!"

Martin had hired a car. He picked up Ashton at a bus stop across the road from the motel. Ashton climbed into the car. Martin sneered, "Hello business partner. This job was supposed to have been done by my staff. Thanks to you, we have to go and pick the parcel up." There was silence as they drove to the international air cargo pick up section.

At the cargo office, Ashton handed over a pick-up slip identification notification and in return handed two forms to fill in. Before he handed back the forms, he slipped the motel's business card into the mix. The officer did a quick check of the two pages, spotted the note and glared at

Ashton who remained absolutely calm. The officer removed the note and gave a knowing nod. He handed him the pick-up document and directed him to the next pick-up area where two parcels would be handed over.

While Ashton was going to the receiving section, the officer picked up the phone and dialled his superiors. The men studied the note before the boss contacted someone higher up. "Let him go. He gave us details and we know where to find him. Pull the CCT in here and all the ones outside. We need to get that car a.s.a.p. That took quite a bit of guts to slip this note while under duress."

As Martin drove casually drove away Ashton could see from his passenger's window an officer watching them drive off. The officer then compared the car details with what was written on the card. It wasn't a match. Instantly he knew there was going to be a car switch. But he smiled at the note: added on the card was a name Martin Shield, his address and phone number and his car details including the number plate. On the other side was a brief message which had raised more eyebrows with the staff.

I am Ashton· Help· Being blackmailed into this· Contraband·

The officers smiled and secretly admired Ashton's coolness.

They rechecked the scanning of the parcels. No drugs but new science equipment which would facilitate the manufacture of drugs. It had slipped past as they were searching for drugs, not manufacturing equipment.

Martin drove for thirty minutes before he turned into the parking area of Marchant Park in Chermside. He pulled up beside an old battered grey Falcon. Ashton didn't know if the car was abandoned or just for the transfer. He remained silent.

Apart from Martin sending a text message, they sat in silence watching the old car. About five minutes later blue ute pulled up on the other side of the grey car. The unknown men pulled out a grubby child's backpack and tossed the bag onto Martin's lap. Martin did a quick count before handing over the two boxes from the airport. Not a word was spoken by either party. The transaction took less than two minutes. The blue ute drove away first. Martin and Ashton in the hired car waited an extra minute before departing.

Martin pulled into a petrol station to fill up the car and then drove the car to the parking bays for hire cars. He reached for the bag of cash which was tossed on to the back seat and removed all of the money. He did a quick recount and gave Ashton the promised half. Martin stuffed his wallet to the maximum with the smaller notes, and then proceeded to stuff all the inside pockets in his jacket with the remainder. Martin pointed to his car parked on the street, pressed the remote control and ordered Ashton to get into his car. "Stay in my car. Don't move and don't say a word." Martin calmly walked towards the service station shop and dumped the backpack in the rubbish bin near the door. He entered the service station shop ready to pay the account in cash.

Martin found himself waiting in a short line when two men rushed in after jumping out of a white car. Inside the shop one bandit pulled out a sawn-off rifle and the other, a butcher's knife. Both were similarly dressed in jeans and faded blue but old T- shirts. Their black caps were pulled down low over their faces.

Martin and the others in the store froze and turned white with fear as the knife and the gun were waved around. "This is a hold up!" screamed the man with the gun. The men herded the people towards the counter before demanding from the attendant, "Open the till and hand over the cash." Shaking with fear the man behind the counter, complied. The men snatched the cash and turned their attention to the customers demanding their wallets. Systematically, they took the wallets from each customer and removed all the cash. When it was Martin's turn, he refused until the gun was placed directly at his head. Slowly, he opened his wallet and removed some of the notes and tossed them into the air. Both men were instantly distracted by the floating notes. Martin seized the moment to kick the man holding gun in the groin. The man dropped to the floor nursing his crotch. Martin swooped down to disarmed man and pointed the gun at directly at the man on the floor. The man holding the knife froze at the reversal of fortune. Martin pointed the gun to the second robber. Martin ordered both to stand near a blank wall with their hands above their heads. Martin snarled, "Game over, punks. Hands up high. To the wall." He turned to the stunned attendant. "Call the cops now." Without hesitation, the attendant complied.

From the parked car Ashton noticed there was a time delay and guessed the two men holding weapons behind their backs were the cause. He looked at his watch. Ten minutes passed and no one was coming out. Not wanting to be involved, he sat while twisting his neck around trying to see what exactly was happening. Nothing. Wrong angle. He sat patiently until four police cars with sirens screamed to the door and ran inside with guns at the ready. After a considerable amount of time, he saw the police pushing the two cuffed bandits into a police car. Two police cars escorted the car with the two bandits. The other police were inside. One by one the customers left. Martin was the last to leave.

As Martin neared the car, Ashton leaned out of the window. "What took you so long and why all the police?" As Martin neared, Ashton could see Martin fuming and didn't respond to his questions. He watched Martin get into the driver's seat and slam the door shut. Ashton was just about to repeat the question when Martin glared at him. "You saw there was trouble, why didn't you come and help?"

Ashton still played dumb. "I was obeying your orders. You said stay here, so I did".

"I could have been killed in there!" growled Martin.

"Doubt it. They were amateurs and you're a professional," said Ashton. "Stop complaining. You're still alive." Ashton could see the hatred in Martin's eyes go up a notch. They sat in silence until they reached the motel.

By the time Martin and Ashton returned to the motel, the news of the foiled robbery was already on all forms of media. As Martin walked through the venue, the staff who had seen the news clapped and congratulated him. Martin smiled and played humble. Ashton kept to the background allowing Martin to lap up the attention. Ashton was about to slip away when Martin called him over. He took Ashton aside and whispered, "At my office at seven tonight."

When he was alone in his room, Ashton dialled Carrie. It went to voice mail. He left a message. He spoke to a person on the Pleiadean Ship.

Keka identified himself. "Hello, Ashton."

"Hello Keka. I need a bit of help. Did you find anything about the people I met at Carries' home on the weekend?"

"Haiten has a vague memory of some people. Tayee and Hammond were right hand men of Prince Alcyn. Tayee was a general who had the task to educate all forms of armed forces which were few and far between, in warfare and create an armed force of some description out of the somewhat complacent population over the two galaxies. Hammond was one of four top research and development people with the portal system Prince Alcyn was working on. As for Patron, he was a diplomat assigned to Beta Genobola. One day he disappeared just before travel between planets by crafts became impossible. Crafts were only used as Alcyn shut down and dismantled the portal system. We did learn only Patron reached Daraxon. His family was on a separate craft with a lot of other families of diplomats. The second craft never made it Daraxon. The craft was hijacked and all on board were jettisoned into space. Other refugee crafts found bodies floating in space and pulled them aboard for identification and a proper burial. All they found were parts of families. Patron's wife was positively identified but the children were never found. Maybe other diplomats from other planets are here as well but just scattered around the planet."

"It was always a rule never to occupy a planet which already had citizens. Did Alcyn find another planet and send other refugees there?" asked Ashton.

"That is a strong possibility. There were orders at the time any refugee ship never received directions to the new planet until they were ready to cross the void or were at the gateways of the waste space. If any came here, then they have already dispersed into this population. If there is another planet, then there is a chance that some of the older people will know about it. The majority of refugees on this hidden planet would have come from Amada. Oberon was quite isolated from Amada. Oberon people dispersed onto other planets outside the system. You already know, we have been searching for them without any form of success."

"I did know search teams were out there. Dad did mention of searches in the early days of settlement. I thought it was all stopped as it was considered a waste of resources and redirected efforts in fighting the Lacertians."

"It was scaled down from three search parties down to one," said Keka.

"What direction in this experiment do I take? Continue living here and being under Shields's thumb or leave and wriggle my way into Daraxon Technologies."

"Leave your current job. Get into Daraxon Technologies. Make it legal this time and don't draw any more attention," said Keka.

"Well, I did keep out of the robbery," said Ashton.

"Yes. Very commendable but you do have a very unique way of dealing with obstacles which always draw attention. That has got to stop."

"What and spoil my fun?" said Ashton in a tongue in cheek manner. "I could have killed them."

"The experiment is for you to live there not become a one-man law enforcer. Leave that to the locals," mused Keka.

"What do you people want me to bring back other than information about Daraxon Technologies?"

"Go on a shopping spree with electronic equipment; computers are high on the list. We can then gauge their advancement. I will send Garyth and Nodin down to collect the items. I will let you know of the pick-up point. It has to be a different location," said Keka. Ashton cut the conversation short when his mobile rang.

"Hi Carrie." said Ashton.

"Hi," said Carrie.

"Do you have go to uni tomorrow?" asked Ashton.

"Yes. Are you going to meet me at the station again?" asked Carrie.

"If that is okay?"

"Of course it is. We can meet again after uni but only for a short time. I finish uni at four. By the time I meet you in the afternoon, it will be close to five. I will pick you up at the motel."

"You have uni the day after don't you?" asked Ashton.

"Yes. How about bringing a change of clothes to stay over-night? Then we could spend more time together and you would not have to worry about public transport. I can hire another room for you to stay in," said Ashton knowing he had to be a perfect gentleman if he wanted to get close to the family.

"I will see you tomorrow morning and breakfast together. Another room sounds fine. Thanks." said Carrie.

Ashton met Carrie at the station and walked Carrie to the bus stop. He held her overnight bag as he walked back to the motel, paid a room for her on the same floor and placed her bag inside his room at the motel. He placed the bag with the growing pile of equipment stacked in one corner. He added extra requested items to the pile through the day. At four-thirty he waited near the door at reception.

An hour had passed, and Carrie hadn't arrived. He phoned her every fifteen minutes but every message went to message bank. He became anxious and felt something had happened to her. He called Jamie, Carrie's father. Ashton could hear the tension in his voice. "Meet me at the river helipad outside Pier One complex. It will take close to an hour for us to reach the helipad."

CHAPTER THIRTEEN
The Search for Carrie

Just over an hour later the Daraxon helicopter landed at the helipad. Ashton rushed to the pad when the blades where at a near stop. Jamie, Jed and one security person, Levi from Daraxon Technologies stepped out. Ashton mentioned when he last saw Carrie and what they had intended to do that evening. The group were still at the helipad when an unmarked police car pulled up. They were whisked to the police station.

The men were separated for their individual stories. Their phones were checked and cross matched. Jed, Jamie and Levi were released early but hung around for Ashton. Ashton became the focus of interest. Ashton cooperated listing the paths he took, and which shops he visited. He pulled out some receipts he had stuffed into his pocket as proof. One CCT which was pulled early into the interview showed Ashton holding the butterfly pendant still attached to Carrie's neck. He kissed the pendant. Carrie lifted the pendant to her lips and pressed it against her lips leaving a smear of lipstick. Ashton was then seen wiping the smear off. Carrie leaned over and gave Ashton a quick kiss on the lips. Ashton was about to be let go when Detective Kirkwood walked in. He was carrying a file about thirty pages thick.

Ashton looked annoyed. "We are wasting time. We have to find Carrie. The longer we wait, the harder it will be to find her." Ignoring Ashton's pleas, Kirkwood began another interview tape. The conversation went for over two more hours. Pictures of himself and others were displayed regarding the Finland incidents and other events at the motel. He was questioned about the gang of four in Milton, the Kerry Smith incident in the car park and then once again about the shoot out in the motel car park. He answered their questions multiple times never tripping over his lies or sequent of events. Ashton had successfully debunked their claims but remained under their suspicion.

The federal police officer who tailed him on the train just a few days ago walked in. Ashton recognised the man and drew a breath of annoyance and hoped he would never be questioned over that incident. Instead, the man began to question him on the note left at the international cargo pick-up. Ashton filled him in on how he discovered Martin Shields and his double life: a respected manager at the motel and a drug lord. The reception desk was the unofficial post office involving innocent and ignorant staff.

The questioning then turned to the laser zaps. Ashton started to fiddle with a pen. He made it roll onto the floor. While picking it up, he made a quick switch with the look-alike. Without prompting, he handed over the glasses. They were examined before they were handed back. Ashton covered his eyes when the glasses were off his face. He explained why the glasses and the hearing aid. Sceptical of his answers but having no evidence to hold him further, he was released in the early hours of the morning. As he left, he saw with Kirkwood, there flurry of activity organising to find Carrie had started well before his release. Carrie's father had left a note at the front desk of the station – they would wait at the reception lounge at the motel.

Kirkwood escorted Ashton to the motel and met with Jed, Jamie and Levi. After quick introductions, Ashton led the way to the buffet. "Have a meal because it is going to be a very long and busy day. This is where Carrie and I intended to have breakfast before she disappeared." Kirkwood filled the others in as to what was happening in the station while Ashton went through detailed questioning. The men formed an additional plan.

*

When Carrie woke up, she found herself duct tapped; hands and feet firmly bound. She looked at the strange, dark surroundings through burry eyes as panic set in. She screamed only to hear the squeaky but solid door above her open. A tall shirtless man wearing a leather vest which concealed some tattoos poked half his body through the door. She could see his shiny bald top with long dangling hair at the sides. "Shut up, sis. If you don't, I will give you something to scream out about." Carrie instantly went silent whimpering to herself. She laid on the bare smelly mattress sobbing more. She wondered how long she had been there.

All she could remember was getting off the bus at the campus bus stop and walking the bush and tree lined path which led from the bus stop to the buildings. She had walked the same path hundreds of times before. Like thousands of other students using the same path, had always considered it safe. She recalled stopping to pick up a book a student walking in front of her had dropped. She saw a shadow and assumed another student was standing behind her waiting for her to stand up. Then she felt a sting in her arm. Carrie looked at her arm and found a small, dried droplet of blood. She recalled the sensation of being dragged between two trees and then nothing until now. She wondered if any other student saw what had happened. *There would have been enough witnesses, surely,* she thought.

She pulled herself up to a sitting position and surveyed the room. *Great,* she thought. *I am in an old cellar. Who has cellars in this country?* The man outside now switched on the only light not long after he closed the door. Her eyes were drawn to the only light in the room which was now emitting a burning smell; layers of dust burning on the naked pendulum. She looked closer and noticed the lead going down to the exposed bulb was so old. It was made of cord and the cord showed signs of fraying to expose the wiring. "The cellar is a death trap," she whispered to herself.

The room was bare of any furnishings other than the mattress she was sitting on. The walls were dark, unpainted with creeping damp showing its tell-tale marks. The steps leading to the door above her head were equally as old. She wondered just how unsafe the treads were. The door was the only way in or out of the glorified hole she was in.

She called out again. The door opened and the same man peered in. "Didn't I tell you to shut up?" "I need to use the dunny," pleaded Carrie. The man threw an old plastic bucket at her. It rolled to the far wall and spun a little before stopping on its side.

"How am I supposed to use that with my hands tied?" she yelled back.

There was no response.

Carrie looked at the ties on her hands and then at her feet. She looked around the room again looking for anything sharp to cut the ties. She wriggled over to the bucket and noticed the bucket had cracked on impact with the ground. She kicked the bucket as hard as she could with her two feet. Eventually, the old plastic cracked more. She kicked the weak point more until a shard came free. Stretching her arms out the best she could, she grabbed the piece of plastic in her hands. She drew her legs up as much as she could and started sawing away at the tape. She managed to cut through one layer before putting the plastic down to check the number of layers. She groaned at the three extra layers. Bit by bit the tape slowly came apart. Using her feet to hold the shard of plastic, she started sawing back and forth on the tape around her wrists. She just managed to make the slightest of nick when the cellar door flung open. Carrie sat still pretending her feet were still tied up.

Two men approached her and pulled her to her feet. Without warning she kicked one in the groin. He fell but the other grabbed her by the arms from the back to restrain her. Carrie swayed from side to side trying to release herself from the grip. Then she suddenly bent forward taking the man off his feet and tossing him over her back. The man landed heavily on top of the first downed man who was just coming to his feet. Carrie ran for the steps. Just as she reached the top of the steps, two more men blocked her way. She had nowhere to go. She felt herself being pulled through the door. Then another jab; she was out to the world again.

This time when she woke up, she found herself bound at the feet again but this time the tape wasn't just at the ankles but up to her knees. There was no old mattress, just an empty room. It was an old shed with a handful of gaps: just enough for her to see out and to allow light to filter through. At this stage she couldn't tell if it was morning or afternoon. She told herself she would have to wait and see if the daylight was going to stay or disappear.

Her eyes were diverted up when she heard a soft noise - rats. Thoughts about being bitten by the creatures were racing through her mind. Another noise came from the left side of the shed. She wriggled closer to the gaps and stared in fear. A deadly King Brown snake forced its way under the bottom rotted slat. She froze as she watched the animal head directly up the frail corner posts, across to the exposed beams and go towards the rats. She watched as the snake gave chase to the rats before giving a fatal bite to secure a small creature. Carrie watched the snake expand its jaws to swallow the rat. She watched the snake make a series of contraction to force the rat down its body. Lazily, the deadly King Brown slid away towards an opening of broken base slats. Carrie gave a sigh of relief but wondered how many more snakes or vermin of any kind would make their way into the shed looking for a meal. It came to her; she could very much be on the menu. She sat vigilantly in the semi-darkness.

The door to the shed opened. She looked at the man carrying a tray of food and a bottle of water. Behind him was a young lady about the same age as herself. The lady was thin, if not looking gaunt. Tattoos were down one arm and around her neck. Her ears were pierced with a simple ring and her nose had a similar ornament going through the base of her nose. She drew out a knife as she approached, "Dunny time," she said to Carrie but waited until the man had put the tray of food down and held Carrie's arms and forced her to a standing position. The lady used the knife to cut the tape binding her legs. Carrie was then led to an old-fashioned outdoor toilet. The tape around her wrists was cut before Carrie was permitted to go through the door.

As the door opened a swarm of horse flies rushed out and the odour nearly made her pass out. Carrie looked down the ancient hole checking to make sure more creatures weren't going to fly or creep out. Down the hole she could see jumbo worms. She gave a second look to be sure they were worms and not snakes. She looked at the ceiling and the open rafters and gave a sigh of relief. No snakes. No spiders. Two dead baby blue tongues were to the side, gizzards and bones exposed contributing to the odour. Carrie looked at the fresh toilet roll hanging by a hook at the side of the toilet and gave a sigh of relief. There was a heavy knock on the door. "Hurry up in there!" yelled the man.

"Okay! Okay! I was checking for creepy crawlies. I'm on the can now!" yelled Carrie.

When Carrie came out, her face was a shade of green. She drew in fresh breaths of air trying to cleanse her lungs and nostrils. "I would like to wash my hands." The lady shoved her towards an outside tap. Carrie washed her hands and face and then held her hands out to be retaped.

"Good girl," said the man. "Now you know the rules. Keep this up and you won't get hurt."

She was led back to the small shed and her legs were rebound but the tape only reached mid-calf before the roll ran out.

The tray of food that was brought to her earlier was still on the ground. "Eat," said the tattooed woman. Both of her guards left the shed. Carrie could hear the bolt sliding into position and click of the lock. She looked at the sorry state of the meal which now had fresh chunks taken out. *Old KFC was that bad,* she thought, *even the rats rejected it.* She forced herself lift one piece, the one piece which was not rat tested or sniffed. It was off. She took a sip of the water hoping it would offer some relief to her now dehydrating body. The water didn't taste right so she spat that out as a strange sensation formed on her tongue and inner cheeks. Her tongue began to itch. Carrie became worried if she had consumed enough drugs to knock her out again. She poured the water out and watched the liquid spill out over the ground. When the bottle was empty, she picked it up again to see what else was in it. She tilted the bottle towards the light and saw traces of a white substance. "Bastards," she whispered angrily to herself. She sat quietly for the rest of the time thinking why all this had happened to her and pondered if she would be saved, assaulted more than she had already been or murdered.

She pulled out the old piece of wire, which was once the toilet roll holder, and tried jabbing the object through the layers of tape around her legs. Each puncture was aimed one beside the other forming a series of holes. With each piece, she tugged with her hands which were not bound as tightly as before. Just when she had removed over half the tape binding her legs, she heard the sound of motor bikes roaring towards her followed by movement of people movement directly outside her jail. She stopped and hid the wire and wriggled over to one of the walls. One by one they parked their noisy precious bikes along the side of the main house. She tried to count them. She knew there were a lot more but from where she was, she counted six bikes. She could hear other voices coming from the other side of the shed. *"Oh, hell. The whole bloody gang. I must be at one of their county safe havens,* thought Carrie as fear slowly took over.

She tried listening to their conversation, but their voices were muffled and softer as the group slowly moved away from the shed. She pulled out the hidden wire and started again punching it into the tape.

Then with her fingers, she peeled the rest of the tape off. Again, she sat down and using her feet to stabilise the wire. She kept slamming her taped hands over the wire until the holes weakened the tape. She jerked her hands apart to test the progress. Her hands came free. She hid the wire again before pulling the residue of the tape off her wrists.

She looked at the side wall where the snake wriggled out. Two old termite damaged slats broke free when she gave them a tug giving her a larger hole but not big enough to squeeze through. She pushed her head through the opening to see what was around. That side showed there was less than a metre of space between the wall and what looked like a steep hill. Bare rock some three metres high blocked that side.

She tugged more at the slats around the opening she had already created then stopped when she noticed the shed swayed with every tug. Fearing the shed would collapse, she stopped. She kicked the side of one slat to ease her frustration. The shed shook again. This time the shed's movement caught the attention of a bikie. She heard them running towards her.

The same tattooed lady opened the door. "You don't learn much do ya?" She drew out the knife she previously used and ordered Carrie to sit down. Carrie obeyed. "Take your clothes off," ordered the lady. Carrie didn't move; too frightened and also stunned at the order. The woman snarled and repeated the order with more venom in her voice. "Take your clothes off or I'll get one of the men to remove them for you."

"Why?" squeaked Carrie. "No tape left to stop you from pissing off. Princesses like you don't like running around in the nuddie in front of men and you cry if you get sunburnt or a few scratches from bushes. Off with the clothes.

Now!" Carrie didn't move. The lady stepped closer and was about to call out when Carrie, whispered, "Okay."

Carrie removed her jeans and blouse and stopped there. The woman looked her up and down. "I like that fancy bra. Take it off. Now." The lady held the knife up in a more threatening manner. Slowly Carrie removed her bra and placed it on the pile of clothes at her feet. "Pick all the clothes up and toss them to me," snapped the lady. Carrie bent over keeping an eye on the lady. Carrie didn't toss the bra over but held it in her hands almost teasing the lady with the delay. Losing patience, the lady yelled out, "Mad Dog! Mad Dog! Come here and have a look at this"

There was sound at the door when a massive bald man appeared. When Mad Dog saw Carrie almost naked, he gave a toothless grin as he approached. He brushed his thick, rough hands over her breast and flicked his tongue at her at the same time exhaling his bad breath into her face. He took the bra from Carrie's hand and held it up for the lady to take. Carrie froze with fear as Mad Dog's hands started to fondle her body more and slowly inch their way down to the under pants. He stopped short and snarled, "Any more funny tricks, it just won't be me having a bit of fun with you. I am making sure I am going in first." He gave her a wink and snapped the elastic of her underpants. "These undies are cute; a real dick teaser," he said with a malicious grin.

Both left her almost naked. The door slammed shut and the sounds of the bolt and lock were heard. A mix of feelings raced through her body: anger, hate, belittlement, desperation, and fear. She sat on the dirt covered floor and cried.

*

Ashton led the group back to his room in the motel. He went through the pile of boxes of electronic equipment he had purchased. As he went through the list, Kirkwood contacted another officer, Cowen. Both officers checked the receipts, noted the time and dates, clearly indicating Ashton was not the abductor. "You spent a small fortune on this equipment, and in cash," said Kirkwood.

Ashton just looked at the now dismantled pile. He cleared the table as he invited the group to help themselves to a drink in the fridge. Ashton picked up a packet which was already opened and pulled out a small square shaped box. He inserted a battery. He saw the light flicker on and then off. Frustrated he muttered, "Carrie is out of range."

Jamie looked at him in horror. "What do you mean, out of range."

Ashton said in a rather cool manner, "I just had a feeling that Carrie could get in trouble. Her being so connected to Daraxon Technologies, I just thought she needed something which could help anyone find her if she got into trouble. Well, she is obviously in trouble and out of range of the tracking devise she is wearing."

Everyone's jaw dropped at the revelation. Jed was first to recover. "What kind of person are you who tags another like some animal?"

"One who was worried about her safety and her well-being," replied Ashton as he repacked the electronics. "I need to have a chat with the commander. Excuse me for a few minutes."

"Hold on. What is going on here?" asked Kirkwood.

Ashton didn't reply.

Ashton spoke in Pleiadean to Jalon. There was a pause for a few minutes. Then Ashton went through each piece of electronic equipment again and held it up to eye view. Some items were returned to the packaging while other items were put on the table.

After twenty minutes of following instructions and piecing bits together, Ashton finally sighed as he said, "Here goes test number two. He turned on the small tracking box. It beeped and shone green. He flipped it over; the digital compass gave a direction. He smiled. "We go north-west. She is somewhere northwest of here. As we get closer, the coordinates will become more precise - within two metres." He said, "Let's get going. She is about fifty kilometres away." Looking around at the stunned group, Ashton said impatiently, "Move. We have a missing person to find, don't we?"

Kirkwood hesitated. "Just how accurate is that tracker since you modified it?"

"Put it this way. Before it wasn't even powerful enough to get a blip and now it is triple the original range. At this distance it is a general direction, but it self-corrects as we get closer."

"Can I have a closer look?" asked Cowan.

Ashton gave the devise to Cowan while Kirkwood phoned the station with the new information. Jamie was also on the phone organising more fuel for the helicopter. Jamie looked at the group, "The helicopter can only hold four people. Can you officers come in another helicopter? We will wait at the helipad and then guide you to the location where Carrie is."

Thirty minutes later the police helicopter waited by the helipad as the last of the fuel was added into the Daraxon Helicopter. Both helicopters turned north-west. Along the way, Ashton gave slight navigational adjustments. When the beeper went into a long blast, he pointed. "Down there. In that house or shed. Fly by and park at the start of the street."

He looked at the extra-long rural block and guessed the distance to be a kilometre away. The police helicopter parked further back, slightly around the corner. The local police cars were not far behind. As soon as they stopped behind the Polair helicopter, they cordoned off the street.

Ashton gave the tracker to Jed. "Look after this. I'm going after Carrie. Tell the others to move forward and around the property. Do not try to raid until I have Carrie out of there." With that Ashton tapped the logo on his shoes and ran up the street leaving Jed and Jamie stunned at his speed and the police in both stunned and annoyed.

Ashton ran six metres up the hill and jumped onto several rocks and crouched down on each planning his path. While looking through the binoculars Jamie said, "What the hell is he doing? He should be waiting for police direction."

Kirkwood walked up to Jed. "Where is Ashton?"

Jed pointed. "Down there already. Jumping around on the hill like some kangaroo on steroids. He has a plan but has told no one other than to wait until he got Carrie out."

Kirkwood, Cowan, Jamie, Jed and Levi slowly walked up the street on the opposite side of the road of the targeted house while the other police fanned themselves around the well-spaced-out homes and in the bushland.

They saw Ashton jumping around the hill. Slowly, he inched his way towards the shed. He would stop and survey the buildings, then jump again going down the hill. Eventually he was on the ground but was out of their sight for a few minutes. They gasped when he landed on the roof of the house. They saw him take something off his jacket and place whatever it was on the rusted corrugated iron roof of the main house. Ashton disappeared from view before he resurfaced on the hill near the old shed.

By this time, Kirkwood's group hid themselves behind bushes directly across the road from the house and waited patiently. They gasped when Ashton levitated across the final hill location and gently landed on the roof of the shed. Kirkwood whispered to Cowan. "The bastard was lying through his teeth at every interview."

Jed overheard the comment and leaped to Ashton's defence. "I would too if I had that equipment."

Ashton looked around the roof looking for a hole to see if Carrie was in the shed. Finding none, he cut a hole. He leaned down to see what was inside. He saw Carrie, semi-naked and covered in dust. He called to her just louder than a whisper, "Carrie! Carrie! Up here!"

Carrie looked up but only walked to the edge of the shadows. "It's me Ashton. The police are here with your father and Jed."

Carrie stepped closer to the voice. "How did you find me?"

Ashton could now see she was trying to cover herself up.

"Shh not now. Later. Did they hurt you?"

"Not yet but they will if I don't cooperate. They gave me a few drugs to knock me out for transport."

"I'll get you some clothes." Jokingly he asked, "Are you fussy about style? The clothesline isn't showing anything too fashionable."

"My own clothes would be nice. But anything will do."

Minutes later, Ashton returned to the hole in the roof. "Carrie, Carrie." She moved to the hole. Ashton dropped down a man's shirt and a pair of men's jeans. They were the smallest size on the line. He knew they were going to be a bit on the large size. He waited until she was dressed. He dropped down into the hole. "Good to see you," said Ashton and without taking a breath, "Not exactly your style, is it?"

"How did you find me?" she asked.

"Later. Hug me. We are getting out." Ashton waited until she embraced him. Ashton turned the levitator on full. They rose up and out of the hole. Ashton guided the controls to the waiting group behind the bushes on the other side of the road. He placed her down beside Kirkwood. Carrie grinned. "Can I have another ride like that?"

"Not now." said Ashton as he looked at Kirkwood.

"Is that all you can say? Later. Not now."

Ashton placed his fingers to his lips. "Shh. There is work to be done. Someone take her to the helicopter and get her out of here."

Jamie tugged on Carrie's hand. "We're leaving. Let them do their work."

Ashton looked at Cowen and Kirkwood. "Do we know how many are in the house?"

"No," they chorused.

"Okay, give me a few minutes to set up a device." Ashton pulled out another pendant - this time of a cross which had at its centre a blackish coloured bead. He gave his mobile phone to Kirkwood after downloading an app. "Watch the screen. I'm going to get some intel." With that, Ashton walked directly to the front door and knocked.

The noisy voices in the house went silent. One man opened the door. "Yeah. What do ya want?" The man was soon joined by a female wearing Carrie's clothes.

Ashton just smiled. "I have come to spread the word of Jesus to those who don't find time to go to church."

"Fuck off, will ya. Bible bashers aren't welcome here," he said in a loud voice so other would hear. Ashton did the sign of the cross and held out his hand. "A gift for the lovely lady standing just behind you; a trinket to go with the studs on such cute ears and the bull ring she is wearing in her nose." The lady reached out and looked a bit perplexed, "Tar. Don't often get a freebie and never by anyone who was told to piss off." She put on the necklace. She nudged the man beside her. He grunted.

Ashton winked. "Lovely ladies need lovely things." He bowed his head and looked both in the eyes. "God bless and deliver these people from evil. I shall go and leave you fine people in peace." He crossed the road checking first to see if the door was shut. He went behind the bushes where Kirkwood and Cowen were hiding.

Cowen shook his head. "You've got some balls."

Ashton ignored the remark. "How many people are inside?"

Kirkwood grinned. "About twenty." He spoke into his phone. A message went to the control room, to Polair and then out to others gathering around the bikie house.

Ashton said, "Let's bring this to an end." He counted to five. There were three small explosions around the house and one on the roof. The house shook but did not collapse. The occupants ran out and scattered through the bushes. Some tried to start their bikes but were furious to see all of them were disabled - the ignitions were melted or faulty. All twenty bikes were history. Just as men started to disperse through the bushes, two more small explosions occurred. It herded about ten bikies directly to the waiting police.

Ashton groaned as the sky filled with helicopters. Polair was circling and giving directions. The Daraxon helicopter was still on the ground wanting to take off but was blocked in by the media helicopters trying to record the action below. Ashton drew Cowen's attention to the small group of bikies escaping up the hill. "I'm going after them."

Ashton touched his shoes and felt the power surging through. He switched to jump mode to beat the escapees up the hill. He positioned himself and aimed as they neared the three-metre mark. "Yellow." One man froze. The others looked back scared. Ashton now gave chase. "Yellow. Yellow. Yellow." The last three men froze. Ashton went to the first and pulled out a cord to tie the man up. He did the same to the others. He dragged the first man towards the other three and tied all four together. Knowing they were balanced on a ledge on the hill, he gave them a reminder, "If one of you moves, you all move down the hill. If you don't want broken necks, stay put." He turned on his levitator and went further up the hill checking for more escapees.

He paused for a few moments to look in the sky. He saw the media circling and heading in his direction. He levitated to the base of the hill, pushed the logo and ran full speed down the street and stopped at the Daraxon helicopter. "Get out of here. Now! The place is going to get nasty. I will find my own way out. Go!" Jamie started the rotors for lift off. Carrie deliberately jumped out when the chopper was just half a metre off the ground. Bent over she ran to a safe distance. Ashton didn't notice her jump until the helicopter was two metres air borne. He was stunned when he saw her standing on the other side. "What the fuck are you doing here?"

"Do you think you are going to have all the fun?" The helicopter started to land again. Jamie screamed out to Carrie, "Get in." Carrie shook her head and ran down the street towards the waiting police cars. Ashton gave chase. He grabbed her and hugged her as he switched on the levitator. He flew her back to the helicopter and tossed through the open door as if she were a sack of potatoes. He flew back to the hill and levitated to the highest point. Out of breath, he hid himself until he recovered. He saw the Daraxon helicopter speed away.

From this vantage point, he could see the police cars and two paddy wagons slowly taking the bikies away. Then his attention was turned to gun fire coming from the other side of the hill. He closed his eyes and swore. Guns were aimed at him. When he looked closer there were five groups below. To the far left was Martin Shields with two men. Ashton frowned at the large weapon Martin was holding and aiming at him. *Christ Almighty. When and where in hell did he get that thing from?* Not far from Martin's group were six more armed bikies. They were shooting at Martin's group and across to the three different groups of police.

Ashton squatted and observed, the state police were more interested in shooting at Martin and the bikies. The federal police and the ASIO groups were looking in his direction but would return fire from any bullet from either Martin's group or the bikies. Martin had obviously figured out the jumbo contraption he was holding on his shoulder and fired the bazooka towards Ashton and another towards the federal police.

The media helicopters which were circling directly above moved away to allow the army helicopter moved in. Martin fired the bazooka at the army. Mistake. They let fly with a series of gunfire which was to scare rather than kill. Martin, again turned the bazooka on the army, fired and missed again. The army moved away to a safer position. Four soldiers holding ropes dropped out.

Ashton had received a message from a four-person pod coming in his direction. He climbed onto a boulder, stood up and sent the pink distress signal. He climbed down when gunfire narrowly missed him. While he was waiting for his rescue, he watched the six-way battle below. The army had now landed and was repossessing their stolen bazooka. They were just about to return to base when the four-man pod appeared. Ashton climbed the rock again. Held his arm up and fired his pink beam. A pink beam came down. Ashton disappeared.

On Board the pod, Kora asked, "What's wrong with these people?"

Before he could answer, Nodin asked, "Just how many people did you piss off down there?"

Ashton pointed. "The state police were upset with me over different things, but I managed to get one on my side. The federal and the other group, I have no idea. The bike gang were upset because I wrecked their bikes, home and had the police with me. And the man with the bazooka, he was my work boss who had a double life. He is really ticked off. That is two ways. Looks like he ticked off the army as well. We better go to my motel room and pick up all the stuff for the ship."

"Guide me," said Kora.

Nodin smirked. "We saw you throw that Earth person in the helicopter. She really likes you."

"The feeling is not mutual."

Ashton was matter-of-fact, "When she realises, I placed a tracking device on her she will be turned off. She's a bit fiery." Nodin slapped him on the back. "That suits you."

"In your dreams," replied Ashton.

Kora laughed. "She has her hooks into you. Big time. She's not going to let go so easily."

Ashton pointed to the motel where he was staying. "Down there. Stay here and I will put the stuff on the balcony."

Ashton jumped out of the pod and placed himself on the motel roof. He walked down the flight of steps before catching the lift to the fourth floor. He placed the items on the balcony.

He signalled for the air lift. The pink beam came down and took the items away. He then called Jamie on his mobile. "Ashton speaking. I want to apologise for the mess I have caused you and your family. I am just letting you all know I will be leaving this planet tomorrow morning. I would appreciate the opportunity to say good-bye in person." Jamie looked at the others who were listening in on speaker. Patron nodded and responded,

"Yes do come. We will all would like to see you again."

"I will be there in the afternoon, after three."

Patron said, "We still have a lot to talk about. And I think Carrie needs to see you before you leave."

"See you then." He clicked off.

Ashton decided to stay in his room as long as possible. He switched on the news and groaned. The day's events and too much footage of the day dominated. Martin Shields was arrested along with twenty plus other men and two ladies. Ashton cursed and switched channels. Not much different and eventually switched off the television. He tried to relax but was disturbed by a knock on the door. Rod, Paul and Gordon were standing there with smirks on their faces. Rod held up a bottle. "Young man, you have some explaining to do."

CHAPTER FOURTEEN
The Siege on Daraxon

Ashton went to the reception desk to checkout. Dayna said. "Mr. Ashton you are not permitted to leave yet. I believe there is an outstanding amount owing in accommodation. Five hundred dollars." Ashton pulled out the reminder of his cash, it was short by two hundred. "Just a minute, I will get a bit extra." He left his bags beside the counter and walked over to a poker machine. He slipped a token in and said, "Green." The wheels spun around and a jackpot of ten thousand sounded. He walked back to Dayna. Take the two hundred owing for the room. Take another five hundred for the reception staff to have a small party on my behalf. I'll take the rest."

He walked around until he found Rod. He found Rod sitting on a stool talking and sipping on water. He got up when he saw Ashton approach. "It's time for me to go," said Ashton.

Rod nodded as a tear formed in his eye. "I'll miss you, spaceman."

Ashton laughed. "A small gift. Something towards retirement."

Ashton handed over five thousand dollars. "It is useless where I am going. Anyway, if I am short, I know how to get more." He smiled as he nodded at the machines. Rod chuckled and gave him a hug.

Do you mind checking the front doors? I don't want media attention." Rod walked outside.

"There are four vans ready to pounce," he said when he returned.

"I'll slip out the back way."

"Before you go, a photo - selfie with the two of us." Before Ashton knew it, there was a line of staff from all sections waiting for a selfie with him.

Ashton walked out of the motel towards the railway station. He pulled his cap low to reduce the risk of recognition. He had had enough of posing. He bought himself a ticket to Beenleigh.

On the platform Kirkwood and Cowen were waiting. "I hope you are not skipping town?" asked Kirkwood. Ashton looked at the two policemen. "Yep. Not coming back. I am going to get a big roasting from the commander."

"I tell you what," said Cowen. "If you can't handle the heat up there, let us know. You can join us." Ashton chuckled, "I've caused enough trouble. ASIO and the Feds still want my ass." Cowen nodded towards two men - one wearing a federal police uniform and the other in plain clothes. Ashton groaned and held out his hands to be cuffed. The federal officer spoke and pushed down the hands and handed Ashton a card. "Next time you and your space buddies come into town, give us a call." Ashton looked at the cards and stuffed it into his pocket. Kirkwood and Cowen each handed him a card. Kirkwood said, "I need to interview Carrie about her kidnapping. Tell her she needs to come in. Tomorrow will do."

Ashton nodded. "You may have to go there and bring some rope. Mark, Titus and Carrie are itching to join me on the main ship. I wouldn't be surprised if they are scheming something up now."

The train pulled into the station. Ashton boarded and waved to the men. He sat down and tried to relax but did not last long. A man wearing a bad disguise sat down beside him. Ashton looked the stranger up and down and almost burst out laughing. To Ashton, the wig looked like it was put on sideways, and the moustache was quite angled. "Ashton?" he whispered as he looked for confirmation. Irritated Ashton responded, "Leave me alone."

"No. Patron sent me. You are in danger. There is a man called Blake Granger. He is transitioning out of ASIO. He has Daraxon Technologies surrounded. He is trying to make a last-minute name for himself. He has carried a twenty-five-year grudge against Daraxon. He is waiting for your return. He has no intentions of letting you disappear into space."

Ashton looked at the stranger. "Just who the hell are you?"

"Reuben. Remember? Carrie has twin brothers. I am one half. I was off the complex doing a job for Patron. He sent me away just after the night of the barbeque. He wanted me to confirm some findings. With some difficulty, I confirmed what he was asking." He handed Ashton a parcel and a flash drive with a tablet. The tablet is set up for you, but it will need extra charging. You can work out a way do that on your spaceship. You won't need internet connections to make it work. Just place the drive into the slot at the side. The password is Ashton on Earth – all lower case. I will accompany you to the station. Then we get into my car, and we go anywhere but to Daraxon."

"What's on the flash drive?"

"The same thing that is written in the parcelled books. The books were created by Jenny and Patron. Jenny wrote it in English. Patron translated it in Pleiadean. It is vital a document and make sure it reaches your government leaders. Make sure they are not corrupt."

"Dad is the president. He is not corrupt." said Ashton.

Reuben looked carefully. "Make sure this never falls into Lacertian hands."

"What is in the paperwork?"

"Our ancient history linking Pleiades, Sirius B, the planet Mars and Earth. Our ancestry. There could be coordinates in there as well."

"Coordinates to where?"

"As a guess… I wasn't privy to that, so it is an educated guess, to Genesis. Genesis is the planet where many Amada refugees went to. If it is not that, then it could be the space warp or wormhole that was accidentally found by our ancestors. That wormhole got you from old Pleiades to here in days, not months."

"Hold on a second, you said our ancestors?" asked Ashton.

Reuben nodded and patted the parcel. "It's all in here. It was Jenny who drew Patron's attention to the cuneiform writing. That is what we call that style of writing, but it is ancient Pleiadean. She asked for Patron's assistance. The information was explosive. She never published it in her thesis in fear of ridicule. She would have had a bad time justifying herself with the long-standing establishment and would have caused tidal waves with all established religions." Ashton nodded absorbing the information. They saw the train fly pass Eden's landing. It was close to the last stop.

"Why the disguise to meet me?" asked Ashton.

"As I said, Granger has the place surrounded. No one can move in or out. It is causing a lot of distress for families who work on the site. The phones are tapped, and they are systematically listening to all mobile phones - a part of Granger's warped conspiracy theory. The man's a dangerous nut. I was outside the complex. Patron was able to contact me before the gates were closed so to speak. The helicopter returning Carrie and the others has now been grounded in the complex."

The train eased its way to the station. Ashton said firmly, "Where are you going after this?" Reuben shrugged. "I can't go to Daraxon. Granger will arrest me on trumped up charges. I will just hide and get some media attention to the situation."

They got off the train. "The car is this way."

Reuben pointed towards the small carpark. When they got into the car, Ashton said, "Do you want to end this crap by Granger?"

"How?" asked Reuben.

"I have contacts. You know the layout." Ashton made a few calls. "We wait now for nearly two hours and help will arrive. Your job now is to ring the media and tell them what is going down in about two hours. Let's have a coffee while we wait and plan things out."

At Daraxon Technologies, Hammond, Tayee and Jed ordered all staff to the mess hall. Concern was across everyone's faces. Jed quizzed as many staff as possible concerning their home situation and what each had observed on the perimeters. Tayee noted on the hastily set up whiteboard where each person had observed on the fast-forming mud-map of the complex. Hammond did a quick calculation. Close to 50 people including Granger had surrounded the property with a mix of firearms and an unknown number of rounds of ammunition. Tayee drew up a crude plan and allocated people to certain tasks. The rest would do their routines and be as normal as possible. On a signal, they would act.

Sirens were heard approaching the complex. Granger's large team turned their attention to the newcomers. Peter Dewy alighted from a van, angry at the situation before him. He tried talking Granger out of his actions. The situation became heated – neither backing down. Dewy cursed. He knew his future career was now in jeopardy.

As he was trying to manoeuvre his people away from the potentially ugly scene, everyone's attention was directed to the sky. Mark and Titus flew the experimental aircraft high into the sky and dived down scattering the mini army surrounding the complex. The aircraft twisted and turned at such a speed, it prevented anyone on the ground from taking aim. The Daraxon helicopter left the complex with four people on board: Jamie, Hammond, Patron and Dalmon. The helicopter disappeared over a hill to the rarely used Ridge Lookout. The helicopter returned. The helicopter did three trips removing female staff to the same location.

Granger ordered a vehicle to the Lookout, to collect and arrest those who had escaped. Mark saw the vehicle and buzzed the van making the driver swerve. Mark noticed a new function button which read 'magnet'. He switched it on guessing it would either lift or stop the van. He buzzed low and with Titus's guidance placed the aircraft directly over the vehicle. There was a loud clunk and the craft shook. Titus chuckled. "We have a payload. Back to Daraxon." The aircraft returned and dumped the load just a metre off the ground. The ashen faced men inside scrambled out as soon as the van bounced onto the ground. Mark and Titus kept circling the men around the property. One pulled a gun out. Mark hit the magnet button again. All the men close by found they were being sucked into the air under the aircraft. The metal on their bodies secured the men to the underbelly. Mark at medium speed flew them high into the sky before depositing them in King George Square, in the heart of Brisbane some 80 kilometres away. Within minutes, the aircraft was back at Daraxon Technologies.

Titus used a loudspeaker to try to communicate with the surrounding army. "Granger, it's time to give up. We will forcibly remove every person and vehicle." Titus and Mark grinned as they circled.

Granger lifted his loudspeaker. "What did you do to my men?"

"They are safe but just embarrassed in King George Square," replied Titus. Mark and Titus chuckled at the expressions on the crowd below.

"Do you want to join them? We can pick you out from the others." He switched off the speaker and to Mark he asked, "Can you do that?"

Mark shrugged. "No. But keep the bluff going." He swooped down near Granger, missing him by metres while everyone scattered. Mark asked, "Do you see any puddles?"

"Go again. Go up vertical and corkscrew down." Mark did a vertical jump into lower space but didn't dive. His mouth and Titus's mouth were agape. In front of them was the spaceship.

Both gasped. The spaceship, The Explorer, stopped approaching Earth. Mark and Titus felt their craft being sucked into the base. Their craft was remotely controlled to a bay where other crafts were lined up. Mark and Titus just sat spell bound. There was a knock on their window and a young blond man signed to open up. Slowly, Titus and Mark opened the cockpit. The man introduced himself, "I'm Eraton. Ashton's friend." Seeing their apprehension, he encouraged, "Come on. It's safe. You are with friends. The commander would like to talk to you both. I have to be with you to translate." Titus was first to move. Mark cautiously followed.

As they approached the upper decks both, Titus and Mark began to grin and then chuckle. Eraton wondered what amused them. Although he wanted to ask, he restrained himself. They were directed to the small conference room. "Please sit," said Eraton. "The commander will be with you as soon as stage one decontamination is complete. A yellow light will come on. The decontamination lights are in every room. The process will take a few minutes." Eraton shut the door. The yellow light came on. Mark looked at his watch to time it. Just three minutes later, the light switched off. Eraton with the commander and a host of others walked into the room.

As the conversation was progressing in the room, neither Mark nor Titus had noticed the spaceship was now hovering over Daraxon Technologies and had deployed a shield. They were directed to look outside. The craft landed. Both swallowed in disbelief.

Those trapped in the complex stood motionless looking at the ramp coming out of the base of the ship. Those outside the complex were kept at bay by the shield. Media, police and army helicopters and the air force jets buzzed the spaceship. Commander Jalon said, "You two are home. Your craft is being unloaded. I would like to meet the people of Daraxon Technologies.

Titus spoke as they all moved towards the exit, "Patron and Dalmon were airlifted to safety on the Ridge Lookout. They will be very disappointed if they missed talking to you."

Commander said and gestured, "We have already returned him and the others to Daraxon. We sent a twelve-man pod and airlifted everyone back." He pointed to Patron and Dalmon who were now walking towards the base of the ramp.

The ship stayed on the ground of Daraxon Technologies for four days. All the time the shield was down it shot baby sized electrical arcs to remind the growing number of onlookers and government personnel to stand back. Ashton and Reuben were able to enter via a temporary gap. There, they joined the rest of the exclusive crowd.

When things settled inside the protected Daraxon Industries, Ashton played tour guide for the small exclusive group consisting of Mark, Titus, Reuben, Andrew, Astra Jenny and Carrie. He left them wander the corridors and peep into each room. Ashton held back Jenny. "Where do I hide this package and the tablet? My room is very small and everything is easily found if Jalon or anyone else know of their existence." Jenny pointed to the air-conditioning duct. "In there," she suggested.

"No too easy."

"Put in in the room below in their air-conditioning duct," suggested Jenny a second time.

"Mark and Titus soon joined them. "Who lives directly under you?" asked Mark when he overheard his older sister and Ashton planning to hide the packages.

"Kora. She's another security person," said Ashton.

Mark said, "Let's plant it in her air-con system before she and everyone returns.

When they reached the door to Kora's room, Ashton pressed the entry code.

Jenny asked, "I thought you said she is in security. How come you know her code?"

Ashton went bashful. "We know each other's codes. We do a bit of room swapping."

Carrie gave a suspicious look and clarified, "You mean, you jump into each other's beds."

Ashton was embarrassed. Carrie stormed out leaving the others with mixed reactions. Ashton didn't go after her. He didn't see the point. Jenny said, "I will talk to her later. She will calm down. She always does."

Later that night DaraxonTechnologies put on a small party to welcome the new arrivals. Carrie cornered Kora. The conversation appeared lengthy. Ashton and Eraton noticed from afar, the girls spoke with interest. What was clearly tension gave way. Their demeanour between the two changed. Later they were like long lost friends – laughing and chatting and rarely giving a glance to anyone else in the place. Icherio also noticed the new clique. He walked over to Ashton and smirked. "Man, you got big girl trouble. When two girls who like you pair up and become friends, you are in the shithole. Good luck." He walked away leaving Ashton wondering what was in store for the trip home.

The ship took on supplies of new foods and tank loads of water. Ashton waved to the departing ship which would anchor again behind the moon until he re-joined it. Carrie stood beside Ashton and with her brothers and cousins. The ship was gone in seconds into the night sky.

The next morning Ashton's phone rang. Kirkwood was on the phone. "Ashton, before you disappear into the blue yonder, I need to get your side of the story. Granger was put into early retirement. When do you think you can come in?"

"No. I have a spaceship to catch. I will be leaving within the hour."

"Can you delay? I really need your side of the story so I can close off the case."

Ashton asked, "Where are you now?"

I'm about halfway to Beenleigh." "

I'll arrange for you to get in." He turned to Carrie, "Who gives clearances here?"

"Jed or Hammond. I will organise it." She walked away to search for the men.

CHAPTER FIFTEEN
Going Home

Ashton spent nearly two hours giving his side of the events over the last few weeks. Kirkwood laughed at the incident at the service station when Martin Shields became a temporary hero before falling into major disgrace by stealing and using the bazooka. He took a selfie with Ashton at the conclusion of the interview. Kirkwood looked at the time. It was now eleven a.m. He walked out of the room and nodded towards Carrie and her parents. "Would it be possible for you to come to the station tomorrow? I need a statement about your kidnapping and other bits of information about the bikie gang. I need to get back to the station." He yawned.

Cassie asked, "You don't look fit to drive. Have a rest in the guest room." Kirkwood considered the question, "I need to get back a.s.a.p. Anyway, it would be too much trouble."

Cassie insisted, "It is less trouble than picking you off the road like some roadkill."

Kirkwood thought of the roadkill image and nodded, "I'll just make a call."

Kirkwood not only slept for a couple of hours but woke to see a tray of food beside his bed. He looked at his watch. It was two-twenty. He quickly ate the fruit and sandwich before tidying himself up. Carrie was ushered to the sealed off lounge room for her interview. At times Kirkwood noticed Carrie's eyes pooling then she would sniff to recompose herself. He eventually asked, "Are those tears of the bad memories of the kidnapping or for your boyfriend who is going away and never coming back?"

Carrie shrugged. "Both, I suppose. It's just taking time for reality to sink in. I didn't like being drugged. I did like levitating but really hated being tossed in the helicopter the way he did. I know he did it to keep me safe, but it was so embarrassing."

Kirkwood and Carrie were interrupted when Ashton knocked on the door. "Just saying good-bye. Levi, that security person who was in the helicopter with us, is driving me to where I need to go to pick up my pod. I have stayed longer than intended. I better get moving." He shook Kirkwood's hand and gave Carrie a peck on a cheek. He handed Kirkwood the altered tracker. "You know what to do with this?"

Kirkwood nodded and turned it on. Carrie jumped at the noise it created. Kirkwood grinned, "It's working. Thanks."

Carrie asked, "What is that thing?"

Ashton left the room quickly leaving Kirkwood to explain. Carrie rushed out of the room yelling, "Ashton! Ashton!" As she ran through the house, she had a glimpse of Ashton outside. She opened the French doors and yelled as she ran towards the car, "Hey! Spaceman." Ashton ran faster to Levi's car, "Drive!" Levi chuckled as the engine clicked over. The car just started to move when Carrie jumped in the back seat.

"Levi, don't stop. Drive to wherever he needs to go," puffed Carrie. "I want to see this pod." She leaned forward pulling Ashton by the shoulder. "Start explaining this," she asked while holding the butterfly pendant.

"I was concerned for your safety. I got into a bad crowd, and I had a feeling if they couldn't get to me, they could get to you."

"So you tagged me like some animal!"

Ashton turned in his seat to face her. "If I hadn't, you could be still there with that mob or six feet under. I didn't tell you because I knew you would toss it away."

Both heard Levi chuckle. Both, at the same time said, "Keep out of this. Just drive."

Levi laughed louder. "Yes. You two sound like my wife and me. Are you two going to tie the knot?" Both chorused, "No!"

"What a shame. So well suited." Levi drove on in silence. Ashton and Carrie didn't speak to each other. Ashton gave directions, past the chalet where Carrie and he first met. Ashton reminded her of first meeting. Carrie grunted. "I should have poured your bottle of water over your head." "I would have loved that. It was just so hot that day."

Levi shook his head. "It sounds as if it wasn't only the day which was hot."

Carrie recoiled in silence glaring a hole into the back of Levi's head.

Levi stopped the car at the end of the road. Ashton grabbed his bags, shook hands with Levi. Carrie got out of the car, "How far is it to the pod?"

"About three kilometres, maybe a bit more." He leaned to give her a kiss on the cheek again. Levi leaned out of the window and called out, "What are you man? Plant a proper one." Both looked towards Levi. Ashton just shook her hand. Levi yelled, "That was the worst goodbye I have ever seen in my life. Both of you step up." Ashton stepped away and switched on the levitator. He was about half a metre off the ground when Carrie gave a football-like tackle.

With Carrie dangling from his feet, Ashton struggled to move. He moved her closer to the car and dropped her on the bonnet. "Stay. I'll be back soon." With that he flew away.

Twenty minutes later, he returned in the pod. He stepped out. To Levi, "Tell the others I will drop Carrie off." he winked at Levi.

Levi looked at Carrie. "What are you waiting for?"

Carrie stepped into the pod and noticed there was only one seat. Ashton placed himself in that seat, strapped himself in and began the usual start-up procedures. "You will have to sit on my lap. Carrie placed herself where indicated. "It won't take long. A short ride. Let's have a look at the space station which Mark is very fond of."

Carrie stared at Ashton. "You're not serious, are you?"

"Very. And we are just about there now. Look out of the window."

Carrie didn't know where to look first: the station, space or the sun appearing around the edges of Earth. She didn't pay any attention to what Ashton was doing or even saying. His voice drifted in the background.

"Space station, this is experimental craft one. Requesting permission to board."

The astronaut inside looked at the commander. "This is the pre-arranged visitor coming. The commander nodded and grinned. "Get ready for some fun. Play along. Everyone will be listening when she boards."

A crackly accented voice said, "Err, experimental craft one, we were unaware of your arrival."

"Didn't mission control tell you?"

"That's typical. Did they tell you I have a delivery?"

"No. Not a word."

"They must have been distracted by the spaceship that landed at Daraxon Technologies."

"We've all been distracted by that ship. That is what I call a very nice ship."

"Are you people going to open up?" asked Ashton.

"Starting procedure now. I can see you coming into view. Gee, that's a radial design and departure from the other styles. Line up for locking." There was a clunk.

Ashton opened the connecting door and was met by the commander. Carrie floated in.

"Where are your suits?" asked the astronaut waiting at the door.

"New craft. No need for suits."

"May I have a look?"

Ashton stepped aside and pulled Carrie out of the man's way.

"You didn't say you have a passenger. And who may this beautiful lady be?"

Carrie introduced herself as she extended her hand. "Carrie."

"Nice to meet you. Please go to the next door. I'll open up after a quick look in here." He turned to Ashton. "Tell me about this baby." He nodded towards the pod.

Ashton gave the astronaut a fist full of chocolate bars when the mini tour came to an end. When the astronaut and Carrie were inside the main part of the space station, Ashton closed the door of the pod and quickly disconnected leaving Carrie trapped inside the space station. He sped off.

The commander and the rest of the crew winked to each other before speaking to Ashton, "This is not a joke. You can't leave her here."

Ashton replied, "I have to, so she doesn't follow me to the spaceship. Bye Carrie."

Carrie yelled through the phone, "You can't leave me here!"

"I just did. You need to be brought down to Earth....Is that the right expression you people use?"

"Fuck you, Ashton!" she screamed through the communication system.

Ashton waved and grinned as he circled the station. "Commander, can you tell Daraxon Technologies, I dropped Carrie off. Mark Lawson will pick her up in the new jet Daraxon created." Ashton saw Carrie's face through one of the windows. He blew her a kiss. All on board the space station saw the pod zoom towards the moon. Carrie was too lost for words as she gazed out the window.

Two hours later, Mark attached the new craft onto the space station. He laughed when he saw Carrie. Carrie ignored him as tears ran down her face. She muttered, "Stop laughing. I have never been so humiliated."

"Come on. You'll be home soon. Get in." Carrie climbed into the jet. She asked Mark, "Does this thing travel under water?"

"No. Why?"

"Does this thing have an eject lever or something like that?"

"Yeah and I'm not telling you where until it's time to use it. What are you planning?"

"Suicide." Mark looked shocked but Carrie slowly began to laugh. "The joke was on me. Ashton always played jokes on me. In Levi's car, we had one doozey of a fight. Levi said we sounded like some married couple."

Mark glanced over. "Oh shit. You've fallen for him, haven't you?"

Carrie didn't reply. Mark glanced again. "Spaceboy was right. You really need to come down to Earth."

"How did you know he said that?"

"Carrie, we were all listening on the communication system: us, every space agency and his ship." Carrie tried to shrink down into the seat further. "You all planned this, didn't you? Whose idea was it?"

"Do I really need to answer that? Ashton just wanted to give you a parting thrill. He noticed you're bit of an adrenaline junkie. Did he succeed?"

She muttered, "Yes." In a louder voice, "So embarrassing. Was the entire conversation in the pod broadcasted?"

"The full three minutes of five minutes of flight and all the conversation in the space station." He paused and looked earnest, "And it's all on video."

"Oh, shit. I just want to die. Where is that eject button? "

"It's too late for that."

"Why?"

Mark nodded to the ground. They were back at Daraxon Technologies.

As they walked towards the first main building, Mark said, "When you were kidnapped, both our mothers searched your room looking for clues as to whom may have threatened you. They found your diary and read the last two months. Nothing really that exciting - mostly your schedules, and appointments. Your comments about Ashton on the first date was more interesting. But there were little footnotes here and there throughout the book: Seen the sunrise this morning at the Ridge Lookout, then from the tower and a few other places including the seaside. Then there was one entry, 'I would love to see the sun from a completely different perspective - space.' That was crossed out with a comment, 'not possible'. While you were being interviewed, Ashton was informed of the search and of the space view of sunrise. He asked if you would be permitted to see the sunrise from space or even from the space station. It was a hurriedly organised thing. It was considered by all agencies as a bit of an experiment, the first tourist to the space station. No one knew for sure if it could be done in such a short time." Mark looked at Carrie with a mild sense of pride knowing Carrie of all people, treasured his flights to the space station. "You noted in your diary you needed to rely on my comments and any photos. 'Jealous.' Are you still jealous?" Carrie shook her head. Mark continued, "Ashton just wanted you to cross that off your bucket list. He says not achieving goals or not doing or not living a dream, causes regrets later in life. Very philosophical."

Mark directed and escorted Carrie back to the mess hall. Her mouth dropped when she saw the hall was lightly decorated and the crowd before her called out, "Happy Birthday!"

CHAPTER SIXTEEN
On Board the Explorer

When Ashton's pod was halfway to the spaceship, a four-person pod met him. Nodin spoke, "Applying decontamination net now and remote control."

Ashton let go of the controls. His pod was being externally decontaminated. The decontamination light inside the pod was activated. "Commencing stage one now," said Ashton. He sat back in his chair and relaxed. The light switched off, "Commencing stage two." Ashton sat back in the seat again and allowed the dark yellow light wash over his body. Frode spoke, "Commencing stage two exterior decontamination." Minutes later, "Commencing stage three. Put on your internal shield. Ashton complied. "All complete. Proceed to the ship. Take bay three," said someone from flight control.

Ashton was met by a small crowd; all his security group, Neo, Dr. Haiten, Commander Jalon and Captain Keka. He was escorted to the small conference room. Commander Jalon and the others took a turn quizzing him over the month's events. "That was very eventful," said Dr. Haiten. You will be confined to your quarters for the next few days. When we have finished the assessment and after more medical checks, you will be free to move around."

After two days of confinement. Ashton was ordered out. He was escorted to the conference room again where Commander Jalon was sitting near a screen showing Ashton with a group of similar aged Earth people. "Sit," ordered Jalon. He pointed to the screen. "Tell me about this event." Jalon listened and wound back the recording a few times for greater details. He pointed to the items he was holding. "Where are those things?"

Ashton stared back not saying a word. "Patron told me you had the items and was instructed only you and I were to see them. Where did you hide them? We have already searched your room." "True. Patron did say for me, dad and you only to look at the parcel. We wait until we get to Beta Cancari."

"Do you have any idea what is in it?"

"Not exactly. I was only given hints. It stays put in its location. Security reasons."

Jalon grunted. "Go back to your room. Haiten will conduct more testing over the next few days. Under the circumstances, you did a passable job. You seem to do better on well-planned missions in Oberon and Amada."

Ashton stood up and was about to leave. Jalon gestured, "Sit. There is another matter which needs to be discussed." He closed down the electronics in the room.

"The girl, Carrie. Do you like her?"

"She's okay. Everyone including Kora says she's my type. I am not convinced. She's fun to be with but only in small doses. I really don't know her that well to make an informed decision."

Jalon nodded. "We have a problem. It was a matter of age. Patron and Dalmon are slowly dying. They want one or two replacements to be trained up to be Guardians. Are you up for the transfer?" Ashton gasped, "That will mean me staying on that planet until the end of my days. I am not sure of that."

"Alcyn declared Earth as a protectorate. Patron and Dalmon need replacements."

"And who else do you think would join me?"

Jalon leaned back. "Someone from the security team. All have volunteered for the position.

Alternatively, Dr. Haiten or Captain Keka."

Ashton sighed. "I need time to think."

Jalon looked firmly, "You have exactly six hours. I don't want to waste too much fuel returning to Earth.

"Am I supposed to be with Carrie while I am there?"

"That's your decision."

"What am I supposed to do there? Give me some information so I can make a decision." Patron and Dalmon said they monitor everything on Earth and liaison and mediate between governments to keep the peace between nations. In short fast track, Earth's development towards unification as one people. Also monitoring their population growth and speeding up care for their planet."

Ashton frowned as he considered the role. "I don't think I have any of those skills and I doubt any of the others on the security team will."

"Whoever goes, will be trained up. Patron has a soft spot for you. Dalmon thinks highly of you."

"Patron is bias. We discovered we were related."

"How? I must have missed that bit of information."

"My grandfather on my mother's side and Patron are brothers. That makes him bias."

Jalon coughed at the revelation. "That works both ways. Generally, diplomacy runs in families. As you say can smack of nepotism. Have a think and let me know of your decision. Just where is the parcel?"

Ashton smirked. "Nice try. Buttering me up and then the punch. If I decide to go, I will tell you then."

Ashton fell asleep when he returned to his room. It was a very deep sleep. When he looked at the time, the time of the deadline had come and gone. He wavered as he considered the information. He thought it strange that Jalon or anyone else in the command section hadn't contacted him. He tried to unlock his door. The code had been reset. He pulled out his unused spare glasses. "Green". The mechanism clicked. He opened the door and walked out. The passageways were empty. Something was wrong. He went back to his room and put on his tactical gear. Cautiously, he walked the empty passageways examining each corridor and rooms as he went. *It's too quiet*, he thought. *Too deserted.*

He approached the mess hall and peered through one of the windows. He gasped. Jalon was held at gun point in front of the others.

The person holding the gun was someone who he had never seen before. He wondered how this person stayed concealed inside the ship.

Ashton moved away and found the nearest air-conditioning duct system. He looked it up by using the maintenance pad near a duct. He looked at the schematics and isolated the mess hall and its surrounds. He traced with his finger a path to the mess hall.

On his belly he slid like a snake and guessed where the tunnel was over the gun wielding person. He wriggled as quietly as he could to a vent to get a view of the scene below. Knowing his angle was wrong, he wriggled to another vent. It wasn't perfect – a bit far away for his likings but it offered a clearer shot. Between the blades of the vent, he aimed the laser. The invisible beam flashed on impact. The stranger fell backwards dead but the gun he was holding fired into Jalon's back. There was a mad rush to restrain the stranger and to assist Jalon. Most of the others rushed out of the room.

Ashton wriggled back to where he entered the system. When he climbed down, he opened the maintenance pad again. This time he was going to the flight deck.

While the others appeared to be rushing in panic, he ran to the nearest duct opening going to the flight deck. Again, he wriggled through the narrow space until he reached the main vent.

He identified three of the original crew all being coerced into flying the craft. Three earth guns were pointed at them and a stranger was in the control seat. Ashton cursed when he heard a noise at the door. Keka and Neo had entered with guns raised. Just as the intruders spun around, Ashton fired a volley of beams killing the person in the chair and two of the strangers. Neo dropped to the floor holding a wound. The remaining stranger dived for cover. Ashton cursed. The person was too well protected. He could see the remaining stranger searching the room for the hidden shooter. Keka was crawling on the floor but was also searching and wondering where the assistance was coming from. The stranger saw Keka make a break for cover. He stood up for a better shot. The stranger dropped to the floor holding an injured arm before passing out. Keka looked around stunned at his fortune. Ashton revealed himself in the vent. "Some help will be nice." Keka undid the screws of the vent while standing on a chair.

"Thanks," said Ashton. "It was a tight squeeze in there. Who are these people?"

Keka searched their bodies for anything that would identify them. Nothing was found.

Ashton frowned. "I have an idea as to who they are. Earth people. These could be some of Granger's hard-core devoted people who had a grudge against Daraxon Technologies. They did very well to smuggle themselves on board and take over the ship for that length of time. What do we do with the injured man?"

There was a groan. Keka and Ashton looked down. Ashton gave the man a small boot near the injury.

"Shut up when we are discussing your future," spat Ashton.

"We jettison the dead. We mend this misguided heap and question him when he recovers."

Keka called in the medics. Dr. Haiten accompanied them. "What do we have here?"

"Neo has been shot by an Earth gun and this man has laser injuries," said Keka. "Watch him." The medics lifted the man onto a stretcher, strapped him up and gave him an injection. The man passed out in seconds. Neo forced himself up from the floor. "Nice work Ashton." Then he passed out. Haiten called for another stretcher team.

As they waited, Keka asked, "How is the commander?"

Haiten shook his head. "Alive. Critical. If he pulls through, he will need a very long recovery period. Earth bullets are messy and cause far more damage than lasers. They really make a big internal mess. They spin inside the body. Nasty. It will be testing my surgery skills. He is being prepped for major surgery now." Dr. Haiten followed the second team of stretcher bearers out.

"Jalon was thinking about two people staying on Earth to be trained up to take over Patron's and Dalmon's roles," said Keka.

Ashton sighed. "I know. We had discussed that. That was one reason I was locked in my room.

I don't think I am the right material."

Keka nodded. "Who do you think should go?"

"Actually, I was thinking we should let President Findlee make that decision. It is a bit of a zoo." Keka chuckled. "You seemed to have done well with all the variables you came across. I believe you have a fan who would very much like you back."

"Don't you start," replied Ashton knowing exactly who Keka was referring to.

"I am going back to Beta Cancari. That is final." Ashton walked out of the flight deck and back to his room. He didn't come out unless it was for meals or to visit Kora in her room. He made it clear to the rest of his team, he wanted alone time.

CHAPTER SEVENTEEN
Beta Cancari
Same Time as the Explorer left Earth

The sirens sounded over the small city. Again, the citizens followed their escape protocol. The control tower alerted the skeleton defence crew and had to determine the exact nature of the threat.

Findlee was briefed, "Sir we have a ship. Bad news. A Lacertian ship but there are other odd signals in the signature. We can't identify them one hundred per cent." Findlee went pale. His nightmares had just become a reality. "Put the shield up. Put the experimental shield up outside that."

"Sir, the new shield hasn't been tested. Will it work?"

"We are going to find out," replied Findlee.

The sound of the outer shield filled the air. The outer shield spread over the city like a giant bubble. It glistened briefly before images of the forest formed. Findlee hoped the approaching ship would just see a heavily forested planet.

A shadow of the Lacertian-like craft passed overhead. It lingered for a while before continuing. The ship was recorded circling and zig-zagging over the planet. It stopped at several locations before moving on. Findlee and the others guessed it was taking samples and making scans. The craft was recorded flying away. Findlee said, "Don't let the citizens out. I think they are fooling around with us. We wait up to a week if necessary. Keep the shields up until we are not out of danger."

For a week the sky above Beta Cancari was scanned. The people were let out to return to their tasks through the day but at night, they returned to the caves. The protective inner shield was lowered but the experimental shield stayed in place. Findlee didn't want all defences down immediately.

It was close to a month when the experimental shield was lowered for maintenance. The city revealed itself. On Findlee's orders, all windows were to be covered with thick shields so interior lights did not act like night beacons. People were now able to stay in the homes. It restored some normality.

Findlee remained on tender hooks. He felt something was amiss. He sent small exploration groups to the locations where the Lacertian-like ship was recorded to stop. If the crews did not return each day, he was certain they would have been attacked. That meant some Lacertian had landed.

On the second day, a small exploration party did not return. A second was dispatched to investigate. They too didn't return. Findlee contemplated the situation. There would not be any more missions. The handful of fighter jets would be sent instead. They had orders to blast the area with a mix of explosives and radars of every kind. The jets returned.

The city's alarm sounded. Once again, the shields went up. The Lacertian-like ship was detected again.

The Lacertian-like mothership approached in stealth mode. It hammered the protective shield with assorted lasers and newly developed missiles. After two days of hammering, the protective shield covering the city fell apart.

The mothership hovered above the city. Shuttle transit pod ferried heavily armed soldiers. Immediately, the soldiers went from door to door searching each room in every surrounding building. They found a handful of people – some of the skeleton above ground crew who hadn't made it to safety. Findlee and many others hid in their assigned locations.

For Findlee, it was the extra tunnel under the administration building which led to a cavity under the library. From the library, he was able to see with the aid of hidden cameras what was going on above ground.

Over two hundred Pleiadeans were rounded up and taken on board. A handful were tortured for information. They gave their lives up rather than expose the rest of the colony. When there was a large gathering of Lacertians and other Lacertian-like 'people' in the city mall, Findlee fired on the group with hidden small missiles. Their screams and blood filled the air. But the captured Pleiadeans in the pods zoomed away.

The mother ship lowered itself and began to shoot out toxic gas. Findlee gave orders to those in other hidden basements, "Fire on the ship. Fire at will." From two different directions, larger missiles fired. The ship exploded spreading nuclear waste and other toxic fumes across the city. The ground shook with the explosion and aftershocks rippled through the area. Findlee prayed that the underground cavities didn't collapse or were blocked. He pushed the warning nuclear button for the hidden citizens to abide by nuclear fallout procedures. This included evacuating through the caves to the overside of the mountain range. Then he set the warning beacon out to space. There it would blip on the known path in the void. Hours later, Findlee with other initial underground survivors, died from radiation poisoning.

One month later a reconnaissance group ventured from the caves. Their movements and progress were slow due to the cumbersome suits and rubble. Remanent of the Lacertian-like ship covered most of the city. Every building was destroyed or declared unsafe. The ground was still soaked with dangerous levels of radiation. The searchers found numerous bodies of Lacertians and another species which were like Lacertians but had different features unique to the new species. The Pleiadeans which were rounded up as prisoners by the invaders were located. All dead inside one part of the downed spaceship. The tortured people were located under some rubble. Ten people were unaccounted for and Findlee was one of those. When the reconnaissance team returned and gave their report, the new temporary leaders of the Pleiadean nation shifted all the survivors to a new location far from this place of death. They left no trail of their survival. They would start again. But the cribs remained in place deep in the cave system. Someone would check them every two days.

CHAPTER SEVENTEEN
The Explorer.

Captain Keka and the crew of the flight deck picked up a feint signal. The navigator, Gippa positioned its location. "I'll send someone to collect it and bring it back."

It was Nodin who was selected to retrieve the shoebox size item floating in space. He bought the beacon to the flight deck. Keka and Neo who still had his arm in a sling, opened the box. A hologram of Findlee speaking gave the warning and a brief description as to the events which had taken place.

He warned that Ashton, Kora, Garth and Eraton were now on the Lacertian most wanted list in the terrorist category. Keka brought in the security team and asked them to watch the hologram. You four named people are going back to Earth. Your days are over. Earth could do with more guardians. You pack your bags and be ready for departure in twelve hours. You will be taking back the sorry specimen of human sitting in the cell. We will make the twelve-seater craft available for your usage. We will return to Earth at a much later date and check on your progress."

Ten hours later, Ashton visited Kora. "Do you mind if I come in?"

Kora stepped aside and let him pass. He pulled up a chair and stood on it to remove the parcel Reuben had given him. "Sorry. I had to hide this somewhere. I was interrogated about this. Actually, it was quite funny. Neo kept questioning me about its location. I just saying it was under his nose. A handy earth expression. It literally was. He was standing on it. They even erected the polygraph right on top of this."

Kora giggled. "You were telling the truth. The only time I have known you to lie was on Earth. The team and I never laughed so much. May I suggest you leave spy work and be a comedian?" Ashton retorted, "Give me a break."

They sat down on her bed. Ashton tried operating the Earth tablet. The low battery message flashed on the screen. "We have to charge it up. He looked at the plug provided and tried placing it in the socket. It didn't fit. Too big. Kora went to her portable charger, "Try this. I hope it doesn't blow." Gingerly Ashton placed it in the socket. It was fit. "Now the power. Try low, very low." Kora changed the settings. The tablet sprung to life. He typed in the password and then inserted the flash drive.

The first part was a bit of history told by Hammond. The next file contained coordinates from the edge of Amada, through the waste space to Earth. The next file contained history about the discovery of Affen Welt and Genesis. The next file contained the path from the edge of Amada to Genesis. Kora and Ashton sat stunned. The main refugee planet was in the same system, but on the other side. Kora asked, "Do we hand this over to Keka?"

Ashton thought for a while. "No Beta Cancari has been compromised. As I see it, we have two choices. We take this back to Earth, or we divert the pod to Genesis. We can make that decision on the craft with everyone in the know. We have a problem, that Earth man, Peters. Do we take him or leave him behind?"

Kora suggested, "I'll make sure we are all settled in first and then we take off leaving him behind. Peters can earn his keep by helping out. He maybe rostered into fighting any Lacertians. It would do him good to learn who the real enemy is. Is that a plan?" Ashton nodded.

On the twelve-seater pod food and other essentials were loaded. Ashton hid the information parcel and the tablet in his bags, making his bag a couple of kilos heavier than usual. The other two were seated. Keka and Neo moved back to allow the escort for Peters to come forward. Ashton and Kora started the pod at top speed and zoomed out of the main ship. The door automatically closed. Garth called out, "what are you two doing?"

Neither answered. Garyth yelled, "We were supposed to take Peters with us back to Earth." Kora and Ashton remained silent. It was close to a light year away when they placed the twelve-seater escape pod into hover. Ashton played back the four files on the tablet. "Now we take a vote. Earth or Genesis or we turn back and tail the Explorer?" There was total silence. Eraton shook his head, "That's a tough decision. Give us time to think."

While each was debating the location, pros, cons and other possible eventualities, a hologram formed inside the pod. They all sat stunned at the image. The man's face was lined with aged wisdom. "May I come aboard? I am Zindel. I am from the army formed by the Lords of the Universe. We have a common enemy, Lizard people. It was the Draconians which have corrupted the Lacertians." The Pleiadeans looked out of the window closet to each of them. They were stunned to see Zindel's miniature pod to the right front side of the pod. All hesitated for a few minutes. Kora opened the pod sealed compartment. Zindel entered the pod.

He walked down the narrow isle. He could see the pod was full of supplies. He said, "You don't have to vote but you will split up but not now. There was an explosion on Beta Cancari. The city is drowned in radiation from the downed Draconian ship which is now sitting on top of the city. It is useless going there. You can return to your ship, but it will be difficult to convince Keka and the others to seek a new planet. Beta Cancari has been overrun with Lacertians and Draconians. Some Pleiadeans have escaped but I have not located them. They are hiding on Beta Cancari."

"I strongly advise you all join me and skill up. Compared to the training I have received; you people are at level one. There are five levels. Each level takes a person about a year to master. Very few achieve each level in less than a year. It has been done. Most people take six years. Put it in a nutshell, I am on a recruiting drive. We need people from all the human races we can find and train them up to fight the Draconians and now the Lacertians. They are moving across the galaxies, enslaving and consuming humans. We have to stop them. Take a few minutes to think this over. I shall return. I am going to your spaceship to give the news to Captain Keka. Oh, there is the part of the training, reading minds." He looked at each individual and placed his hands on their heads. To Nodin and Garyth, "You will be better on Genesis."

To Kora he shook his head. "No, you will be better returning to Earth. You're pregnant. One month maybe two."

Kora mumbled, "Impossible!" Pleiadean women can't naturally conceive and haven't done so for eight hundred years." She paused contemplating the last month and how she was feeling. "Is that why I have been feeling a bit off?"

Zindel drew in a breath and nodded. Zindel looked around, "The father is Ashton."

Ashton gulped. "That's not possible. No Pleiadean female or male can reproduce like that anymore. It's all done artificially. That's why we have the gestation cribs."

Zindel looked at Ashton. "You spent time on Earth. It changed your chemistry. Kora has consumed many food items and water you brought back from Earth. Her chemistry changed a little. It will change back in a few more weeks but the baby will grow. But for now, you're a dad. Get used to the idea." Eraton and Nodin chuckled and patted Ashton on the back. "Ashton, you are not suited to either planet. You are more suited to a job like mine," said Zindel.

"Recruitment?"

"That's just part of it. Training. Spying. Advanced mind control. All of you experienced a degree of mind control before I boarded. I can fake holograms."

Zindel went to the rear door and exited. The Pleiadeans saw his mini pod zoom away.

Nodin asked, "Was that a dream? Mass hypnosis? Or some other side effect from the samples of earth food?"

Ashton closed his eyes and shook his head. "Geez, I really stuffed up, haven't I?" He looked at Kora,

"Sorry. I didn't know. I'm so sorry."

"None of us knew that. That experiment had side effects which no one knew about."

Dr. Haiten would be worried and beside himself. I think I better return to the Explorer."

Eraton spoke, "We all should go back. Beta Cancari is in trouble. We have to save as many as we can."

"I agree, with Eraton," said Nodin.

"Yeah, I don't want my kid growing up without two parents. The Explorer it is," said Ashton.

Nodin asked, "What food did you eat on Earth?"

"I tried as many things as possible I could. Drinks. Food. The water was so fresh. Delicious."

"Maybe it was the water," said Eraton. "It's not what was in the water, but what was left out."

"I got some bottles here. I was going to give it to dad, but I see that may not happen." He pulled out a bottle. The others dived into their bags and pulled out small cups. Kora said, "You gave me two bottles of that stuff. Look at the situation I am in now. Pour me a double. That water is addictive."

The pod pulled up back at the Explorer. The doors opened for it to birth. Kora and Ashton went straight to Dr. Haiten. The others went back to the flight deck but were re-directed to the conference room. Zindel was there giving his speech to Keka, Neo and the other security personnel. Keka looked at the two late arrivals. "Sorry," whispered Nodin. "We decided to come back and help out. Going to Earth is not an option." Eraton and Nodin sat quietly ready to listen to the hard sell Zindel was giving." Zindel gave a fleeting smile. "Welcome back. You obviously are not taking up my offer I take it?"

Both Nodin and Eraton shook their heads.

"Where are Ashton and Kora?" asked Keka.

"Ashton and Kora are with Dr. Haiten."

"Is anything wrong?' asked Keka.

Eraton shook his head. "Nothing but a small case of pregnancy."

"What?" chorused half the people in the room while others were too stunned to say anything.

"The experiment had side effects. Kora is getting a check-up to verify if she and Ashton are going to be parents."

Zindle looked at Nodin and Eraton, "You doubt my skills?"

"Sorry. It was a shock to all of us."

"We think it was the water. Ashton brought some water back. Kora and he were drinking it. We had a sample as well. Ashton kept saying the water quality was fantastic."

Keka recalled, "Yes, he did say it was better than anything he had tasted. We should get back to business."

Neo looked disturbed. "Wait a minute. We refilled this ship with Earth water. All of us have been drinking it." He rushed out of the room and down to Dr. Haiten's surgery.

He knocked and opened the door. He saw Dr. Haiten attending to Ashton and Kora. "There could be a spate of pregnant females. Stop everyone from drinking the water until it is tested." Then he ran to the engineering room, "Turn off the Earth water supply until it is tested! Just all drinking taps!" The engineers looked up surprised at the request by complied. Taps around the ship went dry after the initial trickle was used. Neo ran back to the meeting where Zindel was continuing the hard sell.

Zindel sat down on the only spare seat to allow the other debate what the best course of action would be. The growing indecision and the fragmentation made him stand up. He had enough. "I am going to read your skills and the best course of action you as individuals can make. He placed his hands on their heads. He went into a trance like state.

"Keka it is best for you to continue on this ship and fly as many people to safety as you can. Neo. Your work is cut out training as many people as you can in self-defence. Nodin and Eraton, I read your paths before. No changes. Genesis. Ichiro, hmm, I see a huge change but not in this field of work. Diplomacy on Earth. Frode, you will continue to do this work for many more years before replacing Neo. Eldon, you will do this work before changing into some administration role. The role will be very difficult but you will triumphant in making progress for the people under your administration." He stopped moving around the room. "Take me to Jalon. Immediately."

The group led Zindel to Jalon who was groaning with pain. He was connected to a number of drips. Zindel said with urgency in his voice as he waved his hands over Jalon's body. "The Earth bullet has toxic chemicals. He is reacting to the poisons. He doesn't have much time. Captain Keka, place your hands over Commander Jalon's head." Keka did has he was told. Then Zindel placed his hands over Keka's hands. Zindel briefly looked at Keka. "Get ready for memory transference."

Keka felt a jolt which pushed him halfway across the room. Keka passed out. Zindel held back the others, "Give him time. He will recover." Keka started to groan and rubbed his head.

"Wow. That really did hurt." He continued while seated. Eldon and Nodin pulled him up from the floor and assisted him to a seat. Frode poured water from a jug. Keka took the water and grinned, ''The magic water from Earth, I presume."

Zindel said, "Keka you know have a duplicate memory of Jalon's life experiences and your still have your own. When you sleep over the next few nights, you will have a mixture of dreams and nightmares. It is your brain assimilating the new information. You are now both commander and captain." Jalon groaned and held out his hand. He asked for Keka to come closer. Jalon whispered and tried to smile, "Look after my memories. Good-bye my friend." Jalon gave two long breaths and died.

Zindel went back into a trance state. There is an Earth person among you. Take me to him." Zindel was escorted to Peters's cell. Peters looked defiant. Zindel went into the cell and ordered Peters, "Sit up." Peters didn't comply. Zindel pointed his finger. Peter's was jolted up and held in place. Zindel placed his hands on Perters's head. "Hmm. Primitive. Strong. Dangerous. Traitor with greed and vanity. Untrustworthy. Learned evil." Zindel called in Keka. "Dispose of him. You will have no end of trouble. Left to live, he will sell us and Earth to the Draconians and Lacertians. We should prepare his disposal before you reach Beta Cancari."

Zindel placed Peters into a trance before walking him out of the cell. To Eraton, "Take us to the nearest disposal unit for jettisoning." Eraton led the way but was nervous of Zindel. "Open the top hatch," he said to Eraton. He waited a few seconds as the floor parted to reveal a cavity. To Peters he explained, "This is like your ocean on Earth. Jump into the water from this mini rock." Peters jumped down the hole. Zindel ordered Eraton, "Close the door. Open the lower hatch." Eraton hesitated. "Close it. If he lives, he will join the Lacertians. Greed will motivate him and tell them of Earth. Then they will eat him after he divulges the information." Eraton pushed the lower floor button. Peters was sucked into space. "Now take me to Ashton."

Ashton was sitting in the medical unit with Kora. Haiten had a pile of tablets open. He was flipping between one tablet and to the next trying to find suitable information to give both Ashton and Kora. Zindel walked in after excusing himself. Dr. Haiten looked at Zindel. "What I understand from Pleiadean history, there has not been a case like this for nearly eight hundred years. I am at a loss as to what to advice." He looked at Ashton. "Kora needs to back to Earth. She will receive the best attention there." Zindel flipped through Haiten's small library to an obscure footnote and pointed. "There. That's all you are going to get out of this." He placed his hands on Ashton's head trying to access memories of Earth.

A small bit of information came up. He hummed and nodded. "Kora," he said rather mechanically, "Expect to develop a big tummy. Expect intermittent nausea, food craving, inconvenience at a later stage of gestation, maybe a sore back. Pain and pleasure. Perfect. Hmm." He looked at Ashton, "You didn't take any notice of women down there, except for one." Zindel laughed at some of the memories in Ashton mind as they surfaced.

"Oh. I am so much going to love training you up." Zindel stood back from Ashton, "Look at me." Ashton knew those words too well and diverted his eyes away. "I am not going to use hypnosis on you. I want you to tell me what you see in me."

Ashton cautiously turned his eyes. He said nothing for a while as he looked Zindel over head to toe. "I see an older version of me but one huge difference. I have a person to care for and with luck, another. You never experienced those feelings. I don't want to dry up like you." Zindel looked shocked and then nodded. "No one has ever seen that. The work does dry you up if you allow it. But I know Kora will see that won't happen. I think you will be the best apprentice ever. One who knows when to walk away is rare. Hmm, another Earth side effect. A good one at that."

Zindel looked at the group. "I must depart. Be very careful on Beta Cancari." Zindel vanished.

CHAPTER EIGHTEEN
Beta Cancari

The Explorer arrived at Beta Cancari and circled the planet once upon entry. As the neared their home city, they could see the Draconian ship laid where it was attacked - smack in the middle of the small and only Pleiadean city. Keka noticed the controls blipping a radiation warning. The Explorer moved to the other side of the mountains and went north until radiation did not register. No life registered either. He ordered the ship to follow the range further north. There was a small blip. *Someone is around*, he thought. "Circle the planet again. Heat detecting sonar on." There was nothing except for small, isolated blips which indicated small animal life. In one spot the blips conversed into one continuous sound. *Interesting* he thought. "Mark the spot for further investigation in the very near future," he commanded. Keka didn't like what the control panels were indicating. Too still, too quiet over the rest of the planet. "Go back to the mountain range close to the settlement."

The Explorer gave another blip. "Shield up. Land just south, one kilometre away, in that clearing." He pushed the intercom system. "No one leaves the ship without radiation suits on although this is a radiation free area. Scout team one, be ready to disembark," ordered Keka.

The ramp went down. Five people cautiously walked down the ramp, their guns at the ready. They walked slowly over the rough, uneven sparsely planted terrain towards the blip detected earlier. As they approached, there were more blips which became louder on their hand-held sensors. They stopped and analysed the sounds. The leader of the group, Eldon, nodded. "Slowly now and keep your eyes open."

One of the team members stopped walking and signalled to the others. They squatted with their guns pointed. They focused on the boy standing in the shadows in front of them. The boy was barely in his teens. Eldon threw a stone to the left of the boy. The boy looked in that direction first and then gradually turned. *There was something wrong with the boy,* thought Eldon. The boy stood still and called out, "Flynette! Flynette!" A younger girl who had been concealed from their sight, rushed to his side. She stopped dead in her tracks when she saw the ship not far away. Then she grabbed the boy and led him back to the cave entrance. They could see the girl whispering something into the boy's ear.

Eldon signalled to the others to join him. He spoke to Keka to seek more instructions. Eldon followed the children into the cave entrance. The group stood outside the entrance. Eldon ordered the others to guard the outside. He lifted his mask to see if the bio-scanner had him in the memory banks. The bio-scanner opened the disguised door. He went in.

He slowly went further into the cave which gave way to a tunnel. He stopped dead in his tracks when he entered the first chamber. "Sir we have contact. Pleiadean children. All unsupervised but appear to be in good health." The children stared at Eldon. He took off his gloves. "Hello. I'm Eldon. A Pleiadean. They stared back. Eldon tried to jog their memories. "I was on the ship, the Explorer. President Findlee built the ship. We have been away for just over a year." There was silence but a taller and older teenage girl pushed her way through the group. "I'm Tanke. I remember seeing the Explorer. What is your name again?"

"Eldon." Tanke walked to a screen and typed Eldon in. The screen offered a few details.

She turned to the others. "You're cleared. Are the others guarding outside?" Eldon nodded.

"Tell them to come in and wait near the door. It is dangerous to be outside for an extended period of time monsters are out there." Eldon gave the order for the others to enter.

Eldon walked slowly following Tanke. He noted she was very much the boss. "Give the man room to walk," she ordered the others. They moved away ever so slightly. Tanke led him to a room which had a series of tables and chairs. "Sit down please. You kids sit over here and listen. You will have your turn to speak soon." There was instant silence. Tanke questioned Eldon for a while. Every so often she would allow the younger children ask a question. When she was satisfied, she gave her details.

"The Lacertians came. They rounded up many adults. Killed many as well. Most teens and children are in the cave system, deeper in than where we are. Some have illnesses from the radiation. Some have developed deformities. The gestation cribs, well we don't know what state they are in when it comes to other areas. In here we all take turns pumping the food in, but we had to ration the food as it has almost run out. We don't know how to make the formulas. I think the formula books are in another section in the caves. We don't know if the babies will grow properly. Food has just about run out for all of us. Some of us have died because we tried eating some plants. Some plants made us very ill while others we found were safe. We are building a knowledge of what is safe and what isn't. It's a battle and a gamble in every meal we supplement with plants. Water is rationed. The pumps don't always work. We are slowly figuring out the maintenance. How many people are on the ship?"

"About one hundred," replied Eldon.

"Is there room for all of us?" asked Tanke.

"How many are there?"

"In our section, close to fifty. Other sections, well we don't know. We are not sure of the number of sections there are. The cribs we have been trying to look after number two hundred."

Eldon nodded. "Do you all want to come back to the ship?"

Tanke pulled back with caution. "I won't go. But I will send only Milay and Wilbut. They must return by nightfall. There are wild creatures out here. They eat people."

"What do theses creatures look like?" asked Eldon his attention grabbed a second time by the revelations. Tanke let a tear rolled down her face when she recalled a friend being devoured. She went to the computer and opened a file to show creatures caught on camera. Eldon gasped. He could hardly say the words. "That looks like our enemy, but not quite the same. Fighting Lacertians is my job." He spoke more directly into his headset. "Sir, we have Lacertian look-alike creatures on Beta Cancari.

Repeat, look alike Lacertians on Beta Cancari. They are larger and have different colouring and head shapes. Their tails are much longer. I will try to have the pictures transferred to you."

Tanke looked at Eldon, "I am not sure how to transfer the pictures to the ship. Is Commander Jalon on board? Jalon is my guardian." Eldon looked at the girl. "Sit down." He waited until she sat down. "Jalon was killed by a person who smuggled himself and a few of his friends on board." Eldon stopped talking when tears rolled down the Tanke's face. She wiped them away and sniffed loudly. Eldon hesitated before continuing. "The people were killed. A strange man with some very unique skills came on board. He did something I never seen before. He transferred Commander Jalon's memories into the Captain Keka's head."

Tanke looked up. "Impossible."

Eldon shook his head. "I thought so too."

"I want to see Captain Keka. If that is true, then Commander Jalon's part of his brain will know me. Also, I have to tell him, mum was taken away by the Lacertians."

"Then you better come with us." He looked around the room. "These children too. Not just Milay and Wilbut. I am not sure where we will put you all. We will work out how to transfer the cribs as well."

When the transfer of the children and the cribs were completed, Tanke was guided to the Keka's office. Tanke gave her version of what had happened and how she and the rest of the group had survived so long. She ended, "I want to go to the Lacertian spaceship and see inside."

Keka looked at the girl as if he was her father. "Too dangerous. It's a Draconian ship. We could find Lacertians or Draconians and then there is the radiation."

She said in a very defiant manner, "I will risk that. I need to see what is inside. The only thing stopping me before was the radiation. With suits available, I want to go in." She pouted, crossed her arms and tapped one foot. The Jalon side of Keka's brain kicked in. "No child I raised, will put themselves in that kind of danger."

"Then I will borrow a suit and go by myself," Tanke fired back.

"No. Too dangerous," "Then assign someone to go with me!" Tanke said in a loud demanding voice. Jalon sighed and threw his hands up realising there was some logic to the demand. "You can only go with escorts. I will ask two of my security people to accompany you, but only you can go from your group."

Tanke smiled. "Thanks dad." Keka blushed when Tanke planted a kiss on his cheek. Then realised he was just out manoeuvred by a teenager.

Eraton and Nodin donned radiation protective clothing. Tanke was waiting at the exit for them. Her suit had been adjusted to suit her small frame. They took a four-man pod to the downed ship. They circled before deciding where to land at the nearest possible entry. Not far from their landing position, they decided the best entry was near one of the fighter jet doors. This door was only partially blocked by rubble.

They carefully climbed the rubble making sure each step did not create a tear in the suits. There were many jagged edges; a small slip would create a certain slow death process. Nodin held out his hand for Tanke. She took the assistance to get over the immediate obstacle. Eraton soon joined them. They entered the flight tunnel. Eraton said as he looked, "It's very different to what I expected." He pointed to a script on the wall. "That is not Lacertian. It must be Draconian. There are similarities in the script."

Nodin looked at the script before taking a photo. "Turn on your head cameras. We need to record everything as we go." They moved on going down the tunnel until they reached the landing docks. They pushed on each door until one opened. They went down the passageway and checked out any room which was not blocked by debris or locked. "Gee, this place stinks," said Tanke.

When they reached the semi-destroyed flight deck, Nodin looked stunned. "I have seen pictures of Lacertian flight decks. This is definitely not Lacertian. It is something quite different. On the floor to one side, was a Draconian in an advanced state of decomposing. "That is one source of the odour," said Eraton as he pointed to the carcass.

Tanke said, "That is what we sometimes see in the bushes. They eat people."

Eraton pulled her back. "It's not a Lacertian. It must be a Draconian we were told about. This race of lizards supposed to have corrupted the Lacertians. The Lacertians babies were given a drug which turned them into people-eaters. We were always told the Lacertians invented the drug but now I have my suspicions. I am going to make a big guess, that this lizard race developed the drug and were using Lacertians as pawns."

We better get out of here," said Nodin as he scrapped the skin and flesh of the creature and placed it in a sealed bag.

Tanke moved down the deserted corridor with Nodin and Eraton following. She stopped outside one door which was partially opened. She signalled for them to follow. Nodin's and Eraton's mouths dropped. The room contained three dimensional models of seven galaxies.

Nodin held Tanke back. He pointed to Oberon. "That is the old Obereron. The Oberon before the Lacertians destroyed Pleiades, Andromeda, Sirius B and the two fully occupied planets of Elkondite and Salture." He pointed to another galaxy. "Here is the new Oberon - the way we know it." He pointed to Amada and the waste space and named the planets for Tanke. Then he stopped short. "Eraton, these people know of the white galaxy or as the earth people call it, The Milky Way." He then pointed to another galaxy. That is Julos. That's the galaxy where the Lacertians come from. And that," Nodin stopped as concern entered his voice, "Our galaxy, Enockben."

Eraton looked closer. "This room, I think, is a classroom. These are models for children to learn." Eraton looked at the White Galaxy. He pointed to a planet which was unknown. He touched the planet. It lit up with information. Humanoids appeared. Gaunt pale skinned people with almost transparent hair gave way to their anatomy. That was followed by clips of war where captured people were herded. "That looks so familiar" commented Eraton. All grimaced when the clip changed to cooking instructions. There were lessons on how to cut, cook and consume the unknown race. The clip came to an end.

Eraton touched another planet, Daraxon. Aerial views gave way to views of Lacertians. "Okay, how do we pack this up without destroying this information?"

Tanke pointed to the galaxy where they were currently in, Enockben. She pointed to two other planets in the system. "Dad was talking about these two planets over here. There was talk to explore them." She walked around the models again. She whispered, Julos. We have to attack Julos."

Eraton noticed a cord going from one galaxy to a power outlet. "It's a plug-in system. We can pack up one galaxy and take it with us. Let's take Oberon. We have a fair bit of information on that. It will be the experimental one for testing to make it work. Then we come back for the rest. Actually, this is a valuable find. Thanks, Tanke."

Keka had the galaxies systems set up in the conference room. Through trial and error, they managed to make the models to work. Zindel who had been away from the ship for a couple of days, had returned. He invited himself into the conference room. He looked at the models. He pointed to the White galaxy. "This is the White galaxy as you people call it and as you already know, Earth people call it the Milky Way. This planet here is called Lyra. The Draconians have frequently waged war on the Lyrians. That last war was a distraction for what Draconians were really doing - converting Lacertians into meat eaters with drugs. The Lyrians know of Earth and are doing their best to protect it. The Earth people don't know the Lyrian have been defending Earth. Earth needs to be protected at all costs. If Earth falls, then the other human-like planets fall. Alliances between the human races must accelerated."

Keka asked, "Why would the rest of the planets fall if Earth falls?"

Zindel paused for a minute and threw up a hologram showing the Sphinx in in Egypt. Zindel digressed to explain. "Thousands of years ago, the Sphinx was built as a vault. Earth archaeologists have a theory that powerful information about Earth's early history and possible settlement of Earth is locked deep inside. They don't know it, but theory is true. They are unaware that all humanoid races have buried their DNA in specialised chambers and can be activated. The branches of the human race will redevelop and regenerate to spread over the planet and go back into the stars.

"The Earth people have been searching and theorising where the entrance is. The ideas are close, but not close enough. The last world disaster has ensured the entrance to the Sphinx and any tunnel leading to its Hall of Records inside will be very difficult to uncover. Then when they do uncover it, they won't readily see the vaults containing the DNA storage. It may just take another fifty years for the Hall of Records to be uncovered. I hope they never do. The earth people are not developed enough to handle such information. It would cause chaos as many long held religious beliefs would crumble and then social and political chaos would follow: anarchy, riots, murder of political, social and religious leaders. You don't give babies information they cannot handle. Accessing the DNA vaults when they are not ready would be disastrous for all. If it is not done the correct way, the DNA pool would be permanently destroyed. That is why the vaults are hidden very deep and then disguised." Zindel shut down the hologram and directed attention to the current business.

Zindel looked at their surprised faces. "Each of the different groups on Earth had their origins from other human-like planets. There were a series of experiments done thousands of years ago. The Earth had no people. It had only and still does, what is now termed, ape-like creatures." Zindel saw he wasn't connecting with his audience.

He back tracked and became more animated as his pet subject was given deeper revelation to the captive group. "At the start there was very little on Earth in terms of primates. There were other animals like birds, reptiles and assorted other creatures in the oceans. The Pleiadeans were the first to settle Earth then the others followed." Zindel paused to make sure the group was still with him.

"It is obvious to me; you people don't know your own ancient history when it comes to space travel." Zindel saw all before him nod. He sighed. "I will go back to your distant Pleiadean past."

"Your ancestors over 640,000 years ago came to Earth via an accidental find, a wormhole. It was a unique wormhole which transverses through three galaxies. They went through the wormhole which ended at what the earth people called The Taurid Stream. It is the gap between two earth named constellations – Tauris and Gemini. On the other side of Gemini is another gap called the Gemini Stream It will be worthwhile for you to explore that gap in the future. It maybe another wormhole. Who knows? From The Taurid Stream, they hitched on that anomaly, Marduk, a cross between a planet and a meteor. Marduk circled two stars – a red and a yellow. Earth is at the yellow end of the orbit. Marduk brought them close to Jupiter which they used as a slingshot to Mars and then Earth.

"The Mars base was developed by the Siriusian. It serviced all incoming flights from Oberon's main planets. The site was called Cydonia. Remnants still remain today, a fortress-like structure with a face to the sky as identification for the incoming flights and a pyramid which was a beacon to assist flight deck crew to line the crafts up for landing. Mars was in a different location and was lush with plant life and water, but not much in the way of animals and minerals.

"The Pleiadeans, in particular, were seeking minerals for their growing economy and facilitate the friendly space races which were emerging at the time. Earth was largely a frozen planet but over time and with the influence of the planet-like meteor, Marduk, the Earth changed. It moved a few times and with each movement, most of existing life died off, while others flourished. At times Earth was hit by other asteroids which caused mass destruction. Continuous bombardment from asteroids and the strong forces of Tiamat, caused the Earth to split. The bulk remained as you have all seen and the broken off piece, the moon. These changes altered the dominating life forms on Earth. The changes caused by Marduk and major asteroid hits, caused Earth to have four major ice ages and global warming patterns.

"When your ancestors first visited Earth, it was an ice-covered planet, but it did not stop them from extensive aerial exploration. Later, your ancestors frequently visited Earth, took samples and extracted minerals from the ocean and went back home. As Earth warmed up, their stays became longer. They developed great knowledge where the mineral rich pockets were. As mentioned before, their focus was on extraction from the ocean as that was the only form of mineral extraction they knew how to do. The Earth was warming and was becoming more attractive for longer stays.

"Now we jump 450,000 earth years. The Pleiadean settlement like other settlements from other human planets were by private organisations, consortiums or companies. The start of the first major settlements which created a financial boom for most races, saw Earth carved up into different planetary groups. Each company operated independently and very often in jealous guarded seclusion. This carving up and isolationist approach became set in the human psyche, the beginning of racial discrimination, different histories and the birth of different cultures and languages. Because of this, earth people are still struggling with these divisions. Many with foresight, are working hard to breakdown this ingrained mind-set. Progress is slow.

"Let's just stay with the Pleiadean history otherwise you will get very confused." Zindel reached for a glass of water and smirked. "The last of the Earth water, I presume. It's not the water that is causing the problem of a possible baby explosion, but the quality and richness of the food. You can turn on the water supply." Keka gave a sideway look to Dr. Heiten.

"How much food did we bring on?"

"Wheat based flour, freeze dried fruit and vegetables, tree nuts and some edible seeds." Zindel said rather matter-of- a-fact," Hmm, "Not the real trigger but it may make a few biological shifts. Just monitor it. Now back to business."

"The earth was unpopulated with humans. The diverse animal life was not widely distributed across the planet. Each area had its unique animals and plants. It was largely free pickings for each company.

"The first Pleiadean base was guided by Commander and company director, Enlil. From space he designated, what the Earth people called the Middle East, namely the Persian Gulf and sometimes called the Arabian Gulf. It was the only place at that time in the allocated section, which offered the best flat and driest land. It was also close to the existing intermittent main mining operation. Rich oil and peat deposits were abundant. Fuel on tap made it the most desirable of all settlements. The city of Ur was once coastal and was the main mineral extraction centre from the ocean. It became the gateway for Pleiadean space crafts to land.

"Enki was the first person to be in-charge of the first settlement. Enki was the younger brother of Enlil who governed everything from his hovering space station. Enlil rarely came down to Earth. Enki's men, all engineers and construction workers were termed Neflin. Enki and the Neflin lived in tents until more permanent homes were built. They used stone, the most abundant material in the area. It was very rough conditions at the time.

"Over time the base grew and was very successful. The growth demanded another experiment, agriculture. There was a need for the settlement to be more self-sustaining. Some crops from their home planet were introduced in the northern river system, the most favourable place for agriculture at that time.

"The swampy land between the city of Ur and the coastline was reclaimed, by draining, filling and a small levee was built just to be on the safe side. More settlements started to appear. Each had a purpose: spaceport, mineral extraction, agriculture and so on. The settlements were very small, headed or controlled by two or three families which generally were related. Nepotism in the highest degree.

"As time went on, mineral extraction from the ocean became less and less profitable. The company's very old, if not by then ancient, aerial explorations were re-examined. What they knew was minerals were deep underground and getting them was an issue. Most areas were mountainous, very rugged and offered zero aerial landings. Boat and land transport were the only options. The biggest riches were found in East and South Africa, very much to the south of the existing and thriving base of Ur.

"Boat building began while exploration groups located the mineral rich resources. Minerals were pin-pointed and the area cleared for new settlements. Enki knew he didn't have the time to experiment in deep shaft mining. He delegated the task to other senior engineers who were more willing to experiment and develop techniques. Each shaft or mining location was named after the engineer in-charge. We have Nergal, for example was in-charge of the mines in east Africa. These mines south of Ur and were collectively dubbed the lower world. Later it was called the underworld and a dreadful place to be assigned. Many people died in these mines – cave-ins, suffocation from bad air supply, diseases from the environment, for example insect bites, and poor food. The term underworld became synonymous with death. Later these locations dissolved into Earth mythology and each head engineer which the mines were named after, morphed into gods of the underworld.

"Shaft mining took a major toll on male Pleiadean life. The mortality rate came to the attention of both the company's administrators and that of the Pleiadean government. The situation and the social imbalance of significantly more women and children than men, couldn't last forever.

"The government and the administrators brought in geneticist to experiment on the local animal life with the intention the modified animals would work to reduce the work load of men. They gathered assorted animals and spliced one animal's DNA with another. It was a continuous series of failures. Some creatures died very quickly after birth. Other were physically unsuited to do down the shafts. Cruelty to the surviving genetically modified animals was rife.

"Then one female Pleiadean scientist decided to splice her own DNA with assorted other animals. All failed and those that did survive, were horribly abused. They died. She changed tact to focus on apes. Apes were the most abundant animal life near most mines in East and South

Africa. There were many attempts before success. She found the problem in the culture mix. When she added molybdenum, the DNA took hold. The same female scientists volunteered to be the surrogate mother for the gestation period as all gestation cribs were used on other hybrid animals. The result was a mix of ape and human which had muscle and low but trainable intelligence. She called the first-born Adam. Sub-sequentially, all the following babies, which were all male, were called Adam. Copies were made. Women on the ship were used as surrogates.

"Over time, the ape-modified people were being refined by various Pleiadean geneticists. The city of Ur became the epi centre and profited from the sale of hybrids. In other cities around the world these hybrids trained to do menial work in the cities but more importantly be slaves in the mines. Later, all humanoid cultures later copied the technology. The spread of hybrids became the norm. It was a very gradual progress and modification occurred as the need was required – more efficient workers, more of them, more of this and more of that. The hydrides morphed into look-a-likes to the culture they were born into.

"You must remember, the women of this era across all cultures were expected to be surrogates for these creations which were all male and named Adam. Two things happened. The women began to rebel. They were tired of being pregnant and rightfully claimed it was ruining their relationships with their partners. The other trend was, with improvements people became emotionally attached to the Adams. Adams mistook kindness from the women, their gestational mothers, and from others in society, as approval. They became amorous towards all females."

Zindel gave a sigh and looked around the room and noticed the women present were screwing their faces in disgust and shaking their heads. Ashton's arm slipped further around Kora's shoulders as he studied her face. Disgust.

"The women demanded the geneticists design a female to keep the Adams occupied and let their females do the breeding. That is what happened. The Pleiadean geneticists began new experiments. DNA was removed from the ribs of Adams and used to make a female version. More genetic manipulation. But the creation of Eves caused a new set of social problems.

"Quite often the Eves rejected the Adams. Like the Adams, Eves were supposed to be slaves and assist in the breeding of more Adams. The

Neflin who were either single or married were far away from home, and noticed the Eves were good substitutes for their own women. Soon the Eves caught on being with a Neflin and having his children had distinct advantages. Mind you the same was happening with the female Neflin. The Adams looked pretty attractive when their Neflin partners dumped them for the Eves. It brought about another social change, crossbreed children. Some were immortalised in mythology." Zindel tried to lighten the mood. He referred to modern day Earth and the scientists of the day.

"The Earth people have group called creationists. What a lot of dummies they are. Mind you the evolutionists are not much better. The two groups are always debating each other but none have read the sources or listened to the histories of their own or different cultures. Agh! Those who do listen don't really get the significance and the others want to squash it as humbug. The creationists deny or have failed to understand what is written in most religious books, which borrowed the stories from what they call cuneiform, is Akkadian writing. We call it ancient Pleiadean. The evolutionists have tunnel vision and are constantly looking for the missing link between apes and human. Their search is shared with archaeologists and anthropologists. The archaeologists and the anthropologists have also missed the point or dismissed the oral and written traditions. The last three groups haven't understood what was handed to them on a plate in ancient writings. Simply put, you can't find links of that nature when mass genetic manipulation is involved.

"All the failed experiments by the Pleiadean geneticists were incinerated. Some early Adams did escape the clutches of their creators and ran away to distant parts of the planet. They survived. Some were spared when they showed certain superior attributes and slid into mythology, for example, the centaurs. These centaurs were half person and half horse. There were great for cartage of heavy goods but hopeless for down the mines. Only one became famous, Kyron, and was further immortalised by the constellation of Sagittarius." Zindel flipped his hand around before realising he was going off on another tangent.

"An important point. Earth people have seen patterns in the stars which like us, call constellations. The twelve main ones called the zodiac were used as primitive time measures for different eras of both Pleiadean expansion and human modification on Earth. Keep in mind the Earth was being carved up into racial and cultural settlements. Most were explicitly for mining. Much later, others were out-right free settler colonies. Each race and culture took on different areas of the planet. For example, The Siriusians expanded their Mars outpost, called Cydonia to Earth. They called their new Earth settlement Cairo which is Siriusian for Mars. The Siriusian arrived in the time of the dominant constellation of Leo. They built a jumbo statute in now what earth people call Egypt. This Leo massive statue is very important to all humans which came to Earth or were born of genetic modification. The building of the Sphinx as I said before, is a vault housing valuable information. It was also the start of the Siriusian culture being transported to Earth and over centuries gave rise to the Egyptian pharaohs when the Siriusian departed. They never returned after the catastrophe which occurred just over 20,000 earth years ago."

"What happened 20,000 years ago?" asked Keka.

"Our friend Marduk came very close to Earth. The Earth shook but did not tilt. This caused massive landslides and tidal waves in the Pacific Ocean area. This event has slipped into Earth mythology, especially in the countries surrounding the Pacific Ocean. The continent of Lemiur which occupied most of the southern part of the Pacific Ocean slipped under the sea. The demise of Lemiur occurred in three stages. The first stage saw people make an exodus to the east and west: South America and Australia. Five thousand years on, Marduk caused havoc again. A second reshaping of Earth. All land bridges were destroyed in all directions across the Pacific Ocean and to towards the Indian Ocean. Thirty per cent more of Lemiur disappeared under the sea. The only remains were the highest of mountain peaks which are now the islands of the South Pacific. Parts of the land mass between the Americas and Europe also slipped under the ocean. A partial loss of the continent of Atlantis. This created tidal waves and mass flooding. But more importantly, the land bridges between the Americas and Europe and in the southern hemisphere disappeared forever.

"In the past, people were able to use small boats or rafts to island hop cross the islands to go from one continent to the next. Another important event occurred at the end in this era - about 12,000 to 13,000 years ago. It was the last known recording of Marduk. First event was the Earth stopped rotating for ten days. Then it spun in the opposite direction. The Earth still continues to spin in this direction today. Then as Marduk nearly collided with Earth, the final and major event occurred.

That was the most catastrophic of all. This is where Earth's history takes significant multiple turns.

"All space settlers and workers from all space cultures were ordered back to the circling or hovering spaceships. They all had directives that they must leave their Eves or Adams and their children behind. Many were extremely upset. The commanders saw some people resist the order and gave warning to all, they would not be responsible for those who choose to stay and ignore the directive. The commanders and the company administrative and heads of government had no real choice. Space was limited and the mass evacuation stretched resources well beyond the limits.

"However, the unfolding catastrophe was greater than predicted. The world's population was all but totally abolished. Global devastation was complete. The Siriusian retreated to Cydonia on Mars. But that was later also came under attack by Marduk. The Genobolians, the Nubians, The Andromedans and many others, retreated to their home planets and never returned. However, the massive outcry by the Pleiadeans and the Lyrians saw them return to Earth with a vow never to desert Earth ever again. They vowed to rebuild and society and ensure the Adams and the Eves would thrive under their own resources and ingenuity. They were going to be tutored by volunteer Neflin, many of whom now regarded Earth as their home."

"Exactly what happened?" asked Dr. Haiten who was totally enthralled by the revelations.

"Three major things occurred at the same time – Marduk, a major volcanic explosion assisted by Marduk's appearance and a big solar windstorm that entered the Earths temporary unprotected atmosphere.

"The south pole was and still covered in a massive ice sheet. The ice sheet was so much larger than it is today. Thousands of square kilometres, nearly the size of existing Australia, broke off and slipped under the ocean. The melting ice and the massive displacement of water caused massive tidal waves to rush across the now Indian, Pacific and Atlantic oceans. The cause of the collapse was the reactivation of the large volcano quietly simmering away under the ice sheet. Marduk came close enough to cause a disturbance and the building pressure had to go somewhere. Dirt, volcanic ash, rocks and stones filled the sky. Dark dirt clouds blocked out the sun. The winds stirred up by Marduk and the heat from the volcano, depleted the Earth's atmosphere and exposed it the solar winds. The events combined compounded the disaster. The warming encouraged by the solar winds travelled north soaking up ocean water as it went. At the same time, the remains of the continent of Atlantis, subsided into the now Atlantic Ocean. You can find the last traces of Atlantis on the southern-most tip of southern Spain, just outside what the ancients called the Pillars of Hercules or modern Gibraltar.

"The new land slide, more volcanic eruptions filling the sky, and the rain bearing clouds from the south quickly filled the sky turning day into night. The night became a frightening disorienting darkness. The rain bearing clouds and the growing tidal waves caused by erupting underwater volcanoes coming from the south just took one week to traverse the planet. It rained across the northern hemisphere in a manner no one has ever witnessed before, and never again since. The continents were drowned and battered by strong winds. The forces on the tidal waves ground to dust what the volcanoes didn't burn to ashes. All spaceports in all countries and all forms of civilization, vanished. The sand on the Atlantic Ocean was dumped on across west Africa to Egypt, burying many the great Siriusian structures of the past, except the statue of Leo – the Sphinx, and converting the land to a desert.

"At the same time, the inland area of China and in the highlands of central America, saw the sun stay above the sky and with the solar winds scorch the lands to drying all rivers and evaporate all snow and destroy the crops. People in all areas suffered. For a few days the Earth did not rotate and when it started, it was observed by the few survivors, the Earth spun in the opposite direction, but not before the polarity of the earth flipped.

"As for the Pleiadean settlement, rivers changed direction rendering the land drier and the past draining of the land saw mountains of sand dumped over the land creating a desert. Ur and many other towns built by the Pleiadean were now demolished and now appeared far inland. There was nothing that looked like any form of civilization across any part of the planet. But there were survivors who passed on the events orally. The creation of what was deemed mythology. The same mythology was across the entire planet – just different names for the gods of old but in essence, exactly the same story." Zindle sighed. "All that history has been ignored by Earth people. The connections weren't made and dismissed as mythology. Sad."

"When the Pleiadeans and the Lyrians returned, they began to rebuild society in a vastly different way. Many survivors on different continents were left to their own resources and built their own societies in their unique ways. Due to the trauma of the planetary changes, each jealously guarded their territory and their culture.

"Now, we just focus on the changes in the Persian Gulf area. The greatest of humanitarian rebuilding efforts were undertaken by any space culture. New buildings were made of rocks, the most abundant material left after the devastation. The Neflin taught the crossbreeds and the surviving Adams and Eves, astronomy, agriculture, accounting, limited engineering and government took place. Other cultures which were isolated and knew they were abandoned drew on their memories of the past and began to recreate them with their own unique cultural stamp.

"Remember, the Adams and the Eves along with the cross-bred people were like children, so anything in the sciences, notably, astronomy, had to be in a format they could understand. Underlying complexities like chemistry and physics, were not taught. Their brains were just not ready. Everyday things like reading and basic maths which included measurement of time, distances and weights was all that mattered. Just basic essential stuff was challenging enough for both sides - for the students to learn and for the Neflin to teach. The most proficient were taught to be teachers. Other chosen ones were trained to be emissaries between them and the Neflin-cum-Gods. The chosen ones later morphed into kings, queens, and other assorted rulers and the position was deemed hereditary. Sounds familiar?" Zindel reached for a glass of water and nibbled on some snack which had come into the room as he spoke.

"Now we get to some of the fun bits which have shaped Earth's social, moral, spiritual, political, religious, economic and technological development. Some earth people are trying to shake away these old structures and want to move towards the same structures as we now enjoy. It has been difficult. Some have been readily embraced the ideals. Others who are so steeped in past traditions and the old psyche have resisted. It is too embedded.

"Here is a classic example of the dichotomy which exists. In most of their religious books, it clearly says, 'In the beginning there was darkness. God said, let there be Light.' Look at this in detail. As we said, the children of the Neflin and the Adams and the Eves, were not ready to understand advanced physics and the concept of dark matter. The darkness refers to dark matter. There is no light in dark matter. It was sufficed at the time, there was darkness, meaning nighttime. It was something they could relate to.

""Then there was light.' The earth scientists developed the big bang theory, and they are finding more and more evidence. The traditionalists don't want to hear of it."

Eldon stopped Zindel. S "That's really dumb. You can't create light without making a spark and that is always accompanied by some kind of sound, no matter how small the spark. The sound can be below normal hearing range with specialised equipment."

Zindel clapped his hands in delight, "Colliding and splitting hydrogen and/or helium atoms in dark matter make a spark. BANG!" Zindel clapped his hands again as loud as he could. "At the time when earth people were given this information, they were like toddlers. Concepts in chemistry and dark matter was too much for them to absorb. The Pleiadeans and the rest of the space settlers kept it simple: God created light. This was reinforced by battery or generated powered lights in the buildings used by the Pleiadeans and Lyrians. To the emerging earth races, it was only the Gods who made light. That is what they could understand at that point in time.

"Unfortunately, it became too imbedded into the earth people's psyche. But there are moves of general acceptance of the accuracy of the big bang theory, except for the hardcore creationists." Zindel acknowledged Kora who was trying to ask a question, "I must be missing a point. Gods? Just who were they?" Zindle waved his arm around the group. Primitive human believed we were the gods because of our clothes, technology which included weapons and methods of doing things. The primitive man was smart enough to observe and try to emulate the so-called gods but often failed due to the lack of equipment or whatever they failed to see or lack of techniques. They had to be shown but all were not intellectually bright. The brighter ones or those who showed the most potential were taught to read and do maths. Basically, some administrative stuff like counting bags of harvested crops. So, let's go back to some simplicity which still rages today in the minds of many Earth humans." Ashton nodded and thought, *this must be what is in the documents Jenny refused to publish. She was smart enough, to avoid a meltdown of long held beliefs.*

When Zindel saw the cogs starting to turn in his captive audience, he asked, "Are we going to try to stop those Draconians devouring humans across space?"

He looked at Ashton who asked, "Can I opt out if I find the situation not workable?"

"Many do drop out. You won't be the first and you won't be the last. To train on Earth, will be an experiment in itself. It has never been done before. You seem to handle Earth people in a very unique way."

"Zindel, your explanation cleared up the mental puzzles I was experiencing on Earth. It makes sense and if I am right, the Earth people are a mix which the Pleiadeans had a big hand in shifting them forward in time. But I am puzzled by a couple of aspects. The speed of technological growth on Earth is outstripping their ability to be socially and morally responsible to handle. Many ways they are like young teenagers left to handle adult technology. Is there an explanation for this lop-sided development?"

Zindel nodded. "That is the role of the guardians. Rebalance the lop-sidedness, accelerate the progress of unification and look after the planet. They are all connected. Above all, ensure the planet is ready should the Draconians discover Earth."

Dr. Haiten tried to change the subject and asked, "Just what planet or organisation are you from?" Zindel pondered how he would answer that question. "This universe is broken into twenty-five sectors. Sector twenty is the White Galaxy or as the Earth people call it, the Milky Way, the waste space, Oberon and Amada. This sector is designated for human or humanoids. Sector nineteen is designated for other humanoid creatures on the outside but quite different on the inside. They were wiped out by Draconians. They have invaded sector eighteen and have all but wiped out the gentle Mammalians on this planet, Beta Cancari, and the other two you have in this model. There are four more planets in this sector which the Draconians have not found. Now they are invading sector seventeen. This where Segmar and Xion are located. They have been very hard to defeat. It is a planet at a time.

"The planet I am from, hmm, let's put it this way…. no planet and every planet. I am from the dawn of time. The people I serve are like ghosts or spirits. Their task is to hold together this universe. If the universe goes, they go. They are pure energy. Energy which thinks and creates. To lesser developed people, supreme Gods."

Kora asked, "Then why did they create Draconians."

"They didn't." replied Zindel.

"There is another universe, a parallel universe. The Draconians were a part of that. Somehow, they crossed over, breached the boundary. The closest sector to that breach is sector nineteen. The planets of Lacertra and Turbia are in sector nineteen. That is where we have always tried to focus Draconian containment. But they keep breaching boundaries like getting into sector eighteen and twenty. My organisation? No, its's not an organisation or an army in the traditional sense. Maybe best described as emissaries: report, assist, advice, recruit for the Lords of the Universe and the planets they control within. I just happen to be in charge of sectors twenty to fifteen. With the growing disturbances, I need assistance.

"So, you have set your eyes on Ashton for that position," said Keka.

"Yes. He has the potential. He already has some degree of mind control ability. I was watching your little 'experiment.' Commendable but really, you were just returning to a planet or colony of your own making thousands of years ago. Ashton's antics were quite amusing. However, they do need honing and development."

Garyth thought about what Zindel was saying over the last hour, "Just how old are you?" Zindel was stumped. "I actually have no idea. That's a good question. No one has asked me that before." He went quiet. After few minutes, "From the dawn of time, I think. I am matter. I am energy. I am humanoid. I am everyone and no one. I am spirit in the presence of the Lords of the Universe…… I must look it up".

Ashton asked, "You mean, if I complete my training, I become immortal?"

"Not quite. Self- preservation would be a priority. You would slow down your aging process. Zindel looked Ashton up and down, "You could very much outlive your Earth-bound Kora and child."

There was a knock on the door Tanke, Milway and Wibut walked in. "Sorry to disturb this meeting, but the younger children are crying to go home. I know it is safe here and the, Draconians will be outside our home caves. I can't take them back. I need some help to settle them. Kora and Dr. Haiten left the room and followed Tanke and the others back to the mess hall. The mess hall was now screened off to make temporary accommodation. Nearly every child was either crying or sobbing. Kora asked, "Are they like this every evening?"

"No. This is a strange place for them."

Dr. Haiten walked between the rows of mattresses spread out on the floor. He bent down to speak to the smaller children. Kora did the same. Some settled and fell to sleep, others calmed down. Tanke and the other two were the last to go to their allocated mattresses. Kora asked softly, "What time do they get up?"

"Dawn" replied Tanke. Keka who crept in behind the others, gave Dr. Haiten a sideway look, "We better tell the staff we have early risers. Tomorrow, we search for more cribs and people. God knows where we will put everything. We need to search the other caves for more survivors. There has to be more."

Ashton knocked on Keka's office door. Keka looked up from the reports he was reading. He removed his reading glasses as he indicated for Ashton to sit. "You look concerned. What is it?"

"When my father was alive, he made sure I knew of a tunnel under the administration building. This was an additional tunnel to the regular evacuation tunnel." Keka frowned as he leaned towards Ashton. The Jalon side of Keka's memory kicked in. "Yes, I know of the tunnel."

"Will you come with me and retrieve the original settlement document?" There may be other things hidden in there since we were away. Everything needs to be retrieved before we start searching for a new home. We don't have the resources or personnel to fight these Draconians."

Keka looked at Ashton with an air of seriousness. "We have to get into the entire cave system to see exactly how many survivors there are and the condition of the cribs." We can't access any of the areas from that direction and Tanke did say they were cut off from the rest."

"Sir, the second tunnel under the administration building leads to the library. There is a second exit from under the library to the caves. I was made to learn them through my childhood. It was a precaution."

Keka thought of a strategy. "We can convert a four-seater pod. I will make sure the pod is bubbled to reduce radiation contamination. A decontamination port will need to set up outside. We leave tomorrow morning at five. I think we will ask Ichiro to accompany us. Neo will be in charge of the ship's security."

"Thank you, sir" said Ashton as he stood up.

CHAPTER NINETEEN
Beta Cancari's Cave System

Keka sat in the driver's side of the pod with Ashton beside him. Ichiro was in the back. They were dressed in their suits which doubled their physical size. The pod went slowly south before going over the mountains. The wrecked city came into sight. Keka guided the pod as close as possible to the largely destroyed administration building. When they left the pod, their guns were at the ready. They slowly moved through the rubble, picked their way to what was once the front door. The door was open, but the rubble blocked most of the entrance. They tossed bits of bricks and wire away to make the entrance bigger. When they climbed through, they lit their headlamps.

They walked to the lift and tried pushing the button. No power. They moved to the narrow staircase located in the far corner. The door was jammed. Ichiro cursed. "If it wasn't for the radiation, we could take our head gear off and use those glasses." Ashton smiled at the thought. "Is there something around or in the pod which could lever this?" Keka searched the room and smashed the extinguisher case. He dragged it over to the door. "Try this," he puffed." Ichiro took the extinguisher and slammed it at the critical hinge points. The door held fast. "Stand back," said Ashton. He took out his laser gun and fired. The heat weakened the door hinges. Ichiro slammed the extinguisher against the door. The door slowly creaked under protest. Ichiro gave it another hit. The door slammed inwards to make a ramp over the top ten steps.

Slowly they moved down. The door to the basement was closed. Again, they forced the door open. They stood there silent after entering the room. Their eyes scanning the contents inside. It was the first time Keka and Ichiro had entered this underground chamber. There was an entire defence control system. A mini version of what was above ground and totally buried under the crashed spaceship. Keka examined the panels. "Someone fired missiles from this spot." He pointed to the only control panel. He turned off the flashing buttons which obviously showed waiting missiles were ready for launching. "This entire unit will be taken to the ship. The missiles included. Do you know where the missiles are?"

Ashton shook his head. "I am going to guess – near the control tower."

Keka raised an eyebrow. "That is like a pancake under the ship. The missiles would have exploded."

Ashton led them to the opposite side of the room. Decorating this side of the room was a large panel. Against the panel was glass encased plaques and wall hangings from old Pleiades. The precious artwork concealed for prosperity. Ashton opened the cabinet and turned one artefact. The door opened to reveal another passageway. It was the pathway Ashton knew which would lead to the library.

"Over here!" called Ashton called to the others but it was Ichiro entered first. He didn't take more than a few steps. He hurried back pushing Ashton and Keka back and closing the door behind him. Ichiro held Ashton and slowly shook his head as he looked at Keka. Keka opened the door. President Findlee's advanced decaying body laid in the passageway. The evidence of radiation burns was almost undetectable in the decomposition mix. "No Ashton. Don't look. Ichiro, bring the dust covers for the equipment over." Ichiro and Keka wrapped Findlee's body up and placed it in the room which they were in. Keka held Ashton by the shoulder. "It's not pretty. I don't think it is a good idea to plant this memory of your father in your head."

Ashton drew in a breath. "It still needs to be done, a formal I.D. Just the head will do." Keka let go of Ashton as he nodded. "You're right. But before you do, you may want to bring up the vomit bag first." Ashton pushed an exterior button. A small bag covered his mouth. Ashton looked and bust out crying. It felt like someone punched him very hard in the stomach. He staggered back and went pale. Ichiro caught him before he hit the ground. While they left Ashton alone for a few minutes, Keka organised two retrieval teams: one for the equipment and one to remove Findlee's body for a proper burial.

Ichiro asked Ashton, "Are you right to continue?"

Ashton sobbed, and forgetting he was wearing a suit, tried to wipe his face. He nodded. "Yeah. More determined than ever."

He deflated the vomit bag, stood up and headed for the door to the tunnel.

Ashton guided the others for close to ten minutes before the tunnel opened to another but smaller chamber. They were under the library. He pointed to a glass box. "The original declaration of this colony. We take it with…." He stopped talking. "Keka-cum-Jalon. Do you know what this is?" Keka allowed the Jalon side over. "Absolutely no idea. It is obviously a new addition. It wouldn't be here unless it was important. Open it up and let's all have a look."

Ashton opened the case. A holographic image formed of the planets of Segmar and Xion. Then there were holographic navigational directions. Andromedans and Siriusans had found Beta Cancari. Ashton swallowed hard trying to recall what his father said years ago when he was a teenager concerning anything additional in this glass box.

"We have to go back to his office. He has copies of this spread around the room."

Keka raised an eyebrow at the revelation. "Why? I thought there would be only one copy of the declaration on display in the library. Nothing else stored anywhere. Where is the library from here?" "We are under it." pointed Ashton upwards. "We are directly under the copy on display above. But there is a copy in dad's office as well. He would do the same for anything else retrieved from here. He made sure there were copies and decoys. We can go to his office that is if it is still standing, on another trip. And we also collect the copy above our heads that is if it is not destroyed." Ashton stuffed the valuable finds into two separate bags then stuffed them into another bag. Each time item was securely doubled sealed.

Keka ordered we collect the copy upstairs now. They walked through a short tunnel and up a set of steps. The door to the main display area was ajar and refused to budge. Rubble had to be moved to free it. The library was all but demolished. Some pillars were in pristine condition while other were angled or non-existent. Rubble mixed with damaged equipment had crashed to the floor creating a difficult path to the main display.

The copy of the declaration was intact but its protective glass and pedestal upon which it rested were severely damaged. Ichiro picked up a piece of rubble and tapped the cracked glass and slid the shards away with a piece of scrap metal which was lying close by. He removed the copy. Then he noticed a second item which he and the other assumed was a copy of the information to Xion and Segmar. Like Ashton, he placed the items in a double sealed bag.

Keka looked around. "I thought you said there was another exit. I don't see any."

"We go back to the basement," said Ashton. He led the way back down again. He walked to another spot in the room. He placed a picture of himself on a panel. A door opened. He ushered the others in. "This takes us towards the control tower. Let's just hope the passages are not blocked with rubble. It's about a kilometre walk."

Ashton led the way. They were close just twenty metres from the entrance and stopped. The tunnel had collapsed. There was far too much rubble to shift. "We go back to the administration building. I think we will search dad's office before we go to the caves. We leave the cave for later."

Going into Findlee's office was slow. One rubble obstacle pile after another had to be moved. When they reached the door, the door opened but under protest. Ashton stared at the room. Half was almost in pristine condition and the other half was in a disarray.

In Findlee's office, Ashton searched high and low in in every corner, triggering false bottoms to draws revealed a copy of the settlement declaration. Findlee had placed three sections in different locations. Ashton had retrieved the lot. The search for the new documents revealing Segmar and Xion took much longer. He found sections of the hologram showing Kyrina and the joint Andromedan and Siriusian landing. A match to the beacon. The maps were more difficult to locate. Ashton sat in his father's chair trying to think like his father. *Where did you hide that map, dad?* He thought to himself. He stared at everything in front of him. He swung the chair around to the back of the room. He stared and concentrated hard. A smile broke across his face. "*Yes. Very clever Dad.*" He reached for the damaged enlarged to A3 photo of himself and his father. It was one of the very few fishing trips they went on. Ashton took down the enlarge photo and pulled apart the surrounding frame.

Hidden inside was a miniature data storage unit, no larger than a needle head with a mini spike. It looked very much like the rest of the nails holding the picture together. To an untrained eye, it was a nail. He gave the data pin a test on the phone he was carrying. *Yes!* To the others he called out, "Let's go. I have found everything. Back to the ship." Ashton reassembled the picture frame and stuffed it into another bag.

The next morning, the pod returned close to where the control tower was previously standing. Ashton landed the pod on top of the Draconian ship. They all got out. They stood silently as Ashton slowly rotated. Ashton pointed, "That's the spot. The ship is sitting right on top of the entrance. He cursed. Keka said, "We've struck a dead-end."

Ichiro pointed in another direction. "No, we haven't. The crash has torn off a part of a tunnel. We go that way. We need to levitate."

Ichiro led the way to the exposed opening. Ashton took a few seconds to get his bearings. "This way." He led them downhill in this tunnel until it levelled out. Two chambers were before him. "We go right from here." After a few minutes they came across another chamber. All people inside were dead. The odour and the sight shocked them all. They did a head count – one hundred and sixty-one dead men, women and children. With heavy hearts they went into another chamber marked gestation chamber two. They looked around. All the babies were dead, all two hundred of them. The trio examined the special formula. It was contaminated with radiation. They did a quick search before leaving for the next chamber.

The results in section were the same. Men, women and children all dead. The gestation cribs with dead babies lined the walls. They moved on. Ashton made a note: chambers one and two were lost. They left that chamber and moved to the next. When Ichiro shut that door he said, "Someone placed a radiation warning on the door. Someone must still be alive." Keka and Ashton turned to look at the closed door. "Let's hope we find them," said Keka whose eyes were welling up.

The next chamber, chamber four, showed more promise. It was deeper into the cave system. Critically ill and starving people groaned on their beds. Ten people which looked like animated skeletons feebly smiled. Keka immediately contacted the ship and ordered an emergency evacuation in chamber four. Keka and Ashton examined the cribs. The food was all but gone. The babies were also placed on a ration. Their small hearts were weak.

A young lady who could barely talk, caught Ashton's eye. She pointed to a box. "Take that to the ship. Important things." Ashton went to where she pointed. It was another copy of information to Segmar and Xion. He jammed it into his fresh sack. "Do you know of any manuals for baby formula and maintenance?" The lady nodded and pointed to a worktable not far from where she was lying. Ashton stuffed the book into another bag. Ashton spoke gently, "Are there any more caves with people hiding in them." The lady gave a sigh and struggled to speak, "Cave five and six. The rest are gone." She licked her dry lips. She didn't speak any more. Her heart continued to beat ever so slowly. The trio waited until the rescue team arrived. In that time, they had placed the weakened survivors near the entrance of chamber four ready for a hasty exit. They moved on.

The next chamber was bare of cribs and people. They searched the room. Nothing. Ichiro turned on the CCT. He called to Keka and nudged Ashton. He pointed. Draconians had stripped the chamber: most furnishings and all people. He wondered why they didn't take the CCT. Keka pushed another button on the CCT box. He heard an eerie message. A Draconian prodded a distressed lady to speak. "They know of the cave system. They are taking chamber by chamber when they want to top up their supplies. They will be coming back for more. This is the first chamber they have cleaned out." Static.

Keka looked worried, "We better get moving. Fast."

Chambers five and six saw the rescue of thirty more people who looked slightly healthier. Only half the babies were alive in each chamber. One surviving teenage boy looked at Keka with apologetic eyes. "Sir, were out of food for so long were turned off half the cribs and rationed the baby formula between ourselves and the remaining babies. Just half a cup a day. That is all we consumed for the last three months. Sorry. So sorry." The boy was expecting a reprimand and under normal Pleiadean circumstances, the group would have been prosecuted for murder. Instead, Keka gave the boy a hug and whispered. "You all did what was necessary to keep many alive as possible. That is commendable. No punishment needed. The burden of guilt you all have been carrying, is enough. You're safe now. The rescue teams will be here soon."

On board the Explorer, Keka was concerned. The ship was seriously overcrowded. Five hundred gestation cribs occupied the lounges, the entertainment room, and lining some passageways. The bottom accommodation floors were now jammed three to a room with survivors. The original occupants were now jammed two to a room. All the children and teenagers occupied most of the mess hall. Meals were in inconvenient shifts. The missile firing panels were occupying the flight deck but only three missiles were found. Food and general supplies played on Keka's mind. Keka called Tanke to his office. "You mentioned your small group were making a catalogue of plants which were edible." Tanke nodded. "Can you show me which plants were safe to eat. We will need to harvest them to feed the extra population."

"Sir, it is dangerous to collect them. The Draconians make it dangerous."

"We will go to another location, hopefully a safe location. We need to get more water as well. Can you show us what these safe plants look like?" Tanke nodded again.

The ship slowly lifted from its location. This time Tanke was on the flight deck to observe the foliage below. She gasped when she saw a plain of the safe plants. "Down here! Down here!" she called out smiling with excitement. Neo, Keka and Haiten looked at the crop below. "Something is wrong." said Neo. "It is too organised. Too perfect. It has been planted by some life form. We don't go down but hover and observe what happens."

It was late afternoon when the sonar started to blip. Small statured humans came out of underground burrows. More came out of caves nearby. They tended to the fields. All on the flight deck noticed only half were working the crops while others stood guard. Something triggered an alarm. All scurried back to their hiding places. Draconians marched across the field. They stopped at the evidence of cut crops dumped on the ground. The Draconians spread out searching for any tell-tale sign. One Draconian called the others and pointed to markings on the ground. Keka ordered, "Fire on them. Blast them to pieces."

The limited Pleiadean guns fired on the Draconians. Some tried to escape but were mowed down. All the Draconians they could see were dead. Keka commented, "More will come. But let's scoop up some plants. Take a few whole so we can grow them in the nursery." The ship swooped down and hovered as tubes were dropped from the base. A small group of people, including Tanke, slid down the protective tubes, gathered some plants and other that were harvested. They were packing up their small haul when a small human armed with an arrow approached." Tanke pulled on Garyth's sleeve, "Company." She nodded to towards the small man. "Get inside. Now!" said Garyth.

While still in the tube, Garyth offered the small person a bunch of plants. Then he pointed to the downed Draconians. The small man looked to where Garyth was pointing. The man stared and looked back at Garyth. The man called out. Soon he was joined by others of his group. Garyth thought, *please just go. No time for diplomacy crap.* Cautiously the men circled Garyth. The tube sucked Garyth up at the same time more Draconians entered the scene. The ship fired on the Draconians. Again, all were dead.

The flight deck crew saw the small humans scatter for their lives. The Explorer's shields came down. More Draconians came by air. The Explorer fired small missiles at the assorted two men and four men Draconian pods. More Draconians came by air and land. The Explorer had to resort to the last three missiles taken from the settlement. All three missiles hit their targets but not before The Explorer was rocked by the Draconian weaponry. The ground Draconians fired at The Explorer only to have their shots deflect in random directions. The battle was over in one hour. The Explorer flew at full speed into space leaving the small humans to their own resources.

Keka said as he tried to relax in his command chair. "That was close. Much too close. Those mini humans what were they?"

No one answered but a soft voice which sounded like Zindel's entered his head. "Mammalians." Keka closed his eyes and absorbed the information streaming directly into his mind. When it was over, he gave a new command.

Keka looked at the new maps to Segmar and Xion. He gave directions to Gibba. "We are going to Xion, the closest planet." Gibba studied the three-dimensional map. "Didn't Zindel say the Draconians are heading that way?"

Keka also studied the route. "We don't have too much choice. We have to make contact. We have to help each other. No doubt, we are on the Draconian elimination list. That battle on Beta Centari would make the Draconian and Lacertian alarm bells sound across the galaxies. We cannot return to Beta Cancari. I just hope the Mammalians are not punished for our actions."

"If I were a Draconian, it wouldn't make sense to wipe out one food sources," said Gibba. "But then again, we don't know how the Draconian brain works."

Keka studied the route to Xion. His mind was ticking tactical scenarios. "Go to Segmar," he ordered.

CHAPTER TWENTY
The Explorer

Kora sat on the edge of her bed she now permanently shared with Ashton. She felt ill - her face green. She rubbed her slowly expanding stomach. She nudged Ashton. When he turned, he saw her green complexion. He jumped out of bed and shoved a bowl under her face. She pushed it away but then grabbed it and promptly threw up. "I want to die," she groaned as she tried wiping the remnants of vomit around her mouth. Ashton gave her a glass of water which she used to wash the taste out and spat into the same bowl. Ashton emptied the bowl down the toilet. Through the wall he said in a loud voice, "This is really becoming a habit; you throwing up in the morning. What does Dr. Haiten say about it?"

"He says he thinks it normal," she replied as she looked at Ashton as her colour was slowly changing back to normal. He says he is out of his depth. Earth people are best for this condition. They know what they are doing."

"Do you think we can summon up Zindel to help?"

"Do you know where he is," Kora asked.

"He disappeared. He didn't say where he was going or when he was coming back."

"Then, how do you expect to send him messages for any form of help?"

Ashton shrugged. "The man has his own agenda. Do you want me to try and use my very limited mind control skills?"

Kora threw a pillow at him. "Very funny. That ancient relic is like a freezer when it comes to compassion. Don't you become like him."

Ashton sat down beside her and stroked her back. "I don't want to leave you, certainly not like this" He rubbed her stomach. "It's a bit of a standard joke on the ship now."

"What is?"

"Earth water. Earth food," he replied.

"Oh."

"Don't sound disappointed. On this ship we are celebrities. Did you know people are making bets on whether it's a boy or a girl?"

Kora shook her head and scoffed. "That's what happens when gaming machines are closed off. We have become the entertainment. Next, they will dream up how many mornings a week I throw up. Zindel did say my tummy was going to grow. I am going to have a big problem." Ashton looked at her but only frowned.

"Clothes. My everyday clothes are starting to feel like restrains. I feel constantly bloated."

"Well, we have two options. We visit the people who made up our Earth clothes or you stay here and be naked until its birth time."

Kora gave him a look of death as she stood up. "Let's go and get me measured up."

Neo called a meeting for the security group. Kora sat beside Ashton who had a protective arm around her shoulder. Eldon whispered, "Are you okay? I mean up to this meeting?"

Kora nodded. "It's a distraction. A nice distraction."

Neo looked at the group before him. "We have heard from Zindel. We are diverting to Segmar." There were murmurs around the table. "Both Lacertian and Draconian ships are too close. We could unintentionally lead them to Xion. Be prepared for battle. I am led to believe the Draconians are very different. Very aggressive. Very intelligent. Kora if the call out for battle is announced, you are not going." He held up a hand to stop her speaking. "Your roll will be to make sure all the gestation cribs are secure and assist Dr. Haiten in any manner he wishes.

If you get caught by the Draconians, you will be," Neo stopped for a few seconds and tried to search for the right word but couldn't, "auctioned off. They will see you as some kind of breeding stock. May I suggest after this meeting, you visit Dr. Haiten and start learning new skills. You will not be locked out of any planning meeting we have." Kora nodded as she placed her hand on Ashton's knee and gave a gentle squeeze. "The rest of you, it's down to the gym for practice and training. Meeting closed."

Kora met Ashton back in their room hours later. "How did training go?" asked Kora.

"We are all going to use the earth Equipment again: shoes, glasses but with our more protective uniforms. We did a big session using that stuff." The others on board are going to learn how to use them as well. It looks like most of the crew is going to be fitted out and train to use them. How did your session with Haiten go?"

"Not bad except he was like, as earth people put it, a mother hen. So far it was just measuring out and distributing medicine to those who are still recovering from the caves. It was nice to see some get up and walk. I tell you what, that Tanke girl is a natural. Her two closest friends, Wilbut and Milway are great kids. There is a great future for those three. Tanke kind of shines. There is something fantastic about that girl."

"Does she have essence? Like the essence that Alcyn was supposed to possess?"

"I don't know. Only those who knew Alcyn would know. We both know where they are." Both chorused, "Earth."

"Let's go to the library. Do you recall I brought books back about Earth animals?"

"I have this really crazy idea. I want to show you something. Any way it will pass our time. The crazy idea could make you laugh, if nothing else."

Kora flipped through the pages of a small sample of books Ashton had bought back. Ashton was going through the animal books page by page searching for the information he wanted. Kora stopped at a page. "Hey Ashton. Look at this. Here is a tiny bit about pregnancy." He stopped looking through the pages. He leaned over to her book. He studied the pictures and assisted Kora with the reading. "Okay, this is what we are in for. You better show Haiten that scrap of information. There is next to nothing in our medical library. Eight hundred years is a very long time since the last natural conception. It has kind of dropped out of medical practice."

"Did you find what you are looking for?"

"No. but I did get a few ideas."

"Such as?"

He flipped to the page with lizards. Kora recoiled. These are earth lizards. Generally small creatures which just eat, excrete and mate. There are a few bigger ones like goanna and monitors." The bigger ones tend to be very territorial and somewhat fearless. What a pity we don't have any here. I would like to see if either Lacertians or Draconians do with these creatures. There is nothing intelligent in their brains but survival. What I was looking for are pictures of crocodiles and alligators. They are just eating machines. They eat anything. I would like to see these creatures let loose on one of their ships and see what mayhem they create." He chuckled. "I bet they will view these as cute and have them for pests but not realising they grow very big and get very aggressive."

Kora asked, "How big?"

"Well it won't be practical to have a big one on board. As a rule, the older they get, the bigger they get but seem to stop about five to six metres. Their jaws would snap a leg off in seconds." Kora cringed. "What's the point you are making?"

"We return to Earth. You stay there and get the right medical attention for starters. I want you to be safe. We unload the rescued people and the cribs. We load up on everything else, but we get some of these creatures and poisons from heaps of other creatures like snakes, spiders, and frogs. We go biological. Earth has mastered biological warfare when we never even dreamed of it." "Keka won't agree to any of this," said Kora.

"We will have to get him to change his mind. Oops! Bad pun. We can appeal to the Jalon side of his brain."

Hours later Keka agreed to Ashton's plan. He made the announcement. Neo called another meeting. " We will first go to Segmar and meet the people there and start planning joint operations and then it will be back to Earth. We are going back to Daraxon Technologies on Earth to unload and stock up. We may need to negotiate with Earth people for certain supplies. More orders will be given when we approach Earth."

CHAPTER TWENTY-ONE
Segmar

On Segmar, the alarms sounded. Loudspeakers blared out danger of immediate attack, not a drill. The sirens and the announcements alternated for ten minutes. The power sources to homes were shut down. Only the separate power units to municipal buildings, lifts and to the underground shelters were left on. People walked quickly to their designated locations, checked in and made themselves as comfortable as possible. They whispered between themselves in a bid to glean more information. Every so often a televised announcement broke the television entertainment to give updates. This created more whispers.

After an hour, the back wall to the long narrow shelters opened to reveal a conveyor belt of food and water. As the conveyor moved through the complex, people took their rations. Thirty minutes later another the conveyor belt started. People paced their scraps, plates, cutlery and drink containers back on the belt to be removed for cleaning.

Above ground, some of the governors, some of the military leaders with their armed personnel and the president prepared for a possible invasion.

The Explorer sent out an old Pleiadean signature and began the sequence of identification. Keka and those on board The Explorer, hoped the sequences of identification hadn't been lost or forgotten. The people on the Explorer waited patiently for a response. It took thirty minutes for verification to be acknowledged. The communication systems between Segmar and The Explorer opened.

Keka introduced himself and the crew. The president of Segmar, President Inkanta, reciprocated. The conversations went for twenty minutes before permission was granted to allow The Explorer to land.

The Explorer landed just outside the city's boundary. A small delegation of ministers and military personnel escorted Keka and Neo to the administration building. President Inkanta met Keka and Neo in his office. More discussions occurred: an exchange of the separated history development on their respective planets, their attacks in Oberon and Amada in a bid to reclaim their territories and the losses of people to a common enemy. Captain Keka ended the conversation, "I would like to meet with the families of the crew which found us. Commander Abyr and Captain Zan gave their lives when they dispersed the distress signal which warned us of their capture, and coordinates to here and Xion. All that, no doubt, led to their demise. Can you give more details of the Lacertian rebel group doing their best to assist us?"

Inkanta held a finger to his lips, "Shh. Many on Segmar and Xion are not ready to know of their existence. They are aware both Xion and Segmar would be attacked."

"I have been warned by a spy, Draconians and maybe Lacertians are in the vicinity of Xion. We did plan going to Xion but diverted to here just in case we accidently lead our common enemy to Xion." Inkanta leaned forward with concern, "Who was the informant?"

Keka allowed Jalon to take over, "A strange old man. He comes and goes and invites himself to wherever he needs to be. His information is always accurate. He is on a recruiting drive. He wants half of my security staff to disperse to do different important roles to assist the planets he is defending. His name is Zindel. A brilliant man. He forewarned us of impending Xion trouble. We need his help to defend Xion and he will in turn assist us against the Draconians. He informed us, the Draconians came from a parallel universe. They broke through the boundary. At first the Draconians put all their deformed or rejected citizens in this universe. They were supposed to die off in this universe, but they survived and thrived. Then the so called normal Draconians, decided to step in, convert the Lacertians to meat eaters and be pawns for their expansion in this universe. Finding where they created the hole and patching it up is the only way to slow down and just maybe halt the expansion in this universe. A dangerous mission. It may be impossible to find the gap or rip as no one knows what the hole looks like. Is it a rouge wormhole? A tear caused by a supernova formation? A naturally forming gap in the expanding universes? Who knows. What we do know, more Lacertians led by more and more Draconians are on the way. All the human civilisations will be reduced to food supply."

Inkanta swallowed hard. "This Zindel person, when will he come here?"

Jalon/Keka shook his head. "I just don't know. All I can say I can try to recall him. He is busy defending the human race in other galaxies. He flits about. He is short staffed and that is why he is on a recruitment drive. He needs our help as much as we need his. I can try to contact him, but I cannot guarantee anything."

Inkanta nodded. "Try when you go back to your ship. But wouldn't the communication signals alert the Draconians as to where we are?"

"No. It is all done with the mind. No signals. I have never tried instigating communication with Zindel. It has always been him contacting us. I can try but I am not sure if it will work."

"Regardless, we must plan for an attack on Xion. How many ships are in your fleet?"

Keka looked embarrassed. "Just the Explorer, that's it. Beta Cancari was not generous with minerals. Plenty of water, plants and some animal life including a small statured human race called Mammalians. We didn't know the Mammalians existed until a couple of months ago. We killed a few Draconians for them. I just hope these people are not punished by the other Draconians because of us."

Keka went back to his ship. By now the staff and refugees were able to leave the ship and join the blended society of Andromedans and Siriusians. Days turned over. Daily Keka tried contacting Zindel. Nothing. Plans with the Segmar people of joint assistance to help the people of Xion, were well under way.

Ashton frequently noticed Keka sitting in a trans-like state. When Keka came out of one Ashton asked, "Sir, just what are you trying to do?"

Jalon side responded. "I am trying to reach Zindel. I don't have the power or strength or technique to reach him. Frustrating."

Ashton looked at Jalon. "Next time you try that, maybe I can assist. Maybe it requires two brains. Sorry three brains. Shall we try the experiment and do it together?"

"Give me an hour or two to recover from this trial," replied Jalon. "The man can download information into my head but I can't seem to reach him. It's not two ways."

"I can only guess, he may be receiving you but is indisposed or you are not doing it right. I don't know if I could do it right either. No harm in trying." Ashton walked away thinking about his mind control he had done in the past: on Beta Cancari as a party trick and on Earth to get him out of sticky situations.

Ashton sat opposite Keka in his office. Ashton noticed the chairs had been moved side by side.

"Sit in a chair and make yourself comfortable." Ashton did as instructed.

"Now I want you to try by yourself," said Keka.

"What is the exact message do you want me to try?"

"Zindel, we need your assistance. Draconians are in Julos. Imminent attack on Xion. That should be enough." replied Keka.

Ashton closed his eyes and formed an image of Zindel. He held the picture firmly, and in his mind repeated the statements over and over. Ashton could feel himself drift into nothingness. His body seemed not to exist as his brain appeared to separate and enter a black vacuum. Zindel's image disappeared, and Ashton felt himself reuniting. He slowly opened his eyes, but his body felt incredibly heavy. Slowly his body became lighter. He stretched his body. "That was interesting," he mumbled softly.

Keka looked concerned. "What the hell did you just do?"

"I tried to reach Zindel as instructed. I saw him. Why? What's the problem?" asked Ashton.

Keka paced around the room pushing his hair back with a hand. "You were in such a deep state I wasn't sure if you were alive or dead. What happened? What did you see?"

"I held Zindel's image and then it faded. Blackness all around. Nothingness. Just like a piece of blank black paper. Nothing."

Keka hesitated, "I am not sure if we should continue this experiment. You scared me."

"I would like to try again. This time together. We can have Dr. Haiten present monitoring our vitals," stated Ashton trying to be objective and calmer. Keka sat looking at Ashton considering the monitored idea.

He was about to give a reply when a ghostly image formed in the room. It slowly solidified into Zindel. Zindel wasn't pleased and made it clear. "What! Why!" he stared at Ashton and snarled, "Never do that again. Certainly not without training. You could have killed yourself!" Sheepishly Ashton bowed his head. "Sorry. Sorry Sir."

Zindel turned his back and faced Keka. "I thought you had more sense. Draconians are definitely heading towards Xion. Four mother ships are on their way. They will reach Xion in four days. There is not much time to prepare. Tell president Inkanta of the impending attack. Prepare this ship for battle. I will go to Xion and assist there." He turned to Ashton. "You come with me. We're going to your gym. Your training starts now. No more unsupervised experimental stuff. Zindel, whispered as they walked out odf the room, "Excellent work. That was a late level three. Now let's go back and fill the gaps and start at level two."

As they walked towards the gym, Zindel asked, "Just what did you see. It will gauge the training you must do."

"Separation of the head and body. Darkness and nothingness. That was it. I was focused on your face and the message I had to send to get you're here."

Zindel grunted. "Good. Are you sure you didn't see anything else?"

"Absolutely nothing," replied Ashton.

"Your physical body may be a problem. Was it heavy or light?"

"Heavy. It felt like it was weighed down by heavy building material or I could describe it as being magnetised to the seat. Why?"

"It may not be as bad as I first thought. Still. Just don't do that again without proper training. It may be your natural strength. So, I will focus on that aspect for now as we are short on time. I need to build you up both physically and mentally. You have talent in that area. We can work on the weak spots of level two later." They entered the near deserted gym. The space had been reduced by half. Bedding on the floor occupied the other half.

Ashton walked back to his shared room and flopped on the bed. He fell into a deep sleep but every so often he would wake with a jump. Sweat beads poured out of his body. Kora saw the starts and asked, "What happened? I have never seen you do this before."

"Zindel started my training. It was mentally exhausting. Sorry, I am not permitted to say anything more," said Ashton who noticed the concern in her eyes.

She nodded. "I understand. But were we supposed to start on Earth."

Ashton held a finger to his mouth. "Shh. We are going to prepare for war. Xion is going to be attacked. I want you to help Haiten as much as possible. If you can't, just hide. I don't want you being taken for breeding stock. That disgusts me and scares me no end." Kora nodded.

CHAPTER TWENTY-TWO
Battle for Xion.

The handful of Segmar jets left their base. They flew towards the leading Draconian mother ship which had its shield deployed. The Segmarians saw their missiles and other types of weaponry deflected. The Segmarian crew retreated behind a floating piece of rock which was more than kilometres wide. The leader asked, "Has anyone got a good idea?"

Silence. Then one pilot screwed up his face and uttered in half jest, "Push this rock towards the mothership. Take it out of its orbit and let it fly."

"That's crazy," said the leader of the squad. "I like it. Get ready and line up beside each other, full thrust ahead." The rock didn't move at first. A couple of the jets relocated to another location, a thinner area of rock. "Try again." The rock started to move. The pilots guided the rock towards the mother ship. The ship fired on the rock. The rock didn't shatter as expected. It kept coming with greater momentum.

The Segmarian pilots let go and flew to a safe distance back. The rock continued on its path but for some unknown reason it was attracted to the electromagnetic forces of the shield. The rock penetrated the shield and smashed into the mother ship. The ship disintegrated. The nuclear generator exploded. With the power absorbed by the explosion, the rock sped faster into space and away from Xion. The explosion was detected by the three following ship and the sensors on Xion. The Segmarian jets returned to their base.

The next three mother ships edged closer. All were now going to arrive at the same time. Zindel left the safety of his accommodation on Xion. Mentally he sent a message to Ashton, "*Do me a little favour.*" Ashton shook his head at the clarity of the message. He went immediately to the flight deck. Keka looked at Ashton and immediately realised Ashton was getting messages from Zindel. "Sir, Zindel has instructed me to be here. He wants us to slip behind one mother ship but keep the distance, so we don't register on their screens." When The Explorer was in position, Ashton asked, "Can I borrow your chair." Keka gestured.

Ashton focused on receiving Zindel's instructions and then followed them. He concentrated and jumped into the mind of a Draconian. "Move closer to the ship on your right." He repeated the instruction until the Draconian ship was in position. "Keep this distance. Do not do a thing." In Ashton's mind he instructed the commander of the Draconian ship. "Fire on the ship on your right." The ship fired on its own people. The ship on the far left realising one ship had gone rogue, then fired on the one on the far right. Two ships were down. Only one remained.

Zindel instructed Ashton, "*You get the engineer in the engine room to turn off the power system in the Draconian ship. I will do the rest.*"

Ashton took a while to locate the main engine room. He saw the Draconians switch buttons, pull levers and then remove critical wires. The mother ship slowly came to a halt and was now showing signs of being out of control. Zindel took control of the ship by taking over the commander's mind. The commander pulled out his gun and fired on his own staff. Then he fired the gun on himself. The alarm sounded through the ship. The fighter jets evacuated hastily. None were fully prepared for the next event.

The rock which was pushed out of its stable orbit was now rogue. The shields surrounding the Draconian ship and the fighters attracted the rock. The rock turned towards the fighters before sucking up the mothership. The added debris made the rock a formidable opponent: growing in size at it propelled through space taking everything further and further away from Xion and Segmar.

The area was virtually cleared. No more than twenty Draconian fighters escaped the rock. They went in formation and flew towards

Xion. Their attack was short lived. They were now overpowered by the joint forces Xion and Segmar fighters. This battle was won but all knew, more would be on the way.

On Segmar, Keka met with Inkanta and the President of Xion, Boriser. The exclusive meeting lasted several hours. Then there was a flurry of activity. The Pleiadeans who were rescued on Beta Centari were ordered to stay on Segmar and help defend the planet. All the children and teenagers under the age of 19 and all the gestation cribs were to remain onboard The Explorer to be transported to Earth.

Coming on board would be a team of twenty – a mix of Andromedans, Siriusians, Genobolians and Nubians. The Explorer would still be crowded but not as congested as before. The resupplying of the ship with water, food, medical and horticultural equipment was normal enough. Then at the last minute Segmar and Xion both added two extra fighter jets with their pilots. More arms were added as much as The Explorer could handle.

Nodin and Neo surveyed the last-minute additions. Neo whispered, "The ship is no longer a vessel for exploration, but a second-rate battleship."

Nodin nodded, "I agree." Jokingly he added, "I rename the ship, XSBC" Neo gave a puzzled look.

Nodin clarified. X for Xion, S for Segmar and BC for Beta Cancari."

Neo grinned. "I had other words running through my mind – extra small battle craft. And it is."

"Should we get that painted on the outside?" asked Nodin.

"We have four hours to flit off. Why not. We will let the other discover for themselves the additional letters." Neo winked as he started to give maintenance a call on his communicator.

Now that the number of people were less, the mess hall returned to some form of normality. The newcomers were housed individually in the smaller separate rooms on most floors. The gestation cribs remained as they were – filling some rooms and lining passageways.

Earth was a five-month one-way trip across voids. No one knew if the journey would need detours if the enemy were close by. There would be, like in the past, a total communication black-out.

CHAPTER TWENTY-THREE
The Explorer

Kora was rushed on a stretcher to Dr. Haiten's surgery. The baby was coming. Out of his depth, Dr. Haiten paged Dr. Lawinda. Dr. Lawinda, who was from Xion, ran to the surgery. When she saw Kora in labour, she ordered everyone out. "Ashton. You stay and don't pass out." Ashton went instantly pale. "Hold her hand and talk softly to Kora," ordered Lawinda. Kora gave Ashton a pleading look which said, help.

Four hours later when the contraction became faster and more painful, Kora screamed out and abusive words followed. All locked at Kora as sweat poured out of her body. Ashton felt her hand squeezing his with a strength he had never known before. He whimpered and fought back tears. Kora didn't realise the force she was exerting on Ashton's hand. She heard the soft cry and saw the pooling in his eyes. She screamed again squeezing Ashton hand more than before. "Can I please have my hand back before it is crushed?" he whimpered. She released his now purple hand but grabbed him by the nearest part of his body, his hair. She quickly let go when Ashton involuntarily screamed. "Sorry. I didn't mean it. Want to swap places for a minute?" she panted.

Ashton was still recovering from the attack and rubbed his scalp and sore hand. "I kind of get the idea of pain you are going through." He rubbed his head more and felt a wet patch. Blood. He looked at Kora's hand. A few strands of hair were in her hand. Carefully he took her hand to remove the strands. "Souvenirs of the experience." He held up the strands. Kora looked apologetic and was about to say sorry, but the words were replaced with another scream. There was a sensation to push. The baby was born.

Dr. Lawinda grabbed the baby and quickly checked for its breathing. A few slaps and the cry that rivalled its mother was heard through the surgery. She placed the baby on Kora's chest and draped a cloth over it. "Congratulations," beamed Dr. Lawinda, "It's a boy." She looked over to where Dr. Haiten was last seen. She laughed. Dr. Haiten had passed out and was now slumped over a chair. Ashton and Kora looked briefly at Haiten but quickly turned their eyes to the baby. "What name do we give him from the short list we made? Ashra. Korash. Korton" asked Ashton. Kora looked only at the baby, "Ashra. Yeah. Ashra."

"Ashton grinned as he placed his finger into the baby's hand. The baby's natural reflexes instantly grabbed Ashton's finger. Ashra's hand held firm. Ashton spoke softly, "Ashra, you have your mother's iron grip."

Dr. Lawinda interrupted the family scene. "Sorry to break up this moment. I need to run checks on the child. His name?"

"Ashra," chorused Ashton and Kora.

"Ashton, help Kora have a bath while I run some preliminary checks on Ashra." She nodded towards the cupboard. "Towels are in there. Call me if you see a problem. Don't pass out." Ashton assisted Kora into the shower. "Are you feeling okay?"

She nodded. "I think the gestation cribs are a much better idea." She rubbed her much flatter stomach. She wobbled. Ashton grabber her.

While trying to assist Kora in the shower, he became saturated. He decided to strip off and tossed his wet clothes on the floor outside. They stood under the shower for a minute longer before they were disturbed by a knock. Dr. Lawinda walked in and blushed. "The shower was for her only. It's much too early to start again. Get dressed both of you."

Kora fell asleep in the mini ward. Ashton walked back to his room to change out of his wet clothes. On the way he received some strange looks. When he neared his room, his group of security friends rushed him. "We heard the news. Congratulations. What is it – boy or girl?"

"A boy named Ashra," said Ashton.

Garyth said shyly, "I walked passed the surgery. Was that Kora screaming obscenities?"

"Yep and in different combinations I have never heard before and along with words I never knew existed. Just a word of warning. If you get your girlfriend pregnant, he looked at Eraton, and the baby is on the way, expect to be attacked in the birth process." He held up his now bandaged hand and pointed to the blood stain on his head. "Dr. Lawinda was great. She kept it together. She told me not to pass out. I didn't but Dr. Haiten did." Ashton joked, "I wasn't sure if it was the birth process he was witnessing or the foul language coming out of Kora. I'm going to bed."

"How about a drink in the bar before it closes?" Asked Nodin.

"That sounds good. I'll join you after I change my clothes," replied Ashton.

Ashton was made to sit on one of the few remaining bench seats while the others ordered their drinks and one for him. When they returned, Ashton was slumped across the table and sleeping. "He's an old man already," said Eldon as he placed Ashton's drink on the table. Ichiro tried to prop up Ashton. Ashton barely stirred. When Neo walked in, they all stood to attention, but Ashton fell to the floor and woke up on contact. Neo shook his head. "Great. He gets drunk just when his baby is born."

Nodin came to Ashton's defence. "He fell asleep before the first drink."

"Then get him to his room immediately," ordered Neo.

Two months later the alarm sounded across the ship. Kora took Ashra in her arms and headed for the safety of the nearest room with some of the gestation cribs. She placed Ashra in an empty crib and left the lid open as she busily checked the other babies. When she was satisfied all were secure, she removed Ashra and repeated the process of checking the cribs in all other areas. When she was finished, she reported into the surgery. She secured Ashra into a crib and prepared herself along with the doctors for any possible causalities.

On the flight deck, Captain Keka and Captain Darius form Xion planned their possible attack strategies. The crew had picked up a weak signal coming from behind them. The ship had already stopped moving towards Earth and was now backtracking along the void. The shield was up. Guns deployed. The jets were being readied. It was just a matter of wait and see. The signal slowly became louder. Just one signal meaning one ship. Soon it was identified as a Lacertian ship. Just how big it was, was unknown at that point.

The Lacertian ship stopped moving towards them. There was an attempt for a communication link. The screen on The Explorer flickered before a clear pictured formed. A Lacertian female filled the screen. "Hello, Captain Keka," a raspy Lacertian voice said. "I am not sure if you remember me. Since we last spoke. I have been badly disfigured. I am Kyrina." Keka frowned at the scarred face in front of him but remained sceptical. He allowed the communication to continue as Kyrina identified herself with only conversations they could know. Satisfied about her identity, Keka asked, "How did you acquire a ship and who is with you?"

"I was captured and tortured for many hours. I planted so many lies and a tiny bit of truth in the mix. I caused mistrust in the Lacertian ranks on the Draconian ship." Kyrina gave a twisted grin as her mouth no longer could perform all the actions it once did. Proudly she stated, "I caused a mini rebellion on the ship. Draconians against Lacertians. What a delight to watch. There were more Lacertians than Draconians. Lacertians prevailed. They let me out of prison and transferred me to this Lacertian ship on Shardon. While the ship was being readied with fuel, food and all the rest, the ship was left with an inadequate skeleton crew of ten. With so few on board and virtually no supervision, I was able contact my local supporters. These supporters were rostered to supervise the shipment of Shardonites to Centaria and be sold as slaves. The supporters convinced the transport company they were to divert the Shardonites to this ship and not to another Lacertian ship going to Centaria. My supporters closed the doors and flew off. We dumped the other Lacertians who were pro-Draconian, in space and freed the Shardonites. I have been teaching them how to fly this craft." Kyrina stopped talking and a Shardonite appeared on the screen.

The young girl was shy; years of intimidation and being forced to only talk in Lacertian, had robbed her of her culture, identity and confidence. She gasped at seeing other humans. She stood silent.

"It is okay to speak," encouraged Kyrina. "Go on say something."

The girls coughed and looked around expecting a cue, "What do I say?"

"How about your name for a start," encouraged Kyrina. Instead of a name she rattled her identification number and where she was from.

Everyone from both sides of the screen looked at the girl in shock, "Name," said Kyrina again in a soft tone. The girls looked at Kyrina, "That was my name." Kyrina shook her head sadly.

Keka and Darius shook their heads. Off screen, Neo said softly with a bit of anger and disgust, "They have been reduced to meaningless numbers." Neo could see the rest of the crew looking in disgust. "They have huge and well ingrained psychological damage. This generation doesn't know better or any form of freedom," said Gibba. Keka nodded at Gibba. "We must go gently."

Keka spoke and rattled off the girl's number, "Hello. I'm Captain Keka and this is Captain Boriser." The girl stared at the screen and at the two men. She became nervous. She didn't speak. Keka added, "May I come aboard with three crew members?" asked Keka.

Kyrina smiled, "You are most welcome. Please take landing bay two. It is the closest to the flight deck."

Dr. Haiten, Keka, Frode alighted. The driver of the pod, Nodin, remained inside the pod. The Shardonites were lined up and stared silently at the strangers. They had never seen other humans who walked freely and held any form of authority. "Hello," said Dr. Haiten as he slowly walked past the silent group. Frode smiled but inside he wanted to shout his anger at the subservience of the Shardonites before him. Kyrina hobbled towards them and held out a hand, "Greetings dear friends." To the Shardonites she said gently, "Please relax. These are friends. We are here to help each other." Back to Keka. "We have one hundred and twenty Shardonites on board and four other Lacertians besides me." She glanced at Haiten. "I would like a full medical on each of these Shardonites. Also, I would like assistance as to where we should go. These people are not used to anything other than sitting around or not doing your bidding. They have lost everything that defines them as human."

Dr. Haiten asked, "Where do I set up? It will take a bit of time to do all of them. May I start with the youngest?"

Kyrina called a Shardonite over, "Please guide Dr. Haiten to the medical room. Do not be afraid. He is here to check your health." The Shardonite stopped and looked at Kyrina, "I thought you were supposed to be our friend. Now you are putting us through this examination in preparation for grading and ultimately selling."

"It is not that type of medical examination," Kyrina tried to explain.

Unhappy the Shardonite waved Haiten over. On the way to the medical suite, he said, "I am only here to make sure your health is good. I am not here to grade you for auction preparation. I didn't know that even occurred. Kyrina wants the best for you all." The Shardonite was silent on the way to the room. When they reached the room, the Shardonite held the door open. "Don't go. I want to start with you and then you can stay with me and supervise my medical examinations with the other Shardonites." The Shardonite agreed.

Six hours later, the examinations were completed. Exhausted, Dr. Haiten thanked the supervising Shardonite. "Please lead me back to my pod." The Shardonite was more at ease with Dr. Haiten and was now beginning to ask questions about other human races. To Haiten, that was a breakthrough and a gaining of confidence. He knew that limited information would spread throughout the ship.

In the small conference room on his ship, Keka drew in a breath and surveyed the small group. "We have a problem. We are just over halfway to Earth. I don't think Earth people are ready to extend their hospitality to Shardonites. They have enough racial issues which is largely colour, to sort out. I don't think they could accept another colour. To send Kyrina with the ship could lead the Draconians to Xion or Segmar. We all know, these people need to be placed somewhere safe. Beta Cancari is not an option. The Mammalians have enough to worry about and these people have no ability to look after themselves. I am open to suggestions."

Eldon suggested, "Can we send a beacon to pre-warn Xion of the incoming ship. We supply all details. We send another signal to another planet as a decoy for the Draconians. Then it bounces off in all directions. True, it is risky as the Draconians may get the signal first. The saving aspect is, they are diverted to a dead planet while the rescue mission is undertaken. President Boriser's security team showed me a new technique on beacons. Only those with the known encryption, know where to look. The people are ferried to Xion and the ship moved to another distant location which only the Xion people and Kyrina know. The ship is placed in mothballs in space or given to Kyrina. If the ship is placed in mothballs, the last of the crew are flown back to Xion. If it is given to Kyrina and her rebels, they can go where they wish." Eldon looked at the others and saw a few people considering the concept.

Ichiro broke the silence, "The Lacertian crew is a problem. I doubt if the Xion people will tolerate their existence."

Keka suggested, "The crew goes to Beta Cancari. They can infiltrate their people and offer some protection for the Mammalians. If there are no other suggestions, I will speak to Kyrina about the plans."

Hours later Keka spoke to Kyrina. Kyrina was delighted to unload the Shardonites and to keep the ship. To her it was a reward, the biggest reward she ever dreamed of. When Keka suggested they go to Beta Cancari, she was taken by surprise at the suggestion. "Let me get this clear in my head, you are giving me all of Beta Cancari? We help the Mammalians by keeping them safe and we slowly wipe out the Draconians and other meat-eating Lacertians on Beta Cancari. That's it? What's the catch?" she asked suspiciously.

"No catch. Your ship, your planet. Hopefully, no more war other than fending off Draconians trying to muscle in on the planet. A place where you can start a fresh. You also need a safe haven for your freedom fighters. Just land a good distance from the downed spacecraft. That area only is contaminated. You can have all the contents there after decontamination. Put it bluntly, we are abandoning Beta Cancari forever. It is yours. Your take over will only be known by the presidents of Xion and Segmar and their respective heads of military. The rest of the citizens won't know of your existence. That can be a two-edged sword. Citizens may attack and ask questions later. We will convince the heads of governments you will be under their protection. It will be a no-go zone for all on Segmar and Xion."

Kyrina rubbed her chin. "I will discuss this matter with the rest of my group. I would like a ratified treaty of the proposal. I will get back to you tomorrow." She clicked her screen off.

The next day Kyrina was back on the communication screen. "I have discussed this matter with the other Lacertians on board. We accept the planet of Beta Cancari but we require the following.

1. A treaty to be signed with both Xion and Segmar.

2. Right to peaceful co-existence without fear of attack from any person from either Xion or Segmar. Those who do attack, must be captured in

a timely manner and held accountable for their actions. A member from our community must be included in the proceedings.

3. We will require visitation rights to Xion and Segmar and they will be permitted the same to our planet. We will limit the visitations to no more than six trips for each planet per year. This can alter in the future as the situations change.

4. Two-way trade with no financial barriers such as fees or tariffs.

5. Sharing of plant discoveries for food and medical purposes.

6. Assisting each other (Xion, Segmar and Beta Cancari) if one of us is attacked by Draconians.

7. Be permitted to join forces against Draconians and Lacertians in Oberon and Amada.

8. Cultural exchanges and tours to be discussed at a future date."

Keka smiled and nodded. "I will be more than happy to forward these requests to both governments. The transfer of Shardonites will begin when your ship is one month away from Beta Cancari. The beacon will be set three days prior to that location. You only communicate with this ship. We are setting in place a new communication system which will give you details and acceptance of your requests before either of us move from our current locations in space. The installations will take another two days to perfect. It is experimental at this stage, fingers crossed we can get these requests back and forth without either of us being detected.

One week later, Keka spoke to Kyrina. "The heads of government have agreed to your requests. The transfers will take place as initially planned. You will be given the experiment communication system when you are closer to Beta Cancari. Kyrina, thank you for your assistance. Have a peaceful and successful journey to Beta Cancari. If we return, I would like to meet up with you again." Keka waited for a few seconds for Kyrina's reply. He saw a tear trickle down her face. She wiped it away, "Thank you Captain Keka. I hope we meet again." Kyrina gave a wave before switching off communications. Keka watched the Lacertian ship pick up speed and head towards Beta Cancari. He turned to his staff, we hover for a month. When we get word of the exchange is completed, we go at full speed to Earth.

CHAPTER TWENTY -FOUR
Earth

The Explorer was given permission to land on Earth. Again, it settled on the grounds at Daraxon Technologies. Hammond and Tayee were first to board. Keka met them and guided them to the small conference room. He gave them an update of the last year and how he was now both Jalon and Keka. Tayee asked, "Is that getting any easier in making any decisions?"

Keka chuckled. "Yes. It took a while for the debates to become faster. But time is melding the thoughts as one. It only jumps back when Jalon's daughter is about. I retreat and let Jalon take over. Much simpler."

Keka explained what he needed and asked the best way to achieve the goals. Hammond contacted Jed over the mobile phone and placed it on speaker for all to hear. "The cribs can be left here but we must get government permission. The only country involved will be this one. They know our records of wealth generation and skills in advancing the country and the planet to space activities. The biggest problem will be in acquiring the finances to purchase all the items required. We don't have that amount of spare funds without shutting down our own space craft development program. Closing it down will draw suspicion."

Keka rubbed his chin as he thought. "Just how do we raise funds without eating into your budget?" There was silence. Neo said with some hesitation, "I can send someone down to raise funds. Ashton played the poker machines to kick start his finances. He only used the machines as necessary. I think we should call him in." Neo called Ashton in via the personal communication system.

Ten minutes later, Ashton stood before the group. Neo asked Ashton, "You played the poker machines to kick start your finances down here."

"Yes. I cheated by using the glasses. I still have a couple thousand of Australian dollars." Ashton's eyes flashed around the room and saw the almost stony faces looking back. He added, "If we are going to do the cheating again to buy stuff, we will need to open a bank account or two. Shifting big amounts of cash around is too cumbersome." He looked to Hammond, "How do we open an account?"

Hammond looked at Ashton as his finger rubbed the bottom of the chin. "When you came here last time, you made a birth certificate and a passport. I will come with you to open an account. You will need those items for identification. See me at my office tomorrow and we will go together. Actually, we will need a couple of others to come. Make up two more birth certificates and two more passports. It will be better if there is more than one account. There is a need for more than one card."

"Trouble is not going to happen again. I suspect Detective Kirkwood will make a visit just to keep me in check. He prefers I work with him when I am here. That is not going to happen." The others gave the slightest of smirks as they recalled the comical incident which had occurred when Carrie was being rescued.

Two weeks later, the security team was armed with three with credit cards and given three four-man pods. Ashton studied the map of the world. Let's start in the far north and then we slowly make our way south. Remember the plan?" All in his craft nodded. He heard the other confirm over the communication system. Just remember we can't escape into Finland. Ichiro and I may still be on the wanted list. I have no intention of being incarcerated here but it would be millions of times better than many other countries." He heard a few chuckles.

One person from each pod levitated down close the one of the Swedish casinos. They walked around the poker machines and at random times shot a green beam to a random person. The warm up gave one person a major jackpot and two others a considerable amount of winnings. Ashton then tried a machine as the others standing at a distance watched on. He hit a minor jackpot. Then he used half the tokens to distribute to Frode and Eldon. The other two walked away. They deliberately did not use the glasses the first time round and then with the green beam firing. Both collected their winning. The process was repeated for the next two hours. The winning tokens were converted into the local currency and deposited into their credit card. They walked out with a combined winnings of $150,000. They levitated back to the pods and flew over Norway. The process was repeated. Another $200,000.

Then it was across to Luxemburg, Denmark, and finally Holland. They flew back to Daraxon Technologies. While they rested for the day, the accounts were nearly drained for the purchase of dried and powdered fruit and vegetables and dried assorted meat. The group flew back to Germany where they hit three of four casinos. Then to France and Spain. Ashton led the team, but this time Garyth and Eraton accompanied him. After draining these countries of nearly 500,000 Euro's they headed back home.

They planned their next stops as the money slipped out of their account to top up on electronic parts and assorted tools for the engine room.

In Britain, the team split themselves up. Instead of raiding the casinos as a group of three, they went in pairs to three different Casinos: London, Birmingham and Manchester. When they regrouped, they swapped team members and hit Edenborough, Cardiff and Coventry. They went home with close to another 500,000 Euros.

The next day as they rested, the ship was loaded up with more electronic parts and cleaning equipment. Ashton planned the next series of stops but this time he insisted they wear wigs. He guessed they would slowly come to the attention of staff at the casinos. The casino bosses would conference with each other and their descriptions would start to spread out. Ashton went into Beaudesert, the largest town closest to Daraxon Technologies. He bought three different wigs in three different hair styles and colour: medium brown, red and black. Then he added three different coloured shirts, blue, black and red and white stripped. He bought himself a pair of jeans.

When they were going to return to Europe, he made the others put on the clothes and wigs. They looked at each other and shook their heads before bursting out laughing. Kora who stayed behind grinned widely at Ashton's transformation: jeans, blue shirt and black wig. She added, "The only thing missing is cowboy boots and a moustache." Ashton formed his fingers into a gun and pretend to shoot her. Then he slipped his pretend gun into an invisible holster. She pretended to take the shot and played dead on the chair she was sitting on. "What is that all about?" asked Garyth. "She's just playing around," replied Ashton as he winked at Kora. Kora winked back.

Ashton directed the crafts to France. As they walked past a news stand near the first French casino, they looked at the newspaper heading. Ashton saw his photo and one of Ichiro. Ashton stopped the group, "They are on to us, but they are using photos from Finland. We may need to purchase some caps to hide from the cameras all over the cities. Ichiro walked over to a tourist kiosk and purchased three caps, all had motif of a football team. They entered the first casino; they were directed to remove their caps. They complied. Then they went to work, giving a couple of locals a win before they hit the poker machines. They made appoint of going for the third largest payouts for each machine. By mid-afternoon, they had accumulated 200,000 euros. They would return in the evening and go for the more up-market casino in Paris.

Dressed in slightly more dressy attire, Ashton, Eldon and Frode did their usual routine. Eldon nudged Ashton, "I saw something over here. Come with me and take a look." Eldon led the others to a corner of the room where a sign was written in three languages: French, Chinese and English. LEARN HOW TO PLAY POKER. THIRTY MINUTES OF FREE CLASSES. Under the main heading was a listing: classes in French: 7.00 pm. Ashton looked at the digital clock on the wall. 7.15 pm. Classes in English: 7.30pm. Classes in Chinese: 8.00pm. Ashton whispered we join the English class in fifteen minutes.

After the lesson, the group had a small discussion. The topic was to try another form of gambling and what were the odds. Frode decided he would try one game first. They walked around to find the cheapest entry table. Ashton and Eldon watched. Frode lost his money. Eldon tried. He too lost his money. Ashton tried. He lost. The group moved away. "I want to try again. But this time, using mind reading. I want you two to space yourselves around the table and tell me by thinking only, what the others have. We give it two tries and after that we go back to poker machines." The others nodded.

Ashton sat at the table again. The other two spread themselves around the players. Eldon saw the hand and gave the information to

Ashton. Ashton heard the words form in his mind. Ichiro did the same. Ashton knew the hands of all his opponents. He played the game using the information. He made a small win and left the table. They found another low entry table and he played again. The win was a bit larger. They had recuperated the previous losses and were now even. "I think I have the hang of this game. Let's do one more low entry game."

There was another small win. Frode whispered, can we risk going to another table where the money is a bit higher?" Eldon replied, "Let's do a few pokies first so it doesn't look so obvious. Then back again." Ashton agreed of the tactic. "It's not really gambling but wholesale cheating. Cheating is not addictive." After a few more poker machine wins, they found the next poker table where the start was double that of the first. Ashton had requested that Frode and Eldon not be present for the next first two game. It was a strategy to throw any watching person at the control room off guard. It wasn't a group, just random guys. While the others were away, Ashton tried reading the minds of the other players. He gave up. Too much noise - people telling themselves just one more go before a move to the toilet, men thinking about what the lady across the room would be like in bed, guilt of gambling the family income away and so. Ashton stopped trying to read their minds. *Focus,* he thought to himself. There was a sudden quietening of thoughts. He was then able to read some of the player's hands.

Ashton lost the first two games before Frode and Eldon moved in. Ashton won the hand. The lost money was recovered. Ashton played again going higher. This time he made a large profit. Eldon moved away first as Ashton collected the chips to be cashed in. Frode hung around and watched Ashton head towards the cashier. They all moved to the bar for a drink. "It's back to pokies," said Eldon. It is much faster." They went back to the pokies and pocketed another $100,000 euros before calling it a day. This time they did not return to Daraxon Technologies. The pods were directed to an isolated and hilly countryside. They landed and slept in the pods for the night. The next day they were going to Canada and then to the United States.

When they arrived back at Daraxon Technologies, the next 100,000 in Euros and half a million in a mix of Canadian and U.S dollars were used for supplies : medical books and medical supplies and equipment for The Explorer.for the Explorer. Keka walked in on the group. "Okay, do the local casino and clubs now." Kora you can go with Ashton to shake up any possible detection. Kora said,"It would be nice to go along. Can one of the other females come? Like Tanke? Or Milway?"

The group was ready to set out for Brisbane and the Gold Coast when Carrie and Astra appeared. Carrie said, "Tanke and Milway are too young by law to enter the gaming areas. We are the substitutes." Kora and the men accepted the technicality they had overlooked. "Welcome aboard," said Kora. We females are going to be partnered off. I'm with Ashton at the start and then I am switching to Eraton in the afternoon.

Kora read the partner list. Frode, Eldon and Astra are one group. Nodin, Eraton and Carrie your one group. And Garyth you will be with me and Ashton. We meet at 2 p.m. at the Broadwater beachfront bar for the swap session for the afternoon."

By the afternoon, the small group met at the Broadbeach Bar. They swapped notes. Astra gave Frode a tug on his shirt. "There is a man who has been watching us. Creepy." Frode glanced over his shoulder and then asked Ashton if he recognised the staring stranger. Ashton leaned over to the general direction and planted a peck on Astra's cheek. At the same time, he glanced at the man. He whispered to the group, "He's detective Kirkwood. Nice guy. I am going to invite him over. Staring from afar puts us all on edge. If he is with us, we check each other out. It may be the end of us getting money out of the pokies. Let's play it by ear."

Kirkwood was surprised to be invited into the group and was introduced to all. He wondered what their motive was and asked Ashton why he did not contact him earlier. "Been very busy and in and out of town. This is the first day off," he lied.

Kirkwood suspected that wasn't exactly true. He played along. When it was close to 4 p.m., Frode introduced the idea of going back to Daraxon Technologies. The others agreed and began their good-byes all the time Ashton was sending messages via telepathy where they were to meet.

Kora, Astra, Carrie were left with Kirkwood. Now the men were gone, Kirkwood began quizzing the ladies. They confirmed Ashton and the men were in and out of town, but none told where or what they were doing. Carrie and Astra just didn't know but Kirkwood suspected Kora knew more than what she was letting on. Kirkwood felt uneasy. Something was amiss. Astra and Kora decided to leave giving baby clothes shopping an excuse. Astra confirmed Kora had a boy, born in space. His name was Ashra. "He's so cute," added Astra. "So much like his father, Ashton when it comes to smiling. Poor Kora, she didn't get much of a look-in. …maybe her sparkling eyes." Kirkwood congratulated Kora, "One day I would like to meet the child."

Kora drew out a picture on her mobile phone. She showed him a series of pictures which included a passed-out doctor slumped over a chair. Kirkwood laughed at the sight and the story behind it. He frowned at the model of the phone. "Kora, what type of phone is that?"

"One of our models. Why?"

"What network are you connected to?" he asked. "Our ship's network. The captain likes to know where his staff are," she replied truthfully.

I really must be going. Astra has been patient enough and is starting to get restless over there." Kora pointed to Astra who was pointing to an item in the shop window.

Carrie was left with Kirkwood. As they spoke, she became aware he was starting to hit on her. Her defences went up. She looked at her watch, 4.30 p.m. "I must be heading off. I have a few trains to catch before I get home. No direct lines from the coast to home."

Carrie stood up and as she did so, Kirkwood also stood up and asked, "I would like to meet with you again. A date?"

Carrie felt flattered by the gesture but at the same time played cautious. "I thought you had a wife and kids. Take the wife out, not me."

Kirkwood said, "No wife. Never had one. And no kids. Just me and a dog named 'Cashew'." Carrie paused again in thought and suspected Kirkwood was wanting in and she was the ticket. "The answer is still no. No hard feelings, I prefer younger men." She quickly grabbed her bag and tried to walk away. Kirkwood stopped her again. "Just one date to …." he looked down and grinned but pulled himself together again before continuing, "to keep an 'old man' happy." *Christ,* he thought, *I am not that much older than her. Guess eight years.*

Carrie looked dismayed. "Tell you what, you go home and take Cashew to the dog park. I am sure you'll find like-minded females much closer to your age in that place." She walked off as fast as she could. Kirkwood saw her disappear into the growing afternoon crowd. He called his office.

That evening on Carrie's advice, the group didn't go to any casino. Instead, they went to every football club, every bowling club and every R.S.L. (Returned Service League). They pocked another $50,000 dollars. "Tomorrow, we go south to Sydney and Melbourne and hit the casinos and clubs there" said Eldon who had been studying casino locations on his tablet.

Over the next few weeks, the group played again in the USA and Canada before hitting the Asian countries such as China and Singapore. Then they moved to in many South American countries. Five million in US dollars was quickly added. It was time to stop. The ship had most of its supplies.

The cribs had been unloaded. Milway, Tanke, Wilbut and Ichiro stayed behind. They were assigned to be understudies for Patron and Dalmon. Kora, Ashra and Ashton also stayed behind. Jed had given them permanent accommodation in the new housing complex. Ashton worked in the security section of Daraxon Technologies as well as practising the skills Zindel had taught him. Kora joined in with some of the lower skills while Ashton surged ahead. He received his tuition via telepathy from Zindel. When the lessons came, they were mostly at night and interrupting his sleep.

Kora attended to the cribs as a part of her work day. Five hundred plus cribs kept her busy. Finding foster parents kept her busier. Only ten were placed. No doubt more would have been placed but she had some very tight self-imposed rules – only refugee families from Amada and Oberon were acceptable. Second generation families were also considered but many did not seem too interested just yet. She had to do more selling of the concept. She and Ashton were settling into their new life style.

They had waved their ship good-bye nearly a month ago. The Explorer XSBC was going to Genesis.

CHAPTER TWENTY- FIVE
Genesis and Earth

The Explorer hovered ten light years away from Genesis. Jalon sent a Pleiadean signal and the usual protocol. He hoped someone on Genesis would recognise the signal. He waited for nearly an hour before resending the signal. Then there was a response.

Zantha, who was the diplomat for Prince Alcyn appeared on the communication screen. Surprised at not seeing an Earth based refugee, namely Tayee or Hammond, she instantly grew cautious and asked people of her generation to come into the centre. It was close to an hour before and after much questioning ended. The Explorer XSBC was given approval to land. They were directed to land outside the city just south of their main space port. The space port was closed down and all crafts which would normally be in the open were manoeuvred into the surrounding hangars as a secondary precaution.

As small group of pods from Genesis approached the Explorer and the ramp to the ship came down. Zantha, Patrum, her husband and the other first arrival elders approached. They scanned the people coming out of the craft hoping to see a familiar face. Not one face. Partum drew in a deep breath ready to say something, but he stopped when he saw a mix of people: Pleiadeans, Nubians, Siriusian, Andromedians and Genobolians. He said to Zantha, "What a welcomed sight." He spoke into a communication system, "Get these welcomed guests more transport pods. "The voice on the other end confirmed the instruction, "Where do we take them?"

Patrum had to think for a moment, "To the central administration building. Get the staff to drop what they are doing and set the place up for a banquet. I want the works."

The new arrivals were ushered into the waiting pods and were taken to the centre of the city. The general public stopped whatever they were doing as the convoy arrived. The place was abuzz with phone calls giving descriptions of what was arriving and instructions as what will be required. General excitement.

Liamel met the people at the doorway to the building. Greeting and smiling as never before. As the last of the new arrivals came in, the doors were closed. Patrum addressed the crowd before him. He couldn't help but notice the usual staff had stopped working and were eager to listen in. He gave a quick run-down of their isolated history. How they prospered and were able to build crafts by mining on Affen Welt, well away from the cruel apes which dominated the planet. Minerals were rich on that planet. Genesis was rich with assorted edible plants and high-quality water and what was once considered in Amada, rare minerals. But the main building materials and ore required for building crafts were mostly on Affen Welt.

Keka explained to the absorbed crowd, their experience and discoveries which stretched across six galaxies. He introduced the help of Zindel and forewarned them he may arrive at any time. "He appears at random," said Keka. Then Keka proceeded to tell them how the Lacertians were pawns to Draconians who had breached the parallel universe and entered theirs. Then he handed the floor to Commander Darius who filled them in with the combined histories and developments of Segmar and Xion. He told them how the Explorer had shot down four advancing Draconian mother ships. He also explained the planet of Beta Cancari, the former Pleiadean colony was willingly given over to rebel Lacertians under the leadership of Kyrina, the granddaughter of the disposed President Kyros. "Kyrina's rebel group were given the planet to fend off the Draconians who came in the last eight months and to protect a new human group discovered, the Mammalians." Commander Darius said, "They have their work cut out. Our two planets, Segmar and Xion have a treaty with Beta Cancari. Put simply, we help each other."

The room of invited Genesisian guest, gasped at the revelation. Darius held up a hand. "They do not know of Earth or of this planet, Genesis. In fact, only the very top and then only a handful of administrators of Xion and Segmar know of Earth. They don't know you exist." He paused for a while to allow the questions and murmurs sweep the room. For the next hour, Darius and Keka answered as many questions as possible.

Partum took over the floor, as he cast his eyes to towards the newcomers and finally to Keka he asked, "Will there be more ships and any refugees coming?"

Keka replied, "At this stage, no. We can't guarantee any more in the future. Believe it or not, rescuing people is now very much in the hands of rebel Lacertians. They are growing in number and are infiltrating all aspects of Lacertian and Draconian societies. I can only theorise two things. One, the rebels are becoming appalled at the worsening treatment of humans. And two, they are becoming angry with how they themselves are slowly becoming servants and pawns to advance Draconian causes and expansionism. I suspect there are two groups of rebels, those who want to free humans and free their own society. The other is to just to free themselves of Draconian rule which is sliding into a dictatorship. More and more Lacertians are now seeing themselves as victims. There were more gasps.

The people from the Explorer were driven back to their ship. The door closed. The administrators of Genesis were busy the next day going over and debating the new information. Their quiet world had been rocked. Old wounds opened. Discussions, debates and arguments broke out. A consensus was needed. They were no dispute about the arrivals being who they say they are. It was the other information which had them unsettled. Beta Cancari handed over to Lacertians, attacks on Xion and maybe later Segmar were contentious. They worried for their own safety and debated issues relating to their own matter. Keka had mentioned another human group, the Lyrian. No one on Genesis had heard of them until Keka mentioned. This unknown group were fighting the Lacertians and defending Earth. Like many administrators on Genesis, they wondered why another human race they had never heard of was defending Earth. It was a question they would put to Keka and Darius.

The others, from Beta Cancari, Xion and Segmar, had made raids on the remaining planets in Oberon and Amada. That was something they had never done. One of the administrators put it simply, "They have become war-like and our protectors. They diverted attention away from us. We prospered from that. That we should thank them for."

The next day the leaders of Genesis sat with a small delegation from The Explorer. Zantha asked, "Do you want us to join you in fighting the Lacertians and Draconians?" Commander Darius sighed. "That is entirely up to you. It would be great if this was a refuel and recreational centre but for humans only. There are no other planets that we know of that can serve such a purpose."

Liamel stated, "We have become so used to peace, just like it was when Prince Alcyn ruled. Our peace has been disrupted but it will be disrupted more if the Draconian find us." Keka replied, "The Draconians are already in this galaxy and have been fighting the Lyrians whoever they are."

Liamel suggested, "New allies? Just what do these Lyrian look like?"

Darius took a deep breath, "We can only go on Zendel"s description. Tall gaunt-like and super fine hair which looks a bit transparent."

The administration of Genesis decided to hold a formal meet and greet function. Zantha felt she was in her element. It was something she had done many times before while being a diplomat on Daraxon for the Amada galaxy. She rarely performed this hostess role on the new planet of Genesis and was happy to leave the arrangements to the upcoming younger generation. However, on this occasion, she was not leaving anything to chance. Perfection. Perfection. Perfection.

In the hall which was a tiny bit over capacity by fifty people, she ensured many guests as possible were introduced to the new arrivals and all felt most welcomed. She cast her eyes over to her oldest son, Alcyn, to ensure he was applying all the social graces she had tried to instil in him. She sighed at what she observed and then slowly edged her way towards him.

"Alcyn. Alcyn. Snap out of that now!" hissed Zantha. Alcyn looked at her with apology written all over his face, "Sorry. I didn't mean to."

"What's wrong with you lately? Staring into space. In solitude. In weird trances. Are you taking some of that hallucinatory drug? If you are, I'm putting you away."

"No mum. That's honest."

"Then get yourself together. Socialise," whispered Zantha. Alcyn looked across the room, "I'll stay with the other three Alcyns as much as possible. Unofficial child minders," he grinned as he moved on.

Zantha approached Dr. Haiten, engaged in social chatter before asking for his opinion about Alcyn's trances she wanted another opinion. The local doctors drew a blank. "I will wander over to him. Just where is he?" Zantha pointed to a group of four young men. She said, "Over there. They are all called Alcyn. There was a spate of boys given that name. To differentiate, ask for Alcyn PZ." Zantha saw the puzzled look on Dr. Haiten's face. There were so many boys with that name, the schools added the initials of the parents. P for Patrum and Z for me, Zantha. Tell me what you see. It worries me so much."

Dr. Haiten raised his near empty glass. "Glad to assist."

Twenty minutes later, Dr. Haiten wandered back to Zantha. Partum was standing beside her. Dr. Haiten waited a few minutes until one other guest moved away. "There is nothing wrong with Alcyn PZ. Absolutely nothing. Just a case of telepathy. Seen it before. His brain is just picking up signals or he could be subconsciously sending them. Before we came here, one of Neo's security staff had that gift. We made him and his wife stay on Earth. There is a man called Zindel, weird but wonderful old man is training up our young man, Ashton." Dr. Haiten tried to joke, "I am sure if you put Alcyn and Ashton, in the same room there wouldn't be a sound coming out and both of them. They would be scheming up some of the most incredible pranks or mischief." Dr. Haiten waved his hand. "Relax. Just wait until this Zindel comes along. He is on a recruiting drive. Then worry. "

Patrum gulped the mouthful of drink and cleared his throat, "Recruiting for what?"

"War. Leaders to assist him to stop the Lacertians and Draconians. They are spreading. He can't be everywhere." Dr. Haiten bowed his head, smiled politely, "Excuse me. I see one of your administrators I need to speak to."

Earth. Same Time.

Tanke, Milway, Wilbut, Ashton and Kora sat in the media conference room at Daraxon Technologies. Jenny, Dalmon and Patron sat with them. The wall was covered in a map of the world. Coloured pins littered the map. Jenny spoke to the small group who had examined the research findings of the unpublished manuscript she and Patron had worked on. Patron sat quietly enjoying the now familiar work. It didn't tire him to listen to Jenny. Jenny and Patron considered it a rehearsal for when the information was going to be released. It would be released in dribs and drabs but all arguments and supporting material needed to be in place. Jenny prepared her arguments just like a barrister or Queen's Council prepared to do battle in the courts. Rehearsing rebuttals and dismissing any emotional charges that came her way. Long held beliefs needed to be dismissed and replaced backed by sound evidence – evidence that was already in the ancient literature but interpreted for modern day society. Nothing would be left to chance.

Rewriting the books is never easy – ridicule and threats would be common. Just being prepared with solid facts backing her evidence and separating very clearly what is theory and evidence, was paramount to launching the findings. The group before her, were her sounding boards who were invited to verbally attack, dispute and harshly criticise every word presented. She wanted them to hit her as hard as they could so she would reduce her chances of being off-guard when the time came.

"It was well over two hours of reading, debating and harsh criticism before a break was called. Jenny smiled and thanked all. Tanke sat in the room with Jenny asking more questions. Then she stopped half-way through a sentence. She frowned, blinked her eyes and groaned as she rubbed the back of her neck. She could feel her hackles. "What's wrong," asked Jenny showing some alarm. She recognised the expression on Tanke's face, an expression she had not seen on anyone's face since the time when her Aunt Cassie stayed on the horse stud. Flashbacks of the time when Prince Alcyn was trying to communicate with Cassie via the portal system. Tanke muttered, "I feel as though someone walked across my grave." Hearing the familiar words again after twenty-six years, rattled Jenny. "Tanke, sit. Don't move. I am calling my aunty. She experienced the same thing many years ago. She is the best to help." Tanke nodded as she saw Jenny run out of the room and down the passageway to where both Cassie and Sue, Jenny's mother, were working on a computer.

Both ladies entered the room to see Tanke in a trance. Cassie spoke gently and quietly. "Tanke. Tanke. Can you hear me?" Tanke slowly nodded and then snapped out of the trance. "Weird. I just had a vision.

Well, I think it was a vision. If it's not a vision, then I am slowly going crazy. Maybe too many changes and adjustments since arriving on Earth."

Cassie glanced at both Jenny and Sue as she placed a comforting arm around Tanke's shoulder. "Just tell me what you saw, and I will determine if you are suffering from stress or some form of communication," said Cassie.

Tanke said, "Far away, I don't know where, there is an official function. Many V.I.P.'s. Many different races of people socialising. Then for some unknown reason, my mind settled on a young man. The young man is from some long-established administrative family who seem to command great respect in the community." Tanke flashed her eyes to Cassie. "Am I going nuts?"

Cassie ignored the question but asked a question of her own, "Was the name Alcyn?"

Tanke frowned. "I'm not really sure. There is an older lady called Zantha, maybe his mother, who chastised him for not socialising."

Cassie, Sue and Jenny gasped. "It's Alcyn," said Cassie in a soft voice. "You are not mad or suffering from stress." Cassie spoke into her mobile phone, "Hammond, tell Tayee and the others to come here immediately. We have contact with Alcyn." Although they were rooms away, Cassie could feel the shock vibrating through the airwaves. Hammond arrived with photos of Prince Alcyn as an adult and as a toddler who visited Earth just over twenty-five years ago. Hammond showed the pictures. Tanke looked at the pictures carefully and then slowly pointed to Zantha. "Her. But older." Then she studied the pictures of Alcyn as an adult and as a toddler. She pointed to the adult picture, close in looks but not quite right." Her eyes stared at the toddler she pointed, "Him. The eyes tell me it is him. What does this mean?" asked Tanke.

As Hammond sat down, he glanced at Tayee. "I shall try to explain and make it as simple as possible. It won't be easy for you to grab hold of at first. Ask questions until you fully understand. You must understand everything. It is very important."

Tanke nodded and waited patiently as Hammond's and Tayee's recount of their lives on Daraxon. Hammond went into details how Alcyn downed ten Lacertian motherships all by himself. Cassie stepped in and gave her recount of her experiences with Alcyn. At the end, Tanke asked, "What is the significance of all this?"

Tayee spoke, "I can only guess but I am heavily leaning towards another off-planet war. Alcyn has essence and it has always been his duty to care for and defend his people."

There was a knock on the door as Ashton led the return of others into the room. Wilbut asked,

"What's going on?" Hammond drew in a breath," Visions of war."

The others were shocked. Ashton coughed, "My instructor, Zindel, also foretold of war. This time, not only with a war with Lacertians but more so against the instigators, Draconians. Zindel has been sending lessons via telepathy. Kora has been doing some training as well." Kora asked, "Didn't Prince Alcyn die?"

Sue answered, "Yes. Here on Earth. But something weird happened. When the people from Genesis came to visit, baby Alcyn," She pointed to the picture, "Recognised everyone here. He knew all about us."

Tayee explained, "People having essence re-incarnate over and over until a task is complete. It is only then they can ascend to the next level. Alcyn didn't complete wiping out Lacertians. He's back again." Tayee rubbed his hands, "I doubt at this stage of his rejuvenation, he truly understands what is going on inside his head. If he contacted you, then you can contact him… may be with some difficulty."

Ashton volunteered, "I will help you. If I can speak to Zindel in my training, I think I can speak to Alcyn. Shall we try?" Tankee looked around the room and noted the decision was entirely hers. She slowly nodded. "When do I start? After more of Jenny's interesting talk, or now? Or even later." Hammond said, "That is up to you. Now or later but we shall all be here with you."

Tanke took a deep breath before replying, "Jenny, is this okay with you to do this now?"

Jenny nodded. "You won't be able to concentrate until this is all over and done with."

Cassie gave a warm smile. "She's right. It will drive you to distraction. Now is better."

With Ashton's help, Tanke was back at the party on Genesis. With Ashton by her side, she searched the room. "*There,*" she said to Ashton. "*He's with a group of…damn, all of them are called Alcyn.*" Ashton suggested, "*Which feels right?*" She pointed to the shortest one. "*Short stuff. Yep. That's him and he's going into a trance, now.*"

Genesis.

Alcyn PZ collapsed on the floor. The other three Alcyns gathered around and tried to slap him to. Dr. Haiten who was not far away, rushed over. "Get him outside and some fresh air." Haiten waited until it was done. By that time both Zantha and Patrum had rushed over with concern. Before they could say anything, Dr. Haiten held up his hand. "Another trance-communication episode. We just have to wait and see who he has had conversations with. Patience."

Five minutes later, Alcyn groaned and rubbed his face. Then he realised he was on an armchair on the balcony to the hall. Peering down at him were Dr. Haiten, his parents and the other three Alcyns. As he recovered, he smiled, "I died and went to heaven. I'm in love with an angel called Tanke. There was another one who stood in the background supervising Tanke. A male called Ashton."

Haiten gasped, "Not angels my dear young man. Pleiadeans living on Earth communicating with you. I know them both. I didn't know Tanke had telepathy capabilities. When I see her next time, I will have a chat."

Aclyn asked, "When is the next trip to Earth? I want to meet this," he said loudly in a determined manner, "Angel."

Patrum looked sternly. "You are not going anywhere. You have to finish your studies before you join any spaceship crew. No captain wants someone half trained in anything."

Without warning, Alcyn started to go back into a trance but this time a smile crept across his face.

"Don't need a ship, I can do it without one. Just who is that old man in black clothes standing near the door?"

They all looked towards the door. Zindel was peering in but turned his gaze towards the group. "Dr. Haiten, how nice to see you again," said Zindel who held out his hand. Dr. Haiten quickly introduced Zindel to the group. Zindel bent down and pulled Alcyn up from the armchair. "Young man, you were very hard to find. I'm your tutor, Zindel. Do you remember me?"

Alcyn frowned. "Kind of." Zindel placed his hand on Alcyn's forehead. "Now do you remember me?" Alcyn flew backwards five metres and fell to the floor. He slowly pulled himself up as he said in a dazed manner, "It's all coming back." He stumbled again and fell. Zindel pulled him up. He addressed the others, "He's going to be out of sorts for a few days and a few headaches. He'll live." Patrum finally found words, "What exactly is going on?"

Zindel grinned like a cheeky schoolboy. "Patrum, do you recall being on the royal spaceship and fighting the Lacertians on Centari, Shardon and Octophoria?" Partum nodded.

"Ask Aclyn how it was done and of the battles in the sky?" said Zindel.

Patrum asked question after question. The answers came back. Partum slowly went white. "Not possible. Not possible. …I've been raising Prince Alcyn?"

Alcyn spoke softly as he rubbed his head, "Many years ago, I said I was Alcyn. For a while you agreed and, then forgot."

A waiter carrying a tray of fresh drinks approached. All reached for a glass. He nodded when all the drinks were gone. The waiter walked away as he looked over his shoulder sensing something had occurred in the clique. Something odd. Something important had just happened and it was obviously hush, hush.

Alcyn asked Dr. Haiten, "When you leave for Earth, I going with you."

Zindel raised a hand. "Not until you do a quick refresher of the previous training. It seems you no longer have the need for the neurotransmitter. You now seem to be able to project without that aid. Having two recruits in the one place would be helpful. The Draconians are preparing for a major assault. All planets need to unite and plan for war. Partum when your administrators meet, I want to address the assembly. Genesis is still safe and unknown. Xion has been attacked again but has held back the Draconians. Segmar is next to be attacked. Beta Cancari is odd. There are Lacertian fighting the Draconians. The Mammalians are caught in the crossfire and don't know who to aim their weapons. Captain Keka gifted Beta Cancari to a rebel group of Lacertians. They are best to fight Draconians."

Alcyn frowned. "What's this about a rebel group of Lacertians?"

"They are hardcore sympathisers who are against both Lacertians and Draconians eating and ill-treating all humans. Also, they are very upset that Lacertians are being used as dispensable pawns in the war. The leader of the rebels is the granddaughter of Kyros," said Haiten.

"Alcyn said, "There may be some hope yet."

Earth One Week Later.

Jenny addressed her fist class of graduate students at the Queensland University. She planned to slowly move them towards the concept of relating what was done in the past to modern society. For Jenny, "It was fine to study the past, but it was pointless if it held no bearing on today." She the added a quote from a poet from the 1800's, "'Time past is contained in time present. The present contains time future.' We can learn from the past to prevent disastrous decision making which could leave the future in tatters." At the end she handed out the course plan with suggested reading. She had carefully highlighted three assignments and the date they were due.

Immediately there were murmurs and gasps. She said in a very composed way, "Being able to read the cuneiform writing, the written form of Akkadian language, she thought to herself, *old Pleiadean*, is an interesting bed-time story. But to relate it to modern-day life, that is the challenge for this semester." Jenny watched the group leave the room and muttering about anything and everything.

Carrie met Jenny minutes later. They purchased a takeaway meal at a weekly market stall which now visited the campus every Wednesday. Other stalls appeared were largely fresh fruit and vegetable stands which saved the students not only dollars but also time shopping. They took their food to a shady tree which was shared with several other students.

"It's so nice meeting like this. I really like these impromptu picnics between classes," said Carrie as she stuffed another fork full of food into her mouth.

Jenny replied, "Me too. Sometimes I wonder why half the students are here. It's refreshing to just vege-out with relatives." She looked over to her shoulder and groaned, "Look who is heading this way. Kirkwood. What is he on about now?"

Both watched as Kirkwood invited himself into their space. "Hi Jenny. Hi Carrie." Both women nodded as both had their mouths stuffed. "May I join you?" he asked.

Carrie considered the request, "On the proviso you answer, why you are here?"

"Up grading. Going into accountancy so I can do forensic accountancy for the police force."

"Ah! Sit" Offered Jenny. "No talk about Daraxon Tech stuff."

Kirkwood nodded and placed his books between Jenny and himself.

Carrie read the title of one text, Introductory Accountancy. "That's light going. Done that course. It was almost boring."

Kirkwood looked surprised and tried to push his luck, "If it is boring, how about you show me how to make it less boring?"

Jenny replied as she saw a glint in Kirkwood's eye, a glint she wasn't comfortable with. "It is basic. You add the numbers in one column and add the numbers in another, and see if they match. Simple. You don't need someone to coach you for that. Consider lesson one completed."

Kirkwood and Carrie chuckled. *Nice cut off,* thought Carrie.

Kirkwood changed the subject. He couldn't contain himself, "Just how did the people on the spaceship pay for all the stuff they bought?"

Carrie and Jenny suddenly stood up and walked away leaving Kirkwood alone with his books. He saw them sit on a bench under another tree. He didn't approach but turned on his mobile and then to an app which detected their voices. He listened intently but was disappointed. They spoke about everything but Daraxon Technologies. It was like it never existed. His interest piqued when he heard Carrie speak.

"Jenny, I have been wondering for quite a while, what exactly is the Pleiadean Experiment?' Jenny considered the question before answering. "It depends on who you are. For Keka and the rest of the crew, sending Ashton down was their experiment. In a way it was a good experiment to learn the ways of others. It must have been upsetting for all to discover they were only visiting a lost colony. To me, the experiment was the creation of humans on this planet – the splicing of DNA and getting it to take hold.

"Then came the guilt factor of the floods." She said in a philosophical way, "Did you know that Noah was guided by one of the engineers to build the ark. Some people translated the Akkadian works in detail. The ark was round, not like what the religious groups and even Hollywood depict. It is actually a kuphar or it is also known as a quiffah. If it was an ark was built as the religious organisations constantly depicted, the ark would have capsized in the first four days. But a kuphar is round and covered on top like a sphere, can go with the flow of the water. It spins and rises up and down with big waves. It doesn't capsize so easily. The bigger they are the harder for it to capsize. The measurements were large – the diameter was nearly as long as a football field. When the flood was over and the Earth settled down again, educating the survivors to fend for themselves and some of the Neflin integrated into the population was another experiment in itself. Take your choice on which is the true experiment."

Carrie glanced around the area. She spotted Kirkwood at a distance looking at his phone. "I bet he has some fancy app which listens into conversations. That guy just doesn't get it."

"Get what?"

"He's tried before hitting on me to get information. I suppose he will try on you as he has bombed out with me. Too old. Something slimy about him," said Carrie.

Jenny looked over to where Kirkwood was sitting. He was looking back. "Too old and slimy?" he muttered to himself. "Neither of you are getting any younger." He packed away his phone and collected his books. The words revibrated in his head, *old and slimy. Ouch.*

Back at Daraxon. Ashton, Kora and Jenny were sipping iced drinks on the porch. The sun was beaming down. Jenny casually asked, "How is Ashra going?"

Kora flashed her eyes over to the pram where Ashra was sleeping. "Good. Really good for a child of the stars. You know I had to make up a location for his birth certificate. I couldn't say on The Explorer XSBC or somewhere in a void between Amada and the waste space."

Jenny asked, who added the letters XSBC to the ship's name? I know it is in Pleiadean script." "No one is really sure. No one ever owned up. When Keka saw it, he went ballistic. Funny, he never had it removed."

What does it stand for?" asked Jenny.

"No one really knows for sure. But it smartens up the ship. One rumour it was supposed to be the letters of the planets Xion, Segmar and Beta Cancari. Another guess circulating on the ship was Extra Small Battle Craft."

Ashton interrupted and jested, "Guess three. Experimental Stupidity Before Care. That's my description of my part in the experiment. Who cares?"

Suddenly Ashton went into a trance. Kora looked on with concern. The other stopped chatting. They all waited until Ashton snapped out of it. Then he casually said, "Alcyn is coming."

POSTSCRIPT
A section of Jenny's Unpublished Paper

THE LEGACY OF THE EARLY GODS.

"The first gods to Earth were aliens. The God which modern day religious groups aspire to, is a supreme being who came to Earth much later. The Early or Old Gods should never be confused with the latter. Just who was/is this Supreme Being, we can only conjecture. No matter who or what doctrine you follow, there is only one God.

This paper is about the perception of ancient people who were genetically modified to be in the image of the Old Gods. The Old Gods did it for their own ulterior purposes. The Old Gods were just an advanced society mining Earth for its wealth. The wealth many modern-day corporations and governments of today, and we as common people relate to.

The legacy of the perceived Old Gods persists today and covers every inch of all cultures on this planet: political, social, economic, moral, emotional, religious, culture which includes the arts and sciences. It may never have been the intention of the Old Golds to cause racial tensions and inequalities. That was the working of man – perception of a society thrust upon them by a people who had advanced technology at that point of time. The global disaster which isolated the survivors, forced divisions and protectionism – a psychological response to severe trauma.

The fledgling human race of the past, has evolved, developed and matured and now in many ways reached the technology of what is believed to be gods, the Supreme Being which they were once in awe with. In some areas of science, we have surpassed that level, and we are quickly spearheading into an unknown future – future where technology has and will continue to outstrip the moral, social and emotional advances of society. The circle is now complete. We are now the Old/Early Golds searching for another planet which is suitable to colonise and maybe mine.